Sandra Benns lives in Toronto, Canada and began her writing career full-time in 2019. *49 Parkwood Avenue* is part of her first trilogy; it's sandwiched between *7 Russell Hill Road* and *The Irish Nanny*.

Sandra also penned a series within the last year. To date, this new series includes *Hazel G* and its sequel, *The Delamere Boys*. You can read Q&As and access the playlists for all her books on her website: https://www.sandrabenns.com

Dr. Patel,
Wishing you a
good read!
Peace + love,
Sandra

Although my entire book and its characters are fictional, I wrote the prologue in testament to the courage, intellect, and indomitable spirit of a remarkable woman. Lorraine Rotter was a Polish Jew who was caught in the web of the Third Reich.

In 1944, she was a young married woman, living with her husband in Poland. She was picked up by the Nazis and sent to Auschwitz. Separated forever from her husband, she was transferred from Auschwitz to a work camp in Czechoslovakia where she realized that she was pregnant with her husband's child. She gave birth to her daughter, just weeks before the camp was liberated by the Russians in May, 1945. Lorraine, along with her baby daughter, were moved from camp to camp in Germany after liberation, as the new mother was determined to make a new life for the two of them.

Eventually, this remarkable, resilient woman, her five-year-old daughter and her new husband eventually emigrated to Toronto, Canada, where she currently lives.

She celebrated her ninety-eighth birthday on January 05, 2021, and is treasured by her daughter, son, grandchildren and great-grandchildren.

Lorraine's experiences, along with millions of other immigrants, represent the fluid warp and weft that continues to shape the fabric of our big, homogenous multi-cultural city of Toronto.

I'm eternally grateful to not only Lorraine Rotter, but for all the hard working and hopeful immigrants that come to Canada in search of a better life.

Sandra Benns

49 PARKWOOD AVENUE

AUSTIN MACAULEY PUBLISHERS™

LONDON * CAMBRIDGE * NEW YORK * SHARJAH

Ordering Information
Quantity sales: Special discounts are available on quantity purchases by corporations, associations, and others. For details, contact the publisher at the address below.

Publisher's Cataloging-in-Publication data
Benns, Sandra
49 Parkwood Avenue

ISBN 9781649791580 (Paperback)
ISBN 9781649791597 (ePub e-book)

Library of Congress Control Number: 2021912393

www.austinmacauley.com/us

First Published (2021)
Austin Macauley Publishers LLC
40 Wall Street, 33rd Floor, Suite 3302
New York, NY 10005
USA

mail-usa@austinmacauley.com
+1 (646) 5125767

Thank you, Renee. It's all the little things. All the stories over all the years, your thoughtfulness and caring through all the ups and downs throughout the different stages of our lives. I'm grateful not only for your friendship, but for your mother's stories that you've shared with me.

I promise you; if I ever write a story about the two of us, we'll both be 5'10" tall and weigh 120 lbs. And rich, very rich.

That being said, I love you just the way you are.

Prologue

Their dairy farm was situated in a small, picturesque pocket of north-central Poland, on the outskirts of the quiet village of Wloclawek. It was a 40-minute walk to the main street that hosted the farmer's market, or a five-minute drive back in the days when they could access enough wood gas or tractor-fuel to feed the tractor to pull the wagon loaded with their milk cans and blocks of cheese down to the village.

It was 1943, and one never knew what was going to happen next let alone worrying about not being able to operate the tractor for their weekly delivery down to the market.

***

Martyna checked to see that the children weren't looking as she laughingly swatted his hands off her ass, all at the same time thanking God for her wonderful but much-too-attentive husband. His hands moved up her back and wrapped themselves into her long, perfectly straight, golden hair. She was a good six inches taller than him, so she turned and stooped a little to rub her breasts into his chest with a soft tease and a promise.

"Later, later. Not in front of the kids." She gave him a full kiss on the lips as she pushed him away. "Can't you see I'm busy?" As he backed out of the kitchen, she added, "Ask Milka to run upstairs and get me a ribbon for my hair and then have the others come in here to wash up before dinner."

As Milka's two teenaged brothers and her two nine-year-old twin sisters were being ushered into the kitchen to wash up, she took the stairs of the big old farmhouse two at a time, with her long, well-muscled legs reaching the hallway that led to her parent's bedroom in record time.

She dawdled in front of her mother's dressing-table mirror. She carefully applied a skim of her mother's lipstick, stepped back, and blew her mirrored image a kiss. She had baled hay and milked cows and had won the ribbons to prove it at the local county fair every summer up until the last few years once the ghetto was formed. She was proud of her brains and chutzpah, right along with her height, broad shoulders, and long legs. Her mother had told her that her genes were not only Polish but from the far northern part of the Soviet Union on her maternal side, and that's why she and Milka both ended up with the whitest shade of pale golden hair, bright blue eyes, and long legs. She pivoted a quarter-turn and watched herself as she cupped her full, high, 20-year-old breasts, sighing at the sight. She thought, *Here I am, in the prime of my life, with no chance in hell of a good lay in the hay or a night up on lover's hill under the stars with some good-looking boy any time soon. Fucking Nazis.*

The minute she had that thought, she corrected herself. She was lucky to be alive, and the only reason that her family hadn't been picked up yet was because they ran the only dairy farm in the region. The Nazis had amped up their liquidation of Jews from town over the years, counting back to 1939 when the Wloclawek Jews had numbered 13,500. They were now down to less than 100, in total count, since they burned out the ghetto in town last April, in 1942. The count could be less now, for all she knew. Her life consisted of milking cows and ensuring that her yellow badge with the big 'P' on it was visible on both the front and back of her jacket as she kept her head down and walked past the town out to the mill to pick up the family ration of food that they were expected to live on. Thank God that her family had the dairy farm. Their farm provided a little bit of extra food, as her parents very, very carefully tucked away a little cheese here and there, away from the prying eyes of the Third Reich inspectors that took almost everything for themselves. The Nazis left very little for the town's population that had been living under their occupation over the past four years.

She shook her head, watching her long, perfectly straight, golden hair lift up and fly right from her waist, up, up, and out around her shoulders as if it hadn't a care in the world.

She grabbed one ribbon for herself and the other requested ribbon from the dressing table, and as she headed toward the door, she instinctively felt the hair rise on the nape of her neck.

She stopped, listened, and turned ever so slightly, allowing her peripheral vision to catch the window's pane. Her life, as she knew it in its 20th year, came to a screeching halt.

The truck, making its way up the lane, didn't have the full set of wooden slats set up at the back like it always had before when farmers were free to cart pigs and cattle back and forth. Instead, the side rails were only three or four slats deep, giving her a bird's eye view of the cargo. Said cargo consisted of about two dozen men of all ages, not counting the three Nazi soldiers guarding them, and Milka's quickly sinking heart was fully aware that her family was next to suffer what was known as *a roundup*.

With no time to run downstairs to warn her family, and by the time she had squeezed under her parents' bed, her prayers were interrupted by two sets of boots stepping across the old farmhouse threshold downstairs. The voice commanded, "You. And you. And you. Out. You. And you two. Sit."

Milka's face was plastered to the floor in the tight fit as she attempted to blink away the sweat that was running down from her forehead. Her heart was screaming to upend the bed and run downstairs, and her brain cautioned her to shut up and put up. The argument was settled for her a few minutes later as she heard two sets of footsteps making their way up the stairs. She closed her eyes and gave into the terror that was hers.

A weight forced the one side of the bed down, and she could make out the outline of the heels of his boots, spread about 15 inches apart. He ordered, "Kneel down and unbutton me."

A fold of her mother's blue-and-white printed housedress appeared on the inside of one of his boots. Her heart soared! It was her mother! They hadn't loaded her on the truck! She quickly concluded that the round up was men only this time.

Milka thought that his sounds were exactly like one of the pigs in the barnyard grunting away as they gobbled their feed down with their dirty snouts snotting and snorting their excitement over the clean, pale-yellow grain that her family forfeited from their own meager pantry to fatten them.

However, her distain was short-lived as his grunts subsided and she felt the mattress spring up a little. The boot heels moved out of sight and were replaced by a view of the side of his one boot. She heard him pull his knife out of its sheath.

"Don't move," he ordered my mother.

Milka felt the mattress dip several times, and, with each dip, there was a short, forceful, slicing sound.

It was an eternity until she heard his boots stride back down the hall, skip down the stairs, and then the front door opened and closed with his departure. She closed her eyes once again to say a prayer for her family and to try to gather the courage to squeeze out from under the bed to deal with her mother's remains. She froze at the next sound. Someone or something was rustling in close proximity to the bed.

"Milka, Milka, kochanie, it's okay. It's okay. He just wanted my hair, that's all. He cut off my hair, that's all. Stay put for another few moments while I check the window to see that they're well down the lane. It's okay, kochanie, we're going to be okay. Wait for another minute until I can check to see if we're all clear. Do not come out. Stay put. Then we'll both go downstairs to see if they spared the twins."

***

Later that same evening, after checking once again that the twins were sound asleep, the mother, with a scarf over her shorn locks, stood behind her daughter who was sitting on the small chair in front of her dressing table.

As she gave her beautiful daughter's long, golden hair their nightly one-hundred strokes with her hairbrush, she gave her some advice:

"Never, never, cut your hair. Promise me that you'll never cut your hair. It is your crowning glory. It is your blessing. Coupled with your brains, it will get you far in life." She leaned down and kissed the top of her daughter's head and whispered, *"This may even save your life."*

***

How was this loving, Jewish mother to know at that time that some 73 years later, the heavens above would be transmitting her maternal message of love to yet another young woman with a golden halo far, far away in a big northern country called Canada.

***

The next morning, the same truck returned up the laneway, but this time the back was populated with the remaining Jewish women and children from the village. The day before, the Nazis had diligently loaded the men into a cattle car that was pulled over on a siding near the railway station, and now it was time for the women. Milka, her mother, and her twin sisters joined the others. Once in town, they were herded and lined up in front of the train. They were loaded into a livestock car for a 30-hour hot, then dark and cold, then hot again, journey into the abyss of abject terror.

The four of them stood there, stunned and squinting from the first sunlight they had seen after two days in the dark, dank, cattle car. Milka focused on the sign on the top of the gate. It read *Auschwitz*, and another sign with a large arrow pointing to the right read: *Auschwitz-Birkenau*.

Milka was motioned to the right, and her mother and the twins were motioned to the left.

Milka's last sight of her mother and her nine-year-old twin sisters was from over her shoulder. She could see that her mother had a firm grasp on each of her daughters' hands and that she was holding her head up high, head and shoulders over everyone else, walking along with a definite sense of purpose.

***

As two Nazis shaved her head and then tattooed her arm, much like you would brand a farm animal, she reminded herself over and over again of her mother's dignity and strength. She was determined not to give in to fear, and she welcomed her inner rage. She seethed. She would beat the fucking Nazis at their own game. She was Milka Kaufman, and she was a Jew.

***

She continued to hold onto that rage, and she leaned on her emulated dignity and strength over the next year-and-a-half, bearing the starvation and the seamstress labor of sewing thousands upon thousands of Nazi uniforms right alongside the other women, most of which had been beaten and starved down to existing as mere robotic zombies. She watched the life leave their eyes. Not her, not ever, she vowed. She'd rather die first.

Even at the worst of times, as she witnessed the bodies drop right in front of her from a bullet to their head or through the weekly hangings that they were forced to watch, she never lost her inner rage. It's what kept her alive.

Milka spent the minutes, hours, days, months following, looking forward to their once-daily routine of humbly passing the bowl of something that resembled soup down the line, one to the other, and then to the next, taking a small, measured, and treasured sip, remembering to leave something for the next woman beside her. If, by chance, she was given a crust of bread from the overseer of her work in recognition of her dexterity and speed in completing so many uniforms in so little time, she learned to humbly share it with the workers around her. Solidarity ruled amongst these women, and she never, ever, broke that sisterhood.

***

As time inched on through the days and then the months, and then into her second year, she could feel that changes were afoot as her workload doubled because of all the packing up, shutting down, and burning down certain parts of the mammoth camp. She knew that the Nazis must be losing ground. She had no doubt that the world was coming to save her.

The Nazis were, in fact, facing two enemies, one outside the camp, and one inside the camp. The world had joined forces against them, and every few days they would hear of the worrisome trend of their troops in different parts of Europe being beaten back.

The second enemy, the one that had infiltrated their camp, proved to be another type of headache altogether. The recent typhus epidemic was quietly and slyly making its way through the barracks, one after the other. At the sound of a cough or the lag of a step, a watchful guard would pull the perpetrator from the line and calmly raise his pistol to the worker's forehead. This action would be followed by his motion for others to ensure that the body was deposited into the large pits that swallowed the bodies one by one until another pit could be dug to house the typhus-infected bodies.

However, with sheer determination and guts, and by focusing on the task at hand, and looking forward to her once-daily routine of humbly passing the bowl of soup from sister to sister, Milka never lost sight of the big picture.

During one of the death marches in January, 1945, from Auschwitz-Birkenau to the slave-labor camp called Bergen-Belsen, located up north in Germany, Milka escaped the march on foot. She thought to herself it was because the Nazis knew she was a valuable seamstress; one who could work day in, day out, with her head down in an organized and efficient manner. This was the same trek that was aptly named the *death march* in the history books, as many of the prisoners died from sheer exposure to the German winter.

She was herded onto an open train car, and although some of her sisters froze to death or simply gave up and accepted their fate as they were shot point-blank for resisting in some manner, Milka knew that the train ride was an easier trip than marching on foot in the dead of winter.

She asked for God's forgiveness for her actions on the train, when she took the socks off one of her sisters that had succumbed to the cold to use for herself. After all, she rationalized at the time; the deceased woman that rode on top of the open car had no use for them any longer. Ultimately, it was probably one of the reasons why she survived the ordeal. That, coupled with her inner rage that she had fueled on a daily basis for almost two years, saved her not only physically but mentally as well.

***.

After arriving at Bergen-Belsen, Milka laid her head down on the wooden board of her bunk after politely offering her bunkmate the first choice to sleep either to the right or to the left. It was a narrow bunk, with one blanket to share, but both women knew that the warmth from the other would help keep them alive. At that point, Milka was a 22-year-old dairy farmer that hadn't studied Sigmund Freud and his cohorts, but her survival instincts that she had developed over the past two years told her that the woman lying next to her not only gave her warmth but the human touch as well that we all need to survive.

She closed her eyes, silently mouthing her nightly version of the Kaddish, the prayer for the dead, in memory and in honor of her family that had gone on before her. She gave in to the deep recess of her mind that held the vision of her family sitting around their big dining-room table as her father quietly brought out the extra ration of their very best cheese that he had squirreled away from the Nazis who had commandeered their cheese, milk, and cream since 1939, leaving only the smallest of rations for the villagers and for themselves.

She felt the merciful blanket of sleep wash over her.

***

Once again, with her head bent over her sewing machine, she survived the next three-and-a-half months. The Nazis had recognized her intellect very early on, and she found herself in a sort of management position where she had the opportunity to get up from her machine to help thread another worker's machine or direct her team of ten workers from sewing shirts to sewing pants or whatever the need was that came down from her two Nazi guards. The supervisor, ever-watchful, was never too far away from them. Her intellect had made herself be deemed useful, and she used it with cunning to get the small crusts of bread that two of the guards would bring her after their breakfast, of course, before the supervisor's arrival. She would quickly snatch the bread up and place them carefully in the bottom of her apron pocket to share with the other workers back in their barrack, after being released from the factory that evening.

These two guards were well-aware that their scraps of food were not in the least insignificant to her. It was a toss-up; did they drop the crust on her sewing table out of basic humanity, or did they drop the crusts on her sewing table with the reasoning they knew she would amp up her production and they, in turn, would receive the approval from their supervisor that they craved?

Nevertheless, these same scraps, coupled with their once-daily bowl of soup, kept Milka's team from dying of starvation as the days passed in their new work camp, far from the constant stench of burning flesh and dead corpses of their Auschwitz-Birkenau days.

***

She knew the instant her blue eyes met his that she had made a terrible mistake. In this basic human interaction, she recognized a flicker of humanity in the guard, as his eyes widened to transmit his alarm and concern at her impertinence of raising her eyes from the floor as she spoke to him. She immediately lowered her eyes, but it was too late.

By chance, the supervisor, standing two rows over, was watching his prize worker interact with his guard, indicating her team was ready for a second batch of sleeves.

His eyes narrowed as he saw the unusually tall, Soviet-looking Jew's still-bright-blue eyes lift upward. He automatically reached for his pistol. How dare she! As if he didn't have enough problems! That very morning he had received orders to double the workers' food rations to ensure that they each got a piece of bread with their soup, in their efforts to assuage the world that his camp was merely a well-functioning work camp and nothing more ominous than that. He knew in his gut that the Third Reich's systematic purge of anyone other than the pure Aryan race was coming to an end, and he was faced daily with the desire to cut and run while he could before the typhus took over completely, and, or, before the foreigners' army tanks rolled in to put a final end to it all.

He swallowed his anger and his angst and calmly made his way over to the line that produced twice as much product as any of the others. Having had that minute or two to think it over, he chose a rational rather than a reflexive method to keep his workers in line. He calculated that he wouldn't kill her; that would serve no good purpose. A whipping would suffice. That would ensure that she wouldn't lose any time in her role as a team lead in his factory. He would save his bullet for the very, very stupid guard that had allowed this to happen.

***

Milka was ordered to strip. Two others were ordered to clear the garment rack of product and to bind her hands to the upper rails of the rack.

Upon hearing the supervisor's commands, Milka's heart was full of gratitude with the realization that she was only to receive a whipping to her back instead of receiving the barrel of his pistol to her forehead.

***

There was a little dissention that night, just before they lined up for their daily bowl of soup. The quiet, short debate was based on more than half of her sisters wanting to pass that night's communal bowl on down the line without taking any soup so that Milka, their whipped and weakened leader, could have an extra sip. The other few were so furious with Milka's carelessness that had put their whole team in grave danger that they decided that she shouldn't receive anything let alone an extra helping. The team's decision was a democratic one. The few that wanted to sip stood in the front of the line; Milka was placed in the middle and was urged to finish the bowl completely, sip after sip, as her remaining sisters stood on the other side of her, firmly resolute in their decision to give something back to their leader. After all, she had dutifully shared her crusts of bread that she had gleaned, using such cunning and intellect to coax the guards to drop their breakfast leftovers, along with the daily allotment of thread and buttons on her sewing desk in an almost-daily routine, hours before the supervisor arrived on the floor to oversee the hundreds of workers that were divided up into teams of ten.

***

The hours and days and months that followed did not pass without Milka planning and scheming and organizing in her head in great detail on how she would go back to her family's farm in idyllic Wloclawek once this was all over. She would pass the hours mentally experimenting with new cheeses and safer milk processes. She planned on making the sweetest butter known to Poland, to ensure that the great bakeries in Warsaw would line up to get it. She argued and debated as to the perfect herd size and planned in great detail how to slowly build her herd to include only the best milkers. She named each and every cow in her esteemed herd, and, with a little dose of humor, coupled with a big dose of respect, she named her top ten milkers after her sisters on her team. Her plan didn't stop there. She internally developed a farming system that would allow not only delivery of her milk, cream, butter, and cheese but also a rudimentary pick-up system, along with a storefront of sorts. She would make her parents proud. They would not have died in vain.

She may lose a toe or two from frostbite; she may even lose a limb to the Nazi's brutality, but she would rather die first than to succumb to those monsters getting hold of her dreams, schemes, and basic ability to change like a chameleon lizard to fit the environment that she found herself in.

The young farmer was slowly, ever so slowly, experiencing the metamorphous of her inner rage coming out of its cocoon in the safest way possible. She was giving birth, albeit slowly, to a new, fresh life altogether, even if it was only in her mind. She was a survivor through and through. Her parents would have been so proud of her.

***

It was mid-April, 1945, when the British rolled into Bergen-Belsen.

Milka made herself useful over those first few days and weeks of liberation, helping the British soldiers coax the others to trust them enough to board the passenger train that supplied an individual seat for each of them to start their new lives in a Displaced Persons camp in yet another part of Germany. It was called Foehrenwald.

Every day since arriving, she had made the rounds throughout her new camp, befriending the staff, supervisors, and ONRRA (United Nations Relief and Rehabilitation Administration) workers and constantly scrounging and scavenging for scraps of food and leftovers to deliver to her still-timid and traumatized team from her Bergen-Belsen days.

***

It turned out that her focus on claiming her life back from the day that she was picked up at her family's dairy farm to the day that Bergen-Belsen was liberated, was a large part of her being able to acclimatize relatively quickly at Foehrenwald.

Over the next month, she didn't allow herself to grieve the additional heartbreak of learning that Poland didn't want anything at all to do with her, along with the other Polish Jews that had thought they would return to their old life. Poland, which herself had been completely beaten down and decimated over the years by occupation after occupation, looked upon the Jews that had survived the Holocaust with blame, resentment, and criticism, right along with most of the world.

It seemed that her mother country had stuck her head in the sand, trying to forget that the Holocaust had ever happened. Her past life was gone, all gone.

Letting go of her dreams and plans for her farm was a hard pill to swallow, but she forged ahead. Her choice was made quickly and without delay. The application that the ONRRA worker had placed in front of her spelled out that

Belgium, Britain, and Canada topped the list for taking in the most displaced persons. In a flash, she remembered in the camps that there was a big warehouse that the Polish Jews called *Kanada*. This warehouse was where all the confiscated suitcases and parcels that were taken from the prisoners as they disembarked from the train were stored, sorted, and documented. The finest clothing, the finest leather shoes, family photos, the best jewelry, and pieces of art that the Jews had managed to hold onto until then were then dispatched all over the Third Reich. Amongst the prisoners, it was considered a plum job to be assigned to this warehouse, as the work was not that strenuous. They called the warehouse *Kanada* because it was the land of plenty, just like stories that had come back from their relatives that had settled overseas in the big northern country before things got bad in Poland. Milka also remembered her teacher, way, way, back in her other world, telling the class of the miles and miles and miles of golden wheat that Canada not only produced but shared with poorer countries around the world. She convinced herself that perhaps her plans of returning to dairy farming could be finessed a little to include large fields of wheat. She listed Canada as her first choice, with Belgium and Britain following.

The ONRRA worker smiled and nodded in agreement. How could she argue with the enthusiasm and courage that was leaning across the desk from her? She softly said, "Good choice," as she carefully placed the completed application into her file.

Milka said to the kind, quiet worker, "My mother named me Milka, and in Polish, this name means *queen,* and *leader*. I'm going to make sure that they didn't name me in vain."

Little did Milka know at the time that living her life in Canada, or Belgium, or Britain was not to be. No, not at all.

***

A month after filling out her application to emigrate, Milka met a wonderful, soulful poet-of-a-man who, in turn, was absolutely smitten with her zest for life and her well-honed survival techniques. They fell in love, and they spent hours and hours together up on a hilltop, away from the camp, discovering the all joys of sex that their thin, scarred bodies and hopeful hearts could manage and that the God above had laid out for them to taste on the early summer's grass beneath them.

Their sweet, tender, love affair was to change the course of both their lives forever.

***

One year later, in May, 1946, the 16-year-old UNRRA (United Nations Relief and Rehabilitation Administration) midwife assistant held onto her composure as she filled in the birth form as per the mother's wishes. The completed birth form informed:

Date of birth: She printed: *April 18, 1946*
Name and age of mother. She printed: *Milka Kaufman, age 23*
Name and age of father. She printed: *Unknown*
Given name and sex of live birth: *Martyna Kaufman, female*
Place of birth: Foehrenwald, Wolfratshausen, Germany

The young midwife assistant took another look at the baby. She may have looked like an angel, but she certainly didn't sound like one. She was loudly demanding to be fed, albeit her first breath had been taken less than ten minutes ago.

Milka lay there, and for the first time since she could remember, she was at peace. She felt nothing but joy and love as her noisy daughter latched onto her breast on the third try and finally began to suck. She was well-aware that the last two days struggling to give birth had taken its toll and that she was hemorrhaging to the point that the two nurses couldn't keep up with it. She asked the kind, wide-eyed, young girl that was tending to her under her newly acquired position of 'midwife assistant' to call the rabbi to give her daughter the first blessing and herself the last rites.

Ever since the young midwife had met Milka about five months ago, she was in awe of, no, actually was in love with this articulate, bright, 23-year-old woman who was known as nothing short of a goddess throughout the packed displaced persons' camp. After almost two years at Auschwitz-Birkenau in Poland and a stint at Bergen-Belsen, her pregnant patient had risen from those ashes to become the voice and the heart of the packed, old, army barracks that the Allies had converted to house the Jews that had survived the Holocaust. This heroine's name was Milka Kaufman, and upon arrival, she shared her time and her healing specifically with a man her own age from Poland as they slowly but surely worked together to claw their way out of their trauma. Together, they seized every moment of every day as they befriended every woman and every man in the camp, trying their best to root them out of their stupors that had been inflicted upon them by the Nazis. The two young Survivors had fallen deeply in love.

Everyone in the camp grieved along with Milka as her young lover fell victim all over again to the horrors of the war as suicide took his life. Without warning, he was found hanging by his own hand from a big, strong tree very early one morning. He died before he knew that Milka was pregnant.

This was the midwife assistant's first birth that was, with no doubt, going to claim the life of the mother, and she stepped aside as the rabbi took her place to administer the newborn's first blessing, followed by the last rites of the mother who was slowly succumbing to the hemorrhaging that they couldn't arrest. The mother had fought one hell of a fight to deliver her first child over the past 48 hours, and she was still fiercely holding onto her newborn daughter that had been born with the mop of thick, golden hair of her mother. The baby was greedily sucking on her breast, and the midwife thanked God that the mother's milk had come in early. Tears of sadness rolled down the young UNRRA worker's face as she asked God, "Why her, God, why her? Out of all of them, why her?"

***

An hour later, as the mother's hands relaxed their hold on her sleeping newborn, the midwife assistant continued to write her notes down in the file. Her youth prompted her to write her findings down, not in the prescribed clinical manner but in a personal manner. She wrote of Milka, the mother, that she was known as a goddess throughout the camp. She added line after line of Milka's finest attributes, including that the new mother had named her child after her own mother, Martyna Kaufman, who was a Polish dairy farmer in the town of Wloclawek which was near the city of Warsaw. At the end of her report, she casually added a few notes pertaining to the big, thriving, greedy baby that she herself had helped deliver.

She signed, then printed her full name, Renata Wójcik, along with the date of April 18, 1946, beside her signature in acknowledgment that she had assisted birthing the baby and witnessed the death of the mother. She then handed the paperwork over to the rabbi. She asked the rabbi for a few, extra, appropriate prayers and blessings as he signed off on the birth as well as the death. She decided in her own wisdom that there was simply no rush to notify the other staff of the mother's death, so she sat there quietly as the kind rabbi covered all the bases for the dead and for the living. She smiled a little as he continued with a blessing for UNRRA, her, and all other midwives that helped bring life into the world.

The rabbi had no idea that the young midwife assistant's askance for the additional prayers weren't only for the mother lying there in front of them. It was for her own biological mother; the same mother who had given her to a kind Catholic family to hide away from the clutches of the Nazis. She was five years old when she took the name and identity of being a member of an entirely different family, and it was easy for her as a child to adapt to her new surroundings that included food on the table and two, new, doting Catholic parents. Ever since joining UNRRA, however, she would reach back, way, way back into her childhood, in search of her parents, with quiet thoughts of wondering who she looked like; small, inconsequential things like that. She never spoke of these thoughts to anyone. She always chastised herself for these visits to her other world, as she saw it as a slap in the face for her second mother and father who had taken her in and kept her safe. She was a *'hidden child,'* and she told herself it was the least she could do to forget her early childhood and continue on as an adult with the comforting, solid past of being a nice Catholic girl; an only child to two, kind, hardworking, devout Catholic parents. But there were times, many times, especially of late, of the recurring thoughts of *Who am I?* that she didn't even speak of in her weekly confession to the priest, when her heart cried in vain, "But I'm not a Catholic! I'm a Jew!"

***

Six months later, as 1946 was coming to a close and Germany's trees were losing their leaves, the young midwife and the rest of the staff had to admit to the heart-wrenching realization that Milka's daughter with the golden hair and completely round, bright-blue eyes was profoundly deaf.

However, Renata, the young midwife assistant, finally got an answer to her prayer when her supervisor handed her the good news that came in the form of a letter postmarked Stockholm, Sweden.

The camp had finally received a positive response back from an orphanage that had stepped up to the plate. The big, beautiful, bouncing baby that lived in her own little world of silence was going to start another life far, far away from the aftermath of the Holocaust.

The orphanage was not located in any of the three top countries that Milka had chosen to migrate from. No. Belgium, the United Kingdom, and Canada hadn't responded to Milka's plea. It turned out that a country at the very bottom of the UNRRA's list was the only one willing to take Milka's disabled baby daughter.

A barnhem in Sweden called Stockholm Orphanage for Displaced Children was willing to take Foehrenwald's little, golden angel in. The orphanage recommended that her new Swedish passport be made out as Martina Kaufman Hansson. They suggested that they spell Martyna with a Swedish 'i' in place of the Polish 'y' and that they tack on Hansson, which was a very common Swedish family name, to convince adoptive parents to overlook her two major obstacles: one, that she was born profoundly deaf, and two, that she was born a Polish Jew.

The midwife assistant held the golden angel high above her head, and as the baby smiled and gurgled in return, she said, "Martyna-spelled-with-an-i Kaufman Hansson, you golden angel, you are going to become a Swede and grow up to be a great, great woman just like your mama."

***

It was a bitterly cold night in the dead of winter in Stockholm, in the year 1975, as another new mother, age 29, filled out the top-half of the birth record regarding her newborn daughter. Between gazing at her daughter, she looked around the clean, Swedish hospital where she basked in feelings of peace and love that she had never felt before in her life. Between each line of the form that she read, she leaned over to check on her daughter. Since the new mother couldn't hear anything, she would have to rely on her eyes to tell her when her baby needed her. She carefully printed, spacing each letter perfectly upon the clean, supplied form that the lovely nurse had brought her. The nurse, who had spoken so clearly into her face so that she could lip-read what she was saying, asked her to print clearly to avoid any mistakes made on the final birth certificate.

Date of birth: She printed: *October 10, 1975*
Name and age of mother. She printed: *Martina Kaufman Hansson, age 29*
Name and age of father. She printed: *Unknown.*
Given name and sex of live birth: *Nigella Kaufman Hansson, female*
Place of birth: Stockholm, Sweden

She reread the form over once again and smiled to herself when her eyes read the 'Name of father' line. Oh, he certainly wasn't unknown as she had written on the form. Not to her, anyway. Although she didn't know his last name, she would remember his first name forever. In fact, she had named her baby girl, her love child, after him.

Both of this new baby's parents had had no idea that their fateful, unexpected, one-and-only, afternoon tryst nine months ago could have possibly produced this perfect, little, golden angel. All the new mother knew about the unsuspecting and unknowing father was that his first name was Nigel and that he was a Canadian and that both of them had stupidly parted company that afternoon without any way of reconnecting in the future. They lived in different countries; and to make matters very final, he didn't know her name at all, not her first name and not her family name either. But what she knew about herself was that she would love him with all her heart until the end of her days. His name was Nigel, and it would be in her heart and on her lips forever.

***

25 years later, in the millennial year of 2000, Martina Kaufman Hansson, at the age of 54, carefully printed on the top half of the birth record once again, but this time she was registering her granddaughter.

Martina had been signing, in the sign language of the deaf, feverishly toward her daughter, and smiled as her daughter, refusing to sign with her, spoke clearly into her face.

Her daughter enunciated each word carefully and firmly, "Mor, Mor, listen to me. Don't sign with me. You promised me when I graduated from law school that you would use your words. You know that I don't care about the tonal quality. You know that." The take-charge daughter gave her mother the look and then continued, "Now, about the baby's name. Enough already. I had this baby for both of us. You and me. But I'm the mother, and I'm the boss when it comes to her name. That's it. We're naming the baby after you and that's all I'm going to say about this. You can fill out the form for us."

The new grandmother shrugged her shoulders as she gave in to the wishes of her 25-year-old love child. She smiled and filled out the form:

Date of birth: She printed: *September 25, 2000*
Name and age of mother. She printed: *Nigella Kaufman Hansson, age 25*
Name and age of father. She printed: *Unknown, (in-vitro fertilization), age 30*
Given name and sex of live birth: *Martina Hansson, female*
Place of birth: Stockholm, Sweden

***

Five years later, in 2005, Nigella Kaufman Hansson, the brilliant 30-year-old lawyer and single mother to a precocious five-year-old, put her feet up on the footrest and adjusted her seat back a little. She shook her head in amusement, watching the British Air flight attendant named Linda interact with her beautiful daughter that knew how to work all the angles. The five-year-old was explaining to the flight attendant that she shouldn't have to decide which snack to have. She would just have both of them, thank you very much.

Nigella laughed and said to the kind flight attendant, "What the heck! Why not! We're on holidays! I think that today, just today, we're going to bend the rules a little. After all, this is our very first time in first class, so let's just enjoy it all, shall we?"

Nigella looked out and marveled at the white, fluffy clouds below her that were silently and seamlessly making way for the wing of the plane. Her heart was full as her eyes raised up to the blue, blue heavens, and she whispered to herself, "Mor! Mamma! Are you there? Look at me now! Are you happy for me, Mamma?"

Hours later, with every story book that the airline had to offer scattered over her covers, little Martina had finally submitted to the sandman. Linda, the flight attendant, came to check on 'her girls.' She said to Nigella, "Now, it's time for you, Mom. What would you like? Anything at all. It's on the house."

They chatted easily, and Linda casually inquired, "Is your husband meeting the plane in Toronto?"

"Oh no, Linda, now that would be too, too much to ask for. A pair of first-class tickets *and* a husband? Let's get real!" Nigella laughed and said, "No, there's no doting husband waiting for me. I'm a single parent."

"Welcome to the club, Sister. So, you mentioned earlier that you're on holidays. You mean this isn't a work-related trip?"

Nigella filled in the blanks for her, telling her that she was a lawyer in Stockholm, but this trip was nothing short of a miracle. It could only be classified as the adventure of a lifetime.

Linda looked down at her watch and said, "We've got four more hours to pass. I'm all ears."

As Nigella listened to herself, telling the story of the unexpected turn of events leading up to the holiday, she still could barely comprehend that all of this was happening to her. She told of casually, almost carelessly, registering her DNA with Ancestry.se just because everyone around the water cooler was doing it. To her great surprise, she learned that her biological father was a man named Nigel Royal who was a Canadian Supreme Court Justice who lived in Toronto, Canada. Nigella herself had been born to a single mother who was profoundly deaf, and she never had a father, a stepfather, or any other kind of a father-figure in her whole life.

Linda, with eyebrows raised right up to her hairline, said, "Don't stop now. What happened next?"

Nigella continued with her fairy tale, saying that her newly found father was delighted to hear from her and had immediately arranged for two first-class tickets so that they could meet in Toronto.

Nigella wrapped up her story by summarizing, "So, you see, I don't have a husband waiting for me at the airport, but I do have a much, much better fellow than that! I have a dad that's picking us up. A real dad. A dad that I never knew I had in all my 30 years, until two weeks ago."

Linda continued, "What a way to start the new year of 2006! But wait a minute. How did you end up with his name? You said his name is Nigel, right? And yours is Nigella. What gives with that?"

Nigella told her how her deaf mother was working in a hotel kitchen 31 years ago, and she had an unplanned afternoon tryst with a guest at the hotel after she had delivered room service to him. It was the first time that her mother had ever had sex. He was a young lawyer, age 24, and her mother was 28 years old. They parted company as he was catching his plane back to Toronto that afternoon, and since she was deaf, she was too shy about her language skills and voice to sound her name out to him, so although he asked her, she didn't tell him her name at all. He had written his name 'Nigel' along with his country 'Canada' on a piece of hotel note-paper, and she saved it over all the years. She had given it to Nigella just before she died from cancer, two years ago, at the age of 59 years.

Nigella finished her story by adding that over all the years, her mother never married and stayed true to the love of her life, a man without a last name. Her mother always referred to her as her *love child*, hence the name Nigella, after the father.

"Okay, but what about your beautiful little daughter here? She looks so much like you, so does that mean that you and her are biracial? Is your birth-father an African-Canadian? Was your mother a blonde Swede? Your blonde hair is African, isn't it? And hers too. It's amazing, by the way."

"It's complicated." Nigella explained. "You see, my mother described her lover to me, in that he was a black man, tall, lanky, so yes, I take after him somewhat. And my mother, who was born a Pole, became a Swede when she was six months old. She was born in a displaced persons' camp in Germany right after the war. Her mother was a Holocaust Survivor, a Polish Jew, who died during childbirth. There was no father, so she was an orphan at birth, and Sweden took her in.

"When I was 23 years old, after I became a lawyer, I decided that I would have in-vitro fertilization to have a child to simply keep my mother happy. There was just the two of us for my whole life, and I owed her big time. She was the best. She was always wanting me to marry and to have children, but I simply wasn't wanting or needing a man in my life. I was a young lawyer on the fast-track, and I was in my early 20s. We made a deal that she would take care of the baby while I continued with my career. The three of us, of course, would live together. When I went to the clinic, I chose the donor that was most similar in description to Mom's love of her life. Imagine, finding a black donor in Stockholm, which is like finding a needle in a haystack. But, just for her. I couldn't have cared less to have the baby match up to look like me, but nature takes it course. I know this all sounds crazy, but trust me, it's the truth!"

The British Airways flight attendant shook her head and said, "Here's some advice for you, Nigella Hansson. First, have a wonderful holiday with your father, and then take the next flight directly to Hollywood. Your story would be the blockbuster of the year."

***

Book One

Chapter One
Trouble in Paradise

I had been living in Canada for two years. It was January 03, 2008, in Toronto, and it was freezing cold outside, even to me, a hardy northerner from Stockholm, Sweden. I was pulling out of the drive, and the twins were chattering with each other from their seats behind me. Maureen, my indispensable nanny, was still away for her Christmas break, and I was taking the boys to the part-time daycare that I had arranged. Not that I needed a break, but the boys needed socialization skills implanted early in their life, and staying home with Maureen or me Canadian-style just didn't cut it in my opinion. I was a true-blue believer in the Swedish way of doing things back home where education starts with free daycare and schooling at a very early age.

Dad had pulled out of the driveway just before me, and Martina was blowing kisses to us through the window in his backseat, her one arm around Patou. What would I do without my wonderful dad?

Every morning, rain or shine, Dad was there, making sure Martina's lunch was in her backpack, her homework done, and her jacket zipped up before taking her to school. Just last night he was on the phone with me, giving me Martina's new email address that he had just set up on her new little laptop he had bought her that would stay in his office until she was ready for it, although I knew she was years away from needing an email address. My seven-year-old daughter had a few years to go before emailing anyone, but I graciously accepted his generosity without fighting it. It kept him happy. Today he was coming back to help me organize space in the playroom for all the new Christmas toys and presents. All that, and Mom, seven months pregnant, at the age of 46 with her first pregnancy, was patiently waiting for him to get home for lunch. As much as Mom wanted to be in the thick of things with the kids, the doctor had advised her to lay off all the running around and to just put her feet up, especially with all the cold and ice outside. I would be so happy once their baby, my little half-brother, arrived safe and sound. Her pregnancy, although it had gone so well so far, was a big worry for all of us. She never let on, but I knew she was very conscious of the complications that can arise with a first pregnancy at her age. I don't think Dad had had a good night's sleep ever since they found out she was well into her first trimester way back last fall. And he was getting grayer by the day. They were lucky though; they both doted on each other like I've never seen in my whole life.

And I was the luckiest woman on earth, being their daughter. I never dreamt in my whole life that two years ago, at the age of 30, that I would find my biological father and my stepmom who lived halfway across the world in Toronto, Canada. I had a family. A real family.

I called out to the boys, knowing quite well that they wouldn't understand a word of what I was saying, "Boys, boys, listen up to Mommy. Do you know that you're going to have an uncle that's younger than you? Yeah, we have a crazy, mixed-up family, that's for sure."

***

I saw Dad's Porsche reach my driveway just before me. I pulled up beside him, and he was laughing as he let the dog out of the backseat. He called out, "Ha-ha! Beat you again!"

We both stood there, laughing at Patou who was busy rolling around and around in the snow in the front yard. After all, he was a Great White Pyrenees, and I'm sure he dreamed of snow banks for nine months of the year. I turned up my collar to give him a few minutes of play when all of a sudden, Patou jumped up as if he was on alert or something. He started howling. He ran over to Dad and began to whimper.

"What's wrong, boy?" Dad asked with a worried look on his face.

The dog jumped up on Dad's chest, still whimpering, then took off like a bullet down the street. We stood there watching as the dog turned the corner, heading for his home.

As he turned the corner, we looked at each other and said at the same time, with me saying 'Mom' and him saying 'Denni.'

I drove, and Dad could only say, "Please God, please God," over and over again.

34

We heard the EMS sirens as we turned the corner, and we pulled up right behind them.

Mom was unconscious, lying in the hall. She had managed to unlock the front door for the EMS while calling them to say that she was hemorrhaging. She was lying in a puddle of blood.

I tried to calm Dad; he was like a wild man. "Dad! Dad! Don't look there! Dad! Please! Listen!"

"Whoa, whoa! Step back! Step back right now! We have to get her in the ambulance! Are you her husband? Good. She's still alive. She's just lost consciousness. You come with us. You can ride with her as long as you don't get in our way, do you understand?"

"Dad! Go with them! Right now. Dad! Listen! I'll follow in the car!"

My heart broke as I watched him holding onto the stretcher, head bent over her, assuring her that everything was going to be okay and how much he loved her in between answering the questions that the paramedics were asking him about the pregnancy. It was at that moment I saw my father age 30 years. He turned, in a flash, from a robust, healthy, 56-year-old, albeit a heart patient, into a frail, broken octogenarian.

Luckily, I'm good in times of duress, and I turned to step back inside the door to make sure that the dog was inside before I followed the ambulance. My heart stopped as I watched Patou lay down beside the dark puddle. He wasn't whining any longer; he was crying. Actually crying. I've never heard a dog make that sound before. I kneeled down beside him and cried right along with him. I cried for Dad, for Mom, and for my little baby half-brother that never had a chance. I knew that the baby was gone. I was holding Patou and praying to God that He spare my mother.

I got out my phone to call my husband, François, to meet us at the hospital, and Patou and I both got back in the car and drove to the hospital, leaving the pool of blood unattended to. I couldn't stomach it; I just had to be with Mom and Dad.

Patou had jumped in the front seat beside me, and he rested his paw on my lap for the whole trip to Mount Sinai. When he reached over and licked my face, I knew somehow that Mom was going to be okay. There would be time later to grieve the loss of the baby. I prayed, *Please God, just keep her safe.* I was sure that Dad would die too if we lost her along with the baby.

I saw them sitting there. François had his arm around Dad, and by the time I had reached the two of them on the other side of the room, I allowed myself to fall apart.

Dad held onto me and told me in a soft but calm voice that he'd just been in with Mom and that the doctors were taking good care of her. She had lost a lot of blood, but they were taking care of everything, and she was going to be just fine. He also told me that he and Mom had already signed up for the Neonatal Donation Program at Sick Kids when they had gone to prenatal classes to learn more about being pregnant and going through delivery. Their baby boy would not die in vain. Other newborns would receive his eyes, liver, kidneys, and other organs through Sick Kids Hospital right across the street from where we were sitting at that very moment.

"Pops and Mama are on their way, honey," François said, "And when they get here, I'll take our car to go home to pick up Martina and the twins from school and daycare and get dinner on the table. Where's Patou?"

"In the car here in the hospital parking lot. Can you just take him back to our house so he's with the kids? He took such good care of me all the way to the hospital. He'll be grieving for the baby. He went into the house and saw the blood, so he knows what happened."

Dad said, "Dogs know everything ahead of us. Especially Patou. It's funny, although I love him and take care of him much more than Denni; he's still her dog. I wish we could get him in here just so he can see for himself she's going to be okay."

With that, the doctor came out to speak to us, "I'm back. She's stabilizing nicely, but first and foremost, and once again to you, Mr. Royal, I am so sorry for your loss. This is a heartbreaking situation we've got on our hands, and it's difficult for us all to watch each other having to go through it. Please know she's in very good hands. And the baby, well, the baby is in His hands now. So, here's the plan for going forward. We've got her stabilized, but she's going to stay with us here in ICU for the night at least before we move her into her own room. She's pretty doped up, but you can go in to see her for five minutes tops, and then we're going to top her up with some good drugs to make sure she sleeps right through. She needs plenty of rest. Other than losing too much blood, she's in good shape, no problem with complications like heart, organ failure, etc. We figure she may be well-enough for us to complete a caesarean section in a day or two. Questions?"

"Can I stay in with her tonight?" Dad asked.

"Sorry, Mr. Royal. Not tonight. Not while she's in ICU. However, as soon as we get her into her own room, any of you can stay over as many nights as you like. She'll probably stay with us for a week, just to make sure her C-section incision doesn't give us any trouble and we're sure that her mental health stays strong," the doctor answered.

He added, "Trust me, Mr. Royal, she's not going to know a thing until late tomorrow morning, so I'd advise you to all go home tonight and try to rest. I'd advise that you stay with your daughter for the next night or two. And, there is one other thing that I don't want you worrying or wondering about."

"Yes?" we all asked in unison.

"It doesn't matter what religion, if any at all, that you follow or don't follow. We have a suggestion that may help you when you are making plans for the deceased. The hospital will take care of the cremation or burial if you want us to, or, if you would like to have your own service right here, in Mrs. Royal's room or in the non-denominational chapel, that would be very fitting as well. Of course, we don't know at this moment when the actual delivery will take place, but, meanwhile, keep this information in hand, and you'll know when the time comes how you want to handle everything. And lastly, Mr. Royal, I would like to thank you from the bottom of my heart for your donation to the Neonatal Donation Program. Your baby will help numerous newborns that are in distress. We are at your service, and, once again, I'm sorry for your loss."

Once again, we all spoke in unison, "Thank you, Doctor."

We had all just sat down again when my in-laws came through the door, stress and worry written all over their faces. We all had a cry over the loss of the baby, and Papa, true to form, after a little chat with Dad, took charge, and within ten minutes, we all knew what, when, and how it was all going to go down.

I stood there, watching all the interaction, thinking to myself that from the day I was born until the day I was 30 years old, I didn't have a single male figure in my life. Now I had three of the strongest, most remarkable men in my life on a daily basis.

So, François and Mama left to meet Patou in the car, then to pick up the kids and put dinner on the table. Dad would sleep at our house that night.

Dad and Papa, at Dad's insistence, were first going straight to 7 Russell Hill Road. Dad was very anxious to get home and clean up the front hall; he said that it would give him a sense of closure so he could help Mom through her grief. He also said that he would pack a bag for Mom so she would have her own robe and toiletries, and then he would come back to the hospital to stay with Mom until they kicked him out closing time.

Dad asked me to stay put with Mom until he got back later on. He would bring back dinner for me, and we would eat together, right there in the waiting room, near to Mom.

It all suited me just fine. At that point, I couldn't have left Mom anyway, even if my life had depended on it.

***

Dad and I had just finished the dinner that Mama had packed for us, and we called Uncle Brad to let him know what had happened. He said he'd catch the red-eye up to Toronto, but Dad asked him to wait a few days and come for the little service that we'd have once Mom got out of the woods. I assured Brad again and again that I'd make sure that Dad took his heart meds on time and that I'd give Mom his love until he could get there.

Dad said, "I'm a lucky man to have a brother like Brad. He's always there for me."

The doctor came out to say goodnight to us. "We're definitely all settled in for the night now, so if you'd like to go in and just hang out with her until closing time, it's fine with me. It may give you a little comfort just to sit in there with her, but she's asleep now for the night. And remember, you're going to need your rest to deal with this wallop of grief, so please get home and get into bed early tonight. Doctor's orders!"

We sat there, quietly talking as Mom slept, Dad leaning over her every two minutes to kiss her and smooth her hair back, when he said, "By the way, I was impressed with François earlier. He told me he was thinking about getting a vasectomy, and he asked me if I'd like to get one done at the same time as him, since we know that making babies is out of the question for me from now on. I said yes immediately. I've known ever since last September that I need to have it done to protect Denni from another pregnancy, and now is a perfect time. Denni and I can heal together. I'm going to have my old nurse come and live in with us for the first little while anyway. She took such good care of me when I had the heart attack. May I ask, when did you two decide that three's enough?"

I just looked at him and quietly shook my head. "We didn't. This is the first I heard of it."

Dad reached over and grabbed my hand, and he let out a long sigh. "I'm sorry, honey. Your mom and I have noticed that you two don't share the same kind of relationship as we do, but we thought that it might just be a rough patch."

"Actually, Dad, no one in the whole wide world shares your kind of relationship. What you two have is very special." Tears started rolling down my cheeks. "Wait, Dad, wait; these tears aren't just about my husband and my marriage. I'm crying for your loss mostly. Mom too. The only thing that calms me is the fact that I know you two are going to pull through this just fine. My marriage is another matter. But, yes, please – yes, by all means, yes to the vasectomies. Both of you. Do it next week. I think it's a good idea."

Dad continued, "You know, back to your marriage – maybe we can draw a little solace from one of Canada's great poets. He's a singer as well. His name is Leonard Cohen, and Denni just loves him. Cohen says:

There is a crack in everything, that's how the light gets in."

I smiled a little, and I said, "Now, Dad, you're starting to sound like the wise, old judge that you are in real life. But I agree with you wholeheartedly; there's a lesson to be learned here. Meanwhile, I don't want you and Mom worrying about my marriage. We'll figure it out – or not. But now's not the time to dwell on it."

With that, the nurse came in and whispered that we had five minutes until lights out, so I gave Mom a kiss and left the room to freshen up before going home. I told Dad I would meet him in five minutes at the elevator.

***

A few nights later, I was lying beside my sleeping husband who, once again, had begged for a rain check as I turned to him for love, reassurance, and sex that I was longing for.

I got up and padded into my big en-suite. I stood there, looking into my mirror, searching for my real face. Not this one. I wanted to see the old one; the young, happy, biracial woman with the beautiful, blonde ringlets of African hair brushing her shoulders. No. I was looking into the face of a sad, 30-something woman with a failing marriage on her hands and not knowing how to fix it. The same woman that was sadly coming to realize that she didn't even know if she wanted to fix her marriage if she could. The same woman that talked herself through every day, saying that she should be grateful for all she had. And, now, a new look was beginning to emerge. The look of resentment. I studied my hair with disdain.

I pulled away, away from hearing my Swedish birth-mother's voice in my head, reminding me that my beautiful African hair was my crowning glory and one of my blessings that, coupled with my brains, would get me far in life. My hair over the last year hadn't secured my husband's needing me. Hell, no. He couldn't even get it up for me. If my 'crowning glory' couldn't fix that, there was no hope for me or the marriage.

I rummaged around in the vanity drawer, looking for a pair of scissors. I'd take care of this little problem right now.

I had my left hand high above my head, holding a big chunk of my hair, with the scissors in my right hand, poised to hack, when I heard a new voice in my head. It wasn't Mor, but strangely I felt like I was familiar with this new voice somehow.

I held back on the first cut, and I listened.

I instinctively knew it was my maternal grandmother. Yes, the one that had survived Auschwitz. The same one that lived long enough to give birth to my mother in a displaced person's camp after the war. Yes, the same one that died with the newborn in her arms back in 1946.

I slowly lowered the scissors, and I stood there, eyes riveted straight ahead, fearful that I would miss even a syllable or an inflection as she began her story.

She told me of being shaved bald of her beautiful, full head of golden-blonde hair and of being tattooed like an animal as they attempted to strip her of her identity, her soul, her very being. She told me that she survived both Auschwitz-Birkenau and Bergen-Belsen because she held onto her inner rage. And then she repeated her own mother's last words to her, right along with her story.

"Never, never, cut your hair. Promise me that you'll never cut your hair. It is your crowning glory. It is your blessing. Coupled with your brains, it will get you far in life. It may even save your life."

The voice of my grandmother ended her story by repeating the prayer that she told me she had used nightly in the concentration camp, to honor her family that had gone before her. As I listened to her, I realized that it seemed to be her own version of the Mourner's Kaddish, the Jewish prayer for the dead. I'm not fully versed in my religion's prayers at the best of times let alone hearing them directly from the spirit world, but, nevertheless, I got the message, loud and clear, being the analytical lawyer that I was. I broke down the message into three main points:

Number one was to listen to my mother. Number two was to not cut my hair. Number three was be thankful for my blessings.

I slowly adjusted my focus to look at myself in the mirror; I mean, to really, really look at myself. I put the scissors carefully back in their place, and I just stood there silently while tears began to roll down the sad woman's face that was staring out at me.

Yes, it may have been a sad face, but I never saw that resentment again. Ever.

After a minute or two of feeling sorry for myself, the woman in the mirror was asking me, "Who am I?" I didn't have the answer for her, so I began my journey to find the answers to her age-old question by taking my grandmother's advice. I tried on Grandma's 'inner rage' for size. It was an entirely new way of doing things and I began my journey of self-discovery by taking the first step.

I quickly wrapped a scrunchie around my locks that had just narrowly escaped a terrible fate, smoothed some night cream over my face, and marched over to our bed where François was dead to the world. I grabbed the duvet that was down around his waist with my right hand and pulled hard to release it from the bottom of the bed with my left. I balled the whole thing up, and with a good dose of my very own 'inner rage,' I threw it down into his face.

In response to his sputtering and arm-flailing, I muttered to myself, "Who the fuck needs you anyway!" and I stomped out of the room. It was my first attempt at 'inner rage' and I thought to myself that I was off to a good start. I must admit though, I did jump a little as the big painting in the hall came crashing down immediately following my heartfelt slam of the bedroom door.

By the time I'd reached my office and turned on my computer, the newly found ass-kicking side of my usually sweet disposition had simmered down to a more manageable level.

Although I had had an Ancestry.se account for over five years, I thought I would start from scratch. I applied through Ancestry.ca for two new gene-finding kits, one for myself and one for my daughter, Martina. My main aim was to source new avenues that would lead to my maternal, Kaufman, genes. As I printed out my two receipts, I realized that I was feeling so much better about myself, so I thought that there was no time like the present to start my Kaufman research. You might say that I was on a roll.

I typed in *Auschwitz-Birkenau/Kaufman* that started my search for my grandmother.

What had taken me so long?

***

A few days later, at the service for Baby Nigel Jr. that was being held in Mom's hospital room, I looked at the two men-of-the-cloth beside me, Rabbi Kleiman and Pastor Smith, one on each side of Mom's bed. That's the way we did things in our family. We were such a ragtag bunch. Some of us were Jews, some of us were Christians, and we all sported the different skin tones of our Jamaican, Polish, Swedish, Irish, Vietnamese, French-Canadian, and American backgrounds.

My story, I thought, was typically Canadian. It spoke of the immigrant experience and of the diversity that my new home of Toronto offered to all of us. My grandmother was a Polish Holocaust Survivor; my mother (my Mor) and I were Swedes; my father was born in Jamaica, who had a Caucasian-American brother. My second mother was an Irish-Canadian woman. I was married to a Vietnamese-Canadian, and I had a Jewish daughter that had my African hair. My two Christian sons looked Eurasian, with their father's Asian face, watered down with my Swedish and Jamaican roots. It doesn't get any crazier than that. But somehow it all worked. It all worked seamlessly. Except my marriage of course.

The rabbi's and pastor's prayers were lovely, some in Hebrew and some in English. They set the tone for all of us. I told myself to hold on, to just hold on. It wasn't the time to fall apart now. My parents had set an amazing example of grace and dignity.

Mom was calm, sitting up in the hospital bed, holding her delivered baby wrapped securely in his first hospital swaddle. Dad and I were sitting on either side of her, with our hands resting on the little bundle as his last rites were performed. Uncle Brad was sitting beside Dad, with his arm around his shoulders. In order to keep myself from breaking down completely, I reminded myself that I was a trained lawyer and that I should keep my emotions in check by spending the time analyzing the people around me.

Uncle Brad, who had his arm around Dad's shoulders, was, by anyone's measure, a handsome man. Extremely so. And a rich man. Extremely so. 30-odd years ago, he had moseyed westward from the mid-west states in America across to Lalaland on the coast. It wasn't long after that that Hollywood welcomed him with open arms. Back then, he was a 20-year-old blond, blue-eyed kid that already had enough notches on his bedpost to last a lifetime. He was a charmer to boot, and it wasn't long before he was picking up a gig here and there. His old-fashioned, Midwest manners, work ethic, intellect, and good looks began to show up on the covers of the tabloids, where they had continued to run weekly ever since. All that had changed over the years; according to the tabloids, it was the face and name of the beautiful woman that would be hanging onto his arm. She was sometimes just a hopeful, and at other times a bona fide wife, either at the beginning or the end of their here-today-gone-tomorrow marriage.

But before he got really famous and really rich, he was shooting a little film up in Canada and found himself in a bit of a pickle. That's when he met Dad who, at the time, was also moving up his own ladder as a brilliant, good-looking, well-dressed, black lawyer. They immediately bonded as 'brothers' somehow, and the rest, as they say, is history. Over the ensuing years, Brad would fly in, under the radar of course and away from the paparazzi, and hunker down at 7 Russell Hill Road and have a few days with his 'family,' playing poker and shooting the shit with Dad, Papa, and François before heading back to his home in France or L.A. or on to his next movie's shoot location. Papa always called him 'pretty boy,' with good reason.

I was a little startled as Brad looked up and caught my eye. He gave me an almost-imperceptible nod of assurance and a little wink. He knew exactly that I was playing my ice-queen prosecutor role in order to keep from falling apart. After all, he was a professional actor, playing his own personal role to be able to get through this nightmare, where he just really wanted to hear a director call *Cut!* to be done with it.

My eyes moved to my dad. My God, he was the most handsome man in the whole city. He came to Canada as a nine-year-old Jamaican boy, carrying those good looks that belong to the Caribbean peoples. You know those looks, the ones with the smooth, brown skin and wonderful, dark, brown eyes that were a result of years and years of intermarrying between the Asians and the Africans. That, along with his high cheekbones, wide, wide smile, and his lanky, graceful form completed the package of every woman's dream of the perfect 56-year-old man. Dad too was a hard worker like Brad, but he was an intellectual from the get-go. He ended his career with an early retirement from his position as a Supreme Court Justice of Canada. Over the years, not only did he always have a well-paying job but he had inherited a truckload of money from my granddad, Saul Himmel. Now Saul was not his real father, no, not at all. It's just another story of how they do things in Canada. Saul Himmel was also a Supreme Court Justice and was very well-respected, especially in the Jewish community in Toronto. Back in 1960, he had taken Dad, a small, black boy that attended a Baptist Church every Sunday under his wing. Saul left his extensive estate to Dad when he died years later.

When I met Dad a few short years ago, he shared Saul's money with Mom and me without blinking an eye. And that's the real truth of how I got my big, fancy house at 49 Parkwood Avenue. I hadn't worked as a lawyer in the three years I had been in Canada, and although my husband, François, was a lawyer and made good money, it was Granddad Saul's money that had feathered my nest. It was too bad Granddad Saul wasn't alive to see that he had a Jewish granddaughter, as well as a Jewish great-granddaughter. He would have loved that.

I took a breath and told myself to keep it together as I looked at Mom. She sat there, propped up with the pillows, looking every bit of the queen that she was. It was a very rare occasion that I saw her without her makeup on, but she looked as beautiful as ever. She was such a contrast to Dad, with her white Irish skin and soulful, big, gray, Celtic eyes. Of course, she was ten years younger than him, and that was also part of the contrast, even though the two of them took very good care of themselves. Although I called her Mom, since she was only 14 or 15 years older than I was, and since she was white and I was considered by most as black, the term *Mom* was a bit of a stretch to anyone that met us, but it worked for us. Mom and Dad spent a fortune on their clothes, haircuts, facials, and massages, etc., but really, it was their deep, deep love for each other that kept them both looking like movie stars themselves, never mind Dad's famous brother. She had just had the caesarean section in order to deliver their stillborn son, so I know she was still heavily sedated, but she pulled this whole nightmare off with all the dignity and strength of all the queens around the world before her.

She was another one of us that had had a tough life as a kid; her father had died at a very early age, and she had a mother who just didn't know how to love herself let alone any of her four children. Mom had knocked around the world most of her adult life, using her skills as curriculum designer, teaching English as a second language, and flipping real estate in Canada to augment her travels. She didn't meet Dad until she was 43. It was love at first sight, but that didn't save them from many ups and downs before Dad finally put his foot down and dragged her, heels dug in, all the way to the altar. They had been blissfully happy ever since that day of their little wedding in the backyard of 7 Russell Hill Road. She started her writing career right then and there, and now she was a very-much sought-after author of many, many adventures and misadventures within the pages of her novels. I loved her fiercely.

I smiled as I noticed that Dad had put her big, four-carat, canary-yellow diamond ring back on her finger. Although Dad thought he was head of the family, Mom and I knew differently.

I kept my eyes as far as possible away from the little wrapped-up bundle. There was a limit to my strength, and I told myself that this wasn't the time and place to test it. Some things were best left alone.

I turned around to check on three other members of the family. François was behind me, with his arms around his mom and dad. Papa had been Dad's best friend for 30 years, and his new wife, Diep, loved Mom like a sister. Papa and Mama had come to Canada as boat people from Vietnam in the '70s, and Papa had been with Granddad Saul and Dad ever since. I shook my head a little, and I turned back around to face the music.

Dad read out a poem. The poem was my parents' favorite, and it made a great deal of sense to me. They had explained the poem to me ages ago. It was about loss and resilience, and it was my maternal Granddad Harold's favorite poem from way back in the day when Mom was a young girl. It was Robert Frost's, *The Need Of Being Versed In Country Things.*

I realized there was so much more that I didn't know about this remarkable couple that had become my parents a few years back when I was 30 years old. I made a promise to myself that I wouldn't be so self-absorbed, and to be a better daughter in the future. Their baby son had just died and it was time for me to put my big-boy pants on and be the woman that my birth-mother, my Mor, would have expected.

We all joined in to say *The Lord's Prayer* and then, to the sound of Rabbi Kleiman's tampered-down voice, chanting the appropriate psalms in Hebrew. Mom gave the baby to Dad who, in turn, slowly placed him in Pastor Smith's arms. They walked over to the window, lifted our precious bundle up high into the light as if to offer him to the heavens.

Slowly, ever so slowly, the two of them sung the last psalm as they made their way over to the door, and then they were gone.

In real time, the whole service was a short, perfunctory 10-15 minutes, but, to me, it was a lifetime. I felt a little guilty about just wanting it to be over, as I knew that my poor parents had a lifetime of grieving ahead of them. I promised myself again that I would be a better daughter to them starting that very moment.

The deathly silence was broken by Mom who, up to then, had been perfectly composed. Perhaps she had been playing her own little part, much like Brad and I had done. Her heartbroken wails and wails and wails of grief were muffled into Dad's chest as his ragged, low voice tried to soothe her with his deep baritone. Uncle Brad and I moved over to the window, holding onto each other, trying to keep our tears silent and away from them. I could feel his chest heaving under his jacket as we clung to each other and we cried together in stifled, heart-broken silence. He wiped the tears off my cheeks, and I reached up to wipe his away as well. That's what families do. They hold each other up during the good time and the bad. And this was the worst.

***

Uncle Brad and I both raided the fridge later that night, and I had to laugh as I looked at the two of us standing there in our pajamas, whispering our choices of leftovers to each other over the open fridge door. It had been one hell of a day, but we'd managed to survive it. Dad was staying over in Mom's room at the hospital, my in-laws had gone back to their apartment, the kids were in bed, and François had turned in early. We both turned toward Patou who was lying by the front door. Patou decided day by day which house he was going to spend the day in. Most of the time he slept over at 7 Russell Hill Road, but until Dad and Mom got home from the hospital, he was quite happy to stay with us. The sly, old dog was giving us a little whimper to remind us that he too would like a leftover.

Brad said, "Oh, Patou, you know how to win the heart of the lady of the house. I remember you five years ago when you were nothing but a little white ball of fluff, pissing all on the family-room floor, and lifting your leg up against Nigel and Denni's big ficus trees every five minutes. But don't mind me, Patou, you're a fine dog; I was just walking down memory lane, that's all."

I smiled across the table at Dad's brother as he slathered his roast-beef sandwich with the mustard while I dug into my tuna-melt.

I said, "Yeah, Uncle Brad, hold that thought about memory lane."

Brad interrupted me by putting his sandwich down and giving me the look, "For Christ's sake, Nigella, please, forget this *uncle* business. Just Brad will do. You make me feel like an old man. How many times do I have to tell you?"

"Okay, okay, Brad. Now come on. How often do we have one-on-one time? Just the two of us. Tell me some stories about when you first met Dad. You know, way back when you two were kicking ass, him as a young lawyer in Toronto and you as a young actor in Hollywood."

It all started well enough. After all, he was Hollywood to a 'T,' and I wasn't invincible to his charms. He told me story after story of when he was a little upstart doing his first few films up in Toronto, acting like an asshole and getting out of his little scrapes with the help of his smart, handsome lawyer, namely Nigel Royal. He told of dragging Dad out to party after party where the girls would be lined up outside the hotel suite's door, quite willing to spend time with either him or his good-looking black brother. They were quite a team in the legal sense of the word, but no, not when it came to the girls. My dad would have no part of private parties with the girls. When Brad would insist the very least that he could do was to attend the parties, Nigel would oblige but stand quietly in a corner of the party, quietly nursing a single beer, just waiting to make his escape. Brad went on to say that Dad just couldn't climb out of his inherent shyness. He was simply a tall, good-looking, nerdy intellectual that didn't fare well with the ladies, much to their disappointment. He added that he was a hell of a lawyer though.

All of a sudden, our conversation fell quiet, and we both started bawling our eyes out. It was all brought on of course by the quiet, painful, intimate goodbye we had said earlier to the baby. We sat there at the kitchen table and Patou came over and put his paw up on my lap.

"I'm just such a fucking mess," Hollywood's eye candy sobbed.

"What?" I said, trying to catch on to the change in the topic.

"It's me. It's my fault. If I wasn't such an asshole, I'd still be married to her. And it's always the kids that get hurt the most. It's not fair to them. I've really got to clean up."

"Uncle Brad – I mean Brad, you're my hero. You're being too hard on yourself. Hell, look at me. I'm the worst. I'm just a lazy, spoiled princess. I'm nothing but a daddy's girl. Even my husband doesn't want me anymore."

"This is it. I'm going to go into rehab and clean up my act. I've been boozing way, way too much, and I've got to take better care of myself so I can get back to my family and be a man like your dad. Talk about heroes – now there's a hero for you. He's the best. And for Christ's sake, I'm old! I'm way, way too old to be in Hollywood, tooling around town, still looking for gigs that I know more often than not are going to much younger actors. I'd rather just be directing, but the press and tabloids, once they get their fucking teeth into you, they never let you go. I'm not my own man anymore."

I managed a little smile, shook my head, and I said to him, "Oh, okay, so now we're feeling sorry for ourselves, are we?"

I got a box of Kleenex and we both blew our noses and he said, "Honey, but wait. What did you say about François not wanting you? What's going on here? Do I need to kick someone's ass around the block? Isn't he treating you right?"

"I'm just feeling neglected these days. I don't want to be telling tales out of school, Brad. But it's just that I'm only 34 years old, and the sex went out of my three-year-old marriage two years ago. He just doesn't want me anymore."

48

Brad wiped a tear off my face, and he said, "Who the fuck wouldn't want you, our little Swedish princess? You have a heartbreakingly beautiful face, a big brain, a pure heart, and a very sexy Euro-accent. And standing at 5'10", your long legs make men forget what they're saying mid-sentence. François has lost his fucking mind!"

"Well, maybe he still wants me, but I think he's intimidated or jealous or something with me going back to school to get my doctorate. He doesn't encourage my studies at all. It just boils down to him not coming home at night, or when he does, he can't get it up enough to cover for his insecurities or something. I don't have any experience with other men, so I'm just at a loss. The only thing I know for sure is that I need the sex and the loving from him and I'm not getting any."

"Honey, I don't even know if I should ask you this, but do you think he has a girlfriend at work or something?"

"What? Of course not! He's a married man! He has three children! He wouldn't do that!"

"Okay, honey, okay. Forget I said that. You're right. It must be something else. But one thing I know for sure, it's not you, honey. You're the perfect woman, and the perfect wife, and the perfect daughter. And don't you forget it, d'ya hear me?"

"Yeah. Thanks, Brad. Now I feel like a fool having told you this. Let's forget I said anything. Okay?"

"Just know you can call me anytime, about anything. Anything at all. Call me and tell me when, and I'll come up here and kick his ass into next week for you. We're family and we've got to stick together. Right?"

"Yeah. I love you. And thanks for being here today. Dad and Mom needed you here, but I'll take over for you tomorrow morning. What time is your flight out? Is Papa taking you out to the airport in the blacked-out Benz?"

"Yep. In fact, I'll be gone by the time the kids and you are up. Let's have a hug now; I'm going to turn in. Thanks, honey, for turning down my bed and everything. You must miss your right-hand-nanny, Maureen, right now while she's still on her Christmas break. I wish I could get such a good nanny. Your Maureen O'Reilly is one in a million you know; she's so good with the kids, and she runs your house for you like nobody's business."

As I shut out the kitchen light, my hand automatically went up over the mezuzah on the kitchen doorframe. I said my little prayer to bless everyone, I

49

said an extra one for Dad's fabulous and famous Hollywood eye-candy brother.

He took the stairs, two at a time, and stopped midway. He turned to whisper to me, "Love you, honey."

"Love you too, Uncle Brad. I mean Brad."

***

It was exactly one week later as I looked around their house at 7 Russell Hill Road. The big life-like photos of Granddad Saul and Great-Great-Granddad George looked down at me as I moved around the family room, straightening the chairs around Dad's poker table and wiping imagined dust off the immaculately clean mantle. I smiled as I remembered sketching out the plans with Dad and Mom for this same big room over four years ago when the addition was in its first stages. Back then, when I had just decided to immigrate to Canada, and Mom and Dad had wanted to build a complete apartment for me and Martina, I had convinced them to put their money into a big family room complete with an open-plan kitchen that they could use once Martina and I were able to move out. All of us had never looked back.

This beautiful room was the new hub of Granddad Saul's big old house, and we all felt his presence as he smiled out from the big four-foot by six-foot piece of art that Mom installed for Dad as a surprise when he was coming home from his hospital stay from his heart attack three years ago. She had taken his favorite, old, original photo from 1960 and had it professionally enlarged and touched up to perfection. The photo was of the three of them sitting on the front steps; Granddad Saul, with their new pup named Little Daisy in the middle, who was leaning over, licking Dad's laughing nine-year-old face in delight.

Yes, Saul had bought Dad that pup the same week that Dad emigrated from Jamaica to live with his birth-mother, Mavis Royal, who was Saul Himmel's housekeeper. That was Saul's first overture of kindness toward the nine-year-old who had arrived on Saul's doorstep at 7 Russell Hill Road with nothing but his big smile and a curiosity of life that would lead him, under Saul's careful tutelage, to become first a lawyer, then one of Canada's Supreme Court Justices, following in Saul's footsteps to a 'T.' In the timespan of one five-hour plane ride, the small, thin boy that was labelled a 'pleaser' by his headmaster, the very one with the large keloid scar covering his entire left cheek, had gone from living in a shack with a dirt-floor kitchen to a leafy, upscale neighborhood of Forest Hill in Toronto, Canada.

Saul was the best father-figure a boy could ever dream of, and through the years, he made sure that the bright, lanky boy and his mother that lived in the little apartment attached to the back of his big house never wanted for anything. Saul paid for surgery after surgery to correct Dad's facial scar that was caused by a cricket-bat childhood accident, and by the time Dad graduated from university, all the expensive plastic surgery had paid off. Saul also had quietly bought healthy life-insurance policies for both his protégé and his mother and ensured that he left the bulk of his vast estate, including the house at 7 Russell Hill Road to Dad. And that's how Mom, Martina, and I each acquired a very large chunk of money that would do us a lifetime – given to us by Dad when he generously divvied up his inheritance from Saul. Both Mom and I had no idea of Dad's wealth at the time, but Dad insisted on sharing it all with us as if it was no more than a grilled cheese sandwich and a coffee down at the café.

The only other art on the wall in the big room was just as impressive. It was, once again, an enlargement of an old photograph. This particular, old, black-and-white photo was from Mom's few bits and pieces of her childhood that she kept in an old shoe box up in her office. Apparently, the original photo had been taken by her father when she was a baby. Her father had snapped the priceless classic on a summer day on the back stoop of the old farmhouse; on the very same farm where Dad, Mom, Papa, and Mama were currently setting up their apiary business.

Great-Great-Granddad George's luminescent, blue, Celtic eyes stared out from the picture. He was a tall, spare man with an extravagant, perfectly coifed white-handlebar moustache that drooped slightly at the far edges of his clean-shaven cheeks. A well-worn undershirt with a fraying neckband peaked out from the top of his overalls. In the photo, he was perched on an old, wooden, kitchen chair that had been set up in front of an old screen door that looked like it led from the back stoop into the old farmhouse. He was sitting there, his legs spread apart, and his long frame was stooping forward a little to rest his elbows down on his knees. His rough, old, farm-worn hands gently balanced his great-granddaughter's two tiny hands as she held onto his calloused fingers, trying her best to stay upright. The baby girl was sporting nothing but a cloth diaper, held together with two, big, safety pins. They had named her Denise, but everyone called her Denni. I called her Mom.

However, it wasn't the sweet little baby that was the focus of the photograph. No, not at all. It was her protector's soulful gaze into the camera that spoke volumes of his infinite connection to his little bundle of joy that was sitting on the lap of his old, worn, but clean overalls.

No wonder Mom always referred to him as the Guardian Angel that watched over her. Over the past few years that I had known Mom, she had told me many, many stories of meeting up with her great-grandfather's spirit over the past 20 years up in the bush that had completely taken over the old farm, right along with the old farmhouse and barn years and years before.

As Mom spoke of her other-worldly encounters, she would always add that, to her surprise, spirits didn't respect borders whatsoever. She would tell me the story of the year that he appeared every night as she walked her nightly walk around her neighborhood when she lived on the Gulf of Mexico in Florida. She could never figure out why he was always standing at the end of one particular driveway, under the big palms and well-manicured lawns. His appearance there was such a far cry from his old farm up north in Canada, but then again, she was worlds away from her days on that same farm herself as she sampled life one block from the pristine beaches of the toney neighborhood of Park Shore in Naples, Florida. She had spent all of her adult years, up to when she met Dad in her early 40s, as a gypsy of sorts, living in different cities around the world, and she had experienced life from Caracas, Venezuela, to Nairobi, Kenya, to Nice, France, and everywhere else in between.

But, despite her obvious worldliness and competent manner, Mom was definitely a firm believer in spirits, angels, ghosts, and such that was connected to the spirit world. Of course, Dad used all her stories of her meetings in the bush with her long-departed father and great-grandfather as ammunition to tease her, trying to keep up with the quick wit and storytelling abilities of his wife. It was hard who loved who the most. They were deeply, madly in love with each other despite their differences of him being a home-body and her being an adventurer of sorts. It seemed such a shame that they hadn't met until she was 43 and he was ten years older. When I met them, they had just been married a little over a year.

I made sure everything was perfect for their arrival home from the hospital. I had put fresh flowers in all the rooms, and the nurse had arrived earlier, suitcase in hand. I liked her instantly, and she proceeded to tell me all the stories about taking care of Dad after his heart attack and of how fond she was of both my parents. She couldn't believe how big Patou had grown, and she assured me that she would let him in and out and not give him too many biscuits. She knew Papa and Mama next door and Mary, the dog walker, as well, so I knew my parents were in capable hands. She was going to sleep upstairs in my old room and take care of all the meals to make sure that Mom and Dad didn't overdo it.

She said, "Now, child, don't you be worrying the least little bit. I'm here now. You just relax and take care of yourself and your babies. Your husband just had a vasectomy as well, right? You've got your hands full, girl! And you're just a block or two away, so I'll be sure to call if I need you, and you do the same."

***

She was right. I did have my hands full. I thought back to the other night, watching the old *Sex and the City 2* movie and laughing at the one character's famous line as she was trying to juggle it all. It was a short line meant to be funny, something about losing the nanny, and it really resonated with me somehow. Yes, indeed, thank God for the nanny! François, with his need for constant attention and icepack changes every 20 minutes kept me hopping, but, somehow, the week passed and both men recovered without a scratch; just a lot of bitching and complaining. Mom, as usual, was the most amazing, remarkable woman I have ever known, willingly sharing her big C-section incision with the nurse and myself as we checked her over, time and time again.

***

Five months later, the three, magnificent, dark-gray, smooth, granite stones, all in a row, gleamed and sparkled in the May late-spring sunlight. Dad, who never even knew who his biological father was, had created a literal dynasty which was now on full display in the very well-established Mount Pleasant Cemetery located in the heart of Toronto.

Years and years before, Granddad Saul Himmel, who had raised Dad since he was nine years old, had bought a few plots in the beautiful cemetery, all in

53

one row. He had buried his wife there, and then Dad had buried him in with her way back in 1980. Right after baby Nigel Jr. died in January, he and Mom had a third matching stone made and had it placed in between Saul Himmel and Grandma Mavis Royal who was Dad's Jamaican mother. Today was the day that we had gathered for a formal recognition of the members of our family that weren't with us any longer, in particular Baby Nigel Jr., and to commemorate the three, large, dark-gray, granite stones that carried the names of our loved ones.

I smiled when I read the words scribed into the stone. There it was. The same poem that Dad had read out at the little funeral. The words read: *The Need for Being Versed in Country Things.* Both of my parents' names, Nigel Royal and Denise Royal, were the top two names on the stone. The birthdates were in place, and, of course, the death dates were blank. The baby's name was scribed underneath theirs and read simply: *Baby Nigel Jr., Jan. 03, 2008 - Jan. 03, 2008.* My full given name, Nigella Kaufman Hansson, with my birthdate and the death date left blank followed theirs.

Dad explained to us all that there were three more plots left, one for the kids (meaning François and me and our kids), one for Papa and Mama, and one for good luck. It was his wish that we do whatever we want with them, and actually, no one had to buried there at all; these stones just symbolized the lives lived and had nothing to do with the actual burial of the deceased.

He and Mom had quietly interred Baby Nigel's ashes with Rabbi Kleiman and Pastor Smith earlier in the week in order to protect the family from the image of seeing the remains physically lowered into the earth. He had explained to us earlier that he and Mom were going to scatter the rest of the ashes up in the forest on the farm, under the big oaks and chestnut trees, to be with Mom's deceased family members, her great-granddad, George, and her father, Harold, at a later date.

A few prayers were said and blessings asked for all the lives lived and lost, and the families left behind. Mom and Dad encouraged us all to look at all the stones, monuments, and art that the beautiful cemetery had to offer. I doled out the stones that Jews place so that everyone could have their own private visit at each of our monuments. Papa and François let the boys loose on the grass, and we wandered throughout the beautiful grounds, comparing all the stones and imagining all the lives that had gone before resting here in this beautiful setting.

I caught up with Mom and put my arm around her shoulders. "Mom, how do you do it? You're always busy taking care of all us, and Dad too. You're always cooking and baking and cleaning up, and look at you! You look amazing! I love this pink on you. Is this the new suit that Dad bought you?"

"Thanks, honey. Yeah, it's been a chore shedding the baby weight, so of course my doting husband marched me into Holts and insisted on buying me a few new outfits. I'm afraid my usually perky breasts will never be the same. But really, that baby-weight stuff, it's a tough one. How did you do it in such short order, especially after having the twins?"

"If only it were that easy, Mom. I still have my little pouch that I face in the mirror every morning. We just have to suck it up and bear it like the tough no-nonsense women we are, I suppose. And look at Dad; you've done a remarkable job with the old guy. He's never looked better. Were the dark low lights in his hair your idea? His barber has done an excellent job. In fact, he's more handsome than ever with his new salt-and-pepper look. It takes ten years off his face."

"Yeah, I guess I'll keep him. I've kind of got used to having him around. You know how it is."

I laughed out loud. "Mom, you're the best. I love you to the moon and back. I'm so in awe of you and Dad and how you've handled the last six months."

"Strangely, it hasn't been as bad as you may think. Your dad and I have always had a very, very special love, but now it's just crazy. We've just grown all that much closer, if that's possible. You know how your dad is such a music fan, well, just the other day, he was just summing up our new life together after losing the baby. He says that we've graduated, and now he calls our relationship *A Sunday Kind of Love.* I think that it's one of Etta James's songs from back in the day."

"Well, you have been through a lot. Even going back to the days when he was under the Canadian Witness Protection Program."

"Honey, you have no idea. We've had more ups and downs than an elevator, but nothing seems to break us. And now we have you. It's the icing on our wedding cake, so to speak. Both of us never dreamed in a million years we would have children, and then you came into our lives. That's what helps us with Baby Nigel's death. We still have our daughter."

"Thanks, Mom. I love you."

"Love you too, honey."

It wasn't the time or the place to let her know that François and I didn't seem to share that same loving relationship. I couldn't remember the last time we had sex. I kept my sadness related to my failing marriage to myself.

Dad took us all for lunch at Martina's favorite restaurant, The Rainforest Café, over at Yorkdale Mall after we had all explored the cemetery and said our goodbyes to Brad who was heading straight out to the airport to catch the evening flight back to L.A.

***

I smiled as Papa took charge, making sure that my little twin boys, the hellions, were belted into their highchairs in the restaurant, while Martina dragged Dad from the faux gorillas to the big elephant in the corner of the restaurant. I leaned over and grabbed François hand, and he absentmindedly gave me a little kiss on the cheek. *Better than nothing,* I thought to myself, *Be thankful for small mercies.*

All in all, our day at the cemetery was a way for us adults to set an example of dignity and respect so that our children would follow suit over the years to come. I can't imagine how Mom and Dad must have suffered, reading Baby Nigel Jr.'s name on the big, dark-gray, granite stone.

The noisy restaurant was the perfect foil for our aching hearts to take a little breather from the grief that was choking each and every one of us.

***

Chapter Two
The Farm

We were all visiting my in-laws' farm just north of Toronto. They had a small, 20-acre farm, and they had carved out a beautiful little business of beekeeping in the middle of the big, old, dense, and overrun bush. The farm had been in Mom's family since they arrived from Ireland in 1840. Her Irish ancestors had received the original one-hundred acres of crown land from the government, with the stipulation being that they would settle there. Settle they did, starting out with a log-hewn lean-to shanty that eventually grew into a two-story farmhouse bursting at the seams with their 16 children. Between cutting down section by section of bush every summer and lots of storytelling and fiddle playing during the winter, they thrived. It wasn't too long before they owned cattle, six horses, and took part in the many barn raisings around their little hamlet of Brown Hill, an hour's drive north of Toronto.

Mom was so happy that the last few acres of her farm were back in the family and that my in-laws, who were boat people from Vietnam, were more than happy to partner with her in the business. She was happy to visit her beloved old farm but had no desire to live there on a permanent basis. She may have started out on the farm, but she had evolved into a city girl through and through.

Since there were no buildings on the 20 acres, they hired Tom Oliver, an old school friend of Mom's. He was an arborist who owned a sawmill. He wasto clear the front few acres to plant a flowering meadow to attract the honeybees. Mom loved that old bush like no other, and she had walked it time and time again with Tom, tagging the trees to come down but preserving the big old oaks and chestnut trees that had been standing there forever. Mom was definitely connected to the earth somehow, regardless of her city-slicker outward appearance of Louboutins and designer handbags.

They had bought a nice, new, mobile home for the site, and Papa and Mama called it home until they could build the house of their dreams the next summer. They kept their old apartment over the garage at 7 Russell Hill Road, but it stood empty now most of the time.

The kids and the dog loved going to the farm, and Papa and Mama had a little outdoor shed for all their muddy boots and paraphernalia that kids need in the bush.

Dad and Papa would carry the boys over to the stumpery, to lean them over to feel all the curves and edges of the smooth, gray wood. Papa was quite a gardener, and with a little help from Tom, he had taken numerous stumps from upended fallen trees that Tom had taken out of the bush. He lined them all up, to separate the meadow from the bush. He had painstakingly cleaned and carved and coaxed the stumps into a long, one-hundred-foot, gigantic sculpture that stood between five or six feet tall but rising upward in places to nine or ten feet. He explained to everyone that came to see the spectacle that he had followed the same design that Prince Charles had originated at Highgrove, his estate in England. The stumpery also acted as a wildlife preserve, so my nine-year-old daughter would always be looking for the bunny rabbits that seemed to disappear just as she was almost within reach of them. Mom had quite a time training our dog to give the stumpery a wide birth in order to give the inhabitants a safe haven. Patou had to settle with free range of the whole bush where the small animals had a chance to get away from the big hundred-pound dog that was up from the city for a bit of rough play.

But the best part of the farm were my in-laws. Chi Tran and his wife, Diep, were boat people. They had escaped Vietnam during the '70s, and Canada had taken them in. Chi met my dad who was looking for someone to keep an eye on his aging parents, Saul Himmel and Mavis Royal, way, way back in the late '70s. Chi and his first wife, Duyen, had their baby, François, right there at 7 Russell Hill Road, and Chi never left Dad's side over all these years. It was their dream come true when both their offspring married each other. Actually, it was me that introduced Chi to his new wife, Diep. Chi had been a widower for ten years or so, as his wife had succumbed to cancer, and Diep had been a widow for a couple of years as well when her husband and 28-year-old son were innocent victims in a drunk-driving accident on their way home from the nightshift. Chi and Diep were a match made in heaven when I forced Chi to ask the smiling Diep, who was working as a cashier at Loblaws, out on a date.

That's all it took. Chi and his smiling, sweet, sweet bride were married shortly after that.

***

Sometimes we would all sleep over at the farm, but the bedrooms were tiny. The kids didn't mind in the least of course. No, it was me. For some reason, my husband would always pick this time up at the farm to start riding me on every little thing. I simply couldn't do anything right. He seemed almost jealous that I had decided to go back to school to get my Ph.D., even though my parents and in-laws were encouraging it. He didn't want a nanny either, even though my dad had offered to pay for one. We had the space; our house was big enough to accommodate a team, let alone a nanny. I remember many times in the little bedroom up at the farm, whispering and arguing, and my humiliation of knowing that my in-laws could hear every word of what was going down. The sex had gone out of our marriage after the twins were born, and I must admit, I found it hard to put on a good face up at the farm, with his constant nagging and belittling of me.

***

I remember being up at the farm when I had finally put my foot down about getting a nanny. I had found out the hard way that the full-time job of earning my doctorate with two, very-active, little, look-alike, identical, twin boys, a precocious seven-year-old daughter, and a demanding husband was a recipe for disaster. With the full support of my parents and my in-laws, it was the weekend when we were choosing our nanny from the applications that I had printed out. I squeezed in around the small dining-room table of the trailer between Dad and François and divvied up the ten pages of printouts.

"As you can see, I've highlighted their age, their experience, and what country they live in. All of them are well-qualified for our nanny position, but we need to narrow the field before we have a few Skype interviews."

François immediately started bitching again about not needing a nanny and that I should stay at home with the children instead of working on my doctorate. He complained about the cost, and I reminded him once again that we had the room in our big house so that the room and board would help count toward the salary.

Dad assured him that this was his treat and there would be no expense for 49 Parkwood Avenue.

Mom cried out, "Oh! Oh! Look! This one looks me! Oh! And she lives in Ireland!"

"Yeah, Mom, I know. When I printed it out, I got goose bumps, but I thought maybe it was just me. Both of you have those beautiful Irish eyes. She's 19, and she has been accepted to study at University of Toronto. She says she wants to be a journalist, and the only time off she asks for is to attend mass at a local Catholic church on Sundays, along with her classroom hours."

***

Three weeks later, Dad, Mom, and I stood at the Lester B. Pearson Arrivals Gate, and I held up the sign to give our new nanny a little reassurance. The sign read: Welcome, Maureen O'Reilly.

Mom gave her a big hug and said to her, "Maureen, you're my very own mini-me. Look at us! We look like a mom and daughter duo. We're even the same height!"

Her lovely Irish brogue charmed us all and she said, "Yes, ma'am. You've got the Irish in your eyes. I won't be getting homesick now."

Little did we know at the time that Maureen O'Reilly would become way, way more than just our nanny. She stayed with me through thick and thin over the next nine years, loving each and every one of my eight children like they were her own. She earned a Ph.D. in child psychology at University of Toronto and ended up marrying a doctor, but a hell of a lot of water went under the bridge before all that came to be.

***

We'd bought the big old house almost three years ago, but before now, I didn't really have a reason to finish up the decoration up in the third-floor loft. The real reason I hadn't finished the decoration in a few of the bedrooms and the loft was that I just didn't have the heart for it. I had always wanted more babies right after the twins, but that wasn't going to happen, so the empty rooms were just a sad reminder.

The loft was a beautiful, big, open space with wide arched windows that went up into the peaks of the cathedral ceiling. We had followed the Swedish theme from downstairs all the way up to the rafters of the house. We had installed the same, bleached, birch floors and we'd painted out the ceiling's tongue-and-grove in white, leaving the beams rustic in their natural-colored wood. It was a perfect boys' bedroom and playroom combined.

Since Maureen had joined us, it was time to put the twins and all their toys and paraphernalia upstairs and away from the second floor where Martina would stay in her original room, and Maureen would have her own big room and en-suite. François and I shared the main floor bedroom, so there was enough space for everyone in our big, old house.

***

Mom ran her hands over the freshly lacquered ivory-white armoires. "Can you believe how beautiful these turned out? And they match the two spindle beds perfectly! Who knew that when Saul and Mrs. Himmel bought all this furniture back in the '50s that we'd still have it in the family? I'm so glad that we just left it all up in the attic when Nigel and I got married. And the rest of the pieces in the bedrooms on the second floor are just as perfect there too. It all looks so beautiful, honey. It goes with the overall Swedish look perfectly."

I nodded and smiled at her. I flopped down on one of the beds with the big, white, Swedish down duvet on it and motioned for her to join me. She was carrying the two beautiful quilts that my Vietnamese in-laws had had made by the ladies at their church for the twins. Mom spread the two quilts out beside each other and began to explain what each one meant.

"Okay, so both quilts were copied from two paintings by the famous Vietnamese folk art painter, Don Ho. One is called 'Toad Teaching,' and the other is called 'Rat Wedding.' It's so nice that they're entirely different from each other, but they share the same gold backgrounds, and all the browns, reds, and greens make them good for the boys' room. We'll have many, many hours ahead of us, making up stories with the boys about all the toads and rats and other characters on these quilts. We'll have to take good care of them, as they're definitely family heirlooms."

I looked up at the iconic, Scandinavian, blue-and-white poppy wallpaper that Marimeka had put out way back in 1964, and I said to Mom, "You know, Mom, who would have ever guessed that a girl like me, who grew up with a single mother, living on welfare far, far away in Stockholm, Sweden, would ever be picking out designer wallpaper for my twin's loft?"

"This is only window dressing, honey. You just wait, your real riches, your family, is what is going to give you more happiness than you can ever imagine."

"Don't count my husband in there, Mom. I like the sounds of the rest of it though."

"Just like the Marimeka wallpaper and the big, wide-striped, blue-and-white rug underneath these two beds, husbands can be replaced, you know."

"No, Mom, no. I made my choice three years ago, and part of me still loves him. Some days I think that I should just try a little harder. Look at me, I'm just a spoiled little princess. Dad and you and my in-laws are so good to me. Look at this house that I have, all because of Granddad Saul's money. It's unbelievable. And my beautiful, smart, little Martina and my twins. I couldn't ask for more."

She looked at me and smiled, so I said, "Well, maybe a little sex once in a while. I'm sick and tired of going without."

"I know, honey, I know. For now, though, just concentrate on your doctorate program. You're going to meet some new friends at the university, and that will take your mind off your marriage. François just needs to relax a little. He works so hard at the law office, always trying to make partner. Maybe he's just stressed. Or, do you think he has a girlfriend at the office?"

"Mom! Don't be an idiot! He's a married man! Of course not! That's what Uncle Brad asked me too!"

Just then, I heard the front door open, and Maureen yelled up the stairs, "Just me! How about a tea before it's time to pick up the twins?"

Mom looked at me and said, "See, what did I tell you? Your abundance truck has already arrived. Our Maureen O'Reilly is the best thing that ever hit this old but decorated to a 'T' house."

The three of us sat there, with Maureen chatting away about all the new students and profs down at the university. She stopped talking and looked at us just watching her. Both of us were grinning from ear to ear with our beautiful Irish nanny's '*joie de vivre.*'

"What's got into you two? Can't a girl even tell a little story or two? Denni, you're Irish, you should know better. And you're a writer. The Irish are the best storytellers in the world. Now come on, Nigella Hansson, boss-extraordinaire, can I ask you to get out those Swedish cookies that I love so much? I hope you saved me a few. My skinny little ass needs a few curves. I've got exactly 15 minutes before I pick up the boys."

***

I stood in front of his office for a moment to put on a good face. I had to admit, I was always a little nervous when I was meeting with my doctorate advisor. His name was Dr. Alessandro Camarra, and I knew from the get-go that he was no pushover and that asking for extra time to complete my work was not an option, so I never went there. He had drawn the line in the sand when I first met him as he was considering my application. He told me that our relationship over the next few years would be based on no bullshit on either side and that he expected nothing short of perfection from me.

He told me at that time that he had better things to do than babysit and nurture a half-hearted attempt at a doctorate degree that was applied for, perhaps, for all the wrong reasons. He made it very clear that it just happened that my thesis, which was based on research from stories of incarcerated women in Canada, was of interest to his own doctorate work on police reform in Canada. He added, begrudgingly, that he was pleased that my research was more brilliant than most, and he set that as a barre for my future work.

It was something about the way he looked at me. As if he thought I was nothing more than a princess; a daddy's girl or something. Any compliments he gave me on my work were brief, but I chalked that part of our relationship up to my own shortcomings of always wanting to please the person in front of me. I had been a pleaser from the very beginning, always striving for the best marks in school just to make Mor proud of me. But, really, he had a good point there. Why did I feel the need to be patted on the head for each and every little thing I did? Maybe I was a princess after all. I certainly lived the lifestyle.

I hoped to God that Dr. Alessandro Camarra could read between the lines somehow other than assuming the worst as to why I had come back to school. I knew deep down in my heart that it wasn't all because I was just too lazy to go back to work as a lawyer once I had arrived in Canada, but that's exactly what it looked like to the rest of the people in my small world. Surely, I couldn't be that shallow. But that's what it looked like, and I had no one to blame except myself. When it came to work and business, I learned as a kid that my attitude boiled down to making money, and I was as hard-headed and hard-hearted as the next lawyer, all in my quest to make a good life for Mor and my baby daughter. I found it difficult now to express myself in the professional environment in any other manner. I played my cards close to my chest throughout the application process of my doctorate, so how could I possibly expect a different result than what this brilliant advisor was giving me?

To tell you the truth, after marrying François, and listening to all his stories and accounts of what went on in his office, I was building quite a disdain toward the legal profession. And as for my husband, who I had fell in love with so quickly and so deeply, all that seemed to be up in the air. I knew that I still loved him, but I certainly didn't respect him. And it was beginning to dawn on me that he didn't respect me either. That had gone out the window some time ago. And that's why I simply didn't want any part of the legal world any longer. The desire to be on the other side of the equation came to me slowly as I realized that as a woman, as a single parent, and as an immigrant, that perhaps I could help women that found themselves in trouble with the law, other than representing them in court, time and time again throughout their painful and troubled lives. That's when I started my research on incarcerated women.

And then, late last night, I had received an email from my advisor asking if it was possible to see me the next morning in his office.

I thought to myself, *What now?* My work was up-to-date according to our schedule, and I certainly got along with my team, but my gut was telling me I had something to be worried about.

As I knocked on his door, I had my fingers crossed that he would be wearing my favorite of his two faces.

He was a decidedly handsome man due to his Italian heritage and pitch-black, wavy hair which he wore a little longer at the back that made it curl up at the nape of his neck. He had a narrow aquiline nose and a square jaw. As for his eyes, well, all I can say is that they were his very best feature, hands down. When he would be sitting in amongst our whole team, he would lean back in his chair, and his face would be full of that Italian charm and affability, with his magnificent smile stretching across his face as the conversation dictated.

However, when I would be sitting across from him in his office, just the two of us, it was usually his other face that I would look into. His other face was an experienced, no-nonsense face, whose brown eyes seemed to read right into my innermost thoughts. This face was what made me think twice before I answered his questions.

It seemed to me that I didn't like being interrogated. And he was an interrogator if I ever saw one.

**

Fuck. He had won this round, hands down. I could feel my face flushing as I sat in the chair before his desk. He sat behind his desk, tipping back in his chair, his eyes never leaving mine. If there had been a clock on the wall, it would have been ticking loudly as he waited for me to ask him why the meeting had been called.

I caved. "What's up, Alessandro?"

"You. That's what's up. I've known you now for over a year, and I've finally figured you out."

"What? I mean, pardon? You've never said that my work is not acceptable. I've never missed a deadline. I've been publishing my research as I go along. What are you referring to?"

"You're not a team player. Not at all. And you know the rules. We work as a team around here. Are you so arrogant that you think you can earn your doctorate all by yourself? Are you so arrogant to assume that your team and your advisor's input is of no importance?"

"Alessandro, I'm not quite sure we're on the same page. Forgive me, but I have never missed a team meeting, and this is the first complaint I know about against my team-spirit. And I especially value your input. To put in bluntly, what are you talking about?"

"So, you're going to do this whole graduate program the hard way, Nigella? Let me tell you, it doesn't work that way. How can I help you through the process if you don't share who you really are? I mean, who you really are, never mind all your good looks, your charm, and your obvious big brain. You've proven that you have the potential to develop new knowledge to format into original scholarly work, but you have another thing coming if you think you can get through life without having the humility to share what you're really

65

thinking and what you're really make of. How the hell do you think it will help me help you by not sharing valuable insight into who you really are and what makes you tick? After all this time I've spent here in my office, wondering what makes you tick and what I'm missing in the big picture, I finally dug around and clued into your personal life that could have helped both of us over the last year-and-a-half, if I had known."

By this time, I had had enough of his crap. "Well, Dr. Alessandro Camarra, you're going to have to spit it out for me. Obviously, this is all beyond me. What's got you so riled up?"

I was thunderstruck by his answer.

"Why didn't you tell me who your father was?"

My head snapped back as I responded to his obvious conclusion that I was nothing but a daddy's girl. A princess. A grown woman living off her father's money. I was in full flight-or-fight mode as I lowered my voice and said with my teeth clenched, "What the fuck does it matter who my father is? And who are you to judge me for my interest in pursuing graduate studies?"

His eyebrows went up to match my temper, and he said, "Oh, so we're beyond discussing this in a reasonable manner. Let's try another tac, shall we?"

I sat there, embarrassed at my outburst. In fact, I was acting the part of a spoiled little princess. I said, "Alessandro, please excuse my bad language. Your accusations just confirmed for me what I already know. I'm just a princess, a daddy's girl, living the good life on his dime."

I was a little startled as he jumped up right out of his seat and he exclaimed, "What! That's not what I said at all! And that's certainly not what I meant either! I just meant that if I had known that the Supreme Court Justice Nigel Royal was your father, we could have examined all his work from all his years in the courts just like I did when I was completing my own doctorate on police reform. I simply meant that you were missing a great literature review or a great research opportunity there. Or even toward your data collection. I reached my conclusion with the final thought that you were wanting to do it all by yourself, as an independent researcher, and that you didn't want to lean on your father's credentials in any way. You, Nigella Hansson-Tran, are about the farthest thing from a princess as I have ever known."

"Oh. Oh. You mean to say that I have just embarrassed myself in front of you, my esteemed advisor, for nothing?" I threw my head back and started to laugh like I hadn't laughed in weeks.

His second face, the one that I really liked, laughed right along with me. He said, "I have an idea that may help you explain to me who you really are. Would you mind if I start first? May I share my story with you? I'm just as guilty as you are, always hiding my true feelings behind my dry, boring research. And, my story may make you realize that you and I are cut from the same cloth."

"Yes! Yes, I'd love to hear your story. But I'm laying it on the table right now; I think I've got you beat in the acting-like-an-idiot department. Now, I'm all ears, Alessandro."

He replied, "Maybe so, but I've got you beat when it comes to being a drama queen or, in my case, a drama king. You can't top what I'm going to show you, no matter what, Nigella."

With that, he leaned back and swung one leg up and over the edge of his desk, and he pulled up his jeans by the cuff and said to me, "Feel this."

"What are you doing? What do you mean? This is weird. I don't need to feel your leg."

"No, no. Silly. Not my leg. Just my ankle. Come on, be a sport. I'm trying to show off a little here."

I looked at him as he encouraged me by pulling his pant leg up even further, and then he kicked his shoe off as well.

I stood, and, with the tip of my fingers, I quickly tapped his ankle, and I got the surprise of my life. He was wearing a prosthesis of some sort! He didn't have an ankle at all! I ventured another feel, this time being bold enough to feel down to his toes. All manmade. Every bit of it. What the fuck!

He laughed at my shocked expression, and he explained, "That's why I always sit behind my desk when you come in, and that's why you don't see me running up and down the halls like I've seen you do, taking the stairs two at a time, day after day, over the past year. You see, Nigella, we all have our little personal demons. Yours, of having a rich father doesn't seem so bad now, does it?"

"Well! You're right! You've got my story beat already, and you haven't even started talking!"

And so, he began. He grew up as an immigrant kid. A kid that started public school in Toronto, not speaking any English at all. A kid that was called a *wop* every day of his life. His father and mother, without a word of English themselves, slowly but surely settled into Toronto's 'Little Italy' neighborhood at College Street and Clinton Street. One parent worked his whole life as a brick layer and the other worked her whole life as a seamstress in a dress factory down on Spadina Avenue. They scrimped and saved and bought an old, worn-out Victorian house in their neighborhood and prided themselves in having the best crop of tomatoes out of all their neighbors in their 25-foot-wide patch of a backyard.

Alessandro grew up like most Canadian boys, yelling *'car'* every time the kids had to clear their ball-hockey net from the narrow street right in front of his house during the summer. The only thing that changed was that the kids moved over 200 feet into the park to use the ice rink during the winter. His teenage years were marred by the sudden death of his older sister who was only 17 when she was killed in a motorcycle accident. He worked at the corner grocery and went from Grade 13 high school directly into a job as a police cadet with Toronto Police Department. He first worked as a beat-cop and made detective in record time. The dream soured over the years as police brutality and racial injustice became more and more prevalent in the city. It all came to a head when he was involved in a takedown one night, and he lost his foot due to an errant bullet that shattered every bone from his ankle down into his toes. They said at the time that he was lucky to not need a total limb amputation. They cut below the knee, leaving enough stump to be able to attach a series of prosthesis that he would adapt to over the years.

His amputation was the end of his life as he knew it. The handsome, soulful, sports-playing, Italian cop had not only lost his lower limb but he had lost his active-duty cop job as well. He lost all hope of finding a nice girl to marry. After all, what girl would want a cripple, a man without a job, and a man with no real education? He couldn't even be a bricklayer like his father before him.

He used his insurance payout to pay off his parents' mortgage, and he bought the house right next door to them for himself so he could look after them in their senior years. After a year of concurrent prosthesis tryouts and hobbling around the two old Victorians, helping the construction team as much as he could to renovate his two houses, he evaluated his progress and was finally able to come to terms with his life.

Still on the Toronto Police payroll, he enrolled in university and never looked back. His love for learning took over, and before he knew it, he was receiving his doctorate in police reform, with his proud parents finally accepting the fact that their bachelor son would never give them the grandchildren that they had hoped for, but that he had a Ph.D., was a tenured professor, and owned two houses, side by side, without a mortgage between the two properties. Both parents summed their 43-year-old son up with the same succinct line: *He was un bravo ragazzo. The neighbors all agreed, he was a good boy.*

I shook my head and threw up my hands. "Okay, okay, Alessandro. You win. Hands down. You've got the best story."

"Yes, Nigella, you may be right, but you've got the best legs; each one ends in five toes!"

We sat there grinning at each other, and he said, "What are you waiting for? Spill your guts, try to outdo me if you can. I dare you."

I started from the very beginning, with Mor being born to a Holocaust Survivor in a displaced person's camp in Europe, growing up in the orphanage as a deaf mute, and meeting my father in Stockholm that resulted in my birth nine months later at her age of 29, with my father not knowing any of this. I told him of my childhood's silent world, living off social assistance and handouts from the kitchens of three restaurants, and then using in-vitro fertilization at age 23 to give my mother the grandchild that she wanted so badly once I had secured my first job as a lawyer.

When I told Alessandro the story of meeting my father, Supreme Court Justice Nigel Royal, at age 30 through Ancestry.se, he slammed his hands down on the desk and exclaimed, "No way! No way! You've just got my story beat, Nigella. Are you kidding me?"

"So, you see, I went from a whole lifetime of being a survivor, like my grandma and mother before me, to morphing into a fairytale existence, not only for myself but for my five-year-old daughter as well. And then, I met François that very first year in Canada. Although this is a little too much personal information, I must tell you that I was a virgin until I was 30, so François was my first love and we were married shortly after meeting each other. And then I had my twins right after that. They just turned three, and my daughter is going to be nine this fall."

"Twins! Twins you say! Now you're making this all up. You mean to say that you have three children? You? You're my student that does more work in a day than the rest of them combined!"

"Well, yes, but I do have a wonderful nanny that does everything for me. I'm so grateful for her."

"I've got an idea."

"Which is?"

"Let's call it a draw. Our pasts have had their hurdles, but our futures are bright, wouldn't you say?"

"Absolutely. And I would like to make another appointment with you so you can suggest what areas of my father's papers that deal with his incarceration of women that I should focus on, either as literature review or as part of a research paper. After all, you're my boss, and I don't want to disappoint you again, now do I?"

As I turned to face him at the doorway to say thank you once again, I was happy to see his face – it was the one that I liked. I had made a new friend. I couldn't wait to tell Dad. I smiled to myself as I strode up the hall. There I go again, always the pleaser. Maybe I was just a little bit of a daddy's girl after all.

***

I pressed 'send,' and my very own, first, little, dinner-party invitations went out. I had taken Alessandro's advice to heart and decided to pay a little attention to my study team, who were just as busy with their lives as I was, and it was time I made a friendly little overture toward them. I invited my four team members and their two spouses, as well as Alessandro, Mom and Dad, and my in-laws. This way, I would learn all about my team's ups and downs as well, and my advisor would know that I was turning over a new leaf by opening up a little more. I was going to make some new friends under my own steam, instead of always relying on my parents. At the same time, I knew I could depend on Mom and Dad and my in-laws for mixing in and entertaining everyone with their stories.

***

The dinner party was in full swing; everyone was really enjoying themselves. Maureen had marched the children upstairs to bed just before we started dinner but not before Alessandro had charmed the three of them by taking off his sock and showing them, right along with my other guests, how he could do tricks with his prosthetic foot. My little boys examined it carefully, then wandered off to play with Patou, but Martina was fascinated with it, asking good questions about it as well. I was so proud of her. One by one, the team started with the sly jokes about his amazing piece of equipment, and Alessandro took the teasing in good stride and matched their jokes right along the way.

We all agreed that we would try to top his story with one of our own. Dad told the story of how Mom had attacked the 6'3" deer hunter after he had accidentally shot Dad in his triceps, and how the giant of a man had plucked her off him and threw her down in the sand like he would have plucked a flea from his jacket. Of course, he imitated her wild, Irish, banshee cry as she leapt up to scratch the shooter's eyes out, which she denied, but she was laughing too hard to make her side of the story stick.

I had made a Swedish dinner with soup, salad, main course, dessert, and cheeseboard, and I knew by the scanty leftovers that everyone had enjoyed it all.

The only thing that marred the whole evening was my son-of-a-bitch husband who had refused to attend because I didn't go over the details and the guest list with him before I sent out the invitations. I knew from the get-go he would find something wrong with it; he was just too jealous of me and my studies right along with anyone else remotely involved with it. It was his opinion that I should either be working as a lawyer as I was trained, or stay at home and be a full-time mother. He made an appearance halfway through the dinner, making the excuse that he was out with a client and that he was sorry he couldn't join us as he had to go over a case that he was working on. That was it. A two-minute 'hello' at the table and he disappeared down the hall, not to come out again. I was just sick and tired of placating him by quietly sneaking off to class and keeping all my work to myself. I always made sure I was home in time for dinner which he didn't show up for much anymore anyway; he seemed to work later and later every evening.

After everyone had left except Mom and Dad, I shooed Dad out of the kitchen where he was loading the dishwasher. "Let's just have a decaf and call it a night," I said. "The dishes can wait for me to attend to later."

The dishes certainly could wait. I would need something to do to keep me from going into our bedroom and strangling my husband in frustration.

By the time I opened my inbox the next day, I had a barrage of thank-you notes that had me smiling and laughing out loud as I remembered some of the stories around the dinner table the night before. Yes, I had pulled that one off pretty damn well, I thought to myself.

***

Chapter Three

Addendum: Ditching the Rose-Colored Glasses

Nigel smiled to himself as he looked at his wife from the doorway. She was in her pajamas; her big, old flannel ones that she kept in the office for working hours only. She was staring at her screen, intent on getting her latest story down before the words left her.

She turned around and said, "You look very handsome, Mr. Nigel Royal, in your back-to-school sweater with your backpack slung over your shoulder. Have you packed the gifts for the kids?"

Nigel nodded and smiled a little. "This is one of the sweaters from our days in London. It does remind me of my old days at school somehow. Ever since I started going down to see Nigella at U of T, I've got back in the groove so to speak."

She snuggled under his arm. "Mr. Wonderful, I'm sure GQ will be calling momentarily since you'll be the most perfectly dressed man on campus."

He responded wryly, "Yeah. And the oldest. It's my brilliant daughter that's the student now; I'm just the doting old dad."

They made their way downstairs to the front door. He looked down at her and grinned a little. "I remember the days if I'd interrupt your writing time, you'd throw something at me from across the room to get rid of me. You're being very sweet this morning, walking me to the door, Ms. Brunette. But don't worry, by the time I get home this afternoon, I'll have figured out what you're up to."

"What makes you such a know-it-all?" she teased. "Dinner's at 6:30, so take your time, honey, and enjoy lunch with your son-in-law."

"I'll be home around three at the latest." He grinned and slipped his hands underneath her pajama's waistband to grab her bare ass. "I feel like I need a nap this afternoon."

She opened the door and gave him a little kiss on the lips before pushing him away. "You're insatiable. Go, just go. I love you. I love you, but I've got a book to write."

***

He found himself whistling as he skipped down the steps to the basement level of the university. Nigella had been lucky enough to get a little office of her own in order to finish up her Ph.D. in a timely manner. No, no, he corrected himself, lucky was not the right word. It takes a lot of hard work to get to that point. She had made quite a name for herself this year at University of Toronto. And her doctorate advisor was one hell of a nice guy. He was so proud of her for making time for her graduate studies; she had a busy house with a husband and three kids, yet she made it all work somehow. She even had an assistant of sorts; a student that was wrapping up her Master's thesis who was happy enough to camp out in the little reception space that helped guard Nigella's office from a host of drop-in visitors that his beautiful, friendly daughter seemed to attract.

He opened the door and stepped inside the reception room. No assistant in sight. Everything was quiet.

He paused to listen for conversation at Nigella's closed door; no, she must be on her own. He gave a quick tap and, with his long arm, sprung the door open, and his big baritone's *surprise!* died in his throat at the nightmare presenting itself.

As he met his daughter's eyes, the horror registered for both of them at the same time. No words were spoken.

At this point, the man, who had had his back to the door and who was standing in front of Nigella's desk with his arms bracing the desk on each side of her, with his shirt open and jeans down around his ankles, had no idea five minutes ago that his long-legged Swedish hottie was about to become a distant memory. He felt her push him away and he turned his head, following her eyes toward the door. He gasped a surprised, "Fuck! Fuck!" as he pulled up his jeans

74

and dashed by Nigel out through the door. His shirt tails were flapping as if he was being propelled by the devil himself.

The two remaining parties, left in the room by themselves, both silently wished with all their hearts that they could have escaped that easily.

Nigella sat there, perched on the edge of the visitor's side of her big, old, metal desk, pulling her skirt down over her knees in abject despair. Her panties lay on the floor; a telltale bit of evidence that said it all.

She whispered, "Dad, Dad, I'm so sorry. Dad—"

By then, he had taken a deep breath and interrupted his daughter, "Nigella, I'm leaving now, but I'll be back in ten minutes. We are going to sit down and talk this through. Take the next few minutes to pull yourself together enough in order to tell me that this is the first and last time I'm ever going to witness this. And for Christ's sake, pick up your panties off the floor."

He strode out of the room and flew back up the stairs to wait out his ten minutes of purgatory in solitude. He spotted a Men's Room and locked the cubicle's door with shaking hands. He raked his hands through his hair as his heart began to ache for his daughter. He thought to himself, '*If only it had been her husband there, he would have laughed himself right out of the office, but oh, no, no. His daughter had a lover on the side.*' Tears rolled down his cheeks for his daughter's infidelity and, at the same time, remembering his own pain and loneliness when he was her age. He simply wanted better for her.

***

Upon re-entering the office, she was waiting there, guilt and remorse written all over her face. He took her in his arms, trying to soothe his little girl's heart. He wiped the tears away, both hers and his, with his hanky.

So, they sat there, father and daughter, both hunched over the assistant's desk, nose to nose. She talked; he listened. She talked some more and he began to put the pieces of the puzzle together.

He reminded himself that it takes two to tango, but he boiled it all down to the fact that her husband was not coming home at night. She was lonely, and his side of their bed was empty. Nigella was feeling neglected, unloved by her husband, stressed out by her three, healthy, happy, and active children and the demands of her heavy academic load. She was also worried with her husband's newly acquired habit of smoking weed in the backyard, morning, noon, and night. Denni had mentioned to him before that she didn't think that things were going well at 49 Parkwood Avenue.

Her distraction to her home life's problems came in the form of a handsome, older, savvy professor that started to drop in her office with two coffees in hand, day after day. He was the straw that broke the camel's back.

She wrapped up her story by saying that she was disgusted with herself and was sure that she would never, ever, get herself into this mess again for as long as she lived, husband or no husband.

"I'm going to tell François everything tonight as soon as I see him."

"No, no, honey. Now, now. Not so fast. Let's think this through. Let's see; if you tell him, what good is that going to do? You love your husband, and you're going to dump a lot of pain on him, when really that pain is your burden, not his. Am I right? It may be better to carry this burden of guilt yourself. Just you and a therapist, or maybe just you and me, your dad, who loves you. Maybe book a couple of dates with your husband and a marriage counsellor to understand his side of the story, if he has one. But not today. Wait. I'm pretty sure, honey, that there is another side to this sad story that you're not fully aware of yet. Like we say in court, there's your side, there's his side, and the truth lies somewhere in the middle. Why make a move until you know all the facts? Do you see where I'm going with this?"

"Oh. Yeah. I do love him, although I'm mad at him, but I don't want to hit him over the head with my guilty pain or anything. Yeah, I see. A marriage counsellor seems like a good idea, but down the road a bit." She added, "And I'm going to work from home from now on; I don't deserve this nice office that the university has given me; I've just been taking advantage of everyone and everything. I have a beautiful little office for my studies at home and I should be there with the kids anyway. And I'm halfway to graduating too. I always feel a little guilty about having a nanny. And François has told me again and again that he wants his wife at home. I think he's a little jealous or maybe a little intimidated by my academic work sometimes. And as it turns out, he has good reason to feel like that. I don't deserve him. Or the kids. Or you and Mom."

"How are things in the bedroom, honey? Is everything okay in that department? Do you still feel the same way about him as you did when you were first married?"

"Yes, I'm still in love with him. But things aren't the same anymore in our sex life. He's just not as interested in me as he used to be somehow. I've tried to appeal to him in different ways, but ever since the boys were born, it's just not the same. And then, when I had to find out from you that he was planning a vasectomy, that caused our final breakdown in the sex department. It was totally selfish of me not seeing his point of view, but I was under the impression that we would have more children. That was always my plan and he knew it. I wanted to have lots and lots of kids. After all, we were both only children that buried our birth-mothers early in life, and we wanted more than that for our kids. It all boils down to that I'm just a selfish, cheating bitch."

"Are drugs or alcohol playing a part here, honey?"

"Oh. Oh. Well, yes. On his side only though. I already mentioned the marijuana. That crap smells so terrible. I know it's only marijuana, but he seems to be in his own little world, and it shuts me out. Yes, maybe that's what has cut down his libido too."

"Dad, here I am making excuses for my own bad behavior. I take full responsibility for this big mess. So what if my husband smokes a little pot here and there and he's lost interest in our sex life, that's no reason for me to act like a common whore."

"Hey! Hey! I don't want to hear that kind of language again, do you understand? You're being too hard on yourself." He grabbed my hand and said softly, "Nigella, honey, I love you to the moon and back, and I'm here for you, no matter what. Please, for now, let's just keep this between you and me until you can sort through your feelings. Okay?"

"Well, Dad, yes and no. I agree, let's keep it between ourselves. But I want you to tell Mom everything. Secrets are not good, and I don't want Mom to find out that you and I have been keeping anything from her. I love the two of you so much and I'd never do anything to come between you two."

"Good. You're right. I'll tell her tonight. Yes, she always knows that something's on my mind, so, with your approval, I'll let her in on our secret. Actually, she'll know exactly how to handle this, so we're both in good hands with Denni."

He remembered the gift, and as he handed it to her, he said, "I love you, my beautiful, brilliant lawyer daughter with a Ph.D. almost in her back pocket, Ms. Nigella Kaufman Hansson-Tran."

She unwrapped the Mont Blanc pen, with her initials engraved in gold, NKHT, and with another bout of tears, she said, "You put Mor's – I mean mommy's name in the initials. Thank you, Dad, I love you and Mom so much. But no, I can't accept this. Not today. Will you please hold onto it and give it to me when I graduate? I don't deserve it, or you, today."

***

He looked at his watch. It was 11:30 a.m., just enough time for him to get to François's office to head out for lunch with his son-in-law, the big-shot lawyer, as he fondly called him. As he tucked Nigella's pen away in his backpack, he thought he would also wait to give François his pen at a later date as well. It just didn't seem to be the right day for gifts, somehow.

***

The receptionist waived him through. "You're meeting Mr. Tran for lunch, right? I believe you're a tad early, so please. Go through. He's either in his office or in the smaller conference room down the hall further on the left."

Nigel stuck his head inside the well-appointed office. No François. He ambled down the hall, past the offices, past the large conference room, and saw that the smaller conference room door was ajar.

After having barged into Nigella's office with his loud *surprise* on his lips, he remembered his manners and pushed the half-opened door open quietly. His eyebrows went up as he stood there, watching her straighten his tie as he focused on his phone, up and over her shoulder with one hand while his other hand was on her ass.

She sensed Nigel's presence first, and with a gasp, she quickly stepped away from François, gathered up a pile of briefs from the conference table, and clicked-clacked out of the room, whispering a quiet *excuse me* as she edged passed Nigel who was frozen in the middle of the doorway.

"Sit," Nigel barked in his loud baritone. As he was closing the door behind her, Nigel flipped up the *Meeting in Progress – Do Not Disturb* sign on the door and shut the door firmly.

They sat across from each other in the middle of the long conference room.

"How long has this been going on?"

"About two months," François answered quietly, adding, "Nigel, I'm so sorry."

"I bet you are, Son," Nigel responded dryly, "I'd like to recommend, Counsellor, that you start singing like a canary. Now. Right now. I need to hear the whole story so we can make a good plan together to get you off the *going-to-hell-in-a-hand-basket* route and get you back on track. Do you understand me?"

"Yes, sir. Yes, Nigel. I'm so sorry. I'm so ashamed. Fuck, man, I've really fucked up here."

The prosecutor in Nigel, coupled with the guilt in François, had the whole story laid out on the table within 15 minutes. The perpetrator confessed to being jealous of his brilliant wife's abilities. He went on to whine that although he had got his masters years beforehand, she magically had beaten his timeline not only with her masters but her Ph.D. research as well. He said they met and married so early in their relationship, and then the twins were born right after, and he felt he didn't have a chance to deal with his stress of having a family to feed let alone keeping his sexy, beautiful wife happy. On top of it all, he complained that no matter how hard he worked, day in and day in, working night after night, he still hadn't made partner in his firm. Every time he looked at his beautiful, gifted wife, he was reminded that he was a failure, so he looked elsewhere for the assurance that he needed so badly to boost his lagging confidence.

"Son, I know how you feel. Both our wives are amazing women. Look at me; I'm such a bumbling, nerdy fuck-up, and Denni bails me out time and time and time again. I know that Nigella will bail you out as well. We both married the very best. We both married up. We just have to learn to accept their love and live our lives a little more like Patou, a wagging-tailed puppy dog that will do anything just to get his ears rubbed."

"Are you saying that I should go home and tell Nigella everything?"

"Exactly."

"Is that what you would do with Denni?"

"No, not at all."

"Why not? If I have to do it, why shouldn't you?"

"Well, Denni would listen to my whole sad story, then she would calmly go to the kitchen, get out a big knife, and cut my balls off. That's why not."

With this little tidbit of harsh reality, both men leaned back in their chairs and shared a laugh. However, François's laugh began to waver within the same breath. The anxious, frustrated big-time lawyer laid his head down into his folded arms on the big conference table and cried and sobbed while Nigel got up and louvered the blinds closed to offer them a little more privacy.

"It's all gonna be okay, Son, cry it out, just cry it all out. We're two of the luckiest men on earth to have the wives we have. They're worth every tear that we'll ever shed."

Five minutes later, François had dried his eyes and ordered some lunch in. The wise old judge and the frustrated lawyer both ambled back to the office, with the judge's arm casually draped over the lawyer's shoulders. They both put their feet up on the big desk, munching their takeout corn beef and hot mustard sandwiches and washing it all down with bottles of water. They mapped out their plan of action, just like they had done over all the years before in Saul's old office at 7 Russell Hill Road.

François spoke into the intercom, "Cecilia, would you come in please? Thanks."

Nigel rose from his chair as Cecilia entered. His heart went out to her a little when he saw her face, white and tense with knowing what was coming down the pipe, but he was prepared and held his phone in his hand and clicked 'record.'

François introduced him as The Honorable Nigel Royal, and Nigel responded with a polite, "Pleased to meet you, Ms. Yang." He pulled out her chair a little to indicate that she was to sit down.

Nigel, always a brilliant strategist, was at his very best as he held up his phone from the palm of his big hand and said in a reassuring tone, "Ms. Yang, please be aware that I'm recording this conversation to ensure that we're all on the same page. I'll be happy to send you a copy; but perhaps you'd rather receive it in your personal inbox rather than clogging up your professional email. Same with you, right, François?"

What could François say? He nodded and covered his surprise by uttering a soft, "Absolutely."

Ms. Yang offered a quiet "Of course, my personal email is cyang9084@gmail.com." There was a slight tremor in her voice.

Nigel watched François. The young lawyer switched gears, and he appeared to focus on the task at hand. He pulled it off by looking right at his assistant and saying with a genuinely contrite tone, "Cecilia, please forgive me. I've been acting inappropriately with you over the past couple of months, and I want you to know I'm sorry for everything. As of today, right now, I want to start our working relationship off on a better footing. I have two suggestions to put forward. Would you mind hearing me out?"

"Go ahead."

"Thank you. The first suggestion is to ask you if you'd like to be transferred to another department in our firm in order that you don't have to work with me any longer. I will of course give you a recommendation letter by the end of the day. And, or, my second suggestion comes with a little news of my own. You see, I'm going to be working from home every afternoon now, just coming into the office in the mornings, so I need an assistant that will be willing to cover for me. It's going to mean a lot more work, and I'm willing to raise the pay scale to meet your commitment."

Cecilia smiled a little and said in a relieved voice, "I thought you called me in to fire me." With that, she turned to Nigel and said, "Thank you, Your Honor, for coming into the office today. Your visit has given me quite a wakeup call. You see, I have a wonderful man that works as a lawyer in New York that has been asking me to marry him for the past few months, and I'm going home tonight to accept his proposal."

Both men rose as she stood up. She stretched out her hand to François and simply said, "Friends?"

"Friends."

As Cecilia Yang, the other woman, closed the door behind her, Nigel looked at his son-in-law and said quietly, "Good work, Counsellor. So, we can tick that off the list. However, you'd better keep your eye on that one. She was smart enough not to accept either of your suggestions. She could file a sexual-harassment case against you, and, what's more, win it hands down. I wouldn't put it past her. On the other hand, I wouldn't blame her either. What's the word around the water cooler? Have there been others with her?"

"Yeah. She has a bit of a rep around the office. But we're cool. She knows the score. She'll move on."

"You're her boss, for Christ's sake." Nigel paused to let the gravity of his rebuke sink in. "Now, talking to your wife tonight is next on the list. Good luck with that one; she's no pushover that's for sure. But she loves you enough, I believe, to start fresh."

François got up and came around the desk to give him a heart-felt hug. "I'm sorry, Nigel. Thank you for everything. Thank you from the bottom of my heart. I won't let you down ever again."

Nigel returned the hug and held on a little longer than necessary. "Let's keep this little lunch just between us. Please. You've got this now; you don't need me interfering in your life or your lifestyle. Clean it up and be a man. I have full confidence in you to make it work."

As Nigel was leaving the office, François's phone rang. He motioned for him to wait, and he whispered, "Hold up…it's Nigella. Shhh. Don't let her know you're here; I'll put us on speaker phone." "Hi, beautiful. What's up?"

"François. I'm down here at U of T, in my office, and I've been thinking things over. I think I'd like to give up my office here and work from home. This is crazy, back and forth, back and forth. I need more family time, and, more importantly, more husband time. I love you and I need you. Will that be okay with you if I work from home?"

"On one condition, Blondie."

"And what would that be?"

"That we share the home office. It's funny; I was just thinking the same thing about working from home. I think I'd rather just come into the office here in the mornings. Fuck the billings. Fuck the worry of being made partner. Fuck everything. I don't need the latest Range Rover in the driveway. I just need to spend more time with you and the kids. Like you just said, I love you and I need you. Do you think we can manage on a little less money?"

Nigel could hear her big throaty laugh over the phone, and he and François shared a little smile.

"Oh, honey, you have no idea! I'm the best money-manager in the whole world! We don't need this big lifestyle! We'll cut back and be just fine! But, one thing's for sure; I get first dibs on the big computer though; you'll have to work on the laptop. Deal?"

"Deal."

The moment Nigel had heard his beautiful, unsuspecting daughter's voice over the phone, he was immediately filled with resentment against François for not only cheating on Nigella but what really stung is that he himself had become an accomplice of sorts in his dirty lifestyle. All of a sudden, he remembered Denni confiding in him a long time ago that she thought François may be a bit of a player. She was right. And he had been made a fool by a young whipper-snapper sitting there behind his big desk in a $2400 Italian silk, made-to-measure suit.

He continued watching François's face as he told his wife over the phone that he loved her, and, with all his years of listening to perps telling their lies in court, he instinctively knew that his son-in-law had no intention whatsoever on following through with coming clean with his wife. He was looking at a fucking liar – a fucking fraudster. Every ounce of love and compassion for the struggling lawyer that he had nurtured and coached over the past 37 years disappeared in the blink of an eye. He switched his thoughts over to his daughter's heart-felt remorse that he had listened to two hours earlier. That was an entirely a different matter. She had already proven to him that she was on the right track. She had already called her husband to tell him she had forfeited her university office in order to make plans to forge ahead in the troubled marriage. But no, not her husband, not by a long shot. He knew in his heart that the plan that they had hatched together would never take place.

As he stood at the office door, once again, ready to leave, he looked over his shoulder at the young, smooth lawyer sitting behind his desk. "By the way, François, you better cut back on the weed. I can smell it in your hair, or maybe it's coming from your suit. Not a good look, Counsellor."

***

He took a minute to call Denni before he skipped down the subway stairs. "Hi, honey. Just wondering if we can have a catchup in about 20 minutes, as soon as I get home. Okay with you?"

***

Denni sat across from him, and as he finished his story about catching Nigella not wearing her underwear and then catching François with his hand on his assistant's ass, he watched her face run the gamut through every emotion known to women around the world.

"I'm speechless," she said.

As Nigel pulled out his phone, he said, "So, our little girl is facing more of the same, I'm afraid. I told him I'd stay out of it, but what can we do? I know he's not going to come clean with her, and there she is, all excited about giving the marriage another try. Poor baby. And now I feel that I'm betraying her, right along with him. I listened to her plea as she told him she'd stay home from now on. It makes me sick to my stomach. However, I don't know whether this will come into play, but I'm glad that we have it. Listen to this."

He clicked on *play* and all Denni could say was *'Son-of-a-bitch!'*

"So, she doesn't know that you've spoken to François, right?"Nigel nodded.

Denni continued, "Well, okay, to be fair, we have to wait to see if he does go home and tell her tonight. We'll give him the benefit of the doubt until tomorrow morning and then we can feel free to let her know what you saw. What do you think?"

Nigel watched Denni as she answered the phone and she motioned to him that it was Nigella.

"Hi, honey. Yes, yes, Dad's here. Yes, he told me he saw you. Yes, by all means, please come over tomorrow morning. No, no, honey, no, no. It's okay, everything is okay. I know you can't come right now. Besides, by tomorrow morning, you will know François's plan, and I want details. No, not especially of what went on in your office. I mean of what is going to go on between you and your husband tonight. Your dad and I are wishing you a fabulous, sexy night in with your husband. And tomorrow morning, I want to hear every single bit of your plan and his plan on how you are both going to go forward from now on. Please. I want to hear what he has to say. Okay? Now, go. Just go. Enjoy yourself tonight, honey. I love you, and Dad loves you too. We'll see you tomorrow morning for coffee, after you drop the children off."

Nigel hugged his wife and said, "You're the best. I love you so much."

***

As Nigel spooned his wife later, much later that night, he said softly to her, "Honey, if you ever caught me with another woman, what would you do?"

Denni bolted upright in their bed and turned around to face him. She didn't blink an eye. "I'd cut your balls off." And then she promptly snuggled back down into his open arms.

"I thought so."

***

Chapter Four

A Change of Plans

Dad had left my office 15 minutes ago, and, as crazy as it sounds, I was on top of the world. I quickly wrote an email to the U of T department that took care of the university's office real estate and gave them my notice that I was vacating my office space. I cc'd my team as well as my doctorate advisor, Alessandro, on it. As I typed in his email address, I had a quick pang of regret. I realized that his office was not that far up the corridor from mine; I hoped to hell that he didn't know about the tawdry coffee klatch that I had participated in. How could I have been such a fool!?

Before I shut down the university's computer, I went into my personal email account just to make sure I wiped it clean in case it popped up with the next person that took over my office space. *Oh, what's this? What a welcome diversion!* I thought to myself. How interesting! There was an email for me after all. The email was an invitation of sorts that mapped out an Ancestry.ca get-together and reunion that was going to take place in Toronto, Canada, for the Kaufman family. Six months ago, I had applied to Ancestry.ca with my Kaufman name as well as Martina's Kaufman name in hopes of tracing my Mor's heritage somehow. Of course, with Mom being born in a displaced person's camp in Germany with the Kaufman name of her Holocaust-survivor mother and then growing up as an orphan in Sweden, I didn't have any relatives whatsoever, except for Dad, here in Canada.

I clicked on *'Yes,'* and noted that the meet and greet was in one of University of Toronto's buildings that I was familiar with. I entered the payment without a second thought, and moved the date over into the month of October in my electronic calendar.

I gathered up a few boxes, borrowed a dolly from the janitor, and started packing up my office. I was going to go home and make my marriage work come hell or high water. I was sick of being unhappy. But mostly, I was sick of myself.

I took a last look around at my little office, and, all of a sudden, my initial burst of energy and good will had evaporated. I slowly made my way back to my desk and I sat down. My right hand automatically smoothed over the top of my old, gray, metal desk. That same desk had probably sat in that very office for over 50 years. It was full of dents, nicks, and well-worn corners from all the graduate students that had come before me. The narrow top drawer where I had kept my pens and markers was stained by old ink bottles and fountain pens used years and years before me. The bottom drawer always stuck.

Tears ran down my cheeks as I gave in to another wave of my shame, remorse, and disappointment in myself. I knew Dad and Mom would forgive me, but could I forgive myself? That was the question.

***

I closed the door softly behind me, took a deep breath, and started to slowly push the dolly up the hall.

All of a sudden, I pulled up, made a wide U-turn with the dolly, and went back to my office door. I don't know why. I knew there was no going back. Like a fool, I had burned that bridge. I had thrown it all away for one ten-minute degrading sex act with a sleazy professor. I had allowed myself to be groomed by him with a month of Starbuck's coffee, for the price of $3.79 per cup.

It was then I realized that not only I had cheated on my husband but I was still lying to him about wanting to work from home. I was a liar as well as a cheater. I no more wanted to leave my university office to work at home than the man in the moon. I had just convinced myself that I wanted to leave the office to sweep my bad behavior under the rug so I wouldn't have to examine it any further.

I impatiently turned the doorknob and stepped back into my office.

I took a few minutes, just standing there in the dark. I had left the door open a crack, and a shard of light that the door offered played against the black wall ahead of me. I could make out the outline of the desk and the two visitor chairs in front of it. The old filing cabinet was a black form in the far corner. The dark and the quiet settled me somewhat.

Lifting my head up, facing the darkness, I opened my arms to the darkness and I started talking to God. I left myself out of the conversation all together. I sent up a simple prayer to Him, asking that He bless all the graduate students that had used this office before me, right along with all of them that would follow me. I asked God to spare them my mistakes. It was the least I could do.

Once again, I pushed the dolly up the corridor. I pulled up, and my hand was posed to knock at Alessandro's door to say a neighborly farewell and just to confirm that I would be available to meet regardless of where I was working from.

Whether it was because I was feeling guilty about what had gone on in my office, or whether it was because I was a coward and didn't want to face the music in case Alessandro already knew about my behavior, I didn't knock. No, I took the coward's route. I'm sure I would have died if Alessandro knew about my dalliance, and I just couldn't face it. I reasoned to myself that the most important person in my life had actually caught me in the act, but thinking about it, there was something about Alessandro's second face, the serious one, that I didn't want to mess with either.

I slowly lowered my hand, grabbed hold of the dolly, and pushed forward. I told myself I would phone him and explain that I could get more work done out of my home office.

I turned my thoughts to my immediate plans of working from home. I had it all, and I had been acting like a spoiled brat. I just didn't appreciate my amazing lifestyle, including our wonderful nanny. Maureen was the best; she minded her own business and kept out of family affairs, but she ran my whole house for me with quite efficiency. The kids absolutely loved her, and she loved them in return. She maneuvered her classes down at U of T around the kid's morning schedule, and she disappeared upstairs right after dinner. When it was just her and me, I would find myself laughing along with her; she always saw the humor in a situation. She was Irish; she had that Irish storytelling charm about her somehow. Just like Mom. What would I ever do without her? I'd better smarten up in all departments, not just with my nanny and/or my husband, and/or my doctorate advisor. Thank God for my dad. I knew how I could repay him. I could be the best daughter and the best wife in the world. All this time, my husband had been worrying about making enough money to keep us all; it wasn't that he didn't love me at all – he was just trying to be a good provider. On the other hand, I was very aware that getting caught in my tawdry sex-on-the-side that had forced me to spill my guts to Dad was, in itself, very therapeutic, especially for someone like me that's basically an honest person. Never in a million years would I get myself into that position again. And I wasn't talking about the position of me perched on the edge of my desk. No, not at all.

From now on, I was going to put up and shut up and be a better wife to my husband. Once I was on the main floor, I called an Uber and dialed Mom to see if I could make a date with her for tomorrow morning so I could apologize to her in person for everything. I knew Dad would tell her my whole sad story tonight, and then, by tomorrow morning, I could not only apologize but give her the lowdown on my reunion with my husband that would take place tonight.

I smiled a little; François had no idea what I was planning. I wasn't going to let him sleep a wink. It was going to be a night of nothing but amazing sex that we hadn't shared for whatever reason for quite some time. In fact, I couldn't remember the last time. Our sex life had dwindled down to exactly that, sadly. It was time to turn all that around. Tonight was going to be a night of fantastic sex that neither one of us would ever forget.

***

The next morning, I called out, "Just me," as I scratched Patou's ears at the front door.

"We're down here in the family room!" Dad shouted.

Dad patted the seat next to him as Mom poured me a coffee in the kitchen. I went to her, put my arms around her, and said, "I'm so sorry for my behavior yesterday. I'm ashamed of myself and I hope you can forgive me."

"Nothing to forgive. But I must tell you that I have been a little worried about you lately. You haven't been as happy as you usually are. I've missed your big, gutsy laugh. Maybe it was a little guilt weighing you down. Thank God we don't have to worry about that any longer. I love you all the way. So does your dad. Now come on, let's have a seat. I want to hear about your new plans for working at home with your husband."

We sat down, and, for a moment, I didn't know what to say. I started with, "Well, to tell you the truth, last night was a bit of a letdown. I don't really know why. I think I was just so relieved to be out of my situation at my office that I anticipated a big fairytale reunion or something, and, of course, François was unaware of what I had been up to, so it turned out to be kind of a regular night at home."

Mom sounded disappointed. "Oh, I was hoping to hear stories of wild sex or something."

"Mom, really, give me a break, will you? It's nothing sacred!" She looked a little crestfallen, so I added, "Sorry, Mom. That came out all wrong. I'm just kidding. Don't worry, everything was okay in the bedroom, but I just expected that he would be more enthused about us working together at home in the afternoons. I had to practically pry his thoughts out regarding how we would share the office. He wasn't really in the mood to map it all out with me. I tried to reinitiate the conversation a few times, and he said we'd just go with the flow and not to sweat the small stuff. But we did have a nice dinner, and we both put the kids down early, and that gave us some private time. But you know how it is, he gets up early to get a head start at the office, so it was lights out at 11, kind of. If you know what I mean."

I looked over at Dad who was being very quiet, and I was a little alarmed at his sober face. "Are you still mad at me? You look so serious. You're scaring me a little."

He took my hand and patted it. "No, honey. I'm not mad at you in the least. I'm mad at your husband. And now, I have a dirty job to do, right here in front of me, right now, and what I have to tell you is going to hurt you, and I don't relish that. So please, before I start, forgive me and know I'm telling you this only because I love you."

I said, "Dad! You're definitely scaring me now! What? What is it?"

"I deceived you yesterday. After I left you, I went to have lunch with François, and I was there when you called. I listened in as you told him that you were giving up your office to work at home. I heard him say to you that he was going to work from home in the afternoons. And I pretended that I wasn't there."

"So what? Mom and I put you on speaker phone all the time! What are you getting at?"

"I was wrong in doing that, because François and I had a deal cooking that you were unaware of."

"What are you getting at? Is he buying me a piece of jewelry or something that had to be kept a secret?"

"No. Not at all. It's the exact opposite. He's been lying to you for quite a while, and when I caught him in the lie, he made a deal with me that he'd come clean with you as soon as he got home last night. I was listening on the phone because I couldn't break his confidence. He set me up and then I set you up in return."

I looked at his sorry face. My heart sunk. It sank for me, yes, I admit, but mostly for my poor dad. What the fuck was he about to tell me?

"Out with it, Dad. The whole story. And if you leave anything out, I'll know just by your face. You have the worst poker face in the whole world."

"I was meeting him for lunch, and the receptionist waived me through to his office. I found him in the conference room. His assistant, Ms. Yang, was standing way, way too close to him, adjusting his tie, and his hand was on her ass. I'm sorry, honey. I'm so sorry."

"Keep going. For Christ's sake, don't stop now. I need to hear it all."

"After Ms. Yang left the room, I sat him down, and he spilled his guts. His affair with her had been going on for a few months, he said. We cut a deal. I laid out a plan and he accepted it. I told him he had to come clean with you as soon as he got home last night, and he promised me he would. I had him bring Ms. Yang into the office, in front of me, and he told her it was over, and he offered her a couple of options to work elsewhere. She left the office. Then you called. That's what broke my heart. I could tell by the look on his face when he was speaking with you that he was lying. He had no intention of telling you anything. It just broke my heart. I have loved him like a son for 37 years, and I just found out that he's a liar and a cheat. I couldn't let him continue to do that to you. So, I'm confessing that I set him up to fail, and then I set you up to tell me what happened last night so I could catch him in his lie. I'm sorry, honey, that you're in the middle of this."

I was too disgusted and mad at François to even cry. I couldn't even squeeze a tear out. He had hurt Dad just as much as he'd hurt me over the last year. I looked over at Mom, and I've never seen her look so serious, so I stood up, put my hands on my hips, imitating her when she's mad, and I said, "Okay, Mom. It's all up to you. You're the judge. Who's the bigger fool for loving François Tran? Me or Dad?"

Dad looked up at me in surprise, and then I just let out the biggest laugh out of sheer relief that it was all over. "Dad, don't look so sad! We're all going to be okay! I'm going to kick his ass from here into next week! And then I'm going to slap him in the face with divorce papers! Just watch me!"

It was then that I stopped mid-sentence and thought about it. I remembered one of my old law profs sagely giving us a tidbit of his wisdom. He said to us, "Don't confuse justice with revenge." Here I was, the adulteress, who was going to kick my husband's sorry ass out the door for being an adulterer. Wasn't that a little bit like the pot calling the kettle black?

I came out of that thought and gave me head a little shake. No way! No way! He was going down! Mom was right; he was nothing but a son-of-a-bitch!

Mom got into the swing of things and jumped up off the sofa and chimed in, "Yeah, and right now, the three of us are going to confirm our plan for going forward. Nigel, honey, press *play* to put all the cards on the table."

Dad brought out his phone and clicked. The recording started with Dad's voice asking someone if he could record the conversation, and the female voice gave her email to him, and when I heard Francois's voice come through loud and clear, I began to mentally tally up not only the child support but alimony, the nanny, the house, the car, the savings account, and everything else I was prepared to fight for. I was going to take the bastard to the cleaners. He'd rue the day he ever met me!

As we sat around the table having lunch, we all agreed that we wouldn't say a word to my in-laws until we absolutely had to. No sense in causing them any pain sooner than we had to. They would be devastated. Mom came up with a perfect plan. She proposed that the three of us take the kids to Disney World the next week for a holiday, and what's more, she was going to pick up the tab for it.

"Well, there's just one little amendment to be made. Thank you, Mom, but you can pay for another holiday at another time. I've got a better idea. I'm going to phone François at his office this afternoon. No, in fact, right now. I'm going to suggest that I take the kids on a bit of a holiday next week since he's going to be away in Vancouver on business. I'll keep a lid on the divorce papers until we all get home from our respective trips. I'll let him know I'm using his card to pay for the tickets. He won't mind at all. He's probably taking his little girlfriend, Ms. Cecilia Yang, with him to the coast anyway."

Dad added in, "Okay, I like the idea so far, but may I add in a little bonus? I'm more than happy to pay for Maureen to come along with us. So, Nigella, can you ask her if she'd like to come along? Let her know everything's paid for, and she'll get full wages plus a bonus while we're away. And let's not share the divorce plan with her at this point, okay? We don't want her to worry about anything. It's her holiday too. And it's agreed that we'll leave Chi and Diep at home. Deal?"

The three of us raised our glasses and shouted, "Deal!"

We had no idea at that time that my phone call to François five minutes later would cement our newly hatched plan like nothing else.

***

I put my phone on speaker, laid it on the table between us and dialed. His phone rang several times, and I was just waiting for voicemail to click in to leave him the message that I would be using his card, when, abruptly, a female voice inquired as to who was calling. There was a hint of laughter in her voice and an uneven tone as if she was jumping up to answer the call or grabbing the phone away from someone. Or something.

The voice said, "Mr. Tran's office. Ms. Yang speaking. How may I help you?"

"This is Mrs. Tran. Please have my husband call me at his earliest convenience."

"Yes, Mrs. Tran. Oh, in fact, he's just coming into the office as we speak. One moment please."

The pregnant pause was a long one before his voice said, "Nigella? Hello? Are you there? Sorry, I had just stepped out of the office for a moment, and I had left my cell on my desk. My assistant thought that she had better pick up the call in case it was urgent. What's up?"

"Not too much. But I was just thinking. Since you're in Vancouver next week, I'd like to take the children on a little holiday. We all need a break, and you've been so busy. We'll go this time without you. I'll take Maureen to come along to help with the kids or maybe Mom and Dad will want to come along. You know, we've always spoken about going to Disney World with the kids, and we've never made it. We'll be home by the time you get back from the coast. Is it okay if I use your card to book the tickets? I'll try to get us an all-inclusive deal or something. Is that okay with you?"

"Whatever floats your boat, Blondie. Oh, actually, you'll need a travel letter from me, allowing you to take the kiddos across the border, so I'll email that to you right away to forward to the travel agent, you know, in case they hassle you at the airport."

"Thanks. Will you be home in time for dinner tonight?"

"No, I don't think so. Don't wait up, babe. I'm swamped here. Anything else? By the way, you sound a little down or something. You okay?"

"I'm much better now after talking to you. Try not to be too late tonight."

"Sure thing. Keep the home fires burning."

I clicked off, and Mom said, "He's nothing but a two-timing son-of-a-bitch."

Dad put his arms around me. "I'm sorry about your marriage, honey."

"Dad, would you stop with the sad face!? This is the best thing that's happened to me in a year. And you two need a holiday much more than I do. It hasn't been that long for us since baby Nigel either. This is the start of happier life for me, and for all of us."

"You're right," Mom said, "your soon-to-be-history husband has run out of *get-out-of-jail-free* cards. It's time for us to put it all behind us."

"Now, girls, settle down, settle down. I have an idea for this afternoon. We still have time before picking the kids up, so I'm suggesting that I stay put and I'll book us a nice big suite at the best Disney World hotel there is, and Maureen and I will take the kids out to Swiss Chalet for an early supper. You girls run up to Yorkdale and buy new bathing suits and flip flops for the holiday. Don't rush."

I laughed at him already planning everything out for us. "Yeah, Dad, we'll buy new bathing suits all right. And I'm going to buy you a nice little Speedo. What's your favorite color?"

Mom had already starting running up the stairs to get her handbag. She said, "I'm driving! I called it! Meet me at the door!"

As Dad walked us out to the garage, he said to me quietly on the side, "Please make sure your mom gets a few new bathing suits and some nice little skirts and tee-shirts for our mornings in the park with Minnie and Mickey. She's still so sensitive about her tummy weight from the pregnancy. I just want her to have the time of her life on our holiday."

"Got it, Dad. And a Speedo for you, right?"

I stood there and watched him as he headed back inside, and I was overwhelmed with gratitude for my father. I called out, "Dad, hold up! Wait a sec!" I ran over to him and gave him the biggest hug of my life. "I'm sorry, Dad, for causing you this pain. I love you, and I promise to be the best daughter to you and Mom going forward. Every day I thank God that you accepted me into your life so willingly and so completely a short four years ago. I'm the luckiest girl in the whole world to have a dad like you."

He smiled and looked down at me and pointed to the car. "Look at your mother. She's got the car in gear and you are standing here wasting her valuable shopping time. You know how she loves to shop. Go. Just go. I love you. But don't you dare bring anything that resembles a Speedo home. D'ya hear me?"

***

I looked back and he was out on the sidewalk, waving to me as Mom burned rubber all the way up to the corner.

***

Chapter Five
Holidays

I had to smile at the two flight attendants taking the boys from Maureen and Dad. They were both openly ogling my father like he was a juicy steak at the butcher's counter. I looked over at Mom, and she gave me a little wink and a smile. I had to admit, he looked even more handsome than ever, wearing his white tennis shorts that Mom and I had bought him. He was always impeccably dressed, but he was at his best in sportswear, I thought. He turned and leaned over Mom, smoothing her hair back and kissing her on the lips. Mom, in return, let her left hand, the one with her ostentatious, canary-yellow diamond on the ring finger, slide down his back to rest firmly on his ass where her little pat-pat-pat marked her territory, leaving no question as to who belonged to whom. The flight attendants looked at each other, dropped their fawning looks over the cute, little, identical twins squirming in their arms, and announced that they would be back momentarily to take our orders for drinks.

I was, all of a sudden, overwhelmed with gratefulness for my parents. Here I was, sitting in first class, with a nanny to take care of my three beautiful children, and loving parents who always stood by me through thick and thin.

It wasn't that long ago that I was a kid myself, living in a silent world with a single parent that was profoundly deaf, living on Swedish social-assistance handouts and no knowledge of a world outside our small apartment and my school which was a block away from home. No wonder I was motivated to excel in school; I knew instinctively that an education would mean that my mother and I would be able to buy a few more groceries to make it through the week, and a coat and boots for both of us for the long winters in Stockholm. As a kid, I remember those same coats doing double duty as my Mor would put them over us as an extra blanket on the Swedish, frosty, winter nights.

I smiled to myself as I looked out over the wing as my thoughts traveled through the mounds and mounds of fluffy cotton clouds and I messaged out to the universe, "Mor! Mamma, are you there? Look at me now! Are you happy for me, Mamma?"

***

"Mommy, would it be okay if I went over to ask that girl if she wanted to swim with me?"

"Come on," I said as I jumped up from the poolside lounge, "I'll go with you. It looks like she's with her mom."

At ten years old, my daughter had the skills of a seasoned politician. She had learned quickly, watching her granddad and grandma over the past five years, and she skipped over and said easily with her slight Swedish accent, without hesitation, "Hi, my name is Martina, and I just got here. Do you want to swim with me?"

"Okay," the little girl said while she looked at her mother, "Is it okay, Mom?"

After the two of them held their noses and jumped in the deep end, I could hear Martina explaining to her new friend, "Do you know that I'm a Swede but I live in Canada? And I have a dog."

"My name's Zalia. I'm ten. I live in Miami, and I'm on holidays with my mom. How old are you?"

I turned back to the mom. I reached over the lounge to offer my hand. "Hi. I'm the mom. Nigella. It looks like our girls are going to keep each other entertained." I had no idea as the pretty, smiling woman offered her hand back to reach mine that we would become friends for the rest of our lives. Not just friends, but real girlfriends, like the kind that you share hopes and dreams and fears with, hopes and dreams and fears that you hadn't even spoken out loud before in your whole life.

"Jacquie. My friends call me Jack. With a name like Nigella, you must have been named after a Nigel, am I right?"

"Named after my dad. He's over there with Mom. And where does Jacquie and Jack come from? Are they short for Jacqueline?"

"You got it. Nothing but the best. I was named after the illustrious Jacqueline Bouvier Kennedy of course. You know the one with the perfectly straight, bouffant hairdo."

She continued as I sat down on the end of her daughter's lounge chair, our knees facing each other, "And did I hear your daughter say that you're Swedes? My, you're a long way from home, Sister. I had no idea that Sweden birthed brown sugar women right along with their usual white, blue-eyed beauties. You must have stood out like the north star up there in the frozen hinterlands."

I laughed at her straightforward way of talking. "Well, back at 'cha, girlfriend. I don't imagine the Jacqueline Bouvier Kennedy clan had too many black beauties like you in their midst either. Our African hair would have one hell of a hard time molding into that pillbox-perched-on-bouffant look."

She grinned and leapt up from her chair. She hoisted the bottoms of her two-piece bathing suit up in a cocky manner to semi-cover her navel, stuck out her breasts, and waved me on from behind as she strutted over to the edge of the pool. "I'll race you. Loser buys lunch."

***

I pulled myself up after the lap and laughed as I splashed water at her as she came up behind me. "That'll teach you! You better not challenge me to an arm wrestle either. I'll beat you hands down before you can blink an eye."

"I'll give you this one just because I'm minding my manners, you being a polite Swede or Canuck or whatever you are. You'll learn quick enough not to mess with me. I'm a tough cookie from the projects in Miami, and you don't want to go there."

"You're just like my mom. You've got to meet her. Come on, I want you to meet my folks. You'll love them."

As I pointed over to their chairs, I saw that they were watching me. Their love for me was written all over their faces as my new friend and I sauntered over to their chairs. Dad had jumped up and had a towel all ready to wrap around my shoulders as if I were a child at a swim meet, and Jacquie said, "Oh, I see we have a daddy's girl here. I knew she was a wimp the minute I laid eyes on her."

Mom and Dad were absolutely charmed by her, and all of a sudden I jumped up and said, "Oh my God, I forgot about Martina! I'm supposed to be watching her! What kind of a mother am I!?" I burst out laughing again at my new friend shaking her head at my absentmindedness.

The truth be known, I was on holidays, and I simply didn't give a damn about anything. I hadn't felt this good in over a year, and I dashed over and started flicking my wet towel all over Mom. We were all laughing as Dad pulled up another chair for us as my beautiful, little, ten-year-old daughter and her new friend, Zalia, came running over, asking if they could please, pretty please, have a sleepover that night.

Martina continued with their plan, "Mommy, we have two big beds in our room. We can sleep together, right, Zalia? We'll be good, I promise, Mommy, I promise!"

As Jacquie and I nodded our approval, Mom jumped up and said to the girls, "A real pajama party has to start off on the right foot. Let's see if the gift shop has some Mickey Mouse pajamas for all of us. Come on, girls, let's do a little shopping on Granddad's credit card." She waived Jacquie's offer to put the charge on her room tab and shook her head back and forth. "Not at all. My treat. I'm the grandma here, and it's my biggest pleasure."

Dad laughed and warned Jacquie, "Don't mess with her, Jacquie. You'll see that's she's a woman with a mind of her own, God bless her. And I'm one hell of a lucky man!"

We watched as Mom gathered up the girls and the tall, gangly ten-year-olds happily taking her hand, one on each side of her as they flip-flopped away.

I smiled as I heard Mom explaining that of course they all had to have matching pajamas. She said to them, "You know, girls. Like, we're samesies, right?"

Martina responded, "Grandma, really, samesies? Really? That's not even a word. You're just making it up."

Mom laughed a little and she said, "Girls, samesies is a word, and it's a darn good one. I just made it up, and I think it fits the occasion perfectly."

Zalia offered, "I like it too. Martina, don't be saucy to your grandma. Let's be samesies!"

***

Jacquie switched over to a more professional tone and she asked, "Nigel, may I ask, what line of work are you in?"

98

"You first."

"Oh. I see," she smiled, "ladies first."

"Exactly."

"I'm a pediatric nurse practitioner. I practice at Miami Children's Hospital, an old busy hospital downtown in the big city. Now you. What about you, Nigel?"

Jacquie's profession brought on Dad's memory of losing his son earlier in the year, and pain flashed over his face. I interrupted before he could gather his words. I looked through her saucy exterior and focused on her intelligent, big, brown eyes. I said quietly, "Actually, Jacquie, Dad is familiar with your line of work. He and Mom suffered the neonatal death of their son a while back. Our baby, Nigel Jr., was still born."

Jacquie's hand shot out, patting Dad on the arm. "I'm so sorry for your loss. My chatter has put you in a difficult position here; I'm so sorry. Let's change the conversation, shall we?"

She turned to me. "And you, Princess, what about you? What do you do?"

I leaned back and laughed. "Not much. I sit at home and eat bonbons all day long. But I can tell you about Dad and Mom's careers. Dad is a retired Supreme Court Justice, and Mom is a writer. A novelist."

"Oh really!? Now that's interesting! What genre?"

"Her books are listed under romance, but they're more adventure I'd say. She has lived around the world, and I've noticed a lot of her personal experiences throughout her books. She writes at least three books a year."

Dad added, "She's built a very nice career for herself over the past five years or so."

Jacquie asked again, "And you?"

"I'm a graduate student at University of Toronto. My research is shaping up to be an anthology of stories of Canadian incarcerated women."

"Oh my God. That's deep, man. I owe you an apology. I had you pegged as a princess, a mere piece of beautiful fluff."

All of a sudden, Dad looked over my shoulder, and his eyes lit up as he sprung out of his chair. Jacquie and I turned to follow his big grin. The boys had woken from their nap, and Maureen had them dressed in their little bathing suits and water wings. The three of them were walking hand-in-hand toward our chairs. Dad scooped up the boys and carried them, one under each arm. He placed them both into my lap as they were laughing with their bumpy ride.

They were clapping their hands and both saying, "Mommy, Mommy," all to Jacquie's surprise.

"Oh, oh, oh. So, my new friend turns out to be Ms. United Nations. Another Angelina Jolie Pitt. I wonder what other surprises she has up her sleeve."

"Maureen, I'd like you to meet Jacquie. Jacquie, this is Maureen O'Reilly."

Maureen said in her charming Irish brogue, "Pleased to meet you. And this is Warren and Noah, our wee boys. Don't worry if you can't figure out who's who. No one can."

As Jacquie took Noah from my lap, she balanced him on her one leg and smiled into his face and said, "Noah, or Warren, you beautiful, beautiful little boy, your mommy has a lot of explaining to do. I have a feeling I'm in for a lot of stories over the next few days."

She looked over at me, eyebrows raised, and said, "I'm counting now. There's you, a Swede, there's a Canadian mother who looks like she had you when she was 12, there's a father, probably Jamaican-born, a biracial daughter, two Eurasian identical twins, and with a name like Maureen O'Reilly now in the mix, we can assume there's Irish too. Starting talking, Sister, from the very beginning. I've got all day. And I want details, Sister, all the juicy details."

***

The two of us did a quick grocery shopping in our beach cover-ups and flip-flops as Mom and Dad minded the four kids. Maureen was taking some time for herself and had left the others in search of the other pool. I had to laugh; we had just met that afternoon, and yet we spoke that kind of shorthand that old friends use. I would pick up a box of cereal and raise my eyebrows, and she would give me a quick nod or a 'what-are-you-out-of-your-mind' look that I caught onto quickly. We stood in the lineup and she said to me, "I'm 5'8", but you are towering over me. Are you six feet?"

"Nope. 5'10"," I answered.

"That's okay with me. Perhaps I've got you beat in the brains department. I think we're even with our beautiful little daughters though. It seems to me that they're going to really enjoy our time here together. Now let's get something straight right now, Nigella, before we have our first fight in front of the cashier. You all invited me for dinner and a sleepover, so it's only fair that I pay for these groceries. You don't want to argue with me about this."

I smiled at her and I said, "Thanks, Jacquie, but I'm in between a rock and a hard place here. You see, if my folks ever found out that you paid, they would be very disappointed. They're just like that, and it's from their heart. I've learned to just say thank you. It gives them so much pleasure to treat everyone. And they can afford it; they have more money than God."

"So, I guess this is our first little secret from the old folks, girlfriend. I'm paying. But I hear you. I'll get this one, and you can pick up the next tab. Deal?"

"Deal. But consider yourself warned. Please don't argue with them when they want to pay for the Disney treats tomorrow. They're grandparents; you've gotta give them a bone, Jack. After all, they've never forgotten their humble beginnings, trust me, and it's their biggest pleasure to treat us all."

"Oh! So, you really are a princess! Private school? A pony for your sixth birthday?"

"It's complicated. I grew up on social assistance and food stamps with my birthmother in Sweden. I didn't meet my dad and his wife until five years ago when I was 30. And I didn't know Dad was rich until after that. So, you see what I mean, you've just gotta go with the flow and indulge them. Dad's always trying to make up for all the years we missed. But you know what, I can fill you in on all that later. Let's get out of here and get back to the pool so I can give you some swimming lessons. You were way too slow in your lane earlier. And besides, we're on holidays, right?"

"Aw, so you're not a princess walking around in that $300 bathing suit after all?"

"No. Not at all. I'm a survivor wearing sheep's clothing."

My new friend laughed all the way back to our big suite where we put the groceries away. We made plans for dinner in that first night to make sure that the kids were in bed early to get a good night's sleep before the big day in Disney Park.

It was like we had known each other our whole lives.

***

Since none of us had ever been to Disney World before, it was an eye-opening experience for everyone. I spent the whole morning watching Dad and Mom's reaction to the park, but I have to admit, I think I appreciated it all more than anyone, with Jacquie being a close second. We all agreed to Maureen's suggestion that we would do the park in the mornings and have the boys back to the hotel for an afternoon nap while the rest of us enjoyed the pool. Jacquie and Zalia fit right in. Our meeting up was like it was just meant to be.

The days flew by, and we spent most evenings in, cooking dinner in our little kitchen or ordering in, as everyone needed to be in bed early to rest up for the next day. Our evenings in gave Dad, Mom, Maureen, and I a chance to get to know Jacqueline Dixon, and we found out what made her tick. And that was her ten-year-old daughter, Zalia. Jacquie was a very bright, funny, hardworking, single parent that had grown up in the projects, in the shadows of all the sunshine, white-sand beaches, and fast money in the big city of Miami, Florida.

***

Jacqueline Dixon had had a tough life by anyone's standards. It was further complicated by race.

Her father, Reggie Dixon, was a Vietnam vet who came home with a belly full of PTSD and a sizable drug-and-alcohol problem in the late '60s. He had been drafted as an idealistic, black, 18-year-old kid and came back a shell of a man. When Martin Luther King was assassinated in 1968, he lost a good chunk of his idealism and didn't have the heart to follow through with his activism toward ending racial inequalities that he and his young wife had experienced. He was unable to hold a job and drifted through the years, in and out of Jacquie's life and in and out of jail, usually due to drug charges or basic homelessness. How he was still alive was beyond Jacqui. Since Zalia was born, Jacqueline dealt with her father on a strictly need-be basis, usually with a call to or from the state prison or the local jail who kept her posted as to his comings and goings.

Jacquie's mother, a kid herself when they were married at age 18 just before Reggie was drafted, managed to stay in school to become a nurse. With years and years of never getting a promotion and never getting the good shifts at the hospital because of her black skin, she too lost the will to fight the cause for black America. They had Jacqueline in 1975 and her little brother five years later. The little brother died as a teenager. The police picked him up at home one day, took him to the station, and he died due to a beating while in custody.

Jacquie told us that he was a good kid but a black kid. He didn't have a chance. And as for her mother, she died of cancer the year after Zalia was born. Jacquie took the life-insurance policy payout and bought herself and Zalia a nice two-bedroom condo in a better school district, inching bit by bit out of the old, original 'hood.'

Jacquie's mother was determined that her daughter would have a better life than her, so, following in her mother's encouragement and footsteps, Jacquie became a registered nurse. She continued her studies and worked hard to become a nurse practitioner. For better and for worse, Jacquie, at the age of 23, married a nice, young man full of promise and ambition. He was also a nurse. He thought that he could further his education to become a doctor by joining the U.S.A. Army. Their marriage was sliced into small fragments that took place in between tours of duty and her nightshifts working as a nurse at the hospital. He shipped out to Afghanistan right after Zalia was born in 2000.

His last tour of duty included an honorable discharge as he came home at age 34 as a double amputee. Life dealing with PTSD and confined to a wheelchair wasn't for him, and he died of suicide a year ago when Zalia was nine years old.

A month ago, Jacquie decided that she would exercise her option at work of taking a three-month leave of absence due to stress caused by burnout on the job. She and Zalia had driven up from Miami to Disney World for a much-needed holiday before they struck out on the next leg of their life's journey.

***

We were all quiet as Jacquie finished her story, and then she slapped her hands down on the table and said, "But we all know that it's not what happens to you, it's what you do about it, right?"

Dad's big baritone boomed, "You're exactly right, Jacqueline Dixon. So, what's your plan? We're all ears!"

"Okay, folks. Just know that I am a bit of a drama queen, so I want to show you my plan rather than just tell you about it. Talk is cheap, you know. I'll be right back; I have to go back to our room to get my laptop. Meanwhile, how about a fresh tea, Nigella? If you expect me to entertain you all night long, you've got to keep me hydrated, you know."

Once Jacquie found the email on the screen, she stood up so we could all crowd around and read her 'show and tell' for ourselves. My eyes focused on the screen and I noticed the send date was May 14, 2010; a month beforehand. I couldn't believe what I was reading:

Dear Ms. Dixon,

Just a quick note to confirm that your interview time at Sick Children's Hospital in Toronto is scheduled for Monday, June 28, 2010, at 10:00 p.m.

Please be advised that this is an exploratory measure only and is not an offer of employment nor a work permit for any specific job posting at this time.

We look forward to meeting with you, and, meanwhile, please don't hesitate to call me if you need a recommendation for a nearby hotel for your visit to our city.

Best regards,
Pediatric Medicine, Nurse Practitioner Department, Sick Children's Hospital

***

Maureen broke the silence, and she said quietly, "This is God's work. Nigella, quick, say your prayer; the one you say for a blessing."

I laughed a little and put my arms around Maureen, our good little Catholic, and I repeated my old Jewish prayer:

"Hear, O Israel, the Lord our God, the Lord Is One."

We all said Amen, and then our new friend was bombarded with advice of what rooms and what beds at 49 Parkwood Avenue were the best in our house for her and Zalia, all, of course for the whole duration of her three-month leave of absence. Mom offered to share her car, and Dad said he'd get out and buy Zalia a bike the same as Martina's. Maureen told her that both she and I went to the University of Toronto, which wasn't far from Sick Kid's, so we could take the subway together if Jacquie didn't want to drive downtown.

After we had all assured her that my husband wouldn't mind in the least, it was agreed that she would come up to Canada on Saturday, June 26, with an undetermined return date.

***

I thought to myself, '*That would give me exactly eight days to serve the divorce papers on my cheating husband and kick his sorry ass out the door.*' Dad, Mom, and I didn't mention anything about my marital problems, and, of course, Maureen was still in the dark about the pending divorce.

Jacquie started to tear up and she said, "It was my lucky day the day I met all of you. We Americans always tease you Canadians about being so nice, but it's true."

Mom jumped up and pulled her up out of her chair to give her a big hug. "Welcome to the family, honey. I'm just so happy to have two more wonderful girls to spoil. You're not to worry about anything, and we're treating to your air tickets. We'll make sure you have an open return so you can come and go as you please. Just come up to Canada and then you can make plans to stay forever; never mind this 'exploratory visit' talk, d'ya hear?"

***

Jack and I had whispered long into the night, and I said, "Psst, Jack, are you still awake?"

"Yeah, what do you want now?"

"I just wanted to say how glad I'll be to finally get home."

She turned around to face me. "What? I thought you were having so much fun on your holiday."

"No, it's not the holiday. I'm just sick and tired of you hogging all the covers every night."

I tried not to wake the girls with my laughter as I felt her pillow landing in a thud against the side of my head.

***

Chapter Six
Addendum: François Tran

He had turned away from her and feigned sleep, trying to escape the tedium of her voice. *'The bloom was off the rose,'* he thought to himself, *'for both these fucking long-haul flights to and from Vancouver and Cecilia Yang.'* He'd had it. That was it. It wasn't worth the effort any longer. This was the last goddamn time he was taking her out to the coast. Even the sex which, when it started out, was as hot as any he had ever had in his whole long 20 years of bedding women. Fuck it. Fuck it all.

Over the last hour of the flight, his mind bounced back and forth, from the woman beside him to his wife at home, which was just another source of angst. Nothing suited him these days. And the kids were a handful. Fuck, man. He tried to reason with himself that he had it all. An astoundingly beautiful trophy wife, the big house, three beautiful, healthy kids and a good job, and an assistant that gave him the best head that he'd ever had. Why was he always so anxious? Why was he never satisfied?

He couldn't wait to get off the fucking plane to have a few tokes off the last few reefers that he had in his pocket. That would mellow him out enough to face the Swedish princess whose beautiful, innocent heart was just too much for him to deal with these days. He always felt like a complete failure with her. It had even affected him when he was fucking her. Or trying to. More often than not, lately, he wasn't even able to get it up with her.

No, he decided, he wouldn't go home tonight. On the other hand, he sure as hell didn't want to spend another night with Cecilia. She didn't know it yet, but he had decided over the last day or two that he wasn't going to be dipping his pen into her inkwell from this day forward.

It had nothing to do with the fact that Nigel had caught him with her last week in the boardroom, although that was unfortunate. He loved Nigel and it just added to his stress that he had caused him any pain. Fuck, man!

His mind wandered back to the present, when it dawned on him. Ah ha! Bingo! That was it! He had ordered a crate of B.C. salmon, all packed in dry ice, that would be waiting for him to pick up once they landed. He would give his parents a call and suggest that he run it up to them, right from the airport, and simply stay the night with them up at the farm. He'd call Nigella and tell her where he was and that he'd be home first thing in the morning. Yeah. Smooth move, Counsellor.

***

He lay there in his parents' small second bedroom, unable to sleep. Worn weary from his week's work on the coast and the long flight home, he was unable to unwind. He rolled out of bed and reached into his club-bag for a pair of jeans and a tee-shirt. He tried not to make any noise as he tiptoed toward the door. He had heard Pops and Mama shut out all the lights and close their bedroom door about an hour ago, so he thought he would go for a run down the back lane through the bush to see if that would ease his insomnia.

It was a hot summer night up there at the farm, and he found the night sounds of the frogs and the wind ruffling up through the bush somewhat comforting. His feet crackled under the dry grass as he stepped on it before hitting the sandy lane. He realized that even though it was only mid-June, the hot, dry summer had dried out the bush to the extent that it had lost its usual cool lushness somehow. He just stood there, silently counting all the beehives thriving in the family's apiary business. He breathed in the country sounds emanating from the insects and life in the meadow that was full of field flowers that his parents had planted in order to encourage the honeybees. He pulled out a reefer and took a couple of deep drags, waiting for it to kick in. His eyes rested on the first few of the beehives that were stationed every ten feet or so throughout the meadow in front of the bush, all bordered by the stumpery. His parents had done one hell of a good job here on the farm. That meadow had taken a lot of hard work, clearing the land and planting all the flowering plants and foliage that were natural to the habitat. Yeah, it all worked. Pops and his new wife, who insisted that he call her Mama, were so happy working their farm. It was their dream come true. They had managed to keep the big, old bush cut back enough to give the meadow the direct sunlight it needed to survive, and, in turn, to attract the honeybees.

He smiled a little, the first smile all day, and he scouted the night sky for the full moon. Although he was a true-blue city slicker, he felt a kinship of sorts with the bush that night just standing there, listening to the wind pick up and looking up, up, and up, following the clouds that were scuttling at quite a pace over the black sky. He watched as a single star revealed itself to him as its cloud-cover sailed silently past it.

As he stood there in the night, he sucked in his breath as he watched a shooting star falling down, down, and then fading into nothingness as it burned itself out. All in the flash of a moment.

Way back in his memory, the old nursery rhyme, *I wish, I wish upon a star,* vaguely came to mind, but he shook his head, tossed down the tail end of his reefer, and began an easy jog down the long lane past the 100-year-old oaks and chestnut trees and past all the brush and bramble that calls such a property its home. Nothing had changed really since the year 1850 when the Canadian government had sold it as crown land to Denni's ancestors who cleared a patch in that first bush to build their little lean-to shanty. *We've all come a long way,* he thought to himself, remembering the stories Pops and his birth-Mama had told him about their journey to Canada as the 'boat people from Vietnam' back in 1975. Even Uncle Nigel, with more money than God, came from a dirt-floor kitchen in rural Jamaica when he was a nine-year-old boy. And his wife's grandma was a Holocaust Survivor, for Chrissake. And Nigella's first mother, a deaf mute, who grew up in an orphanage. He didn't have anything to complain about. He made up his mind right then and there that he was going to turn his life around and be the son and the husband and the father that his family deserved.

He knew he was halfway down the lane when his eye caught the plaque that Denni had insisted be installed in the bush. Pops had carved the whole thing for her, and it was truly a piece of art. The wording that Pops had meticulously carved out had been filled in a little with black paint to make the words pop out of the old piece of timber. It said simply that the plaque was in honor of all the first nations' people that had lived on this land over all the years. "Yeah," he reminded himself, "this old farm was still near-and-dear to Denni, although you'd never know it with her big-city look."

He was looking forward to just sitting on the old, long-retired, railroad tracks at the very back of his parents' farm. He just needed some peace and quiet. Maybe, with any luck at all, he'd see another shooting star.

Yeah, he'd have to bring his boys back here once they got a little older to appreciate the wonders and beauty of a night in the country. Yeah. They could even bring a tent or sleep under the stars. Yeah. As soon as they got a little older. What the fuck, they were only three; he would have to wait a couple of years yet.

30 minutes later, after skipping over railway ties down the track a bit, he turned back to head home. He was fixated on the sky which hosted a full moon. While he was looking up at the man in the moon, he said to the glorious, silent, perfectly mystical sphere, "Fuck, man, that's pretty good weed." Realizing that he was talking to an inanimate object, he laughed out loud and was startled by the sound, turning around to see if it was someone else that was laughing. He couldn't even feel his fingers. Fuck, man!

He lit up one more reefer for the road.

As he started jogging back up the lane, with the summer branches of foliage arching over him in the dark, he felt he was finally ready to turn in for the night. As he jogged through the hot, black night, with the full moon way, way up behind him, something in the humid air caught in his throat, and he felt a searing pain rip deep down into his chest. He stopped and threw his head back to try to get a deep breath of air as both his hands instinctively rubbed his chest.

The second attack knocked him completely off his feet. He lay on the ground, gasping for air and clutching his chest from the searing pain. As it subsided, he cautiously took several shorter breaths to test the water, so to speak. He knew instinctively that he should get back to the trailer, but, as soon as he was once again fully upright, he was hit once again with the pain that ripped through his chest like an axe ripping through a block of wood.

It was then, as he was down on his knees, with both hands clutching his chest, that he smelled the smoke. As the horror registered in his mind, he pleaded with his eyes to tell him that the bush in front of him was not all gray and full of rolling smoke and that those flames way, way up the lane near the beehives were not real.

Through his panic and his slowed reaction due to the weed, he still knew to keep low and to follow the sandy laneway. He needed to get his parents out of the trailer before the wind switched course which would lead the fire their way.

He crawled along, keeping low to the ground, and he had made about 20 meters of headway, when a sly, silent gust of wind swooped down and delivered the final bout of the old bush's smoke deep, deep down into his lungs.

He came to after the final attack, and he lay on his back, facing west, back toward the railroad tracks where the sky was clear and pitch black. The man in the moon still hung in the black sky, smiling benevolently down at him in silence. The stars were stationed by the millions, twinkling above the big, old, silent moon.

François's eyes widened as a shooting star fell down, down, directly in front of him as if it were going to reach down and pluck him out of his pain to start afresh in an alternate universe.

He reached up with both arms in acceptance of the lift being offered, and he finally felt the peace that had always eluded him up until now.

***

He hovered, looking down at earth's version of himself. He had spent 37 years in that body. It lay face up, eyes still open, a small smile on the lips as his last breath exhaled softly.

***

He felt the pull of the long, white light that would take him to his next station.

***

Chapter Seven
Loss and Resilience

I threw back my covers for the umpteenth time that night and gave in to my insomnia. I thought I may as well be productive, so I put on a robe with the idea that I would get up and take care of a few emails. I left our bedroom and first padded up to the third floor to once again check on the boys, tiptoeing carefully over the array of stray Legos and a train set that they had been setting up in the middle of the floor before I had caught them and tucked them into bed for the third time that night. They were a handful.

They lay there, sleeping blissfully, unaware of their parents' troubles. Oh my God, how did I get into such a mess? My heart went out to these two, little, innocent, lookalike, three-year-old boys, with their curly hair and beautiful Eurasian faces. I was so blessed.

They had had such a good time in Disney World, still being young enough to be filled with wonderment with the rides and attractions and the pool. How would we tell them that their parents were going to live separate lives? I pulled their sheets up over their waists and folded their quilts across the bottom of their beds. I made my way over to the big dormer window. I just stood there, half of my heart grieving for my marriage and the other half full of wonderment at how I had ended up with three beautiful children, living in the house of my dreams with my loving parents two blocks away. It was a sweltering, hot, summer night in the city, and the full moon lit up the quiet street. *Not a creature was stirring,* as the old story goes.

I craned my neck for a full view of the sky and smiled a little to myself as I sent out my question to the universe, *Mor, Mamma, are you there? Tell me what to do with this mess I've got myself into, will you!? Mor!? Are you listening to me!?*

I turned to take one last look at my little boys, and my hand automatically went up to touch the mezuzah mounted on the doorframe that Rabbi Kleiman had given to me. He told me at that time that mezuzahs were nice to have on my home's interior doors as well as the front door, because their meaning was *to protect the inhabitants.* I repeated my nightly prayer standing in their doorway, *Hear, O Israel, the Lord our God, the Lord Is One.*

I left the loft to check on Martina. She was snuggled under her duvet, so I bent over and lightly kissed her curls before backing up and sitting down in the little chair at her desk. She was so different from the boys. Always had been. She was more like me, I suppose, but who she really took after was Mom. Strange, they weren't blood relatives at all, but ever since she had met her grandma when she was five, she emulated her. Not as much now that she was older, but she had spent those first, few, formative years of kindergarten and grade school saying over and over again, *But Grandma does it this way; but Grandma says this; but Grandma wouldn't do that.* Dad always thought she was his little girl, and Mom and I never told him any differently. Martina's grandma was her idol. And she was tough like her grandma too. She didn't take fools lightly, and she held no prisoners.

I stood up and lifted up her *Canadiana* quilt that her grandma had bought for her. The quilt was an exquisite piece of Canadian art and was in pristine condition, although it was over 50 years old. Upon receiving it, Martina had sat Grandma down and explained that although she really liked it, Grandma had to take it back and ask them to add all the family's country flags along the bottom of it. Grandma, of course, complied. She meticulously handcrafted tiny bits and pieces of colorful quilter's cotton to make the flags of Sweden, Ireland, Jamaica, Vietnam, United States of America, and Canada, which she carefully hand-stitched all along the lower edge of the old quilt. Martina and her grandma shared many of these little plans and projects. They had quite a bond.

My eye rested on the beautiful dollhouse that my father-in-law had made her. Chi Tran was so talented in many areas. He had run the greenhouse food-bank business for years, planted all the beautiful gardens at both 7 Russell Hill Road and 49 Parkwood Avenue, and, of late, in his spare time, he had built a beautiful dollhouse for Martina. It was a real work of art, and he had made all the furnishings for it as well. We kept it up on a table, away from the little boys' curiosity. Now he and his wife were fully entrenched with running the apiary. It had always been their dream to have a farm, and I was so happy for them that their dream had come to fruition.

Mom and I had Martina's room painted out in 'Sugar Plum' which was a pale lavender paint with a corresponding pale, pale toile wall covering that you had to really look at closely to decipher the delicate French story lines of the vignettes.

Martina had doted on both her grandparents while we were in Disney World, always asking them if she could rub sunscreen on their face and arms poolside. '*Grandma,*' she would say, '*you have white skin! You have to be careful, Grandma!*'

As I refolded the treasured quilt, I thanked God for Mom and Dad. Now this was one area of my life where I really got lucky. I sighed. My husband troubles were a different matter altogether. Once again, I put my hand over Martina's mezuzah and whispered the prayer before I closed her door halfway and made my way downstairs.

***

I made myself an herbal tea, thinking it would help me sleep. I wandered into my office and turned on my computer to check for emails. As I clicked on my computer, I was startled by the front door chime.

I jumped up, thinking that François had changed his mind about staying at the farm with his parents for the night. He must have forgotten his keys. I felt my stomach tighten with the thought of seeing my husband that had become more of a stranger to me than a partner.

"Where the hell is your key!?" I said icily as I swung the door open. I froze. It wasn't François at all. It was two uniformed policemen.

"Oh, oh, excuse me. I thought it was my husband."

"Good evening. Is François Tran home, and may we speak with him?"

"No, he's not home. I'm his wife. Is something wrong?"

"May we come in?"

"Of course. What is it? What's wrong? Oh please, come in. Come in."

"It's about Mr. Tran's parents."

"Oh my God. What's happened!?"

"We don't have all the details yet, but it appears there was a fire in the bush on their farm, and Mr. Tran's parents have lost their lives trying to save their beehives from the fire that took the bush down."

I stood there, stunned. I couldn't move. I couldn't speak. I saw the one officer step toward me. He took me by the arm and led me to the sofa in the living room. He sat me down and peered into my face.

"Mrs. Tran, Mrs. Tran, can you hear me? May I get you a drink of water?" All I could do was nod in the affirmative and point to the kitchen.

The officer brought me a glass of water, but my hands were shaking so much that I couldn't grasp the glass. He gently raised the glass to my lips and I took a sip before leaning back on the sofa. The two officers just sat there, one beside me and one in front of me, quietly, waiting until I recovered.

I heard myself saying quietly, "I'm going to be okay. Please tell me everything."

"Are you sure, Mrs. Tran? Would you rather wait until your husband came home? We tried his cellphone, but there was no answer."

"He's not coming home," I said dully.

"Oh. Well then. Does he have an alternate number where we can reach him?"

"No, he's not coming home. Ever. You can't reach him, and neither can I," I said. I started to sob as I gave them the whereabouts of my husband. "He's with his parents at the farm."

I felt the officer's arms go around me as the other officer sat there. All he could say was, "Fuck man, fuck!" and then he added a quiet, "Please excuse my French, Ma'am."

"Please call my dad. I want my dad," I said quietly into the dark-blue jacket that was pressed against my face.

The one police officer stepped out on the front porch to make the call to Mom and Dad, and I just stood there in front of the window, waiting for their car lights to pull into the driveway. There was a small beacon of comedy I witnessed as Patou leapt out of the car's backseat and charged toward the officer. Thank God Patou listened as Mom ordered him to heel.

Patou gave me a few licks on my face before disappearing upstairs to check on the kids, and I allowed myself to fall apart once Dad gathered me up into his arms.

Dad said quietly, "The officer who was waiting outside told me that the dispatcher had just called in that they had found a third body that appears to be an Asian male in his 30s. His body was located at the back of the farm, near the railway tracks. It looked like he died from smoke inhalation. His body suffered no burns."

This piece of follow-up information was not news to me. Oh no, not at all. I knew in my gut as soon as I saw the two officers in the doorway that my husband was dead.

Dad whispered, "There, there, there, baby. Cry it all out. Just cry it all out. I'm here, honey, I'm here."

My world, as I knew it, had collapsed. Nothing but ashes left.

Mom put coffee on and volunteered to fill in the blanks as to the Tran family for the officers and their paperwork while Dad held me, rocking me back and forth and patting my back as he tried to soothe me.

I sobbed, "But, Dad, what about you? Papa was your best friend. And Mama. Poor Mama. They loved each other so much and had been married such a short time."

As we all sat up to the dining-room table to Mom's coffee, I heard Martina's voice from the stairs, "Mommy? Mommy? What's going on?"

Dad jumped up and returned with his little girl, who wasn't such a little girl any longer, in his arms. He held her on his lap as the police officers explained to her that there had been a fire.

She suffered the worst loss. She had lost her dad, the dad that had adopted her when we married. She also lost her paternal grandparents, all in one fell swoop.

Patou was up on his hind paws, licking her face and crying right along with her. Right along with all of us, in fact, including the two officers.

***

After the police officers left, Mom went home to pack an overnight bag for her and dad, with a promise to be back in 15 minutes. I smiled a little at Martina. True to form, she wasn't willing to hear the softer version of what happens after you die that Dad was trying to tell her.

She said in a very analytical voice, "Now, Granddad, how can Grandmère and Grandpère and Dad be all together with Grandmère's first husband and her son that died so many years ago? You know in Canada that we aren't allowed to have two husbands at the same time. I think that you've got your facts mixed up a little bit, Granddad."

She continued, "You'd better check your story with Grandma as soon as she gets back. I bet that she'll call your story a bunch of hogwash."

"You're right, honey, you're right. Let's leave it up to Grandma to tell us how they sort and manage families in heaven. I learned a long time ago that Grandma knows everything."

***

I glanced over at Martina, who had fallen asleep, snuggled down in between Mom and me in my big king bed. I nodded to Dad sitting in the big easy chair that he had pulled up to my side of the bed, and I said, "She's out like a light. It's time to get down to business, Dad."

And so, the planning began. It was my job to call Jacquie the next morning to ask her if she could come up to Canada right away rather than waiting until the next week. It was Dad's job to call Rabbi Kleiman and Mom's job to call Pastor Smith. Those two pillars of their respective faiths would arrange for a beautiful service to be held as soon as possible at the interdenominational church down on St. Clair Avenue where my in-laws attended Sunday Services and where my mother-in-law sang in the choir. (I corrected myself; she used to sing.) The pastor would officiate, and the rabbi would be his second. After all, François's adopted ten-year-old daughter was a Jew, and his three-year-old twin sons were Christians. That's how we did things in our family. We would follow the service with the interment up at Mount Pleasant Cemetery so the three members of the Tran family would take their place right along with Baby Nigel Jr., Saul Himmel, and Mavis Royal.

We would have a separate, non-religious Celebration of Life service a few weeks later to honor the Tran family, designed for Mom and Dad's friends and a few of our neighbors, and, of course, so that François's law office, colleagues, and friends could come together to pay their respects, once our small family had had a chance to grapple with the church service and actual burial in private.

I insisted, over Dad's protests, since I was listed as executor in his will that we had made when we were married, that I would do all the paperwork; the death certificates, François's life-insurance policy, closing the bank accounts for the three of them, and all the other notifications that come with death. I thought it would be a good way to encourage closure, and, really, I was the next of kin as well as being executor, and it was my duty to step up.

"Listen to me, Dad. I'm a lawyer. I'm good with paperwork, and I'll need something to keep me busy. Trust me, I'll let you know if I need your help. You've got enough to do."

I continued before they could argue, "I need you two to listen to me. What I'm going to say now is written in stone. Everything else is flexible, but there's one thing that I insist on and I won't budge on either," I said firmly.

"Shoot, honey. What's up?" Dad said.

"For continuity's sake, and, if you can, I'm asking you two to take care of all the costs and bills until François's life-insurance policy is paid out. I'll get it all back to you, every cent of it, as soon as I receive his payout. Will this work for you?"

"Now, honey, don't be worrying about money. We're paying for everything; you put the insurance payout away for you and the kids."

"That's not the way it works, Dad. And trust me, you don't want to argue this point with me right now, or ever, in fact. It's your job to keep an exact record of all monies you spend, and it's my job to use the insurance money to return what I owe back to you. You can run the show, the funeral, the cremation, the burial, the whole works. This is the only thing that I insist on. No arguing. I won't have it. Now, have I got your word on this?"

Mom spoke up. "You probably haven't thought about this yet, but you won't have to be worrying about budgeting or money again in your lifetime, Nigella. We know that Chi and Diep have life-insurance policies that are going to be paid out to you as well, and many years ago, when François was born, your dad and Chi set up a life-insurance policy with baby François being the second beneficiary after his mother. As you know, his mother died 15 years ago. It's the same as how your granddad Saul took care of Dad, you, me, and Martina long, long before Saul knew that Dad would have a family of his own."

Dad added, "And you have mortgage insurance, right? That will pay off the mortgage on the house. We don't think it would be wise for you to sell the house, honey. You've lost so much already, and you love this big, old place. Just stay put. Please."

"Oh. Oh. Well, this news just strengthens my case. Mom, Dad, do we have a deal? You pay upfront and I'll reimburse you."

They looked at each other and nodded their heads in unison. "Deal," they said.

We also decided that Mom and Dad would sort through my in-laws' apartment and decide on what keepsakes to save for the children and what to donate, but this would come later; there was certainly no rush to open that can of worms.

We all agreed that the farm and the land itself would just have to wait. None of us had the guts to face it. We weren't in any condition to see the remains of the fire, especially Mom who loved that old bush with her whole heart. It was the connection that she and Papa had shared passionately. It was obvious to us 'outsiders' that they were people of the land and shared a special affinity for trees and plant-life somehow. I suggested that down the road we hire back Mom's old friend, Tom Oliver, the arborist, to deal with the physical wreckage until we had time and foresight to talk about reforestation.

Next on our list was calling Uncle Brad. I insisted, over Dad's pleading, that I call him right then and there. After all, it was three hours earlier on the coast.

"Uncle Brad, it's Nigella."

"Hi, darlin'! For Chrissake, my beautiful niece, I thought that we had put that *uncle* business behind us. I'm just Brad, honey, just Brad. Are you all home from Disney World?"

In the second where I was gathering my courage up to speak, he caught on that something was wrong.

"Honey, is Nigel okay? What's wrong, honey? Tell me, is Nigel and Denni okay?"

"They're both okay. In fact, they're right beside me. Uncle Brad, I have bad news to tell you." I just blurted it out to spare him as best I could, "We just found out an hour ago that François and both his parents have been killed in a fire at the farm."

"Oh, honey. I'm so sorry. I'm so sorry. Shit. Fuck, fuck, fuck! No way! Oh, honey. I'll be up right away. Are you okay? Are the kids okay? How's Nigel and Denni taking this? Is there anything I can do right now?"

"No, but thanks. Everyone here is as well as can be expected, Uncle Brad. Mom and Dad are right beside me. Martina knows already; she's asleep right beside me right now. But we haven't made any arrangements yet, so don't come up tomorrow night until we know what day the funeral is, okay? Are you in the middle of a shoot? I don't want you taking time away from work. And it's a long flight from L.A."

I hesitated for a second, then changed my mind. "Wait. Wait. Contrary to what I've just said, I'm going to need you here for Dad. He and Mom are going to need you here." I looked up at Dad, and I smiled a little as I said, "You know what a boob he is." With that, we said our *I love you* and I passed the phone over to Dad who took the phone and started to cry with his head sunk down into his chest.

"My best friend is gone. Gone. The kids' daddy too. They're all gone." He got up and left the room so he could give Brad the details of the fire without me and Mom having to hear it all over again.

Mom propped herself up on one elbow and leaned over Martina as she whispered, "Thanks, honey, for making the call to Brad for your dad. I must tell you that even more than I love you, I respect and admire you. You are one hell of a tough cookie to handle all this as cool as a cucumber. Listen, between you and me, we have a big job ahead of us taking care of Dad and the kids, especially Martina. We can't afford to fall apart now. We'll have time to fall apart later. Can you just keep it together for the sake of them? I'm here for you, honey, and you're here for me. But back to Martina for a minute. Our little ten-year-old is going on 30, if you know what I mean. She may take on a mothering role toward you, and that's no good for a little girl. I know how to handle her, so if it's okay with you, leave her to me, and you focus on your dad. And Jacquie will be here tomorrow, and she'll also take care of you and me. She's a nurse, and she knows how to do this. Speaking of her, we're both so blessed that we met her. So, she'll take care of us while I focus on Martina and you focus on Dad. Deal?"

"Deal. You're the best. I love you."

"And I love you, baby."

She settled back down into the bed, and I had her voice float up from under the covers, "And one last thing, baby. Please, please go easy on yourself. Try to put the whole divorce issue out of your mind permanently. You don't need to be beating yourself up over that issue that's not relevant any longer. You have other things on your plate. I'd pick grief over guilt every time, if I had to make a choice. That guilt business is a bitch to deal with."

"Like Dad always says, you're right, Mom. You're always right."

***

The morning sun was peeking through the shade's edge as my eyes opened to face my first day of being a widow. I turned to check on Martina who was still sound asleep. I quietly padded out to the kitchen to see Dad, Mom, and Maureen sitting there, nursing coffees.

I stood there in the doorway, and I gave them a little smile. I lifted my hand to cover the kitchen's mezuzah to remind them that we were all in God's hands as I repeated the old blessing, "Hear, O Israel, the Lord our God, the Lord Is One."

Maureen met me there in the doorway and, holding me tight, recited her very own Irish blessing to the three of us from over my shoulder. Her lovely Irish brogue lilted through the words:

"*May the road rise to meet you,*
And the wind always be at your back.
May the sun shine warm on your face,
And the rains fall softly on your fields.
And until we meet again,
May God hold you gently in the palm of his hand."

"I love you, and I'm so grateful that you're here with us."

She responded with her usual aplomb as if I was one of her small charges, "I have no doubt, dearie. The good Lord will take care of us all."

We all settled around the kitchen table to have a morning coffee and to sort out the daily schedule.

***

I phoned Jacquie after the coffee. "Hi, Jack. We've run into stormy weather here."

As I finished delivering my news, I didn't have to ask her to move the date up for traveling.

"We'll come on the next flight and stay for as long as you need us. I've got you covered, Sis."

"Thanks, Jack. So, would it be okay if Dad changed the tickets to leaving tomorrow morning, with an open return? He'll call you later this morning to confirm the flight time."

"Absolutely. Meanwhile, please take care of yourself. The kids will be just fine. Just hold on, baby, we're on our way. I'll see you tomorrow around noon, and we'll get through this together."

***

Mom made a big lunch, trying to juggle everyone's favorites, and Rabbi Kleiman and Pastor Smith and his wife joined us around the table. Maureen took the kids to the park, and between all of us, we put together the church funeral service and luncheon that would follow downstairs where Papa and Mama had been married a few short years ago. We opted for a private interment, and our two 'men of the cloth' said they would handle all those details. It was all to take place on the Monday, so Dad called Uncle Brad to confirm our plans.

"Rabbi and Pastor Smith, I have a little chore that I think you two will handle so well."

"Anything, anything at all, Nigella," they both responded.

"Will you please put your heads together and come up with a synergistic story of how the kids' Daddy, Grandmère, and Grandpère are living in heaven now. I know the boys won't understand too much, as they're only three, but Martina is going to need you to answer all her questions. They'll be home from the park very soon, so perhaps we can sit down, all together, and take care of this right away. Whatever you say is good with me, and I'll follow along over the days to come."

That afternoon, while the boys were napping, and Dad, Maureen, and Martina went out to Canadian Tire to buy a bike for Zalia, Mom and I went upstairs to prepare for Jackie and Zalia's arrival. We both agreed that Martina's twin-sized princess bed would be too small for the two girls who probably would want to sleep together like they did in Disney World, so we set up the one guestroom for them and the other guestroom for Jacquie. Both rooms were joined by a Jack 'n Jill bathroom, like my old room at Mom and Dad's house. We stood there, on opposite sides of the bed, pulling up the fresh sheets, and I looked up and caught Mom's eye. All of a sudden, my beautiful, youthful-looking 49-year-old Mom looked old and worn out. By the time I got to her, she had sunk down on the bed, and, with sobs shaking her shoulders, her hands up covering her face, I held her as her tears finally flowed.

"Now listen up, Mom, here's what we're going to do." We shared the box of Kleenex between us. "You can cry all the tears you want for Papa and Mama, but you're not allowed to shed one tear for François. He doesn't deserve your sympathy. Not right now anyway. I'm still too mad at him for cheating on me. I reserve judgment to change my mind on this, but for now, our tears are for his parents only. Do you understand?"

She smiled a little and nodded. "Okay for now. But I know from personal experience that suppressing tears is not a healthy way to go. I'm hoping you'll change your mind about crying for François. Not that he deserves it, but you do. You can't afford the luxury of lugging around any unforgiven, past events. Let them go. Learn to forgive fully and completely. Let go and let God. That's what I did when I was staying in London one year, and it helped me let go of my broken family. I don't want you getting sick and ending up in the psych ward in the hospital, like I did way back in France, when I was mad at your dad."

"Hold up here! What do you say? You were in the psych ward because of Dad?"

"Yeah. Right after we had fallen in love in Paris, we had arrived home, and he saw some pictures of me and an old friend and he became so jealous that he changed his phone number and didn't call me again. I, in turn, thought his absence was all my fault and that I didn't deserve him. So, I packed my bag and left Toronto. A long story made short, I lived in Nice, France, for almost a year. It was then, in Nice, after too much boozing and too much missing Nigel and too much getting involved with another man that I had a complete nervous breakdown and was hospitalized in the psych ward for a month. Auntie Catharine came down from the château to take care of me until I was well enough to come back to Canada. All because I didn't, or wouldn't, face my loss. Now do you see what I'm getting at? I'm worried that you may have a breakdown."

My mouth was open, and I was speechless. My mom and dad having a fight of epic proportions! No! No way! They were the perfect couple! And they loved each other more than Liz and Dick did through all their multiple marriages and breakups combined!

"Don't stop now, Mom! Come on! What happened next!?"

She smiled and looked down at her big, flashy, canary-yellow diamond. "Well, I came back home to Toronto and bumped into him at the café quite by accident. Both of us were so furious at each other and so heartbroken at the same time. He grabbed my hand and literally dragged me all the way up Heath Street to 7 Russell Hill Road to ensure that we hammer things out, being the big-time know-it-all judge that he thinks he is. Less than 24 hours later, he surprised me by putting this ring on my finger, and we were married immediately in his backyard under the big maple tree. Rabbi Kleiman married us, even though neither of us is Jewish. You know, you've seen our little wedding video. We've never looked back."

I sprung away from her, throwing my head back, howling with laughter as I landed on my back with arms outspread on the big half-made bed.

"Oh, Mom, oh, Mom! This is the best Nigel-Denni story I've heard to date! Why didn't you tell me this before? You two are simply too much!" I was still laughing as she lay down beside me and propped herself up on one elbow in order to get the last word in.

"Listen, missy, I don't tell you half of what goes on because you're too much like your father. I spend my whole life getting teased day in, day out, by the two of you. I don't want to give you any more ammunition than I have to."

***

Before I knew it, we were all squeezed into the two limos to attend the funeral service at Papa and Mama's interdenominational church on St. Clair Avenue West, three blocks from the house. Uncle Brad had arrived from L.A. right on time, followed by Auntie Catharine and Uncle Edouard who had flown in from Avignon, France. Catharine and Edouard were not actually related to either Mom or Dad but were old friends of Mom's from her single days out in Vancouver years and years ago. They were a lovely couple that lived in a big ancestral château in the south of France but were down-to-earth just like Uncle Brad with all his fame and fortune. Ann-Marie and Walt, another couple that were best friends of Mom's from her days at her old farm in Marlbank, had driven up from Napanee to stay a few days at 7 Russell Hill Road to keep my parents company. All of them, Brad, Catharine and Edouard, and Ann-Marie and Walt had made extra efforts to ensure that Jacquie and little Zalia were included in all conversations.

Anyone else would have been intimidated by the Hollywood icon and the two French aristocrats, but Jacquie took it all in stride without batting an eye. She was the best.

I looked at Mom squeezed in beside Catharine. She looked so beautiful with her dark brunette hair up and carefully applied makeup. She had made sure we were all decked out in new dresses, Jacquie and Maureen included, and she had gone out and bought matching navy-blue dresses with little white-lace collars for Martina and Zalia, and navy suits with short pants, white shirts, and clip-on ties for the boys.

I sat there in the front pew, with Jacquie on one side of me and Mom on the other. Brad was on the other side of Mom, right beside Maureen. I leaned forward and waved to my boys who were firmly under Maureen's careful watch. Dad was between the two girls, with his arms around both of them. Catharine and Edouard and Ann-Marie and Walt were right behind Mom and Dad so they could lean in to be close to them if need be. All in all, we were all holding up remarkably well. No tears, just nice and calm and organized. Of course, Mom, Dad, and Brad had set a lively tone beforehand in the limo, playing with the boys and keeping the conversation light for everyone.

***

I laughed along with everyone else as Rabbi Kleiman, who had known Chi Tran for over 30 years, and Pastor Smith, who had known Diep for almost as long, joined together to deliver a funny but poignant little story about how the couple were so competitive with each other, always trying to outdo each other with their crops of tomatoes and veggies, as they provided year-round food out of their greenhouse and from their farm for the local food bank.

Dad got up and spoke of the early years, over 30 years ago, when he and Chi both sported full heads of glorious black hair that Chi always insisted that black straight Asian hair was far superior to curly African hair. Dad went on to say that they shared a young pup named 'Little Daisy' who, during the course of living with them for 16 years, gradually became 'Old Daisy.' He told us of Chi's dedication in taking care of his aging parents, Saul and Mavis, and then of Chi joining forces with the Intelligence Department of the Canadian

Government that helped bring down a major, global, money-laundering operation. He spoke of Chi's pride, right along with his own, when Chi's son, François, was born, and of how proud Chi and Nuyen, who passed away shortly after that, were when François passed the bar and got his first job with a law firm downtown. He ended his heartfelt sentiments by saying that Chi had confided in him on his wedding day to Diep, that it was the happiest day of his life.

Mom stood up and told a few funny stories of how her and Diep strategized over many cups of coffee on how to beat the boys in their weekly card games, and of how Diep was a devoted wife and grandmother to her three grandchildren. She told of Diep's passion for all things around her choir at the church, and of how much Diep loved her choir sisters as they practiced and sang, and practiced and sang, week after week for the many years in the beautiful interdenominational church that made everyone feel so welcome. That was Diep in a nutshell, Mom said, she made everyone always feel so loved and so welcome.

The local food bank manager told us of Chi's twenty years of dedicated service, delivering fresh food all summer, and preserves all winter, year after year.

The service ended with Maureen and my three beautiful children all filing up and across to the center of the altar. Martina started, saying in a loud and confident voice, "Hello, my name is Martina Hansson-Tran. These are my brothers, Warren and Noah. This is our nanny, Maureen O-Reilly. I am a Jew. My brothers are Christians, and Maureen is a Catholic. That's how we do things in our family. That's how you do things in our church." With a quick look over to Maureen to confirm that she had said everything that she was supposed to say, she finished up by saying, "Thank you for coming today and for being such good friends to our family. Please come downstairs right after the last prayer to have some lunch with us."

All of a sudden, someone way in the back of the church stood up and starting clapping for her, and I smiled a little over at Jacquie and Zalia as we could feel the pews and pews of people behind us rise to applaud my ten-year-old daughter.

Warren and Noah, still up at the altar, broke away from Maureen's firm grip and started clapping and jumping up and down, and everyone started laughing until Maureen, laughing herself, motioned for everyone to sit down.

She stood there, once again holding hands with the boys and Martina, and in her beautiful Irish brogue, she wrapped up the service with her Irish prayer:

"May the road rise to meet you,
And the wind always be at your back.
May the sun shine warm on your face,
And the rains fall softly on your fields.
And until we meet again,
May God hold you gently in the palm of his hand."

***

According to our laid-out plan of action, Mom, Jacquie, Catharine, Ann-Marie, and I worked the room downstairs in the church's community room where the ladies from the church had put up a beautiful luncheon. This was right up Ann-Marie's alley, as she had made up lunches for many church socials, weddings, and funerals upcountry where she still cooked in the old hotel's big kitchen. We passed around trays of sandwiches, brownies, and butter-tarts and served tea and coffee like we'd been cafeteria waitresses our whole life.

Actually, it gave us something to do, as small talk doesn't come easy at a time like this. This way, we could say hello to all the people from Papa and Mama's church that had come out for the funeral service as well as keeping our pain a little closer to our chest while we were out in public. It suited me just fine.

Dad and Maureen took the boys in hand, while Brad kept his arms around Martina and Zalia, taking them all around from table to table to say hello and to thank the guests for coming out. As a few people started to recognize his familiar face from the movies, he quickly confirmed their suspicions that it was indeed him, and then he smoothly guided their attention back to the girls, prompting them to mind their manners and speak up to say hello to the guests. I caught his eye and gave him a wink. He was such a pro. No wonder women around the world slept with his picture under their pillow. Of course, what made it so funny to me as I watched him was that our two little ten-year-old girls who were being cocooned in his big, strong arms hadn't a clue as to their Uncle Brad's effect on women around the world.

Dad signaled Mom from across the room by tapping his watch-wrist, and before I knew it, I was in the limo once again, watching the kids wave out the back window to Rabbi Kleiman and Pastor Smith and the others who were right behind us in the second limo. We seamlessly pulled away from Papa and Mama's lovely interdenominational church on our way to the interment at Mount Pleasant Cemetery.

***

The part of the day that I had been dreading, of course, was the interment. Not for me especially, but I knew it was going to be hard for Mom, Dad, Brad, and Martina. It turned out that I had been worrying for nothing.

Rabbi Kleiman and Pastor Smith had everything planned perfectly. Although our monument hadn't been scribed yet, let alone placed in the cemetery, they had dug a small hole in the ground and placed a huge floral display behind it that took away a bit of the harshness. It was just behind our big, gray monument for Baby Nigel Jr., which was sandwiched between our monuments for my granddad, Saul Himmel, and my grandma, Mavis Royal. I stood there in amazement, with Brad and Jacquie on each side of me, as we watched the cemetery attendant explain to the children about the two beautiful white doves that he was holding in a cage. He explained that they symbolized everlasting love and peace, and he told them that he was going to release them so they could fly up to the heavens along with the spirits of the loved ones that had passed away.

He stood in the middle of the circle and asked the four children to help him open the cage. After they all had a turn, practicing opening and closing the latch a few times, he released his thumb from the door, and he lifted the opened cage up to the heavens. All of a sudden, the two beautiful white doves came out, sat for a moment on the roof of the cage, then they fluttered about us. We were all awed with their beauty and the magic of the moment. They ruffled out their feathers, spoke a little to each other, and then soared away into the azure, blue, summer sky that was painted with white, fluffy, cumulus clouds.

Without further ado, Rabbi Kleiman and Pastor Smith quickly took the single box that held all of the ashes of the Tran family together and started to lower it into the prepared ground. Dad lost no time starting the Lord's Prayer as he gathered the kids up to divert their attention away from the hole in the ground. We all chimed in, and upon the last Amen, Dad, Brad, and Mom took us all under their wings and ushered us away from the site of the box of ashes that had been quietly interred into the ground. We meandered through the beautiful grounds full of monuments to lives lost while Rabbi Kleiman and Pastor Smith wrapped up the process at the burial site, saying their prayers in both Hebrew and English, as the box of ashes disappeared from their sight with their shovels working evenly and without pause.

***

All the adults sat with our feet in the kiddies' pool. The four kids had been stripped out of their fancy funeral clothes and into their bathing suits, paddling and playing in the manmade water feature which was a long, narrow stream which ran down the side of Mom and Dad's big backyard. Patou was firmly ensconced in his regular spot in the middle of the narrow stream, causing the water to back up and pool, as it would in a dam, before gradually spilling over the top of the big white dog in its quest to reach the bottom of its run, only to recycle with the help of Papa's ingenious engineering, all to start its journey over once again. The boys were trying to push Patou out of the way, but the hundred-pound dog wasn't about to leave his territory for the two little hellions and their wagon full of boats and rubber duckies.

Jacquie smiled as she kicked a little water around in the kiddie pool. "This is like we used to do in the projects."

Brad chimed in, "Yeah, Nigel's saving up for a big pool someday. Times are tough at 7 Russell Hill Road."

Dad was quick to respond, pointing to the shorts that he had loaned Brad. He said the shorts seemed a little too big in the crotch area. We laughed at Mom warning him to behave himself in front of company, while Catharine and Edouard starting teasing Brad about his tabloid image in France that had him pegged as a womanizer of epic proportions.

"Aw, come on, guys, I'm trying to impress Ms. Jacqueline Dixon here. For Chrisake, give me a break, will you?" Brad asked.

Jacquie said in response, "Brad, you old dog, I know exactly who you are. Don't try to pull the wool over my eyes."

To Brad's relief, Dad changed tac and said, "Okay, everyone, in memory of Chi, who gardened this backyard every day over the past 30 years, I want to give you some background on how our beautiful oasis in the heart of the city came about. May I tell you about just a few of our beautiful shrubs, trees, and flowers surrounding us?"

And as we followed him from the hydrangeas, through the variety of beds of English country gardens and more formal ones framed with miniature boxwood hedges, we ended up at Papa's prize rose garden.

"This particular rose was the prototype from Chi's first attempt at hybrid gardening. He named this pink rose, *Duyen*, after his first wife, and then this brilliant red-and-orange hybrid, named after *Denni*, was created about four or five years ago at my request. The yellow one here was cross-pollinated for not only beauty but resilience. He named it Diep, and it was in memory of her first husband and her son. And these miniatures were grafted as *Martinas*. His project to name after the boys is still in the works in the greenhouse."

Jacquie raised her glass and said quietly, "Here's to your best friend, Nigel. These gardens will serve as a wonderful memory of all your years together."

We all lifted our glasses, and she continued, "And, Nigel, kudos to you and your family for pulling off the most beautiful funeral I've ever been to. Thank you for including me. Please know, I'm here to help in any way I can. May God bless you and give you strength in the days ahead."

Dad responded, "Here's to the Tran family, may God bless them."

"Okay, okay, folks," Brad said, "it's time for me to get to work. I'm going to fire up the barbeque. Jack and I put the potatoes in the oven an hour ago, and the salad is in the fridge." He put his arm around Jacquie and smooched her a little on the cheek as he said, "Come on, Jack, give me a hand; we're going to show these Canucks a thing or two about grilling the perfect steak."

As we watched them, arm in arm, walking back toward the terrace, Maureen said in a matter-of-fact voice, "Um, um, um. He's turning up the heat in more than the barbeque! Look out, Jacqueline, here comes Hollywood!"

We all roared with laughter, and Brad looked back and lifted both arms up in the air and mouthed a silent 'What?' before his innocent look morphed into a wolfish grin. He turned back to whisper something into Jack's ear.

She, in turn, wheeled around to face us and, laughing, started to 'play the violin' for our benefit, letting us know that she was fully tuned in to his smooth moves.

Walt chimed in and said, "Never mind, folks. Brad is A-okay in my books. It wasn't that many years ago when his son, who was only 16 at the time, came down to the old farm in Marlbank with his friend and we had a terrible day that Brad's son pulled through with flying colors. His son went from a boy to a man in one terrible afternoon, and I knew right then that he must have remarkable parents behind him."

Edouard added, "Oh, I remember now. That's when the two boys were staying with you, right, Nigel?"

Nigel shook his head. "That was hell. Pure hell. You see, it was Chi, once again, that got us all through that. And, yes, the two boys were only 16; my nephew, Brad's son, and the other, Stéphane, who was his best friend. They were holidaying with me, as the two boys lived in France at the time. His little friend lost his life to suicide that day, down in Denni's old barn. Chi helped me cut the body down from the noose that Stéphane had fashioned from the swing rope in the hay loft. I couldn't do it on my own; I didn't have the guts. Chi stepped up to the plate and got the job done. He was one hell of a man and one hell of a friend."

Denni added, "I know, I know, honey. I remember the time he pulled me out of a real mess too. It was when you, Nigel, had your heart attack. He was tough on me at the time and shouted right into my face that I was the toughest woman he had ever met in my life and to get my act together and do my part."

I said, "I'll always remember when I first met him. We just connected somehow. I knew instinctively that he loved me from the get-go. Here I was, a complete stranger, presenting to a very, very tight family as a long-lost daughter, and Chi didn't bat an eye. He accepted me immediately. He never told me, but he told François at that time that he wanted his son to marry me."

***

I wasn't concerned in the least that I hadn't shed a tear over the past day or two. There was lots of time stretching ahead of me for that. At that very moment, I was going to focus on what was happening in real time. I looked over and saw my beautiful kids floating rubber duckies in the water and the dog swiping at their toys. I got up to give Maureen a hug as we laughed at Dad trying to grab Mom's ass as she stepped out of the kiddie pool.

***

I looked up into the big maple tree where I had married François under the chuppa four short years ago. I smiled a little to myself as I beamed up a message to my Mor, "I'm doing just fine, Mor. Everything's gonna be okay, Mor."

I stood there for a moment silently when all of a sudden, my mood shifted ever so slightly.

As my little smile began to waiver in its transition into a silent scream, I felt my dad's arms wrap around me, and he lifted me up to get me over to a chair. My mouth was still wide open with the silent scream, and from somewhere in the back of my mind, I saw Maureen and Mom running over to the get the kids out of the water and into the house.

I sat there on my dad's lap, completely undone. An utter torrent of pent-up tears of loss and misery soaked through his shirt as he smoothed my hair down and coaxed me to cry it out, just to cry it all out. My pain was literally palpable.

***

As I lay there, later that night, all snuggled under my duvet, I watched Jack as she came out of the bathroom. She had an exaggerated pout on her face. She stomped loudly over to the other side of the bed. As she threw back the covers in mock anger, she said to me, trying not to smile, "That's my luck! That's my fucking luck! My one and only chance to make whoopy with one of Hollywood's best, and I get stuck playing nursemaid to my sis for the night! What the hell!"

"Go on! Just go on! Get out of here! He'll still be up waiting for you! But don't let Mom and Dad hear you go in. They'll tease you until the day you die!"

"No, Sis. Seriously, though, I look at it this way. He might be the famous pretty-boy Brad from Hollywood, but I don't run after any man. But you – you're still to blame! You're not off the hook! You owe me, Sister, and you owe me big-time. I'll let you know what the payback is as soon as I can figure it out."

"Oh, now, Jack. You sound a little like a poor loser to me."

I started a little sing-song under my breath, "Na na na na na! Jacquie is a loser! Jacquie is a loser!"

"Now just a minute, here, smartass. Think about it. Exactly who has been the focus of his wooing over the past two days? It hasn't been you, now has it? Straighten up and fly right, princess. You have to admit, he was hot to trot and I was the object of his desire."

As I laughed at her faux huffiness, she reached up to turn off the light, and she sighed and said, "It doesn't matter any way. Even if it did happen, I could never tell anyone about it."

"Why not? You're a single woman; he's a single man. What's not to tell?"

"Nobody would ever fucking believe me!"

With that, we both lay on our backs, laughing our heads off at the craziness of the whole short-lived, not-to-be-consummated, hotter-than-a-firecracker, lust affair between the hardworking pediatric-nurse practitioner from Miami and the famous, filthy-rich pretty-boy from Hollywood.

We had finally quieted down and Jacquie said, "You're going to be okay, honey. You did good. A gold star on the fridge door for you today."

"Thanks, Sis. I love you."

"Love you too. Night-night."

***

The next morning, I answered the door to a florist delivery. Of course, I was thinking that the glorious, over-the-top bouquet of 24 long-stemmed red roses was for me, perhaps from Mom and Dad, or Rabbi Kleiman, or someone from the funeral the day before. You can imagine my surprise when I read the name on the sealed envelope. It was marked:

Ms. Jacqueline Dixon.

I was hanging over her shoulder, trying to read the card as she opened the envelope.

She read it, and, as she passed it over to me, she leaned back and roared with laughter.

The card read:

> *As the old Streisand song goes, 'We almost had it all, didn't we, love?'*
> It was signed, *Hot and Bothered in Hollywood.*

Chapter Eight
The Boat People

The funeral director addressed the room, stating that the Celebration of Life Service for the Tran family was about to begin and that there would be only one speaker, namely Nigella Kaufman Hansson-Tran. He thanked our guests for wearing the Canadian maple-leaf pins that were handed out earlier, and he asked everyone to please move into the adjoining room for refreshments after Mrs. Hansson-Tran's speech.

With his introduction, I sprinted up the few steps in my high-heels, remembering Mom's last words to put my chin up and shoulders back. I completed my somewhat modified strut to the podium. I knew I looked good, and, thanks to all the coaching from Maureen, Jack, and Mom, I was pretty confident that my exactly ten-minute speech would sit well among the hundred guests.

I looked out over the crowd of Francois's colleagues, his clients, our neighbors, Dad and Mom's friends, Brad sitting between Jack and Maureen, my team from the university along with Dr. Alessandro Camarra, my wonderful advisor. I saw some church friends of my in-laws, Rabbi Kleiman with a big smile for me, as well as a few people from the food bank that Papa had worked with over the years, and many others that I didn't recognize. I knew that some of François's colleagues and friends had attended my wedding four short years ago, so they knew who I was, but I really hadn't a clue. That all seemed so long ago. I was thankful that the four children were at home with the babysitter; this was a day to celebrate the immediate Tran family and it was more of a corporate event than something that the children could participate in.

Way, way back in law school, I had learned the art of grabbing the audience's attention within the first minute or two by getting them to smile a little, so I started my speech from the podium. I turned my head from side to side as if I was looking for someone in particular. I finally focused on my parents as if I needed their reassurance, just like a little grade-four girl would do. I gave them a big, cheesy grin and sent out a little wave to them. "Hi, Dad. Hi, Mom." I laughed a little; Dad and Mom laughed a lot; and everyone followed. I was off to a good start.

I began in a loud, clear voice. I thanked them all for coming to honor the lives of the Tran family. I had planned that throughout my speech, I would refer to the three of them as the 'Tran family.' I didn't want to have to mention François personally. It would have been disingenuous of me to do so. I couldn't even think about him let alone speak of him. On the other hand, no one else had to know about my feelings toward my dead husband. Dad, Mom, and I knew exactly how I felt about him, and I was willing to play my part respectfully for the sake of everyone else.

I stepped away from the podium and my notes. I stood in the center of the platform to continue my speech from my heart:

"They were boat people. They were survivors. Their world in Vietnam as crop farmers came crashing down around them as they witnessed the slaughter of their people and the burning of their villages. In 1975, by the grace of God, they found themselves on Canada's roll call, and they joined the rest of us as immigrants, here, north of the 49th parallel."

I told the story of Chi Tran and his young wife meeting my father in Montreal, and then of them taking care of my grandparents while having their only son, François, and being so proud when he became a lawyer 25 years later. I told them of Chi's wife dying of cancer and his loneliness until he met Diep just four years ago. I added that Chi and Diep Tran finally bought their very own farm and started an apiary, a honeybee farm, which was their dream come true.

I wrapped up the Tran family story by saying,

"I mean, really, we're all immigrants. Some of us are brand-new, like myself, and some of us are second-generation immigrants like my mom with her Irish roots. But deep down, we all have our stories. And some of us are survivors, like Chi and Diep Tran. My maternal grandmother was

a Holocaust Survivor, and my birthmother was a profoundly deaf baby who grew up in an orphanage in Sweden, who never spoke out loud until she was 42 years old. My paternal grandmother emigrated from Jamaica and worked her whole life as a housekeeper for another immigrant, Supreme Court Justice Saul Himmel, who was a French Jew who came to Canada just before the war with nothing but the shirt on his back.

And, as I see the faces in front of me, I see my neighbor, Ursula Sipaki, who indeed has her own story. It was 1956 in Hungary which was under Soviet occupation. She was 14 years old and hiding under a blanket in the back of a pickup truck when the Soviets discovered her. The truck hit the gas, and she remembers to this day the sound of the bullets that tried to shoot the tires out. She waited out five years in Austria and Ireland until Canada took her in. More recently, my doctorate advisor, Dr. Alessandro Camarra, told me of his own story of starting public school over in Little Italy on the west side of our city, not speaking a word of English as his father worked as a brick layer and his mother worked as a sewing-machine operator, saving every nickel to buy a house for their family in the early '70s.

My Uncle Brad, who is an American, and my extended-family sister, Jacqueline Dixon, also an American, reminded me of their country's definition of Canada. It goes like this: Years ago, the Underground Railroad started down in the American South and ended way up north, just north of the 49th parallel in Canada. The travelers on that journey slipped from safe house to safe house, following the river north. They described Canada as the North Star. In 1967, Martin Luther King Jr. spoke at the University of Toronto, right here in our beautiful city of Toronto. He reiterated this truth that the African-Americans living in those times held: 'Canada was the North Star.'

So today, I urge you not to dwell on this crushing blow to the remaining Tran family but to celebrate their lives lived. As you know, François and I had three beautiful children. Even with this blow, they will survive. Not only survive, but they will thrive. I mean, after all, they come from hardy stock, right? Boat people and Holocaust Survivors. I'd put my money on this new generation every time.

I want to thank you for wearing your Canadian maple-leaf pins that we handed our earlier. Please wear these symbols of Canada, not only in

135

memory of the role that Canada has played in the Tran family but of your own families as well. Think of the lives that we all enjoy today because of those who have gone before us.

And once we're all together in the reception room, please share your own stories with others around you. By delving into these experiences, some our own, some from our parents and grandparents, we find out who we really are. Yes, who we are in our guts deep down beyond the law degrees and the marriages and the kids, the joys, the heartaches, and the disappointments. We have to really dig deep into ourselves so that we can pay it forward just like my whole family has done, generation after generation, through the thick and the thin of it, and just like Canadians have been doing since the beginning.

In closing, thank you from the bottom of my heart for all your thoughts and prayers during my family's time of loss. Please join us for some fellowship in the adjoining room. Thank you. Thank you."

I looked over at Dad and Mom. They were on their feet, along with everyone else, clapping for me. Little old me. Mom gave me a thumbs up, and Dad's smile couldn't have been wider. I blew them a kiss, Hollywood style, before I threw my shoulders back and strode off the stage like I did this every day of my life. I whispered to myself, "Mor! Mor! Are you there!? How do you like me now, Morsa? Are you proud of me, Mor?"

***

My plan of asking the crowd to talk about their own stories worked perfectly. I avoided having to talk about my husband and my kids by responding to each inquiry with, "You first. I want to hear your story. I've already told you mine." And so the afternoon, from everyone's take, went swimmingly well. I made my way over to Dad who was standing there with Uncle Brad and Alessandro.

Alessandro, my advisor, gave me a little kiss on the cheek, and all of a sudden, he wrapped his arms around me and gave me a big hug. He whispered, "Yeah, just like I told you in the office that day. You're no princess, Nigella. You, my dear, are a full-fledged Swedish queen! Kudos, colleague, you knocked 'em dead."

Dad said, "Quite a crowd, honey. Good thing we booked the two rooms for the whole afternoon. Nobody's leaving! And take a look at your squad over there. They look like they're planning something. Do you know what they're up to?"

"No, Dad. But I know those three. I'm going over there to check on them, and I'll let you know. Whatever is going down is because Mom is at the helm of things. Don't blame me, got it?"

Brad said, "Oh my God, Alessandro. The four of them together. This is should be rich. Just stay put and don't take your eyes off them. We're in for a treat."

Sure enough, the minute I was in front of Jack, Maureen, and Mom, they put their arms around me and walked me down to the side of the room, where the crowd had thinned out somewhat.

Maureen leaned into my ear and said, "This is just for you, Nigella. All you."

My eyebrows went up a little as the light went on. Over the past weeks, Mom and I had told Jacquie and Maureen the whole story of François's office affair with Cecelia Yang and my plans to divorce him.

The squad, as Dad called us, stopped right in front of a trio of women. They were women from François's law office. Two of them took one look at us and disappeared, leaving the Asian woman alone to fend for herself. Mom took the right side of her, and Jack took the left. I noticed that both of them were carrying little pieces of paper. Maureen held onto me tightly so I couldn't go anywhere, and we stood our ground. With my heels on, I stood there, over six feet tall, towering over the petite Asian woman.

Maureen spoke quietly, "Cecelia Yang?"

Cecilia Yang was no fool. She couldn't cut and run, so she played it cool. She immediately lifted her head up and looked me dead in the eye and stuck out her hand.

"I'm so sorry for your loss, Mrs. Tran."

Maureen slapped my hand down before I could return the handshake, and she started on a tirade in her Irish Gaelic language, which I couldn't decipher. Not a word. But the timber and inflection of Maureen's fury was quite evident. She tore a strip off Cecilia Yang's cheating, whoring hide like I've never heard before.

Maureen's eyes narrowed, and she spit out, "*Is ceann de's na h-singseacha diablhail thú! Feckin eejit. Bodach. Mallacht mo chait ort!*"

Jack jumped in and hissed into Cecilia Yang's left ear, "Yeah. And here's the translation from Irish-Gaelic to plain English, *You are one of the Devil's fools. An idiot. A boor, a pig, a lowlife, a churl, and a lout.* And what's more, Maureen has just laid a curse upon you, and it goes like this, *A widow's curse upon you.*"

Maureen leaned in, heaping a second stream of abuse onto the terrified captive, "*Omadhaun! Náire agus aithir chugat! Dul go h-olc ort! Lagú cléibh ort!*"

By then, although I was feeling a little sorry for Cecilia Yang, I struggled to keep the smile off my face as Mom leaned in from the other side and whispered into her right ear, "Yeah. And here's my translation, *You are a fool. A home wrecker. A whore, and the other woman.* You have been further cursed with, *Weariness of the heart upon you! That you may be shamed and disgraced!* And to wrap it all up, Maureen issues her final curse upon you, which you will rue to the end of your days. She says, *Bad luck to you!*"

Right then, the punished and properly flogged captive looked passed my shoulder, and I read further dismay wash over her face. I heard Dad's voice from behind me. His deep baritone said, "Hello, Ms. Yang. I understand you're leaving. Come on now. I'll walk you out."

Once again, the squad, as Dad called the four of us, put their arms around me, and Mom said, "It's okay, honey, it's okay. Now you can forget what François did to you."

I looked down into Mom's caring, protective face and I said calmly, "François who?"

The three of them leaned into our huddle, heads down, to cover their laughter at my haughty, Swedish queen response.

And that's when Maureen and Jack stopped calling me *princess* and started calling me *Your Majesty*.

***

Later in the afternoon, as the crowd finally thinned out, Brad came over to me and put his arm around me. "Honey, I won't be coming over for dinner tonight, and I won't be sleeping over at Nigel's either. I've got a room down at the Four Seasons for the night, and I'll be flying out early tomorrow morning, so I'll say my goodbye now, if that's okay with you."

I was a little surprised with his news, and he continued with what was really on his mind, "Well, actually, um, um, I want to ask you something. Um, um, it's this way. I want to treat Jacquie to a night out on the town, and I figure that she'll stay with me downtown for the night, but only, and I really mean this, only, if you say it's okay with you that Jack and I spend some private time together. You know what I mean. And I already spoke to Nigel about it."

I threw back my head and roared with laughter. "Oh, Uncle Brad, I love you so much! You're the best! If you and Jack can handle all the teasing that's bound to come your way about all of this, please, by all means, jump from the frying pan into the fire with my blessing."

***

I was a little surprised after the Celebration of Life service, as we were arranging who was driving with whom, when Dad casually mentioned that he had asked Alessandro to join us for dinner. Dad was always so thoughtful, and, to tell you the truth, now that I knew Brad wouldn't be spending the night with Dad, I thought it would be a good idea to round out the table a little for both Dad and Mom who were missing their best friends, Chi and Diep, every minute of every day.

Mom and I put dinner in the oven, and I glanced out over the porch to watch Dad and Alessandro out on the sidewalk, checking to see that all four kids on their bikes had their helmets done up before they all headed over to the park. Alessandro was riding François's old bike and Dad was riding his. I think that was the first time I really gave Alessandro's presence any real thought. Ever since I had had that little dinner party and introduced the two of them, Dad and him had been spending time together, and it seemed more often than not that if Dad popped into the house, Alessandro would be right behind him. Just another great man in my life. And a handsome one at that.

The squad reconvened in Jack's room. Maureen and I stretched out on Jack's bed as Mom and her packed her overnight bag for her big night out downtown with Hollywood's finest.

Maureen said, "Now, Jacqueline, do you want to me to pick you up? Whatever time, it's okay. I'll get you home. I mean, after all, you really don't know Brad all that well, and you may have second thoughts about spending the whole night with him."

"Trust me, Maureen, I know I won't be wanting to come home tonight. Now that's a certainty. I know Brad well enough to be packing my fancy nightie and toothbrush, don't you worry."

Maureen continued like the mother hen she was, "You only met him a month ago, and we all know how that went down. Disaster. You chose Nigella over him. How do you know that you two will hit it off in bed, with this being your first time with him?"

By this time, Mom and I were laughing out loud at Maureen's naivety, and Jack threw her silk robe over Maureen's head as she said, "Maureen, honey, I'm going to tell you about the birds and the bees. I've been with Brad every single night since we met last month when he flew in for the funeral."

Maureen, struggling to untangle the robe from her hair, said, "Now that's nothing short of a lie, missy. You know very well he's been out in L.A. and you've been right here, sleeping in your own bed."

By this time, Mom and I were starting to goad her a little as well, "Yeah, Jack, how do you know if he's up to your high standards? Maybe it's all just Hollywood talk. Maybe he's nothing but a dud."

Jack had a little smile on her face as she explained to us how things are done in Hollywood. "I know every one of his moves. And oh my God, he's the best."

Mom dropped what she was holding; I sat upright in the bed, and Maureen whined, "What are you talking about?"

Jack sighed. "Maureen, my innocent, good, Irish-Catholic girl, I'm talking about phone sex. Brad and I have been together every night over the last month, and he's the best I've ever had, long distance, short distance, face to face, or otherwise."

You could hear us laughing all the way to Heath Street.

We had all just settled down when Maureen asked in a quiet voice, "But, Jacqueline, do you know how old he is? I mean really, he's ten years older than my father. He's an old man. How could you?"

Jacqui sighed in mock exasperation, and she said, "Look at it this way, honey. You know the term *friends with benefits*, don't you? Well, it's something like that. And you're only 20. You see, I'm 35 years old, and I've only been with one man in my whole life. That was my husband. He died almost two years ago. It's a little awkward getting back into the swing of things, especially when you don't have any real experience. Brad is a women's best friend. He just takes care of everything. He makes you feel like a woman again, but he sets it up so you just stay good friends with him, and there are no hard feelings either way. No one falls in love, but you both have a night of wonderful, fun-filled sex that everybody needs. Brad is a loving, caring man that knows what women need and want from him, with no strings attached. After tonight, we'll probably never have sex again, but we'll be best friends until the day we die. Now, do you get it?"

Mom said, "Jacquie, you should be a sex-ed teacher! You're the best! I went through my whole life never understanding the concept of *friends with benefits* and it caused me years and years of grief and two terrible marriages because I always thought you had to be in love to have sex with the guy. I wish I had heard this 40 years ago!"

It was then that the three of us older women got the shock of our lives. Our naïve 20-year-old virginal Irish-Catholic nanny dropped the bombshell of all bombshells.

"Yeah, okay. I see your point. I guess I'm still too young and inexperienced yet to really know what I would do in your case. Although that's not really my problem."

I asked, "Well, what's your problem? Spit it out, sugar."

She answered so calmly in her beautiful Irish brogue, "My problem is that I can't make up my mind if I like girls better than I like boys. One day I'm lusting after some girl, and the next day I'm lusting after some boy. Maybe I'll just stay that way. Besides, who says I have to be gay or straight? I kind of like being bisexual. Have any of you women had any experience fooling around with girls?"

Our collective gasp was audible. Maureen looked from one of us to the other, waiting for an answer.

Mom was the first to recover from our howls of laughter. She said, "Oh, honey, oh, honey, we're not laughing at you. We're laughing at ourselves! We think we know everything and you could teach us so much if we would just stop talking long enough to listen you."

I piped up and said, "Yes, Maureen. Exactly. We love you just the way you are. Never, ever change. Not for us, or for any girl or any boy. We'll be right here, cheering you on through all your love affairs to come, boys and girls alike."

Maureen sat up and clapped her hands to get our attention, and she warned, "Okay. Okay. Everybody better stop looking at me or shit will go down!"

More howls of laughter followed, and Mom summed it up with, "Words to live by!"

Jacquie was shaking her head as she zipped up her overnight bag. She said, "Maureen O'Reilly, I'm coming to you for advice from now on. You've got your head on straight. These other two members of the squad are just as fucked up as I am. We've got a lot to learn from you, honey."

***

Chapter Nine

Cutting Off the Nose to Spite the Face

I immediately sunk to the floor, fighting down the waves of nausea and focusing my eyes on the light bulb above, trying not to pass out from the pain. I was shaking so badly, it took me several attempts to wrestle my phone from my back pocket.

"Jack, help. Help me."

"Where are you?"

"In the garage."

I lost grip on my cell once again, and I lay there, the sweat dripping from my face. The cement floor felt cold underneath my back.

I heard the door open, and I managed a quiet, "It's my foot. I think I've broken it."

The experienced nurse practitioner took 30 seconds to evaluate the situation and said, "You're right on this note, honey. Don't move. We're going to call an ambulance, as I'm afraid I will hurt you getting you into the car. And besides, I don't know where the hospital is. Okay?"

The next thing I knew, I was being very competently moved onto a stretcher and placed in the back of an ambulance while Jacquie dashed inside to get our handbags to make the trip to Sunnybrook.

Jacquie was magnificent. She held my hand as she took control in the back of the ambulance. She spoke med-talk to the two attendants, rhyming off the damage to the toes as well as the foot and filling them in on my general health which included no drugs, no prescriptions, and no alcohol. She leaned over me and said softly, "Can you tell us what happened, honey?"

By then, the pain of having to tell her how I had brought this upon myself was greater than the broken bones. I stayed silent, not willing to accept the teasing for the rest of my life that was sure to follow as my due punishment.

Her voice sharpened. "Nigella, are you okay? Can you talk to me?"

"Yes, for Christ's sake, I can talk to you. It's just that I'm too embarrassed to tell you what happened."

Her eyebrows went up a little, and she leaned into my face. A little smile was beginning to emerge. "Spit it out, Sister."

By this time, the two attendants knew that I was in no immediate danger, and they were also leaning over me, eager to hear what I had to say.

"I lost my temper. My aim was off. I missed the tire, and I kicked the fucking, fancy, wheel spokes of his fucking, fancy, vintage, Alpha Romeo convertible. I'm going to sell his fucking little party-on-wheels before the sun goes down, mark my words."

The howls of laughter not only from the three of them but from the driver as well, who had us on intercom, was worse punishment than the walking cast that I would have to deal with over the next six weeks.

I said to the three of them once their laughter had subsided enough for me to think straight, "It's not all that funny."

"You're right, Mrs. Hansson. It's not all that funny – it's the combination of your posh accent with the potty mouth that's so hilarious! You're quite a storyteller! You should be on Jimmy Kimmel!"

At that moment, I realized that I was becoming my mother. That's when my humor began to peek through to make its appearance once again in my topsy-turvy, complicated, little world.

Two hours later, as the pain pills took hold, I had fully gotten over myself. I heard myself telling the story to the attending doctor and nurses with a self-depreciating humor that would have made Mom and Dad proud. Their little Swedish princess was growing up, albeit with the temper of a three-year-old and the mouth of a truck driver.

***

He sat on my porch and shook his head. "You're killing me, Mrs. Hansson. I know, I know, your husband died recently and you can't keep these two vehicles any longer, and on top of everything, you're wearing a cast on your right foot, but, Mrs. Hansson, you've got to see my point here."

The Volvo dealership had sent this salesman down to the house to check out my trade-ins and to try to seal the deal. I had pulled both vehicles out to the driveway, and he and I were sitting on the porch, with a pitcher of lemonade between us. I was playing the victim with my casted foot perched up on a footstool.

I had already calculated that my Range Rover and Francois's vintage Alpha Romeo would amount to a fairly even trade for the two Volvos that I had picked out of the lot yesterday. I figured I would buy the big XC-90 SE Lux 7-seater Volvo to use as the family car, and I was going to buy the Volvo smaller hatchback for Maureen. After all, it was me that insisted that she get her Canadian driver's license. She had passed her driver's exam on the first try, and she drove my big Range Rover and Dad's Porsche all the time without a nick or a scratch. This would be the first time that she had her very own car. Not to cart the kids around or to pick up groceries. This was just for herself. She was the best. And the kids loved her. She was part of the family. She deserved everything and anything I could ever think of, and a car of her own may help pay her back for all she went through, day in and day out in our big, busy house. I would put the ownership in her name and I would cover the insurance as well. Mom was adamant about always taking her shopping for clothes and was always picking her up a new pair of jeans or a new hoodie. She was the best-dressed student at University of Toronto. Dad was already paying her university tuition and books so that she could quietly salt away her salary to take a holiday once in a while. I didn't want her to struggle like I had to at that age, and I knew Dad and Mom felt the same way.

I had noticed that on her days off, her friends would be there in our driveway, waiting to pick her up. I knew by the looks of their cars that it was either their family car that they had borrowed from their parents or it was their first car that they'd bought with their summer jobs. Those cars were usually a little patched up, rusted out shit-box that was cheap on gas.

Yes, it was time that Maureen could have the pleasure of picking her friends up in her own car; a nice, new, clean, reliable Volvo instead of relying on her friends as well as the subway day in and day out. I was just happy that Maureen had a nice little circle of friends to round out her experience of living so far away from her home back in the countryside in Ireland. She never mentioned again about being bisexual, and I didn't ask. It simply didn't matter in the big scheme of things.

However, I knew exactly why she very rarely brought her friends into the house, even though I was constantly asking her to bring them in to hang out at home; her home. Whenever I would step out on the porch to wave her friends in, they were always polite as the window of the car would go down and they would yell out a respectful, *"Hello, Mrs. Hansson-Tran."* No, Maureen was smart enough not to present as an Irish country girl from humble beginnings, living in another family's posh neighborhood in the big city, working her way through life as a lowly nanny. Not at all. She was going to become a very successful journalist and marry money. Big money. And she was determined to do it her way. And I had no doubt that she would grab the golden ring without batting an eye. She was a force to be reckoned with. I admired and respected her for all her determination and resolve.

I was a little startled as I tuned back into the salesman's voice once again after drifting off in thoughts of Maureen. I don't know why or how the salesman had come to the conclusion that he was not going to able to squeeze a dollar out of me to seal the deal, but he sat there, nodding his head up and down judiciously and saying, "Well, Mrs. Hansson, although I'll have to call into my boss to get final approval, and I'm not going to make a nickel on this transaction, can we shake hands right here and now and I'll have your cars picked up later this afternoon? Do we have a deal?"

"Deal. But please remember, I want the hatchback delivered with your biggest and best, big, red ribbon tied around it, right?" I gave him my very best firm handshake.

As I waved goodbye to him as he pulled away, I grabbed my phone to call Dad, just like any little girl does when she's a pleaser and they're looking for a little reassurance from Daddy that she is indeed the smartest and most capable girl in the whole world. I laughed a little as I recognized my need for this little pat on the head, and when I heard Dad's big baritone say, "Hi, honey. What's up?" I answered true to form.

"Dad! You're never going to guess what I did today!"

***

The next morning, the two cars were delivered precisely at 10:00 a.m. I had the hatchback complete with a huge, red ribbon threaded through the windows, driven straight into the garage, and left the big new family car outside in the drive so as to not spoil the surprise for Maureen.

Maureen grumbled from the kitchen, "I don't see why Nigel and Denni need to have everyone out on the front porch at 10:30 a.m. I like to have the kids home from the park by then. What could possibly be so important that they need everyone here at that hour?"

Dad, Mom, and Patou arrived with Maureen's favorite cake in hand. I put a pot of coffee on and grabbed the lemonade out of the fridge. Jacquie was reminding Martina and Zalia not to spoil the surprise. They were busy rounding up the twins to get everyone all out on the porch.

I cleared the driveway, and exactly at 10:30, I backed the beribboned Volvo hatchback out carefully. By the time I had joined them all on the front porch, Maureen was looking from one to the other, realizing that she was the only one that didn't get the memo, so to speak.

Martina and Zalia gave her a gift box, and as she opened the box to pull out the set of car keys, she still didn't clue in. The girls said excitedly, "This is your new car, Maureen! It's just yours, and we're not allowed in it! No kids allowed! Just you!"

Dad, Mom, Jack, and I sat there, watching the kids jump up and down when Maureen said they were allowed to sit in the new car but only after they washed their hands.

She was in true Nanny mode, as she admonished the boys to keep their feet off the seats as she allowed them, one by one, carefully, to have their little tryout but only if they didn't touch anything.

Dad announced he was taking the kids to the park, and he insisted that Maureen was to take the day off and just drive around town in her car, picking up boys, like all beautiful, young women should do. Martina and Zalia got all four kids' bikes as well as Dad's out and lined them up near the sidewalk, far, far away from Maureen's new, shining fenders.

Later that night, when Jack and I were in our pajamas in the kitchen having a tea, Maureen came in, holding the same gift box from her car keys in her hand.

She gave the box to Jack and said, "Jacqueline, I want you to have the second set of keys to my car. We'll share it. You're the newest member of the family, and that's how we do things here. Use it anytime. Just don't let the kids with their grubby little hands in it."

I smiled and held up my coffee mug as if to toast, "Here's to girl power. We're quite a team, aren't we?"

We sat there for a moment, and Jack said to Maureen in a serious voice, "Maureen, you know what I'm really happy about, don't you?"

"No, Jacqueline, what are you really happy about?"

I should have known that they were teaming up against me. I never caught onto the two of them until it was too late.

"I'm just happy that our little vintage Alpha Romeo will never have to suffer that kind of abuse again. I'm mean really, Her Majesty kicked him right in the teeth. I'm so glad he's gone now to a better home."

***

Book Two

Chapter Ten
Addendum: Nigel Royal

Nigel saw her at the corner of Heath and Spadina Road, running in place, looking as cool as a cucumber on that perfect early summer morning while the dawn's dew was still glistening on the flowers and lawns through the neighborhood. He tucked his head down and gave it his all. He stopped up short, held out his arm and she took his pulse, and he settled down enough to say, "Good morning, boss." He held out his other arm so she could check his Fitbit. "How're my vitals this morning?"

"Not bad for an old guy," Jacquie offered him, "Come on, I'm buying the coffee this morning."

The barista looked at them ordering their regular brew, and she waived Jacquie's debit card away, "You know your money's no good here. Nigel would have me fired if I ever let you pay."

They sat down in their regular booth, and he started by saying, "Jacquie, I've been thinking."

"Oh oh."

"I need you to do me a huge favor."

"You're just lucky that I'm in a very good mood today, so you may possibly get an affirmative answer, but I ask you, isn't it enough that I have to crack the whip every morning just to keep you in shape so that you can keep up with your young wife? What's on your mind so early in the morning?"

"Family business, as usual. But particularly, this pertains to my beautiful daughter. Denni and I are just waiting for the other shoe to drop, you know what I mean. You live with her. She's just too damn calm after all she's been through with the fire and the deaths and everything. I mean really, her husband died, her in-laws died, and yet it doesn't seem to faze her in the least. She even went out on impulse last week and bought two new cars without even asking me for my opinion. And you know, Jacquie, I don't want her spending her money like that; I'd rather pay for those big expenses. Oh, I don't know, maybe I'm just feeling a little left out or something. But, Jacquie, you're a nurse, and you're also a young widow. You've coached all of us through our grieving, even our little Martina. Denni and I are still devastated; there are days we think that it will never get any better. However, Nigella is too calm, cool, and collected, and it's worrying us. We don't want her to get sick. As you know, both Denni and I have suffered with mental-health issues years ago, and we want to avoid her following our poor examples of not handling our issues properly. We just want the best for our little girl. I don't want her crashing and burning."

"Yeah. I hear you. Sometimes, you know, she makes me laugh. I know it's rather unconventional, but she does let off a little steam here and there. She'll go on a big rant about what a son-of-a-bitch François was, and how she wishes he were still alive so she could kick his ass around the block. Like when she kicked his poor unsuspecting car and broke her foot for instance. I think she may still be in the anger stage of her grief. I wouldn't worry too much, not right now anyway. Everybody grieves a different way. But you know, Nigel, she told me of her little dabble into sex-on-the-side with that sleazy professor and you finding her there in the middle of it all. That's not like her. Oh, I can see her having lots and lots of sex partners, but from what I understand, there was no fun involved there. It was just a disgusting act of an older teacher preying on an innocent student who was feeling lost in her marriage. I think she's been grieving the loss of her marriage for over three years now, ever since the boys were born, so don't worry too much about her not having any feelings about the death of her husband. He said goodbye to her years ago. And it really hurt her. That's the hurt that she needs some professional help with. You're right. When it's the right time, I'll get her set up with a good mental-health professional."

The nurse in Jacquie continued, "But you know, Nigel, after watching her every move, I think that she's going through something other than grieving for the husband and even grieving for the lost marriage."

"Oh no! Is there something else? Is something wrong with her health? Are the kids okay?"

"No, no, no. Sorry. I mean something good. Really good. Nigel, have we got time this morning? I tend to ramble on when I'm thinking things over. Do we have time for a refill? And remember, we haven't even discussed the favor that you're begging me for yet."

Nigel caught the barista's eye to indicate a refill was in order, and he used his old, wise judge's voice as he sat back, arms crossed, "Now, Jacquie, please start from the beginning. The very beginning, and don't leave anything out. I'm listening."

"The executive summary line always comes first, Nigel, so here it is: I think our little girl is growing up, despite our best intentions of trying to keep her smack dab in the middle of the fairytale existence that she lives in at 49 Parkwood Avenue."

"You mean that I've spoiled her?"

"Not at all. It has very little to do with you, Nigel. And it has everything to do with her. She's morphing from a little protected princess into a full-fledged, regal queen who occasionally emulates her mom, who is the ass-kicker of all ass-kickers I've ever known. Nigella is on the verge of finding out who she really is. You know, it's like that age-old question we all face at one time or another, *who am I?*"

"Oh. So, you think she has growing pains?"

"Exactly. And there's not a damn thing we can do about it. And what's more, there's not a damn thing that we should do about it. Allow her, her wings. Let her fly. She's like one of your beautiful, miraculous, Canadian Monarch butterflies. She's a survivor, through and through, and burying a husband or two along the way isn't going to keep her down."

"So, okay. What have you witnessed that makes you think she's evolving into her full magnificence?"

"Nigel, please know that I usually don't share confidences. Not that she said not to tell anyone, but I know that she doesn't share her past easily. So please, please, keep this to yourself and Denni only and know that I'm telling you not to make you feel badly but to help us help her."

"Deal. It stays between you, me, and Denni."

"When we first met in Disney World, and her and I shared the same bed for a sleepover, just like our ten-year-old girls, she told me that it was her first sleepover in her whole life. She could never have a sleepover, because her mother and she only had the one bed. Their kitchen did not have the proverbial box of cornflakes there to make sure a little friend had some breakfast after a sleepover. Nigella told me that she grew up with her deaf mother who went to the backdoor door of three restaurants daily to pick up leftovers from the kitchen so that her little girl would have some lunch to take to school the next day. Their tiny home had no telephone, no television, and during the winter months, her mother would lay their coats over their blankets to keep them warm at night. Nigella's daily chatter of what went on at school that day was answered with the silent signing of her adoring but profoundly deaf mother. She lived in a very quiet but loving home. That's what motivated her to excel in school. She knew it was up to her to provide a better life for her and her mother. Once she became a lawyer, her mother was always urging her to find a man and marry him and have children. Nigella was only 23. She couldn't even think about dating a man, let alone marrying one. She had a good job, and she was going to work hard and earn money. She had no desire for a husband or a child. She never really had a childhood herself. She finally relented and got pregnant through in-vitro fertilization just to give her mother a baby. Her pregnancy wasn't for herself. It was for her mother. She felt it would give her mother a sense of purpose as she would care for the baby while Nigella paid attention to her young career. Of course, the moment the baby was born, she fell deeply in love with her, and the mother, the baby, and Nigella had a very, very, happy and full life for three years before the mother died of cancer. And then she met you and Denni two years later. The rest is history, as they say."

Nigel, through his silent tears that were running freely down his cheeks, could only whisper, "My poor baby, my poor baby."

"I know, I know, Nigel. I felt the same way as she told me her story. But you know our Nigella, she is so smart and so witty. She had me laughing so hard at the end of her story that I almost fell out of the bed. She summed everything up by saying, "*Listen, girlfriend, the only reason I told you this long, sad tale was to refute the name that you were calling me out at the pool.*"

Jacqui continued, "I thought back and, yes, I had to agree with her; I had name-called her right to her face. Actually, when I first met her at the pool in Disney World that day, she was wearing a 300-dollar bathing suit, and then she introduced me to her mom that was sporting the biggest canary-yellow diamond that I've ever seen in my life, so I promptly labelled her as a princess and the name stuck. So, she made sure she cleared that little misconception up. She told me flat out she was no princess. She said that she was simply a fraud. She was nothing but a survivor in sheep's clothing."

Nigel tilted his head back, and his big baritone filled the whole café as he roared with laughter at his witty, charming daughter's confession as to her real identity.

Jacquie added, "But just to bring my observations up to date, Nigel, there is another positive sign that lets us know she's going to be okay. She's had wonderful results with all her research into her family roots that she started a little while ago. She has learned her grandmother's full name, and it turns out that there are records of her being at both Auschwitz-Birkenau and Bergen-Belson, as well as the displaced person's camp in Germany where her grandmother gave birth to her mother. And that same camp has a record of the midwife's name and notes that the midwife wrote at the time of the birth. She also has found out that her grandmother's family owned a dairy farm in Poland before the Nazis occupied the town."

Nigel's mouth was open in surprise, and all he could get out was, "No! Are you kidding me!?"

Jacquie reached over the table and patted Nigel's hand reassuringly. "See, Nigel, she's going to be okay. She's ready now to leave your beautifully and lovingly feathered nest to become the strong, independent head of her family under her own steam. She's ready to fly, and we just have to let her go. It's all good, please don't worry about our girl. And I'm here, and I'm not going anywhere."

Nigel jumped out of his seat and walked a few long strides back and forth, back and forth, until Jacquie started to laugh and she said to him, "Nigel, people are beginning to stare. Please, sit. Can't you think while you're sitting down?"

Nigel shook his head a little and sat down abruptly. He said, "Jacquie, we can work all this information into my little plan. May I tell you the favor I need of you now?"

"Shoot. I've got all morning."

"I was going to ask you to please help me convince Nigella that you, Maureen, and all the kids, along with Denni and me, go to Auntie Catharine and Uncle Edouard's château in the south of France for a holiday before school goes back in. Denni and I thought it would be a nice treat for you and Zalia, and it would be good for Nigella to take her mind off the fire. Nigella and the children have never been there either. And when Catharine and Edouard were here last month for the funeral, they pleaded with us to come over for a break away from it all. But now, here's where you really come in. If we all go to France to stay at the château, then maybe you and Nigella could slip up to Germany and Poland so she could pay her respects to her grandmother. You two could go visit the family dairy-farm or at least what's left of it. The kids and us would stay back at the château while you two take a few days and maybe Nigella would be able to connect in some small way with her grandmother or at least her past. That would help her in her quest to find out who she really is. Would you please help Denni and I pull this off, Jacquie? Please, Jacquie. It's what our girl needs right now. And you could use a holiday too."

Jacquie sat there, quietly looking into Nigel's handsome, earnest face. She said, "Here I sit, staring into the face of a wonderful man that has become one of my best friends, who is responsible for my new life in Canada, who now wants me to take my daughter and me on a holiday with his family. Up until this summer, I had never left the shores of the U.S.A., and now my daughter and I are becoming jet setters. I can understand fully how Nigella gratefully and gracefully entered her four-year hiatus from real life to live as a princess in your kingdom, Nigel. And yes, the answer is yes. Actually, I think between the two of us, we've hatched a perfect plan. I'll broach the subject with our little survivor in sheep's clothing tonight, and by tomorrow morning, she'll be calling you, asking if you want to come along with her to Europe. Deal, Nigel?"

"Deal, Jacquie. Let's get out of here. We've got work to do."

As they walked back up through the neighborhood, Nigel said, "Back to my daughter's mental health and her grieving process, if we can, Jacquie."

"Shoot."

"Nigella has a lot to look forward to that she hasn't even clued into yet, and that's a good thing. The timing is all off right now. We don't want to complicate matters. But this has been happening since the spring, before we met you, and actually only myself, Denni, and one other person knows about it."

"Knows what?"

"Well, you know Nigella's graduate advisor, Alessandro Camarra?"

"Yeah, he comes over to the house with you. He's a great guy. A good looker, that's for sure. What about him?"

"He's in love with Nigella."

Jacquie stopped in her tracks and looked into Nigel's face. "Oh no. Fuck, man. She's in no shape for affairs of the heart. It's way too early. It would end in disaster for both of them."

"Lucky for us, he's a very principled and ethical man. He wouldn't touch her with a ten-foot pole as long as she's his student. He actually has talked to me already and told me he is going to wait until after her graduation, hoping by then she will have managed her grieving enough to allow him to court her. He's Italian, you know. It has to be done properly and respectfully. We don't have to worry about Alessandro; he's perfect for her, but he wants her forever and ever. He knows how to keep it in his pants. He's a family man. So, there is something only you can help her with, Jacquie."

"You can count on me, Nigel. What can I do?"

"Take care of her, but on the other hand, make sure she gets out there and has some fun being a girl. I never in a million years thought I'd ever be saying this, but my daughter needs to get out there, and, safely, mind you, but, well – she needs to put a few notches on her bedpost, so to speak. Away from the house of course. Far away from the house. Oh my God, this all sounds so crass. But, do you understand what I'm saying?"

"I hear you loud and clear. And it doesn't sound crass at all, Nigel. It sounds like a loving father who wants the best for his daughter. In fact, that's pretty good advice for me as well. It's time we both cut loose. But in a safe way, Nigel. You and Denni don't have anything to worry about. I've got this. And, hey, I'm a girl that doesn't kiss and tell, so don't expect any updates on this matter. Got it? Deal?"

"Oh my God, an update? I would die first! Please, I've forgotten this whole convo already! But one last thing. Let's keep this news of Alessandro being in love with her between ourselves. This is going to take time for her, and we can't have her rushing into something just because she's lonely or trying to replace her marriage. She's got a lot of emotional baggage to sort through beforehand, and when she does fall in love with him, it's got to be just between the two of them. I trust Alessandro implicitly. But my little girl has a mind of her own, as you know. I remember I tried to rush Denni into love, and it caused both of us one hell of a lot of trouble, and I wouldn't wish that on my worst enemy."

"We have nothing to worry about. This reminds me of that old saying, *When the student is ready, the teacher arrives.*"

Nigel stopped in his tracks and looked at Jacquie and shook his head. "I haven't heard that expression for years. *When the student is ready, the teacher arrives.* Jacquie, have we got time for one last story? And it's the real reason why I want our girl to get out there and have some fun as a single woman."

Nigel proceeded to tell her about his painful shyness and being a black boy in a white world that had kept him from having a normal, healthy sex life or even a high-school dating life that would have allowed him to get to second base, as they called it back in the day. He told her that he was a virgin until the age of 24, and that his first time was with Nigella's birthmother in a little hotel room on a cold day in Stockholm, Sweden. His partner was also a virgin who was also profoundly deaf and mute as well.

"You can imagine, Jacquie, how all that went down. And yet, I can honestly say that the two of us fell in love that afternoon. I mean that. Seriously. Both of us, with no experience whatsoever – and with no talking – well – we just connected, deeply somehow."

"Well, Nigel, what exactly happened? Why did it end so abruptly?"

"Yeah. My fault. Back to me having no experience with girls and being a shy, polite lawyer. And she was deaf. After spending the afternoon in bed with her, I realized I was going to miss my plane, so she got dressed and was waiting at the door for me. I got some money out of my wallet to give her for taxi fare, and when I told her it was taxi fare, she didn't hear me. She thought I was paying her for sex. She slapped my face so hard and ran away before I could stop crying from the humiliation of it all. I didn't even know her name. I thought it was because I was a black man and I was too stupid or naïve to realize she hadn't heard my offer to taxi fare. I had written down my name for her on a piece of paper, and she kept it for 23 years and gave it to Nigella after Nigella graduated from law school. That was the proof that Nigella gave me that I was indeed her father. And, of course, the DNA results from Ancestry.ca."

"You're making this up, right, Nigel?"

"Scout's honor. But let me finish my sad story of the rest of my 20s. It gets worse."

"You're exaggerating. How could things get possibly worse?"

"After my first time with my golden angel, I toughened up a little and decided I would find a nice girl and get married. A black girl. This new articling student walked through my office door and I was a goner, in 30 seconds flat. She was a beautiful black girl, in town from Kingston, Jamaica, with an agenda to finish her law degree and to find a husband that would take her out of the slums and into a better world. I was her mark. I couldn't eat. I couldn't sleep. She groomed me from the get-go."

He paused and looked at Jacquie. "Jacquie, I'm a little embarrassed to give you these details, but I want you to know this, so if it happens to Nigella or yourself, you'll recognize a hustler if you come across one."

"For Chrissake, Nigel, I'm not a kid. Tell me, my good friend. Your pain is written all over your face."

"On our first date, she showed me how to strip-tease for a woman. She showed me how to please her and she did things to me that I never could have even dreamed of. We were insatiable. Or, thinking back now, maybe it was just me that couldn't get enough of her. Over that first month, she didn't let up. So, when I heard you say, *When the student is ready, the teacher arrives,* I remembered all too well my sad tale of being a student. I was sucked into the deepest vortex I've ever experienced. A real maelstrom. And she was smart, and funny too, which appealed to me."

Jacquie prompted him, "So, it sounds pretty good to me. What was your problem with having an experienced teacher? You weren't a kid, Nigel. You already said you didn't know what you were doing in the sex department beforehand."

Nigel sighed. "We were married in the surf on a Jamaican beach about a month later. After the ceremony, that same day, after the sun went down, I found her fucking one of the musicians in the back garden of the hotel."

"No! No way! You're kidding, right?"

"He was sitting in a lawn chair, with his pants down around his ankles, and she was sitting on his lap with her white wedding dress bouncing up and down in the moonlight to his thrusts."

Jacquie said quietly to him, "So now you're going to tell me that you met Denni and you lived happily ever after, right?"

Nigel smiled at her wanting the fairytale ending. "Not so fast. I didn't meet Denni for another 28 years."

"Please tell me that your next woman treated you a little better. Please, Nigel."

"Honey, life is never that simple. You see, there was no other woman. Not one. I just drifted through life alone. I stayed celibate until I met Denni 28 years later."

Jacquie looked at him in disbelief. "You're telling me that a handsome, successful, brilliant, sexy, charming man like yourself went without having sex with a partner for 28 years?"

"Yup. As Seinfeld said in his old sitcom, *I was the master of my own domain.*"

"This is sounding now like you're just bringing all this on yourself. Surely there were lots and lots of girls for you to bed."

"I guess so. But right from the very beginning, I had to be in love with the girl. Saul Himmel taught me how to be a gentleman. And I'm just funny that way. What can I say? I'm the world's biggest romantic it seems. I'm not a hit-it and quit-it kind of guy. I'd rather die first. And I'm basically a shy person, and then any game that I thought I had was shot down completely when I was put under the Canadian Witness Protection Program. So that's why I like Alessandro Camarra so much. He's exactly like me. And that's why I know he's the man for our Nigella. He'll never cheat on her. But back to my story and to wrap it up on a positive note, when I finally met Denni, I fell deeply in love with her the first time I laid eyes on her. I didn't know her, or anything about her, but from the moment I saw her, I thought of nothing else. I was so nervous about our first time together, even more nervous than her, but I found out that sex was like riding a bicycle, and all my lessons learned from my black hustler wife paid off big time. And then, after many ups and downs, fate brought us together once again, and she finally accepted my love. Now, Denni and I have a fantastic sex life, thanks to my lessons learned at the hands of an accomplished teacher."

"Does Denni know your *Mrs. Robinson* story?"

"Hell no. She just thinks I'm naturally gifted in that department."

***

160

Chapter Eleven
I Found My Thrill on Blueberry Hill

You might say the light went on. I slowly turned around, put my hands on my hips, and narrowed my eyes and I went nose to nose with her. "Just a minute, Jacqueline Dixon, something smells fishy here. Everything sounded good until all of a sudden Dad's name popped up in your little suggestion. Have you and him hatched this plan and tried to pass it off to me as my own idea? Have the two of you been sneakily making plans for me behind my back? Do the two of you think I'm falling apart? Is that it?"

Jacquie was on it like a fly to a fresh string of flypaper. "Don't even go there, Sis. Now think about it, even if your dad and I did come up with this brilliant idea, all for your wellbeing by the way, don't start with me. Don't shoot the messenger! Or your dad, your wonderful, loving, caring, generous-to-a-fault father who wants nothing but the best for his pain-in-the-ass Swedish princess. Please know that I'm going to be sitting right here, drinking my coffee for the next ten minutes, so you will have enough time to rethink this situation and be the graceful daughter that I know you are while you phone your dad to tell him that we're going to Europe and you want him and your mom to come along. They can mind the kids at the château along with Maureen while you and I go up to visit your grandma's old dairy farm up in Poland. Now put your big-boy pants on and phone him right now."

I was a little taken back with her firm tone, and it made me realize that I was indeed a spoiled brat. I said to her, "You'll have to get up off your ass so I can give you a proper hug and a proper apology for my bratty behavior. Come on now, Sis, get up here."

She responded by jumping up and giving me a big bear-hug, lifting me right off my feet. She whirled me around in the air, exclaiming loudly, "Oh the little princess has come to her senses." She laughed in my face and said, "I love you, Sis. I'd better learn not to get you so riled up, or you might go out to the garage and kick your new car and break your other foot if I'm not careful. Now if you'll take a minute and listen to me, I'll tell you what I talked to your dad about."

I said rather nonchalantly, "Oh. What would that be, Jack?"

"I told him that I was going to give up calling you a princess. I've figured out that you're not a princess after all. You're in the middle of morphing into a real, true-blue ass-kicker, just like Denni. I also told him that I couldn't be prouder of you for the way that you're handling your grieving process. You're one hell of a woman, Sis."

"Yeah. I know. It felt so good to buy the two new cars last week. And did you know I didn't even ask Dad what I should do. I went to the dealership all by myself and I made the deal myself. Do you know it's my first car I've bought in my whole life and I'm 35 years old? I used some of my husband's insurance money, but that money is mine, not my dad's. I earned it. Every penny of it. Putting up with a cheating, lying son-of-a-bitch husband for four years. My God! I'm such a late bloomer with both men and cars. Poor Dad. He probably thinks I'm losing my mind or something. I've just made up my mind to do things for myself from now on. I have to be king of my own castle right now. I hope he understands that. But let me tell you, it feels damn good to take back control of my life once in a while."

"I hear you, Sis. But you know what, tell your dad exactly what you just told me. He worries about you, and it's up to you to convince him that you're on the right track."

I said, "You're right, Jack. I'm going to phone him right now and have a nice long chat with him. When he insists on paying for the air tickets and all, I'm not going to fight it like I usually do. Maybe he's feeling a little like he's losing his little girl or something. My God, Jack, do you think I'm finally growing up?"

"Is the Pope a catholic?"

**

It was a long haul; no doubt about it, but we had dressed the kids in their pajamas to catch the 11:30 p.m. Toronto-Avignon flight, and they were conked out in their sleeper cabins along with Maureen.

Jacquie whispered to me, "Look at the two lovers. What a couple. They are the most in-love lovebirds I've ever known."

I looked over at Mom and Dad. He was smoothing her hair out, and she was half-talking, half-kissing him through a conversation. "Do you know, Jack, at their age, they still belong to the twice-a-day club?"

Jack sighed. "Lucky them. Even at the best of times, my husband and I weren't members. But, on the other hand, she is ten years younger than him. Actually, she's only 15 years older than us. And she takes care of herself. She looks much younger than she is. I hope I look as good at her age."

"Yeah, me too," I laughed and shook my head at the two of them as I watched her touch his chest, "Their close proximity for the next seven hours is going to cramp their style, I'm sure. It's a good thing we're taking a hotel in Avignon for the first day and night of our trip, so they'll be able to make up for lost time."

I was just dozing off when Jack whispered, "Sis, how the hell did we get here?"

"What? What do mean?"

"Think about it. Two black girls who grew up on food stamps and backdoor restaurant leftovers. Flying first class to Europe with our four beautiful children, a nanny, and the most loving grandparents on earth. What are the chances?"

"As Mom says, *Pinch me. Just pinch me.*"

***

I stood there in the warm summer night, with Dad's arm around my shoulders. The horses glistened and the riders all wore that same ridiculous, animated smile plastered on their faces, one hand held up in the wave as the beautiful antique carrousel went round and round, with the classic European music piping out over the square. We were in *Old Town, Centre Ville,* in Avignon, France, watching Mom holding onto Warren on her steed, Jacqui with Noah on hers, Maureen, Martina, and Zalia all on their own mounts.

Dad said, "You see why I didn't want to ride, honey? Just watching them all is my biggest treat. Look at them. That's our family there. I'm so proud of you all. Every one of you, but especially you, Nigella. You're one hell of a woman."

"I get it from my dad. But, Dad, look at Mom. She's the most beautiful woman on the carrousel. She's so in love with you. I was watching the two of you on the plane. She couldn't stop herself from kissing you all the time the two of you were talking."

"Yeah. I know. I'm one hell of a lucky man! She makes me feel like a kid in a candy store. How'd I get so lucky? How'd I get so damn lucky?"

***

Every time I looked at her, I laughed. Of course, she was playing the part, I must admit, but Mom just looked so cute driving the huge nine-seater van all the way from Avignon upcountry to the château. She had pulled her ponytail through the back loop of her Blue Jays ball cap and was quite happy playing chauffeur and pointing out the sights as we headed northwest to pass over the mountains. She couldn't wait to get us all there – to her and Dad's favorite place in the whole world, Auntie Catharine and Uncle Edouard's big, old, ancestral château. They had arranged for horseback riding lessons for all of us, and Auntie Catharine had a local artist coming in a couple of afternoons to give us all painting lessons as well.

Jack and I would slip away and travel up northeast to Poland so that I could complete my journey to walk in my grandma's footsteps, right from her farm in Wloclawek, Poland, to Auschwitz-Birkenau, then up to Bergen-Belson and then over to Foehrenwald, the displaced person's camp in Northern Germany, where my mother was actually born.

***

Dad's big laugh couldn't drown out all the excited oohs and awes as Mom drove slowly down the long, winding driveway. The château's four painted turrets had caught little Noah's eyes, and he cried, "Mommy, Mommy, this is where the fairytale princess lives!"

All Jack could say was, "Are you kidding me!? Is this for real? Nigella, are you kidding me?"

Dad had warned us all that their dog's name was also Patou, and he was our dog's father and that they looked exactly alike. Dad said he'd get out first just in case the dog charged him, and he didn't want the boys to be knocked over.

Mom pulled up in the middle of the courtyard, and, sure enough, the minute Dad stepped out of the van, the Great White Pyrenees tucked his massive white head down into his chest and made a beeline for Dad who, by this time, was down on his knees with his arms out. Apparently, the first time they had met years ago, the dog knocked him right off his feet and ran away with one of his socks. We all bailed out of the van while Dad and old Patou rolled over and over on the great lawn.

Mom looked at her husband and man's best friend, and she said to Auntie Catharine, "Look at them. Two old dogs and not a new trick between them. God bless them."

I turned around to see that Maureen was chasing after the twins that were scrambling up over the balustrade that surrounded the big fountain. We had arrived.

***

Two days later, while the kids were down at the stables, taking their riding lessons, Dad walked Jack and I out to the car to see us off to Germany and Poland in my search for my family's roots. He gave us a plastic bag that held 100 beautiful, small, gold-colored, Canadian maple-leaf pins, the same as what we had used at the Tran family celebration of life service. He insisted that we wear one at all times and give everyone that we came into contact with a pin. He reminded us that we were guests in these countries and that we were representing Canada. He was every bit the Supreme Court Justice at that moment as he'd ever been.

Catharine and Maureen gave us a lift to the nearest airport, and Jack and I were off and running, with loud admonishments from Maureen to behave ourselves. Jack and I were giggling like schoolgirls as we boarded our first of several flights. Those giggles were the last we would have for the next few days.

I had revised our trip a little to put the solemn visits first, so, after our first night in a hotel in Krakow, Germany, we arrived at Auschwitz where I had made an appointment the month before to speak to one of the historians on

165

sight that would show me my grandmother's documentation that was on record.

Dad was right about the pins. Having studied international law myself, it was an excellent way of putting theory into practice. As I pinned the maple leaf on the historian's lapel, she gave Jack and me a big hug and a thank you. I wasn't prepared at all for her research, however.

The historian guided Jack and I through the records, and, all of a sudden, I began to tremble from head to foot when I read Milka Kaufman in the middle of a long list of names that had disembarked from the train on that particular summer day in 1943.

Neatly written and well-preserved, there were three other names underneath that I wasn't expecting. The names read: *Martyna Kaufman, first-twin girl Kaufman, second-twin girl Kaufman.*

The historian explained that my grandmother, Milka, at age 20, was directed to the left, and her mother, Martyna, at age 43, and her nine-year-old twin daughters were directed to the right. She explained that there were no further records for Martyna and her twin girls, but she would be happy to give us photocopies of everything they had on the four Kaufmans that had boarded the train in the Polish city of Wloclawek.

Jacquie said quietly, "We just need a minute. We have two ten-year-old girls and a pair of three-year-old twins ourselves, so this is hitting us very close to home."

The historian was such a pro. She chatted us through the worst of it and actually filled in with a lot of detail that eased our pain considerably. She was interested in our African heritage, as the Nazis were just as hard on African heritage as they were on Jews. By the time we were ready to join a tour group, I was somewhat composed, but I knew I would never be the same. Talk about growing up; that day I felt like I was ancient.

Jack and I held hands throughout the whole tour. We reminded each other time and time again to save our grieving for later. We were here, right now, learning that Milka Kaufman was as tough as nails and she had survived this nightmare. I can't imagine the guts that my grandma would have had to have.

There was one part of the tour that I wished for a second that my dad could have heard. Not that I wished that hellhole of a place on anyone, but I knew that he would have liked the little story that the tour guide told us as she pointed out to a building which she described as a 'warehouse.' The Polish prisoners had dubbed this particular warehouse *Kanada* because this was where the Nazis stored all the suitcases and bundles of personal treasures that the prisoners had brought with them. It was a treasury of family photographs, small pieces of art, jewelry, best clothes, fine leather shoes, and mementos from home. It was systematically stockpiled and then shipped out all over the Third Reich. The prisoners named it *Kanada* because Canada was known as the land of plenty. Although this name started out as prison slang, it was adopted by the camp administration and the name stuck.

I looked into Jack's face and squeezed her hand a little, hoping that she had heard the reference to Canada, but her face was blanketed with pain and her eyes were swimming with tears, so I made a mental note to save this little tidbit for Dad. After all, Jack was an American and I couldn't expect her to feel the same pride in Canada as I did.

***

We took our next flight that afternoon, heading north to Hanover, to visit the nearby Bergen-Belsen 'labour-camp' site. By this time, Jacquie and I realized that we were over the worst of it, and we filled our time on the flight in wonderment in how the two of us, who shared a history of African slavery and Jewish genocide, met in Disney World of all places – a place so far removed from our history, it was almost implausible that we had met at all.

Just like clockwork, the local historian met us early the next morning at the comprehensive Visitor Centre at Belsen. This visit was not as traumatic as Auschwitz for us, as all the buildings had been razed by the British upon liberation, but the grassy mounds that were the mass graves were enough of a visual reminder of what had happened here. Once again, we left with photocopies of Grandma's name on several lists, the best one being the copy of her name on the British Army's list of Survivors that they put on a train headed for the Displaced Person's camp in yet another part of Germany.

It was our next stop that we hit real gold. We had caught an early afternoon flight from Hanover down to Munich, which was near Grandma's displaced person's camp, called Foehrenwald, and located in Wolfratshausen at the time.

The historian's face was beaming as she shook both our hands and said, "Welcome! Welcome! Since our last email, I have discovered something very interesting from UNRRA, that is, the *United Relief and Rehabilitation Administration* files that pertains to your grandmother."

I was astounded with her news. "You mean to tell me that the Catholic midwife that helped birth my mother is alive and actually wants to meet with me?"

"Yes, and she lives about five minutes from here in a senior's residence, and she has invited us over for tea."

***

The historian, armed with photocopies of everything she had on file pertaining to Grandma and her newborn, who was my mother, along with Jack and I, knocked on Renata Wójcik's apartment door. My heart was pounding.

The woman that opened the door just stood there, listening as the historian introduced us. She nodded her head slightly before bluntly saying, "Yeah. You're tall like Milka was. You've got the same broad shoulders. And her baby girl who she named Martyna was a big, long baby too. But they both had bright blue eyes and straight golden hair, and not like yours at all."

She was a pleasant, sharp-as-a-tack octogenarian, having had her 80th birthday three weeks beforehand. As we settled into her sparsely furnished senior's apartment, she told us of being a Catholic, marrying another Catholic at the age of 20, but never having children. She had been a widow for many years, and she was very pleased a few years ago to get into the senior's residence where her small pension was enough to cover the rent.

Renata, it appeared, was quite a character and definitely not suffering from any problems related to aging other than having to use the old, beat-up walker that was stationed in her small foyer. There was nothing at all wrong with her brain; she was simply not quite up-to-date with the current ways of the world.

***

Jack had offered to carry the teapot in from the kitchen, and once Jack had left the assumed earshot, Renata turned her head away from me and said to the historian in a lowered pitch as if I wasn't sitting right next to her, "Well, this is the first time I've ever had Negros in my house. I suppose it's not as bad as I would have thought."

I laid my cards on the table as if we were discussing the weather, and I said very pleasantly, almost offhandedly, "Yes, my father is a black man. He is a Supreme Court Justice in Canada, so he has a very important job with the government. I look a little like him with my African hair, but my skin tones are a little lighter, since my mother was, as you know, a Polish Jew. That's how we do things in Canada. Everybody mixes with everybody else. We hardly notice our skin color anymore. And as for me, I got a good education, and I'm a lawyer, and my friend here is a pediatric nurse who ran a whole division for babies in a big hospital in America, so the two of you have a lot in common, with you being a midwife and all. And another thing the three of us have in common is that we're all widows. Our husbands died when they were in their 30s, and now we raise our kids on our own. And you're a widow too."

I continued, "May I?" She nodded to allow me to pin the Canadian maple leaf onto her cardigan. The historian was laughing by then, as she hugged me after putting her own maple leaf on.

Jack came back into the living room, and she had a huge grin plastered all over her face. I knew that I couldn't look at her or I would have burst out laughing myself.

Renata looked at us, shaking her head, disbelieving what she was hearing. "You mean to tell me that you're a lawyer and she's a nurse? Really! Times are achangin'!"

I said, "Renata, please! I can't wait another minute! May you tell me the story of how you met my grandma?"

And so, she began. Her memory recall was excellent. She told us that she was a 16-year-old midwife assistant, and it was the spring of 1946. Grandma was already pregnant when they met. She told of how the father of Milka's baby died of suicide, but she didn't know his name anymore, and how my grandma was the queen of the camp. It was Renata's first birth where the mother had died. She told of how she called the rabbi to give Milka her last rites and to give the baby her first blessing. She told of how peaceful Milka was when she died.

Renata's whole demeanor changed as she began her story of the baby; my Mor. It was like Mor was her own baby. The 16-year-old had nursed baby Martyna Kaufman for six months before Sweden took her in as a deaf orphan. The Swedish orphanage changed her name from Martyna Kaufman to Martina Kaufman Hansson in hopes that the Swedish name would lead to adoption.

As Renata ended her story, the historian took out the photocopies, and Renata excitedly pointed to her signature where she had signed off on the death as well as the birth records.

Tears ran down my face as I saw the teenaged European handwriting outlining a detailed accounting of Grandma's last four months of her life, and my mother's first six months of her life.

"Renata, now I know how it came to be that my profoundly deaf mother was such a loving and kind woman. She got it from you during the first six months of her life. All the love that you poured into her stuck with her, and then she was able to pass it along to me. Thank you."

By this time, Jacquie was playing her part as the Negro kitchen help, and on her way out of the dining room, she whispered to the historian to ask if she had an envelope. I excused myself and asked if I could use the toilet and saw that Jacquie was stuffing a bunch of Euros into the envelope and writing something on the front of the envelope. It read:

Please buy yourself a new walker. After all, us widows have to take care of ourselves! Love from Nigella, Canada, and Jacqueline, U.S.A.

Jack nodded as I quickly and quietly added my euros to the envelope as well.

By the time Jacquie and I had come back into the room, the historian asked if we were ready to go, but Renata stood up quickly and said, "Wait! Wait just a minute! I have something else to say to you!"

We sat, facing the small, white-haired elder, and she started tearing up with her own story. Her real story. It turned out that our visit was just as much a growing up experience for her as it was for me.

She looked a little desperate and she asked us to understand, "Look. I've never said this before in my life. To anyone. Not even my husband."

I said softly, "It's okay, Renata. We're friends. What is it?"

Her tone became a little defensive and she said, "Well, Nigella, if you can say it, and you're a Negro, then I can be brave and say it too."

"Say what, Renata?" I coaxed.

She put her head down into her hands and she exclaimed, "I'm a Jew! I'm not a Catholic! I was a hidden child since I was five years old, and I have lived a lie my whole life! I'm a Jew!"

I put my arms around her and rocked her back and forth like I do with the boys when they've scraped a knee.

Jacquie lightened the mood by saying quietly to the historian, "Well, I'm a Baptist. What are you?"

The historian's wit kicked in and she said, "I'm Swiss and I'm neutral. Don't be bringing me into your crazy, mixed-up worlds of race and religion!"

I must say, it was a brilliant move on my part. I said to the historian, "Olga, I'm going to e-transfer you some money so that you can set up an account for Renata. I want you and Renata to work together to see if you can hire a rabbi to come and visit Renata to explore all the options that are available to her. Perhaps you can help trace her birth family like you did for me as well. Anything that Renata wants. It's my treat, and I'm paying for everything. Can we do this together as a team?"

***

On our way out of the senior's residence, I pulled the historian and Jack into the management office on the first floor. The administrator looked up, a little surprised to see the three of us standing there, and she said, "May I help you?"

"Yes," I said. "I would like to prepay Renata Wójcik's rent for the next 12 months."

"Of course, madam. Cash or card? Polish Zloty or Euros?"

***

Our next flight took us to Warsaw, and within the hour we found ourselves in downtown Wloclawek, the town where my grandmother, Milka, lived on her dairy farm. As we made our way into the small hotel lobby that was situated downtown, Jacquie warned me, "Now, Nigella, today may seem to be a little of a letdown after meeting Renata yesterday. Please remember that this town-planner guy that you've been working with has already said that your grandma's farm doesn't exist any longer."

"I know, Jack, I know. But we've come this far, so it's only right that we just stand on the ground where the farm was, or something. It's okay, I'm not going to be disappointed or anything. It's a good way to wrap up the whole 'finding myself' experience though, you must admit."

We unpacked, had a quick lunch in the hotel's little restaurant, and then made our way back to the hotel lobby where we were meeting the town planner, Mr. Jakub Kowalski.

Jackie elbowed me. "Take a look. Eye-candy at four o'clock. See him? That's the man of my dreams. He makes me forget Brad. I mean really, Brad who?"

Said man looked at us and, not taking his eyes off of Jacquie, came over and introduced himself, "Jakub Kowalski at your service, ladies."

Jacqui and I gave each other a little schoolgirl-crush look and started to giggle. This giggling swept the sadness and pain of the last two days under the proverbial carpet, and I shook my head as I looked at Jack. Her face was flushed, and she was still laughing and totally tongue-tied. We were acting like idiots. I gathered myself together and elbowed her and said, "And I'm Nigella. It's so good to meet you in person. Thank you so much for agreeing to meet with me. This is my best friend, Jacqueline Dixon."

His eyes were still on Jacquie as he shook my hand first. He held onto hers as he spoke, "Well, well, well. It's my lucky day. Two beautiful ladies to squire around town. And, to top it all off, my cousin, Filip, is going to meet us in ten minutes, and he's going to help me show you two ladies around town. We can even take in the county fair if you like." With this, he smiled a very rakish smile into Jacquie's beaming face and said, "I'll treat you to the best Polish sausage you've ever had."

Jack and I looked at each other, with our eyes wide from his suggestive innuendo of the Polish sausage. Jacquie was the first one to lean back and roar with laughter, and I followed. All the while our new best friend, Jakub, was chuckling and saying, "Ladies, ladies, we're attracting attention here. Come on. I'm taking you to a café where we'll meet up with my cousin. By the way, Nigella, he's a lawyer, the same as you. You'll like him. And he has better manners than I have. Well, sometimes."

Jakub's cousin, Filip, came striding into the beautiful, classic, European café shortly after we had arrived. He looked like Jakub's brother, and they explained that their fathers were brothers and that's how they looked so much alike. Both of these 30-year-old 'boys' had a typical Slavic look; blond straight hair, very blue eyes, high cheekbones, just over six feet tall, buffed out pecs, with slim builds. They dressed like the young, euro eye-candy that they were. Jack and I obviously had a few years on them; but their obvious experience and charm in dealing with the opposite sex was light years ahead of us two moms-let-loose-on-a-holiday-without-the-kids. It was very evident that we were in for a day of fun, fun, fun.

Jacquie, still not taking her eyes off of Jakub, elbowed me and asked me to get out the Canadian maple-leaf pins. I looked at her as she pinned the boys. I thought to myself, this is how it should be; people of different nationalities all coming together for coffee and pastries in a beautiful European café.

Jakub's cousin, Filip, the lawyer, who was the more polished and soulful of the two, had been watching me as if he could read my mind. He interjected a bit of reality into the conversation, albeit in a very respectful and woke manner.

He said in his sexy, euro-accented, perfect English, "Ladies, I need to tell you a little about our town's demographics before we leave for our tour and the county fair. But first things first. Please be assured that Jakub and I are here to show you the best time you've ever had, and you have nothing at all to worry about in our city, either with us two or by yourselves. You're in good hands. Both my cousin and myself are professionals, and we both sit on town council, so we are established voices for our community. However, as women of color, you may come across attitudes during your stay that could be called racist. But rest assured, it's not racism at all. It's just friendly ignorance that's based on the fact that we don't have any people of color that live in our town at all. None. Not one. You are both our town's exotic beauties for the day, and I beg you not to be insulted if someone approaches you to ask if they can take a picture of you. It's not meant to offend. Please look at it as if you're educating them. They mean no malice. They're just curious, never having seen black people before, let alone gorgeous, educated women such as yourselves. The way that you gave us your Canadian maple-leaf pins, well, that's exactly the right tone you're setting."

I leaned back and pursed my lips and said to Jacquie, "So, Jack, can you handle being a celebrity for the day? Shall we make our own family celebrity, Uncle Brad, proud of us?"

"You bet your sweet ass, Sis. Bring 'em on."

I looked at the two young, big-shot, Wloclawek businessmen who obviously wanted a photo of them and their catch-of-the-day, and I leaned in and said, "Boys, I have an idea. If you two can come up with some decent press in town, I mean perhaps the local newspaper, and a local rabbi, if you have one, we could put a nice little story of two international visitors coming to town. The story would read that a Jewish Swedish lawyer, who is also an African-Canadian, along with her best friend, an African-American pediatric nurse practitioner, came to town to visit the Jewish grandma's old dairy farm, as well as to visit the old Jewish ghetto from the '30s. We're ready and willing for as many photo ops as you want, as long as the press tells my grandma's story which I can have emailed to you within the next day or two."

I reached my hand out to Filip and said, "Deal?"

He was smiling from ear to ear, and his hand shot out and grasped mine. "Deal."

***

I let out a low whistle as he opened the door of his pristine, CLK 550 Mercedes Benz convertible. I said, "I must say, Counsellor, you're obviously doing very well for yourself. Business must be good."

Filip laughed a little but with obvious pride on his face, and he motioned for Jakub and Jack to take the backseats as he whispered in my ear, "You sit in the front right beside me. Your beautiful long, long legs need a little more legroom. Besides, we're both lawyers. Maybe we can talk a little business."

"Filip, let's forget the business today, okay? It's like the song goes, *Girls Just Want to Have Fun*."

"Don't worry, Nigella, I just meant monkey business. Is that off the table as well?"

"Just to be very clear on the agenda, Filip. About monkey business – bring it on!"

***

The four of us stood there silent, just looking at the old, worn-out playground. There wasn't even any grass left. The weeds were high all along the perimeter of the small park, and there were deep ruts where the children would start their swing in the bank of six seats of the rusty set. The teeter-totter pointed upward toward the clear, blue, sunny sky. 30 feet away, I could make out the diameter of the cement splash pad that had weeds growing up from its cracks. A lone pole without its basketball hoop stood over the entire area.

Filip said to his town-planner cousin, "Fuck, man. Are you sure this is it? Is this really the old Jewish ghetto or did you bring us here just to show us your pet project that you can't sell to council?"

"Easy, Filip, easy. Actually, it's a little bit of both. So, girls, I'd better come clean with you right now and tell you how I found out that this is the center of the old Jewish ghetto."

And so, he began his story. We all have our stories, and this seemingly carefree 30-year-old town planner shared a little of his hopes and dreams that weren't necessarily planned as a part of his fun day out with a hot black chick from Miami, Florida.

He walked us away from the wire fencing of the playground and out to the street to view the narrow streets lined with cars and motorcycles, with a hodgepodge of older houses and four-story walkups that had seen better days that circled the old playground. He waved from left to right as he explained that the four-street square neighborhood was the Jewish ghetto that the Nazis had formed in 1940. He told us that according to town records, there were 13,500 Jews living in Wloclawek in 1939, and by 1941, 3,000 of the Jews had been killed by the Nazis. All the rest were forced into the Jewish ghetto, and their systematic dispatch of Jews to the concentration camps and work camps continued until there was no Jewish population left at all. The Nazis set fire to the ghetto and burned every building down to the ground before the war ended in 1946.

Jakub continued with his story. The war had completely devastated the town, and the Polish towns and cities across the country didn't want anything to do with the Holocaust Survivors as they struggled to make their way back home.

In the early '50s, the government decided to rebuild the razed ghetto into an area of affordable housing to try to attract new business to the impoverished town.

By 1970, the neighborhood had lost its edge of its new start 20 years beforehand, and the community was currently full of social problems, government-sponsored housing, complete with drugs and way, way too much alcohol consumption. As for the Jews, the last remaining Jewish congregation consisting of a handful of hangers-on ceased to operate in the '70s, and there were no Jews whatsoever documented in town records to date in 2010, the same as no people of color.

Jakub continued, and he put his arm around my shoulders as he said, "So, Nigella, look around here all you like, but you won't feel your grandma's presence here. And that's a good thing. She was safe from all this horror for that time-being because she was on the dairy farm, and the Nazis needed her family to run the farm to feed them, the Soviets, and the non-Jewish townspeople. And I'm going to take you to where the farm was, but I wanted to show you this first."

Filip said, "Okay, Jake, but first, before we go, tell them about your pet project here, the shit-box playground. Tell the girls why you showed it to them."

"Okay, I'll confess, but I'm going to add a disclaimer first."

He looked at me and said, "Nigella, when I got your email and you hired me to do some research, I had no idea at all where the Jewish ghetto was. You can imagine my surprise when I found out it was smack dab in the middle of where I grew up in the '80s. You see, I grew up here in the 'hood' myself, right over there in that second, shitty, old, four-story apartment building. And about the playground, well, this was my childhood park. I played in this park from morning until nightfall, to keep away from my father who was a mean drunk. This playground kept me safe. Ever since I graduated from university and got my job as the town planner, I have been trying to get government funding to refurbish this little patch but to no avail. And my smart cousin here has helped me write many proposals in my quest, but our town is poor, man, dirt poor. There's just no money available for a vanity project like my playground."

I said offhandedly, "So let's take a closer look at it, shall we?"

We all moved back to the fence, hopped it, and as I settled into the seat of the squeaking swing, I said to Jakub, "Okay, you're on, Mr. Town Planner. Give me the bottom line first and then explain your breakdown. And I want a timeline as well."

It was definitely his passion. It was his life's work. That young town planner had a vision that he just couldn't shake. He had it down to the last 50 cents, and he said the playground equipment supplier in Warsaw had already told him it was a three-month project after the specs had been approved by council. The total cost came in at just under 50,000 euros, as the town owned the land and would be responsible for the upkeep.

I said, "Now, Jakub, if I were at the helm of this project, I would be adding in an additional 5,000 euros for signage."

"What would the signage read, Nigella?"

"I'll tell you what it would read in English and then you follow with what it would read in Polish. In English, it would read: *The Milka Kaufman Children's Playground.*"

He thought about it for a minute and jumped up out of the swing seat. He spread his arms out wide, and he shouted at the top of his lungs, *"Park dla dzieci Milka Kaufman."*

After that, the four of us were dead silent. Filip broke the silence by asking me, "What exactly are you suggesting?"

"I'm suggesting that I transfer your town council 50,000 euros along with the artwork for the big sign over the front entrance, as well as a plaque stating who my grandma was, so that Jakub can build this playground out to his specs, with you acting as legal counsel for the town. Jacquie and I will come back to town next spring to cut the ribbon."

Once again, silence reigned. All of a sudden, Jakub, the young, good-looking skirt-chaser with his heart of gold broke down completely and sobbed in his cousin's arms. That same cousin said to me as he continued patting Jakub's back to console him, "Nigella, you and I can work out the details over email, and I'll make sure that the legal and financials are all taken care of. You have my word."

***

Jakub unrolled the town's plan on the hood of the car, and the four of us peered down into his careful markings of where Grandma's farm used to be.

"So, Nigella, I would think that we are standing right now somewhere between your family's barn and the farmhouse. I hope that you can accept the fact that the actual farm is long gone. It was redeveloped by the town when we made room for the water tower up behind us, up on Blueberry Hill."

Sure enough, with Filip's arm around me to cushion the blow of my crushed dreams of at least seeing the pastureland, I followed Jakub's pointing finger up the rough, open, grassy hill where the huge water tower with the big, black letters of 'W L O C L A W E K' spanning its circumference. It looked down on us like we were ants making little ant-tracks in our small, little, ant existence.

I looked at the three of them solemnly watching me, and I repeated what Dad had told me long ago regarding my disappointment in my flailing marriage, "It's okay, guys. I can handle this. It's like Leonard Cohen, Canada's great poet and singer said, *'There is a crack in everything, that's how the light gets in.'*"

***

In an attempt to grab back the fun into the afternoon, I said, "Come on, guys. Let's go to the county fair. I want a ride on the Ferris wheel and a big cone of cotton candy. What are we waiting for!?"

Once again, Jack and I put on our ball caps that Filip had supplied us out of his glove box of his beautiful convertible in order to save our hair-dos from the ride back to the county fair.

I looked back at my very best friend, my sis. She was snuggled up against her boy-toy, and she had her one hand resting on his thigh. I turned back around and looked at the handsome, charming, young lawyer driving his big, fancy car as if he owned the whole town. *Um um,* I thought to myself, *nothing like a man with confidence.*

I leaned back in the seat, facing upward into the summer day, and I stretched my arm over to him and followed Jack's lead. Filip grabbed my hand and lifted it to his lips, then placed it firmly on his upper thigh.

We had slowed down on the main street. The farmer's market was packing up, and we could hear the carnival with all the music from a few blocks away. All of a sudden, Jacquie leaned forward and said, "Nigella, if you see a pharmacy, would you run in for me since I'm in the backseat? I need some gum."

I looked at her. "Gum?" I said. "Since when do you chew gum?"

"Yeah. You know. The kind of gum that I liked when Brad was in town. I got it at the drug store."

I shook my head and laughed as I patted Filip's thigh, and I said, "Filip, Jack and I really want to stop at a pharmacy to buy some gum. Is there one right around here?"

178

He looked at me. "Beautiful, there's gum right in my glove box. Help yourself."

"No, no, Filip. This is a special kind of gum that we want. You don't have to come in. I'll just run in and get it for myself. I'll be quick. Trust me."

He shrugged his shoulders a little and said, "Whatever you want, beautiful. I'm just here to make you happy. Oh here, take some Polish zloty. They may not take euros."

As I swung the pharmacy door open, I could hear Filip wolf-whistle me. I didn't turn around to face him; I just wriggled my ass for him to let him know that I appreciated his interest. I was on a mission to buy condoms for my responsible sis, and this was no time to get sidetracked.

I jumped back into the car and looked back at Jack. "We're good to go."

As Filip grabbed the gear shift, he leaned over to kiss me on the cheek and said, "I'm the slow cousin. Jakub just told me what kind of gum you were looking for. Duh. But please know that when you're out with me, I've got you covered. Always."

***

I had never had such a fun day in my whole life. Jakub and Filip were the best. They were so witty and energetic and sexy. They hugged us; they kissed us; they smooched and spoiled us throughout the day. They had me banging down the targets at the shooting range like I was a sharpshooter from the old west. We rode every ride, some of them twice. We ate all the food that county fair offered, including the Polish sausage complete with sauerkraut, and Jacquie even won Jakub a teddy bear in the dart throw.

True to their word, the boys set up the press and it all went off without a hitch. I asked Jakub not to tell the press about our playground deal and suggested that we save it for a future press release once we had signed the deal. But I insisted that the press knew of the nature of our visit, which was to visit my Jewish grandma's dairy farm. I made sure that the reporters had spelled out our names and our specified credentials to my liking. Jack wanted to see their notes to make sure that they didn't use the word 'Negro' anywhere.

I watched them out of the corner of my eye for a few moments as we stood in line to go on the Ferris wheel. Finally, I gave them a little wave and a smile, and that's all they needed. The three little teenage girls, just a little older than

Martina and Zalia, approached me and asked in their halted English if they could take my picture with the three of them. Jacquie jumped in and the five of us posed and clowned around for a multitude of phone cameras that seemed to appear out of nowhere.

It was dark by the time we made it to the dance tent. It was a hot, slow, sexy dance, and I could feel his big erection grinding up against me. Oh my God, he felt so good. His tongue was in my mouth, and his hand was on my ass. My panties, I knew, were wet right through. He dragged me back to our table where Jacquie was all over Jakub and his hand was down the ass of her jeans. He came up for air and said to Filip, "Filip, we need to show our girls Blueberry Hill. I mean, after all, they can't go back home without experiencing laying out under the big blanket of stars on Blueberry Hill, can they?"

As we were once again buckling up in the convertible, I said to them, "So it's called Blueberry Hill. Is there a big blueberry business here in town?"

With that, the boys broke out into laughter, and Filip kissed me and said, "No, beautiful. It's just that over all the years, that big old hill has been responsible for many, many, many of us finding our thrill on Blueberry Hill, you know, like the old Fats Domino song."

With that, the four of us broke out into the song as if we had sung the old '50s American blues tune our whole lives.

***

As Filip popped the trunk to bring out two blankets, he said, "This hill has been here for lovers, years and years and years before your family farmed down below it. I can assure you, beautiful, that your grandma had her fair share of nights on Blueberry Hill, finding her thrill, the same as her parents before her, even though it must have had another name back in the '30s and '40s."

I said, "Well, that makes it a family tradition. I can't wait. Do you know any star constellations? I want you to show me the Big Dipper. Are you up for it?"

Jacquie and I had a quick moment to ourselves as I passed her half of the condoms out of the box, and the boys were polite enough to give us a little space. Jakub held Jacquie's hand all the way up the big hill in the dark, and every time she would turn around to look at me, we would break out laughing like schoolgirls. Jakub reassured Filip that he had lots of his own gum and wanted to know if Filip wanted any.

We divvyed up the six-pack of beer, and Jack and Jakub took one side of the knoll, and Filip and I took the other side. Once in a while, their laughter would float over to us, and Filip would call out to them to keep it down; they were spoiling the mood. And then it would be us, questioning which one of them was the screamer. And the sex. Oh my God. I never knew that sex could be like that. I surprised myself at being so uninhibited, laying there totally naked under the stars, whispering to my lover where to touch me and where to kiss me. I howled with laughter as I spilled the can of beer all down the front of me, and Filip licked it off, saying it was the best beer he'd ever had.

All I said was that I wondered how Polish sausage tasted with a beer marinade, and he asked me in a soft whisper if he could show me how they do it on Blueberry Hill. I learned a lot from my skillful, caring lover that night as I had peeled out of my shyness right along with my clothes. At one point, I looked down at Filip, with his arms holding my ass as I pumped him, and I leaned forward and giggled into his mouth. "Filip, you have no idea how good you make me feel." For some reason, the Canadian singer, Shania Twain's, song, *Man! I Feel Like A Woman!* came to mind, and I whispered a couple of lines of it.

He said out loud to the voices behind us, "Jakub, you know the song, I Feel Like A Woman – give us the first stanza."

I don't know who was the loudest. I think it was Jacquie. The four of us belted out the song like there was no tomorrow. It was the perfect song for the perfect occasion.

***

Here I was, 35-years-old, a black Jew, in a town in Poland that had forgotten Jews a long time ago and had yet to know any black folks. And yet, under those rather bleak circumstances, I was having the time of my life. I was being tended to very skillfully by my third lover in my 35 years, and I was making plans to not wait so long for my fourth. It felt so good to have this kind of fun, spontaneous, and carefree sex without a care in the world. Of course, I knew that tomorrow I was back to my regular life of being mommy to my three beautiful children and daddy's little girl, but for right now, I was going to enjoy every moment that my eager, confident, young lover could bestow upon me. I meant it wholeheartedly as I whispered in his ear, "Filip, baby, you're the best! Show me how to get you big and hard again. You make me feel so good. I need to feel you inside me – again."

***

Just before we packed up to leave, there was one poignant note between Jack and myself that I'll never forget. I'm not sure if the Polish boys really got the significance of what Jack was talking about, but it wasn't lost on me. It happened when we were all laughing at the same time and I heard Jack call out from the other side of the knoll, "Hey, guys, you see the very, very bright, lead star out there? Yeah, the brightest one. That's called the North Star. And way, way back in the day, when my people were making their way out of slavery to freedom on the Underground Railroad, they used the North Star to guide them up north to Canada. My people knew way back then that Canada was the North Star, just like I know now. And during the war, the Polish Jews named a warehouse in Auschwitz *Kanada* because they thought that Canada was the land of plenty. So, right at this very moment, this big North Star up above us has just confirmed everything for me. I've just decided that I'm going to apply for Canadian citizenship just as soon as I can. I'm going to become a Canadian."

***

We stood on the sidewalk in front of our little hotel and waved to the boys as they drove up the street and out of sight.

I put my arm around Jack and I said, "Jack, I'll never be able to repay you for being here for me over the past few days."

"Aw, shucks. It was nothing. I'm just a big, bossy, Negro nurse taking care of my sister who's a Negro Jewish lawyer."

As she pressed the elevator button, she said, "But you know, Nigella, all kidding aside, I'm a teensy-weensy bit worried about you."

"Me? Why?"

"It's this way, honey. Your baby brother died not that long ago. Your husband died a short eight weeks ago. Your in-laws died eight weeks ago. A devastating fire is as bad as a death. Over the past few days, you've witnessed six million Jews being murdered. It's a big shock to my system, let alone yours. I'm just tagging along for the ride, but you, honey, you're experiencing all this firsthand. You're carrying a lot on your shoulders right now, and the grieving process is very, very sneaky. You think you're okay, and all of a sudden you're in a big emotional mess that can really do some serious damage."

"Do you think I'm a meshuggeneh? Don't you think I should have gone up to Blueberry Hill?"

"What do I know, Sis? Speaking for myself, it was the best night of sex I've ever had, and it sounds like yours too, but, really, I think we were just acting out a little, trying to overcome all the horror we saw up at Auschwitz-Birkenau and Bergen-Belsen. Thank God that we hooked up with two, fine, caring gentlemen. What I'm trying to say is when we get back home, I want you to start seeing a doctor so that you can sort through all your grief in a nice, safe manner."

"But you're my grief counsellor, and we work together so well."

"No, no. Don't give me any bullshit. I'm your friend, I'm not the medical professional that you could benefit from. Please. I love you. I don't want you to fuck this up. I want you to stay strong for your own sake."

I gave her a big hug and said, "I love you, Jacqueline Dixon. It was the best day of my life when I met you at the pool at Disney World."

"Yeah. Just remember, Your Majesty, I let you win that swim race because I felt sorry for you having to live your sorry life with all those African blonde ringlets and those disgustingly long, long legs. You've got enough of a burden to carry."

Jack was a lot like Mom, in that she always had to have the last word.

She added in, "But seriously, Nigella, I think your troubles started long before François died. I think you've been grieving your lost marriage ever since the twins were born. And then, a few months ago, fucking the sleazy professor on the edge of your desk, well, that's not who you really are at all, honey. That little episode was definitely tied into grieving your dead marriage. You just didn't know it at the time."

I laughed a little. "You're probably right, Jack. But the good news is that I don't go all crazy and fall in love or anything like that. I know the scoop. Think about it; today with the tall blond Polish lawyer, tooling around in his fancy

Benz. He's just a facsimile of that first sleazy professor underneath his blond fabulousness. But a much, much better lover, for sure."

She laughed and hugged me. "Hey, us two widows need the occasional lover to scratch our itch. Don't start dissing the Polish sausage boys. Today was a day I'll never forget in my whole life. Even better than the month of phone sex with Brad."

"Really? That good?"

"No comparison."

"But what about the night you spent with Brad at the Four Seasons?"

"Nah. By that time, we had become such good friends that we spent most of the night talking about his ex-wives and my sad, disabled, war-vet husband. Mind you, the sex was good. But when friends-with-benefits' pure sex turns into something akin to making love, it's time to say goodbye. You've gotta know when to hold 'em and when to fold 'em."

"Jack, you're too much."

"I know, honey. I know."

***

Within 15 minutes, we both had quick showers, and we were in bed, sound asleep, with our African curls still full of grass and the smaller twigs from Blueberry Hill.

My heart was full of love for all the wonderful people that I had met and shared lives with over the past few days. It was a time in my life that I would treasure for always.

***

Little did I know that at the very same time I was taking my shower in Poland, Maureen was tiptoeing into hers back at the château. The handsome boy, Lucas, who worked at the stables, who had been teaching her as well as the children to ride over the past week, had taken Maureen out on a date that night. Mom and Dad had waved them off as Lucas pulled Maureen up onto his horse behind him so that she could ride bareback with him, just like Hiawatha and Minnehaha would have done. He had planned a night-time picnic, complete with his guitar, down at a little campsite that he had prepared just for

184

the two of them. Mom had made sure that Maureen packed the same kind of gum that I had bought earlier in the day to take along on her first date, just as Jack and I would have done if we had been there.

As it turned out, Maureen laid there under the very stars that I had and marveled at the fact that she was a virgin no longer. She smiled up at Lucas and told him that she wanted to try it on top this time. She was getting into the swing of things, you might say.

***

It was our last day of holidays at the château, and the whole afternoon was nothing but, "Mommy, Mommy, look at me!" coming from the kids. Lucas and Maureen had set up a big portion of the front lawn to showcase the children's new skills that they had been working on. They had built a bit of a riding ring, and the two horses and two ponies were still grazing on the front lawn. I laughed as a big bay mare lifted her tail and deposited a huge pile of fertilizer on the beautiful grounds. It didn't seem to phase Edouard or Catharine in the least. Little Noah forgot to hold on when he was up there on his pony and took a dive. He scrambled back on the pony and remembered to wave with just one hand after that first tumble. At my insistence, Mom got on the big mare and showed us how to clear a couple of jumps that Lucas had set up, so of course Martina wouldn't rest until she too could manage a bit of a jump. I looked over at Dad and he was just bursting with pride. He loved all of us so much. As he would often say, "How did I get so lucky? How did I get so damn lucky?"

The badminton net was set up, and Edouard and Dad had to step over and around the little boys as they lobbed the birdie in the main direction of the net against Mom and Catharine.

All the art easels were up, and the art teacher had set up a clothes line affair, and all the art was flapping gently from the clothespins. As I took a close look at all the art, it was very evident that one of my boys had a talent. The teacher explained to me that he had watched her mix the paint, and without saying a word, he was grabbing the paint brush and swiping big splashes of perfectly mixed colors, one up beside the other, as if he was a veteran painter. Of course, she didn't know if it was Noah or Warren, but one of them showed a lot of promise. Dad's art too was quite good, although he had never had any lessons in his whole life.

We had a big picnic supper outside in the middle of it all, and as soon as the sun went down, Maureen brought out the four sleeping bags and the kids were allowed to sleep out around the campfire but only if they were all good. The four of them were dead to the world by 20:45 p.m., and Maureen announced that she was officially off duty for the rest of the night. She snuggled down into Lucas's lap, and then the adults started the storytelling.

***

Jack and I were already in bed, and for whatever reason, the two of us couldn't sleep. It was our last night at the château, and we had all turned in early.

We tiptoed down the big staircase in our pajamas, holding onto our running shoes to take a last stroll under the stars. We opened the big, double, ten-foot doors, and old Patou, who slept right there, didn't even give us as much as a woof. I guess he was tired out after having all the kids and us around over the past week. He'd had enough.

The courtyard's pea-gravel was loud under our feet, so Jack motioned to the center of the great lawn that stretched all the way out to the big main gates at the end of the drive. Both of us felt the same way. Our walk out there was somehow sacred. Too sacred to spoil with talk. We walked in silence, listening to the night life around us. The crickets, the frogs, the fireflies were all a part of the music. They were communicating their night moves. It was a ten-minute walk, and we reached the black wrought-iron fence to turn around for our last look where, as Noah had said the week before, the fairytale princess lived.

I stood there, and I could make out the hulking form of the château in the dark summer night in the distance. A thousand stars were bouncing off the tiled turrets.

The center lawn was shining with the night's dew, and we could hear the resident owl from up in the fir trees over on the west lawn. It hooted, *"Whoo. Whoo. Whooooooo."*

All of a sudden, there was a definite conversation being held to the left of us in the dark, near the pond. Jack's eyes widened as we both realized that we were encroaching on someone's private moment and that we should just keep quiet so as to not steal their privacy from them.

The pond was where all nature's music was stemming from, so we were pretty sure that the voices there wouldn't have heard us walking along the dewy lawn.

We didn't want to listen, but there we were, smack dab in the middle of it. The two of us had to hold onto each other as we were shaking with our silent laughter as we heard the woman say, "Nigie, Nigie, don't cum yet. I want it to last all night long; oh, baby, baby, and I'm so ready for you. You're my man and I need you."

The deep baritone pleaded, "Hey, hey, whoa, baby. Nice and easy, honey, I want to last for you. I love you. Cum for me, baby. I want to make you feel good. Oh, honey, you make me crazy."

She cried, "Nigie…ohhhhh…Nigieeeee. Ohhhhhh – ohhhhh…Nigieeeee."

***

Jack and I never spoke of our accidental eavesdropping incident again. The four of us, the squad, as Dad called us, talked about sex all the time, and even over the past days since we had been home back at the château, Mom, Catharine, Maureen, Jack, and I had shared every moment and every move that the young stable guy, Lucas, had laid on the virginal, good, Catholic girl, Maureen, as well as all the Polish sausage that Jack and I had sampled. But that was fair game. That was just sex. What Jack and I witnessed that night out on the great lawn between Mom and Dad was lovemaking. And that was strictly off limits in everyone's book.

Maybe, just maybe, I'd be lucky enough to find a love like that someday.

***

It seemed to all of us that Jacquie and Zalia had been with us forever. We couldn't separate the girls, and Jack and I were just as bad. The twins liked having them with us, and they were quite savvy at both answering to both of their names, as most of the time, none of us knew who was who. They were only three years old, but they knew how to work it. I think it helped them get through the initial stage of missing their dad. Maureen and Mom rounded out the 'squad,' as Dad called us, so it all helped with Mom's grieving the loss of my in-laws a great deal. Jacquie had followed through with her decision to immigrate to Canada, so Dad was helping her with that. She had enrolled in the government-sponsored program for internationally trained medical professionals to get her equivalency, and she had secured an invitation from Sick Kids Hospital to complete her internship with them and to start applying for jobs with them as soon as she was through her equivalency and once her work permit came through.

Dad had insisted to Maureen that he would be over every morning to see that the children got off to school and I worked on the paperwork to wrap up all the legalities surrounding the deaths as well as the charred remains of the farm. We hired Mom's old friend, Tom Oliver, to assemble a crew to work on clearing the farm land with plans for reforestation as soon as the town permits were secured. None of us had the guts to consider starting the apiary business up again, but it was therapeutic in a way, just to clear the land and leave it to heal itself.

***

Mrs. Bosworth had her no-nonsense face on as she cut a deal with the girls. She looked from one face to the other, "Okay, Martina and Zalia, from what I understand, you're asking me if the two of you can sit beside each other for grade five, since Zalia is new to our school and since, Martina, you're looking out for her."

Martina quickly spoke up, sounding more like me than I cared to admit, "Yes, Mrs. Bosworth, and trust me, there won't be any trouble. We'll be so good, you won't even know we're in your class."

The stern old teacher had trouble keeping the smile down. "What? You mean you're not going to contribute anything at all? You're just going to sit there like a pair of duds?"

Both girls started to giggle as they sensed the teacher was about to grant them their request. Mrs. Bosworth softened ever so slightly, and she turned to focus on her new student, "And you, Zalia. I've had the chance to look over your grade-four report card from Miami, Florida, and it looks like I'm going to be counting on you to help me out when the odd student needs a little help.

188

You're very bright and you have such nice manners. If I call on you to help out, will you do that?"

Zalia was beaming. "Yes, Mrs. Bosworth. I'm good at writing on the board. And I'm taking French lessons at home, because we went to France this summer and I want to speak French like the rest of the family."

"Well, I think we should give your requested seating arrangement a try, girls, but don't think for a moment you can take advantage of this one favor."

She continued, "And meanwhile, to the four of you, Mrs. Hansson, Mrs. Dixon, Martina, and Zalia, I know that the fire at your farm and losing Mr. Hansson and his parents happened way back in June, but I just want to tell you that I'm here and our school counsellor is here as well if any of you want to talk things over with us. And that includes you, Zalia. I understand that your dad died last year, so both you and Martina will be coming into grade five missing your dads. We have lots of students here in the school with only one parent, so you're not alone. And you can tell me anything at all."

She turned to Martina and on a brighter note said, "Martina, ever since you joined our school four years ago, we've all enjoyed having you and your whole family here so much. Remember the day that your granddad brought your dog in so that you could show the class his tricks? How is he, anyway? Is he still behaving himself?"

I piped up, "Who? The dog or the granddad?"

We all laughed and that was the end of our preschool visit to meet the teacher, and we were all set for grade five. Zalia and Martina raced ahead and hopped on their bikes, and Jack and I stood there, catching up on all our news with Mrs. Bosworth. Ever since I had come to Canada, she always made a point of asking me how my studies were going after Martina told her that I was going to school and I was studying 'ladies who got into trouble and had to go to jail.' I filled her in on Jacquie going back to school to get her Canadian equivalency for pediatric-nurse practitioner and she added, "Well, your two daughters are bright enough to help you both with your homework. They're going to rule the world one of the days."

Before we left her, Mrs. Bosworth confirmed that I could send over Martina and Zalia's birthday-party invitations for her to hand out. She assured me that no one would be left out. Martina's birthday party at her granddad's house had become a bit of a tradition over the past four years, and lucky for us, Zalia's birthday was in September as well.

***

Dad's birthday party for the two girls was quite an event. As in previous years, the parents and Martina's, and now Zalia's classmates as well, were out in full force, but this year we had Jacquie and Zalia to introduce around. It took some of the sting away from missing François and his parents. Dad had become pretty good friends with Alessandro, so that was very helpful for him, as it had always been Dad and his best friend, Chi Tran, that had taken care of setting everything up. I was a little concerned as I looked across the backyard to see Rabbi Kleiman standing there talking to some of the parents. He had aged a lot over the year, and I hadn't noticed until now. Of course, he must have been about 80 years old at the time, but, still, I felt a quick pang as I noticed how his shoulders were thinning out, just like all elderly men's physiques change with ageing. I was so grateful that Jacquie had come into my life. There she was, right by my side to help me through all the emotion as the parents of all Martina and Zalia's classmates came up to me, one by one, to offer their condolences for my loss. On the other hand, it was a fun, noisy afternoon, and everyone had a great time. Mom and Dad were such excellent hosts, and, as usual, they had hired a kid's party-planning organization to help out with the food and entertainment.

I was just standing there alone, looking around the big crowd, when my eyes wandered back to the big, old maple where François and I had been married a short four years ago. I wheeled around, keeping my head down so no one could see my tears. By the time I made it down the side hall and into the laundry room, I was having a hard time breathing. Fucking grief. It just sneaks up on you. I grabbed a piece of paper toweling and was blowing my nose when I sensed someone behind me.

He was standing in the doorway, just looking helpless and impossibly handsome as he stood there watching me. "Nigella, I'm sorry. I didn't mean to sneak up on you. I saw you rush out of the party, and I thought maybe I could help in some small way."

He stepped into the room, and all of a sudden, I was in his arms, crying all over his shirt. "Oh, Alessandro, I'm sorry that you're seeing me like this. Every once in a while, it just hits me that my husband and his parents aren't here to see the kids having such fun. My husband may have been a bastard, but his parents were the finest people on earth."

190

He whispered, "*Bella, bella*, it's okay. It's okay. You need to cry, and scream, and shout all you want. It's tough, but let me tell you, you're doing an amazing job. And I'm here for you."

He wiped the tears off my face and smiled a little. "Even Wonder Woman needs time out once in a while you know. Hey, I just thought of something I can do for you the next time a certain situation comes up."

I sniffled and looked into his handsome face which had changed from a caring, loving face into a face that was about to impart a little humor.

He said, "Look at my foot, *bella*. It's a surgical plastic toe with a 23-inch aluminum post. Next time you go kicking the spokes out of a car wheel, call me. I'll be happy to do that little job for you. We can't have you spoiling those long, long beautiful legs of yours in a fit of temper, can we?"

I struggled to get out of his arms that were holding me ever so gently so he couldn't see me smiling at his little joke, and I said as I squeezed past him, "Don't you have a party to go to, or, even better, papers to grade, Professor?"

***

Chapter Twelve
Addendum: The Molecular Biologist

"Oh," he said to himself, "this looks interesting." The email was an Ancestry.co.uk alert which indicated that possibly some long-lost family member who was registered with the worldwide genealogy site was looking for him.

He gave an exasperated sigh after reading it over for the third time. It must be some kind of mistake. The email turned out to be an invitation to go to a Kaufman reunion in October, in Toronto, Canada.

He leaned back in his chair and lifted his arms up and said out loud to his computer, "My name's Hansson, not Kaufman, you robotic piece of crap! Get your records straight!"

With that, as he was shutting everything down, he gave the email a small bit of recognition; at least the computer had given a date and place that fit right into his schedule. He was due in Toronto in October to accept an award for work done in Brazil the year before.

He got up and wandered over to the window. It was late, well after midnight as he looked down onto the rainy streets of Oxford, England. He admitted to himself that his latest appointment with Oxford was not all that it cracked to be. He was bored. Bored out of his mind. He'd much rather be working in the field. Fuck this seemingly esteemed life of a molecular-biologist professor at Oxford. It wasn't for him. Perhaps he had made a big mistake in leaving Stockholm years ago. He should have known better. He had accepted many offers around the world during his career, but the bloom went off the rose every goddamn time, for this reason or that. He had squandered his youth wandering from place to place, always with his nose in a book, never quite fitting in but not willing to quit the gig either. He tried going back home; to settle back in Stockholm, but you know what they say, *you can never go back*. And the fairer sex – well, that was just another disappointment. He couldn't really put his finger on it, but he just never found the love of his life, it seemed. He was just too fussy, it seemed. A fussy, aging, old nerd that enjoyed his lab more than the company of a good woman, it seemed.

It wasn't that he really regretted his time spent at Oxford. It was actually a very prestigious position. But there was just something missing. And, for some reason, he couldn't face signing the papers that had been sitting on his desk for a month now. These papers, upon his signature, would confirm that he would stay on in the new year, which, at that time, seemed like a lifetime away.

***

He had been a good son, an only child to his Swedish parents who had adopted him as a baby when they were in their late 30s. They had moved to England with Dad's job once he was in settled in postgrad studies in Stockholm. They settled in nicely and never returned back to Sweden. Earlier this year, he had got them into in a nice senior's residence in London, and both of them, turning 80 this year, appeared to be in good health and very happy with their circumstances. At least he did that right.

Throughout his career and solitary lifestyle, he had moved from place to place, country to country, always looking for something that he couldn't put his finger on. Never married, no kids, no family, and few friends. It all added up to a lonely lifestyle, a Ph.D. hanging on the wall, along with a hell of a pile of awards and honorariums for scientific discoveries in the field of biology.

The next morning, over his first coffee, he clicked on his personal email as an afterthought and was surprised to see a second alert from Ancestry.co.uk.

"Oh! Now this is more like it! This is what we're talkin' about!" It was, what the Ancestry gene pool calls, a 'match.'

The 'match' indicated that it was a close relative, and he or she had applied through Ancestry.ca a few months ago. He or she lived in Toronto, Ontario, and the last name, strangely enough, was Kaufman. Could it be possible that it was a relative from his birthmother or father who he never knew? On the other hand, Kaufman was a Jewish name, and he was a black man. Even his adoptive parents, the Hanssons, were a white couple. He smiled wryly to himself. That narrowed the genetic field down considerably; how many black Jews with the name of Kaufman could there be?

193

Many, many years ago, when he had tried to find out who his birthparents were, the Swedish Children's Aid had told him that the file was closed, meaning that there were no records available to him. At the time, he accepted that and went on with his life, thankful for the wonderful parents that had adopted him as a baby. He had never given it another thought.

He stood there, lost in thought, when his phone rang. He said a quiet 'good morning' to the caller and, at the same time, clicked on 'shut down' and grabbed a jacket for his daily morning walk to Oxford.

**

Canada's famous maples were putting on a show with their reds and oranges. It was October, and he could hear the leaves crunching under his feet as he cut through the park en route to the University of Toronto to check out the Ancestry.ca Kaufman invitation that he had received months ago.

He thanked the friendly woman at the Ancestry.ca sign-in desk for the Sharpie and wrote his name in bold letters on the supplied paper name-badge, *Lars Hansson*. He strolled up the hall toward the conference room, hands in pockets, trying to look at ease. He was shy to say the least, and usually he had an assistant with him to break the ice.

He took a deep breath and stepped into the room. Most of the people milling around were either very old and accompanied by their 60-year-old children or by their 30-year-old grandchildren. He supposed, that with a name like Kaufman, they were looking for Survivors' family units from the Holocaust days of the '30s and '40s.

He was making his way to the bar at the other end of the room, when someone, not watching where they were going, bumped into him from behind.

"Oh, I'm so sorry. I'm so clumsy, excuse me!"

He turned to put a face to the female's husky voice. He drew in his breath and just stood there, unable to speak. She was almost as tall as him, so they were pretty well nose to nose. Her hair, a magnificent bundle of blonde African ringlets, created a huge halo around her breathtakingly beautiful face.

As he was recovering, she smiled, and he was once again overwhelmed and completely tongue-tied.

"Are you okay? I'm sorry for bumping into you. Oh, where are my manners?" With that, she stuck out her hand. His, on autopilot, reached out to receive it.

"My name is Nigella Hansson – oh – I see your name badge – your name is Hansson too! Oh! My goodness! And it's spelled the Swedish way! You must be a Swede! Are you a Swede? I know Hansson is a very common surname though. I'm from Stockholm, where are you from?"

He nodded, unable to tear his eyes away from her smile, wanting to speak but unable to do so.

Her eyebrows raised ever so slightly, indicating that he was supposed to say something.

"Oh!" his voice finally burst forward, "no, no not at all. Wait. I mean to say yes. I'm a Swede. But I meant that it's not your fault. I'm never sure where I'm going, and I must have stepped back instead of going forward. Excuse me. And, yes, indeed, my name is Lars Hansson, and yes, I'm a Swede. But I don't live there. In Sweden I mean. I live in the U.K." He realized he was still holding onto her hand, so he dropped it like a hot potato, totally embarrassed with his awkwardness.

They just stood there, looking into each other's face, when the beauty leaned her head back and let loose with a big gutsy laugh with such amazing ease. It was contagious. He found himself laughing right along with her. He hoped to hell she was laughing with him and not at him.

She waved her two free-drink tickets that came with admission in front of his face and said, "If you accompany me to the bar, I'll buy the first round."

He was a goner. Here he stood, a very-well-established 40-year-old scientist that had earned awards around the world for his work in the field of molecular biology, and he was tongue-tied beyond belief. The most beautiful woman in the world was offering to buy him a drink.

She was a skilled communicator, and, coupled with her warmth, wit, and charm, he found himself inexplicitly talking a mile a minute. It turned out that they had both graduated from the same university in Stockholm with their undergraduate degrees, him five years before her, before him splitting off into science and her into law. So, she had brains as well as beauty. What a package!

After some time, she leaned in a little and said, "I'm sure you've noticed, but I'd like to comment on the fact that I'm pretty certain that we were the only two black students that our university ever graduated, aren't we? Stockholm, back then, didn't have what you would call a diverse population. Actually," she continued, "I must clarify. I'm not really black. I'm biracial, hence the lighter skin tones and the almost-blonde hair. I get my African curls though from my Jamaican-Canadian father. My mother was born in a displaced person's camp right after the war. She grew up in an orphanage in Stockholm as Martina Hansson, but her birth name was Martyna Kaufman. What about you? Where do you get your handsome looks from?"

Lars replied, "I never knew my birthparents. I was adopted by a Swedish couple as a baby. But, after looking all over the world for people that look similar to me, I think you can safely say that at the very least, one of my parents must have been a person of color, don't you agree?"

His dream-woman was saying in wonderment, "This is amazing. We have the same African hair, and we have the same accent. It's been so long since I've heard that accent! I'm a little homesick all of a sudden! I love the way you sound!"

He started to laugh. "Well, we do sound exactly alike. I'm happy that you like my accent, but I'm thinking here – I guess that means that you like to hear yourself talk, am I right?"

"Are you making fun of me?"

"How perceptive; you catch on quickly, Nigella!" he teased.

He gathered up his courage, and, with his fingers crossed, he asked a polite yet very pointed question, "What about your husband, is he a Swede? Is he a black man too?"

She laughed a little, recognizing his interest in her marital status, and she said softly, "No, my husband was Asian-Canadian. His parents were Vietnamese boat people that came to Canada back in the '70s. And, a second no in answer to your question if I'm married. I'm not married. I'm a widow; my husband died in an accident a while ago."

"Oh my God! I'm so sorry!" Lars responded.

"Oh, please, please. It's okay. It's okay. I've come to terms with it, and I have wonderful parents that live two blocks from me, and they pamper me every day. Now what about you? Do you live with your wife in the U.K., and where, exactly, in the U.K. do you live?"

Lars eagerly responded, "No, no wife. I'm a bachelor. Never married. I live in Oxford where I teach."

As the afternoon flew by, she flashed one of her million-dollar smiles and said, "Lars, I'm going to be very bold here and make a suggestion. Please don't feel obliged to say yes. It's just that I'm enjoying your company so much, and our hosts are going to be kicking us all out shortly. Here's what I propose. First, let's both run around the room here and check all the nametags and ask all the questions as to why we are here and as to who we are looking for. That is, you're looking for your birthparents' family, and I'm looking for my birthmother's family, right? Secondly, let's meet back here at the bar in say 15 minutes so I can ask you if you'd like to come home with me and have dinner with me and my parents. What do you think?"

He couldn't believe his ears. She was suggesting that he meet her parents. Oh my God, had she read his mind as he imagined her in a white dress walking down the aisle to meet him at the altar? He responded with, "Brilliant! See you in 15!"

As she lightly put her hand on his arm, he felt his face flush. She said with a wicked smile on her face, "Good. Don't be late now, handsome."

He was grinning like a fool as he watched her halo of curls bouncing as she walked away from him.

All of a sudden, she wheeled around and walked quickly back to him, saying, "Are you a vegetarian? Mom will want to know what you like. She's a fabulous cook and will make you anything at all."

He stared at her and thought to himself, *This just keeps getting better and better*. "I eat everything and anything. But I must confess, I absolutely love chocolate ice-cream."

She smiled and blonde ringlets jiggled from side to side, and she shook her head. "My kind of man," was all she said. She nodded quickly and wheeled back around, pulling out her phone as she walked. My God, her legs went on and on for miles. And that ass! What a combination!

He wandered through the crowd, berating himself for giving her the childish choice of chocolate ice-cream. Determined to calm down, he attempted to focus on the crowd for some glimmer into why he had received notices and alerts as to the Kaufman family name. A few minutes later, after hurriedly making the rounds, he admitted to himself that he'd had lost interest in all things unrelated to the blonde bombshell that had befriended him. He hadn't the slightest inclination to spoil his romantic thoughts by being jarred out of it by trying to sort out his puzzling invitation to a Kaufman reunion.

"Since dinner is at seven, Nigella, may I suggest we get a drink somewhere around here before we hop in a taxi? I don't want to arrive too early and interrupt your parent's afternoon. And you're sure that I shouldn't go back to the hotel to change into a jacket?"

"Absolutely no to the jacket idea. You're perfect just the way you are. And about the drink; it sounds like a good idea, Lars, however, I'm not much of a drinker, and there'll be plenty of wine over dinner. Could you settle for *Starbucks*? It's right across the street from us, and I'd love to hear more about your work."

***

He stopped himself midsentence and said, "Enough about me. Tell me about your dissertation, mystery woman. And tell me about your parents. Help me out here; I'm going to their home, and I don't even know their names. What do they do? Are they Canadian or Swedes living in Canada?"

He listened as she started sharing small tidbits about her parents. They were Canadians, her father was a retired Supreme Court Justice, and her mother was technically her stepmother, as her birthmother had died some years ago in Stockholm. The current 'Mom,' as she referred to her, was a novelist whose publisher was always hounding her for another book. She kept it simple, but he read between the lines enough to know that she loved them fiercely.

She went on her explanation that her academic work's original research was based on Canadian women in jail. He smiled as she lifted her hand up in the air as if she was writing on a blackboard, and as her hand wrote in invisible ink, she called out: *Anthology: Stories Told by Canadian Incarcerated Women.* She lowered her hand, leaned in a little, and said, "What do you think?"

As they were leaving the coffee shop to catch a taxi, she wrapped up the conversation with a little laugh and said, "There's not enough time to tell you about my best friend, Jacquie, but trust me, you'd love her. She's the best. But we'll save that story for another day. Dinner awaits."

***

The taxi dropped them off in front of a beautiful home complete with an amazing, well-cared-for front garden. It was obvious from the façade of the big home that someone in the family was doing very, very well for themselves. Nigella deftly punched in a code to open the front door. As she opened the door, it sounded a chime. He froze for a moment and stepped back, trying to gather his composure.

He was facing a huge, very quiet, white dog with very serious brown eyes that were glued to his. She leaned over to give the monstrosity a hug around his massive chest. The dog didn't take his eyes off him as he said timidly, "Hello, boy. What's your name?"

Nigella said, "This is Patou. Don't worry, he's friendly; he just looks scary, that's all."

As he tentatively patted the guard's head, he looked up as the two parents made their way to the front door. He could see immediately where his dream woman got her big smile from. He shook her dad's hand as the man that looked like he could be his own father grinned from ear to ear.

He said in a booming voice, "So pleased to meet you, Lars. Let me take your coat. This is my wife, Denni."

As he shook the father's hand, he wondered what had happened to his left cheek. It looked like an old scar, but it was still quite evident. It was shaped like a hook and followed his high cheekbone, and it covered most of his closely shaved cheek. Other than that, he was a very handsome man; a black man with skin tones very similar to his own. He wore his thick, African, graying hair similar to Lars, a little longer, almost a shaggy look on top, but a trimmed nape that spoke to a good barber somewhere in the mix. His jet-black eyebrows that framed obvious intelligence showing in his dark brown eyes. He was, no doubt, a man that took good care of himself.

It wasn't lost on Lars that in some strange way, he and the father looked alike. Perhaps it was just their dark skin and African hair, or maybe it was the thick, black eyebrows. He felt a little like a fool though, as he noticed that the father was wearing the identical vee-neck navy sweater to his. *Strange,* he thought to himself before turning to the mother who was speaking to him.

"Welcome, Lars. We're so glad that you could join us. Nothing too fancy on the menu tonight, Coquille St. Jacques, then roast chicken. Are you okay with shellfish, Lars? Is this your first time in Toronto?"

Remembering his manners, he bent down to untie his Doc Martins as his dream woman right beside him zipped out of her thigh-high boots. He looked up to see the mother smiling a little, watching him ogle her daughter's long, beautiful legs. He chastised himself, *Down, Hansson, down! Behave! Fuck, man!*

He walked through the big, beautiful living room, guided by the mom who had her hand resting on his back, like she had known him all his life. He asked her about a Simon Bull painting that was presenting itself boldly on the designer-white wall, and the mom chatted easily.

He looked at her as she talked. She was also a beauty, but in a different way altogether from her daughter. She was white, with the look of the Irish around her eyes, about 5'7" or 5'8", and definitely much younger than her husband. In fact, she was more his age. Perhaps she was the second or third wife of the old judge. In any case, it looked like she had been spending her husband's money though, according to her longer, gathered-into-soft-pleats, cream-colored, leather skirt that she wore with a matching silk top tucked into it. The outfit allowed her big emerald earrings to act as the showstopper. As he neared the end of his appraisal of her, he checked out her footwear. She definitely had toned her upscale look way, way down. She was walking along in her bare feet, sporting bright red nail lacquer on her well-manicured toes. As he recognized that she was quite twinkly, he had a feeling that she had a very, very big personality. Lars decided that the upscale boho look that she wore so well was no indication whatsoever that she would be a pushover. Quite the opposite; the wife of the old judge would probably be a formidable opponent in any sort of a scuffle. He knew who wore the proverbial pants in that family.

His dream woman was tucked under the arm of the dad, walking ahead of them, and she was calling out to yet another person that was standing in the doorway of yet another room.

Nigella broke out of her dad's hold enough to give the other man a big hug and a kiss. She said, "Lars, I'd like you to meet Rabbi Kleiman. Rabbi, this is Lars Hansson. Lars works in the field of bio-molecular science, and he's in town in from the U.K."

"Please call me David, Lars," the rabbi was saying as he eagerly pumped his arm with a firm handshake. He smiled as he noticed Lars's lookalike navy sweater and he reached over and pulled the hem of Nigel's sweater with a tug.

"Looks like I didn't get the memo!" He gave a big laugh as he put his arm around Lars's shoulders. "Come on in. Now, what are you drinking? I'm acting as the official barkeep tonight."

***

As they all sat together, on two big leather sofas in the beautiful room, he couldn't believe his good fortune in meeting this remarkable family, let alone his dream woman. It was very few and far between get-togethers like this when he wasn't bored right out of his mind. Most of the time, he avoided such social interactions like the plague.

This time, he found the conversation entertaining and even bordering on scintillating as the old judge and his young wife told their witty stories of how they met and how they lurched from crisis to crisis, managing to extricate themselves out of one mess and into another. He was a little surprised, as in every story the esteemed Supreme Court Justice came across as a clumsy, bumbling nerd that was saved time and time again by the savvy and knowing younger woman that seemed to dote on him hand and foot. Their deep love for each other was a very rare thing indeed. In fact, he couldn't remember meeting such a devoted couple in his lifetime, except for maybe his parents who were much, much quieter and didn't share the pizzazz of this pair. He had watched them as the evening progressed. The two of them had left the confines of the sofas, and they were back behind the kitchen island. She had her head down, and he was standing close behind her. He had put both his hands into her thick brunette hair, and then, ever so gently, lifted it all up and began to kiss the nape of her neck. It was a long, sexy moment, and Lars felt a little like a peeping Tom of sorts as he watched her close her eyes and lean back a little into his lips.

All of a sudden, Lars felt a pang of loss and regret that he had never found the love of his life, a woman that could not only be his lover but that could take the place of his passion for his world of science that he was so devoted to.

Lars turned his attention to their daughter, and he studied her face intently. Maybe, just maybe, this time.

***

There was some light jazz playing in the background, and the rabbi started telling jokes. Lars was laughing so hard, he felt the tears running down his cheeks, and the dad, the old judge, was literally on the floor, rolling around, with the dog playfully jumping to and away from him, tail wagging and growling in fake distemper. (The dog, not the old judge.)

The mother interjected, "You know, I heard a remarkable story on the news yesterday about a disabled teacher. Did you hear it?" She paused a little before delivering the punch line, "The crossed-eyed teacher couldn't keep track of her pupils."

It was such a silly, politically incorrect schoolgirl joke, but by this time, they were all well beyond the threshold of polite first meetings, and Lars found himself throwing his head back and howling in laughter like he hadn't howled before. He was having the time of his life.

As they all savored the first course, the mother piped up with a routine that all the others around the table, including the rabbi, seemed to be familiar with.

"Okay, everyone, let's start the storytelling. I'll set it up for us. Tell us the story behind the last time and place that you ate Coquilles St. Jacques. Details, man, we need details. You know, use the 5wh formula, meaning who, what, where, when, why, and how."

And so, it began. He surprised himself, actually, by jumping in, feet first, as the dinner progressed, sharing stories of meals that he had had around the world while delivering papers or attending conferences in his field of bio-molecular science. The father was delighted to hear him tell of all the notes that he had made in his little notebook, describing the tastes and flavors of all the delectable food that he had sampled over all the years.

The old judge's big voice boomed out with laughter as he said to his wife who was shaking her head in disbelief, "See, honey, I'm not crazy! Lars does the very same thing as me!"

Nigel continued, "Lars, give me your take on this. Over these past years, I could never break the habit of handwriting in my little notebook. I should have been able to transfer over to using my phone to simply key in the notes, but, for some reason, it's not the same. What about you? How did you make the changeover?"

"No, man, absolutely not! Never, ever! It's pen and ink all the way for me too!"

Denni, the mother, raised her glass and said simply, "Here's to our handsome, nerdy, intellectually burdened note-takers. Gotta love 'em!"

Denni looked at Lars and then at her husband and said on a more serious note, "Excuse me for getting a little personal here, but, Lars, I must ask you, did you notice when you met Nigel that the two of you look like you could be brothers or something!? Are your good looks from your parents being from Jamaica? And, on top of that strange coincidence, may I ask, what's your connection to the Kaufman clan? I thought our beautiful daughter was the only Swedish black Jew that would ever show up at a Kaufman reunion in Canada! And then, to top it all off, you both have the same last name as well as the same African hair! Really, now, what are the chances of this all happening?"

The rabbi added, "Well, when I first met you, Lars, I thought that you looked like Nigella. You could be her brother, never mind Nigel's. Actually, the three of you share the same build too. You're all tall and lanky." He patted his round stomach and said, "Unlike me!"

Lars laughed and was a little surprised at his ease and eagerness to join in the discussion. "It beats me! It's as much a serendipitous mystery to me as it is to all of you!"

Nigel said, "Now, now, Professor. You are a scientist. I doubt very much if you will be able to chock this up to a mistake made in the Ancestry.uk lab. Tell us all what you know for sure."

"All I know is that I'm the luckiest man in the world to have met you all today! May I make a toast to the beautiful woman sitting beside me. The one that bumped into me, insisted on buying me a drink, and then brought me home to meet her parents, all in the same breath."

"To Nigella!" was shouted out by the four of them in unison.

So, Lars began to untangle the mystery by explaining to them that his name Lars Hansson was given to him by his adoptive parents who had adopted him when he was a month old.

Nigella confirmed for everyone that Hansson was a very common name in Sweden, so that part of the mystery was easily solved. He told them that he had joined Ancestry.se in vague hopes of learning something about his birthparents, never dreaming of the email that popped up on his computer, first inviting him to a Kaufman reunion in Canada, and the second alert that told him there was a direct match with a person named 'Kaufman' that lived in Toronto, Canada.

Nigel's arms went up in the air, and he smiled. "Well, there you go! You and Nigella must be related in some way, either through your Hansson name or through Nigella's Kaufman name."

"No, Dad, No! You're not understanding!" Nigella interrupted. She continued, "Okay, between all of us here, we should be able to figure this out. But, Dad, think about it. My name Hansson is not my biological name. It was a name that the government agency in Sweden gave my mother at birth before she was shipped from Poland to the orphanage in Sweden. And Lars's last name, Hansson, is not his biological name either. His adoptive parents gave it to him. He doesn't know his birthparents' names."

"Okay, we'll start with the facts," Lars said. "One, Hansson is my adoptive name, which is very common, and I don't know my birthparents' names. Two, I received one message from Ancestry.ca, inviting me to a Kaufman reunion in Canada. Three, I received a separate, unrelated alert from Ancestry.ca, saying that I had a direct hit which means someone closely related to me within the last two generations, that has Kaufman genes, lives in Toronto, Canada. Four, I checked with the others at the reunion, including Nigella, and none of them that I asked had a hit saying they had a relative that lived in Sweden or anywhere else in Scandinavia."

Nigella spoke up, "So, here's my facts. One, Hansson is also my adoptive name. Two, my mother's middle name was Kaufman which probably was her family name because we know that her mother was a Polish Jew who died giving her birth. Three, I received an invitation to the Kaufman reunion in Canada because, obviously, I have Kaufman blood from Poland. Four, I did not receive a direct hit or any other kind of hit from Ancestry.se, saying that I had a relative at all, either in Sweden or anywhere else in the world."

Nigel, nodded his head. "So, we know that both your names of Hansson is nothing but a coincidence and not a surprising one at that, being that a Swedish adoption played a part on both sides of the equation. We also know that the Kaufman that you are related to, Lars, didn't attend the reunion and hasn't contacted you by email. Nigella, we know that if, in fact, you have any Kaufman relatives alive, they too did not attend the reunion, and they have not contacted you by email either. So, it boils down to if the two of you were related, the Ancestry lab would have alerted both of you as soon as the genes were matched. In summary, it appears that the two of you are not related in any way. Right?"

We all responded by shouting, "Right!" and Nigella added, "Whew. This handsome man that I'm sitting beside is not my cousin or, God forbid, my brother!"

Nigella's mother raised her glass and said, "Let's toast to chance encounters of the best kind." We all raised our glasses and shouted out, "To chance encounters!"

By the end of the evening, Lars couldn't decide who he was infatuated with more, the stunning Swede with the long legs, or her Canadian parents.

***

He was up, pacing back and forth in his hotel room, reviewing the whole night, going over and over again every piece of every conversation and reveling in the fact that they all wanted to attend his award ceremony the next afternoon at University of Toronto where he was receiving an award for work done in Brazil the year before. He had offered to treat to dinner right after the ceremony, so it meant that he would see them all once again before heading back to Oxford. There was only one nagging little thought in the back of his mind that he wasn't really willing to examine right then and there. It definitely deserved a little more time to know for sure what was happening in that particular department.

He fell into bed, tossing and turning, to finally give into his insomnia. He got up once again to face that little thought that he had brushed off over the last few hours. It's not that he didn't believe the little bitchy, nagging message. No, not at all. It was simply because he didn't want to face the truth of the matter at hand.

It all started as Nigella decided to walk him up the street to hail a cab after the best night of his life. They had both laughed as her mother buttoned up his jacket for him like he was a child, saying, "It's cold out, Lars, and we can't have you getting sick now." She had kissed him on the cheek, adding, "Until tomorrow."

It was evident that Nigella felt the same way about him as he felt about her. From the moment they had met that afternoon, until right now, he couldn't dissuade his impetuous dick to behave. He had lugged his huge erection around all afternoon, all through dinner, and although it had simmered down a little as the savvy mother buttoned up his coat, it now looked like Nigella was bound and determined to address their state of affairs head-on. They had barely reached the sidewalk, when she laughed and turned to press up against him. He could feel her thighs against his. She unbuttoned his jacket and slid in closer, her arms reaching around him, her hands sliding up and down the back of his shirt. Lars thought, *'Oh my God, this all feels so good.'*

His erection pressed into her as they shared their first kiss. Her mouth opened to invite his tongue to meet hers. By this time, he had taken his hands out of her hair, and he placed them up under the back of her blouse on her warm, silky skin. His smooth moves were quite foreign to him; it was like he was taking instructions from her tongue as he snapped her bra open.

Lars thought to himself, *'I'm no ladies' man, and I'm not what you'd call a skilled lover. I swear to God, I don't know where my moves are coming from, but she seems more than happy to indulge me.'*

Her breasts were warm, and he felt her nipples harden. He reached back behind him and took her one hand and guided it to his shaft which felt like it was going to explode. He panicked a little, thinking that he may cum right then and there with her touch. One half of his brain was saying, *Whoa, whoa! Down, boy!* and the other half was saying, *What the fuck! Go for it!*

She pulled away from his mouth and laughed a little and teased, "Oh my! You're a big boy! All this for little old me?"

"You talk too much," he said as his hands slid to cup down her ass. He felt like a teenager who was emboldened by getting to second base. Her hands returned to his back once again to pull his shirt out so that she could reach his skin.

It was then that man's worst nightmare came calling while he was making love to her beautiful full lips and her tongue that was definitely speaking the same language as his. When all this hotness and passion was going on in their mouths, all of a sudden, he felt his erection fading away, and his dismay at this sudden turn of events quickly finished it off completely. His tongue became clumsy in her mouth, and it retreated back into home base. He quickly removed his hands from her round, beautiful ass up to the much-safer territory of her glorious blonde African hair, all at the same time trying to ease back a little so she wouldn't notice his flagging manhood. What the fuck!

His lips, by this time, were whispering his lies into her ear, "Baby, baby, I'm sorry. I'm acting like a complete boar. Forgive me. I'm not acting like a gentleman should on his very first date with a beautiful woman at all. I'd better get a taxi before I really mess this up."

She pulled back a little in surprise and looked him right in the eye. She covered well enough, he had to admit, when she said coolly, "Not at all. I was just as bad as you were. And, besides, it's late." She gave him a quick little kiss on the lips and ended by saying, "We'll pick up where we left off at a later date, handsome," as she made a little space between them to re-button his jacket. He couldn't read her poker face at all, so, five minutes later, humiliated to no end, he scrambled into the taxi, not knowing if his little excuse covered his embarrassing flat tire well enough or she knew straight out that he was a fraud. Fuck. Fuck. Fuck.

So, there he was, at 4:30 a.m., wrapping up his latest analysis of how his dick works and how his dick has a mind of its own. He laid out the facts, similar to the way that Nigel had coached them through earlier while they were analyzing the facts surrounding his genealogy.

Fact number one was that he knew for certain that he wasn't gay, and that fact is what forced him to face the music. He asked himself with a sinking heart, '*Could it be at all possible? Could it be that this stunningly beautiful, sexy, long-legged woman and I simply didn't share that chemistry – that spark – that* je n'est se quoi *– that lovers share? Could it be that we were doomed to be friends instead of lovers?*'

He sat there, absorbing this disappointing news, when he thought that maybe the problem lay elsewhere. Maybe he was just off his game. Maybe he had suffered a reaction to the shellfish. He reached down into his pajama, and, with both hands, he had his culprit cock up in full working order within the span of 45 seconds. He closed his eyes, savoring the immediate pleasure that the release gave him, and, as he wiped himself off, he admitted to himself, *Nope, it wasn't the shellfish.*

He wearily laid his head down on his pillow once again. He knew that his dick was nobody's fool, and, with a sinking heart, he resigned himself to the fact that it was his destiny to be a 40-year-old, single, nerdy intellectual who had, up to this very moment, never met his soul mate. He would continue on, living the single life, puttering about in the lab, solving the puzzles that life and science seemed to offer up to him one after the other.

He just had to accept, once and for all, that it was just his bad, fucking luck – science was his mistress of choice, and Ms. Nigella Hansson's long legs and fabulous ass weren't going to change anything.

He sighed, punched the hotel's pillow into a side-sleeper shape, and closed his eyes. As he was dozing off, he smiled a little to himself. All was not lost; he was going to see his new best friend and her fabulous family tomorrow afternoon.

***

Chapter Thirteen
A Quick Trip Back Home

I leaned out a little from my seat to smile at Dad. I was sitting between Rabbi Kleiman and Mom, with Dad on the other side of her. I straightened back up as I heard them call out Lars's name, and I watched as this handsome, lanky, nerdy intellectual posed for the press, one hand on his award and the other firmly pumping the other scientist's hand. Even from our seats, it was evident that Lars looked like Dad. I automatically clapped, along with everyone else, and for some reason, I felt a little let down. I was just tired, that's all, I told myself.

I must admit that I hadn't slept well. I tossed and turned all night long as I reviewed my immediate, explosive reaction to Lars's first kiss out on the sidewalk the night before. Oh my God, it had felt so good. It had been so long. I needed a man so badly, and when I felt his big erection pressing into me, I was quickly formulating exactly how many minutes it would take to drag him around the corner and get him into my big, lonely bed so that I could wrap my arms and legs around his beautiful, eager body.

In the middle of my scheming, right when his hands were all over my ass, I don't know what came over me, but his tongue, all of a sudden, didn't seem to fit in my mouth somehow. I think he clued into what I was thinking, because he backed off a little. My passion, that had my knees buckling seconds before, was just like one of those shooting stars that you see; it takes your breath away for a minute, and then it fizzles out to nothing.

Could it be that I simply was coming down with the flu or something? Or, more worrisome, had I become a daddy's girl that no man could ever match up to? God forbid! No, I was smarter than that, surely!

I shook my head to get away from my thoughts, and I focused on the stage. I listened and smiled a little as my very own accent floated down from him over the crowd as he delivered his warm but professional acceptance speech. I guess it was just his accent, but all of a sudden, I was homesick for Sweden.

I felt Mom's hand on my arm. "Well, what do you think, honey? Is he the one? You know that Dad and I would be so happy for you."

Mom and I had no secrets from each other, so I looked her right in the eye and let out a long sigh.

"Oh. It's that way," she said quietly.

"Yeah. Unfortunately."

"No spark?"

"There was a definite two-way spark but it fizzled out within two minutes."

"Maybe you aren't feeling well. Maybe you're tired. Maybe he looks too much like your dad for you. Maybe his accent reminds you of your other life back in Sweden."

I nodded my head in agreement, and she patted my hand and said, "Maybe we shouldn't be making such big decisions without further investigation."

"You're right, Mom. Let's give it a little more time."

"But wait a moment. What about him? Did you kiss him? What was his reaction?"

I laughed, "Mom, get real. I'm your daughter. I couldn't wait to get him into my bed, let alone kiss him! Of course, I kissed him. As soon as we left your house, right on the sidewalk. And he kissed me back. I felt his erection. My God, it was magnificent. It all started to fall apart when I realized that I didn't seem to want his tongue in my mouth. By the time that I pressed back into him to check to see if he felt the same way, his big erection had disappeared entirely!"

Her eyebrows went up. "Well, honey, this changes everything! A bad kisser is something that we can fix. Let's not be too hasty here! He's so perfect for you!"

"Sorry, Mom, it wasn't him. He's a man with all the right moves. He had unclipped my bra within ten seconds of the first kiss. It was me. All of a sudden, it felt like I was kissing my brother."

"Hm…this doesn't sound good, honey."

"I know, Mom."

I sat back and looked at her. She and Dad were always so open about their robust sex life, so I knew that she could take a little teasing. I whispered, "Mom, has dad ever lost his erection in the middle of your kiss?"

She gave me a deadpan look and never missed a beat. "Not on my watch, girlfriend."

She sighed. "Men! You can't live with them, and you can't live without them!"

Dad and Rabbi Kleiman leaned in to get in on the joke, but Mom brushed them off by shaking her head and saying, "It's nothing, boys; just girl talk."

She leaned over and whispered in my ear, "You know, darling, it hasn't been that long since François died; that may be a factor to consider."

"Yeah, I know, Mom. You're right. But as you and Dad know, my marriage ended long, long before my husband lost his life. It's just that I don't even know who I am these days. I look into the mirror and I don't recognize myself somehow."

***

Rabbi Kleiman couldn't stay for our dinner that was to follow the presentation at the university, so there were just the four of us. Lars gave the Maître d the name 'Dr. Hansson,' and the older, dark-suited restaurateur took a moment to look at the four of us. As he walked us to our table, I heard him say to Lars, "Dr. Hansson, you have one hell of a good-looking family. Enjoy your dinner with your parents and your sister."

That said it all. That's when Mom and I shared a little look, and I realized that the whole world knew my often-wished-for and badly needed lover was definitely nowhere in sight.

***

Over the delicious dinner, I watched Dad and Lars delve into conversation, and I realized that there was more than just me figuring into this equation. It seemed like my father and Lars were developing quite a bromance.

As Dad was sharing the dessert menu with Mom, I straightened up, put on my happy face, and faced the elephant in the room. I leaned into Lars's handsome face, and, nose to nose, I whispered, "Lars, Lars, Lars, I can't make up my mind. You're just so damn cute! Is it your handsome face, or is it just your Swedish accent?" I looked him square in the eye and laughed, challenging him a little. "Dr. Lars Hansson, what's really going on here?"

Just before he laughed and kissed me on my cheek, I detected a flicker of acknowledgment in his beautiful brown eyes. His face flushed a little as if he had been caught in a little lie. Ah ha! I knew right then and there that he understood what I was saying. His part of the spark that had caused his big erection the night before had also been short-lived. We were both in the same boat. We were doomed to be just friends. Luck of the draw, I supposed to myself, but I felt a deep pang of disappointment come over me. Fuck. I couldn't get anything right. I didn't even know who I was, let alone trying to navigate my messy life forward. I felt like I was in life's boat without a paddle.

***

The night, however, ended on a surprising high note for me just as I was acclimatizing to the sad fact that my love life was back to square one. As we were finishing dessert, Lars invited me to meet him in London so that he could take me back home to Stockholm just to look around and to prove to myself that I wasn't missing anything.

His offer was delivered with such warmth and kindness that I backtracked to think that maybe we did need to take another look at our options. I searched his face, hoping against hope that the illusive spark would make a second appearance. Maybe, just maybe we could make this work.

Nope. Nothing. Zip. Nada. It was that very moment, I think, that we both committed to a deeply loving yet platonic relationship. Little did I know at the time that our future spouses would have to learn to work around the wonder and the weirdness of our very close, loving relationship.

I jumped out of my chair and landed right on Lars's lap, kissing him on the lips and tousling his gorgeous hair. He was beaming, and I saw him give a little wink to Dad as if to say he would take good care of his little girl.

***

I sat on the edge of their bed, explaining to Martina that I was only going to be gone for five days and that she and Zalia had to help Jacquie and Maureen take care of the boys.

"Don't worry, Mom, I'm 11 now. I can do this. Just go and have fun. I'll take care of Granddad and Grandma too. But, Mom, I can't even remember now where we lived. Will you know how to get there? Will Lars take care of you?"

Zalia piped up and she patted Martina's arm and said, "Don't worry, I'll take care of Martina for you."

I sat there, smiling down at the two of them, with their wild, curly, African hair and matching pajamas. "Girls, I have a great idea. How about once I get home, we go out shopping for two nice matching beds for this room so you'll have a little room to stretch out."

That idea was met with two loud *no's*, so I retreated toward the door. I put my hand up over the mezuzah and motioned for the girls to join me in our nightly prayer:

"Hear, O Israel, the Lord our God, the Lord Is One."

***

'This should keep them happy,' I thought to myself as I stepped back to view my travel wardrobe that I had laid out on the bed so that my bossy mother, my nanny, and my take-charge girlfriend could nod their approval.

Mom, with wide, questioning eyes, said, "Where's the La Perla? You can't take flannel pajamas! No man wants to see his girl in flannels!"

"Mom, how many times have I told you? Lars and I are just friends. Not friends with benefits. Just buddies. Not fuck-buddies. I'm not going to make a fool out of myself by packing sexy nightwear."

Mom, who only wanted the best for me, looked so disappointed, so I quickly added, "But thank you so much for going out and buying me this beautiful suit and silk shirt to wear when I'm having lunch with my old boss at the law office. I'll knock 'em dead, Mom, don't worry about a thing."

Jacqui said, "Listen up. Here's what we'll do. Right now. Go get your very best, very hottest little La Perla number, and we'll tuck it in a corner of the suitcase just to bring you good luck. You never know. Maybe there'll be some sexy lawyer at your old office that won't be able to take his eyes off the long-legged Swede that got away."

At the mention of a sexy lawyer in the law office, we all said in the same breath, "Remember Cecilia?" and, with that, we collapsed on the bed, howling

213

with laughter, remembering Maureen tearing a strip off Cecilia Yang's cheating little ass at François's Celebration of Life party.

I added the final punch line, "François who?"

***

I stood there, hair pulled back, leaning over the small sink as I balanced myself against the subtle movement of the plane. I rolled up the sleeves of my British Airways pajama top and carefully applied first the eye cream, then the night cream. As I looked into the mirror, I blew the woman in the mirror a kiss and said, "Not bad for an old widow with four kids, a girlfriend, two parents, a platonic boyfriend, a nanny, and a dog to look after."

The night sky was lit with the full moon, and black striations formed perfectly sharp edges and wedges through the luminous stratus clouds that seemed to glide by the window in deference to the big plane populated with members of the human race.

"Mor! Morsa! Can you hear me? I'm coming home, Mor! Are you happy for me, Morsa?"

***

I couldn't help but grin as I watched him. The tall, lanky, handsome Swede placed my luggage into the 'boot,' as he called it, and I said, with a little smile still on my face, "Really, Lars? A Volvo? Why a Volvo?"

He looked over quickly, and when he saw that I was teasing him, he reminded me, "Yeah. The best damn car in the world, thanks to us Swedes. We're world-famous for more than just flat-packed furniture and brilliant scientists, you know. And pray-tell, Ms. Smart-Ass, what do you drive in the frozen outback called Canada?"

"Same."

"I thought you might. Now, are you ready for the best holiday of your life? I told your father that I would spoil you rotten, and that's what I intend to do."

I laughed a little and said, "That's exactly what I told him I was going to do to you! So, I guess we're both in for a treat, right?"

We had already made our plans that would cover our five-day adventure, so I leaned back to enjoy the drive into London, to go to his parents' home for tea. My protests to meeting the parents had fallen upon deaf ears. All he said was *'Tit for tat'* and it made me realize that, actually, his parents, who were both turning 80 that year, would be happy to see Lars bringing home a friend. Lars was just being a good son.

Since my jetlag was inevitable, we would travel right up to Oxford after meeting the folks so he could tuck me into bed to rest up for the flight to Stockholm the next afternoon. He told me that his kitchen was fully stocked in case I woke up in the middle of the night, looking for dinner on Canadian time.

As Lars maneuvered London's traffic, driving on the left side of the road, he quickly filled me in on the status of his parents. When they both started using canes, walkers, and hearing aids, Lars knew it was time for them to give up their home. He had put them in a big, brand-new retirement home where they had their own private apartment. The residence offered complete care, all meals in a big, communal, dining room, entertainment, the works. He summed it up by saying that they were always a devoted couple, and they seemed very happy with their lot in life.

This little tidbit of information did not prepare me for the shock when I first saw them.

***

Lars had taken my hand as we entered his folks' residence, and my eyes were roaming around the big, beautiful, reception lounge when Lars called out in Swedish, "*Mor! Pappa!* There you are!"

He guided me toward them.

Oh my God! They were old! Really old! And so frail-looking, gripping their walkers to secure a good stance as they stood there in the lobby, eagerly awaiting the arrival of their only child who was finally bringing a girl home. And they were white! I mean really white; with snow-white skin and snow-white hair! For some reason, I thought they would be people of color, like Lars. I had an immediate outpouring of love for this Swedish couple that, 40 years ago, had adopted a little black baby instead of taking the safe route of choosing a baby that would match their own skin tones.

I changed tac immediately and put my formal, stiff, lawyer-like manners behind me. I stooped over her to give her a big bear-hug, and when it was time to greet Lars's old father, he had let go of his walker to offer me the same big hug back.

We walked at a snail's pace as they proudly gave us the cook's tour of the residence. Of course, they had to introduce us to each and every nurse, every employee, every neighbor that we passed along the way to see the craft room, the pub, the gym, the hair salon, and the big dining room, already beautifully set for tea which would be served at 14:00 hour sharp.

The elevator that would take us up to their apartment was also slow. While I was absorbing all these geriatric measures and slow, aged ways, it gave me pause to think of the absolute contrast between them and my own parents. I had no idea whatsoever that this is what parents looked and acted like when they were getting up in years. I promised myself that I would never, ever allow my mother to cook another meal for me while I sat there on a kitchen stool lazily watching her, as long as I lived. I had just been taking advantage of her! And my dad, always carting the kids back and forth, jumping up every two minutes from his seat to get them a snack. What had I been thinking!?

I spoke in Swedish to the three of them, "Oh my! These Swedish biscuits are making me homesick! All of a sudden, I can't wait to get back home tomorrow!"

Lars's father patted my hand from across the table, and he said quietly, "Don't be in too much of a rush to go back, Nigella. Sometimes, in life, you find that going back home is best kept on the backburner."

Lars jumped in with a quick, "Oh, don't worry about Nigella. She's going back Stockholm to work on that age-old question that we all seem to have. It has nothing to do with geography or old loves from her past."

I sat back and asked him, "Oh really? Now, tell us, Lars, tell us all, what's the age-old question that you think I'm asking myself?"

The three of them all shrugged their shoulders in unison, and they all said together, "Who am I?"

I sat there, a little stunned with this revelation that I hadn't actually verbalized, even in my most soul-searching moments since the day I had met Lars. My ego had been so tied up with the idea of Lars not being interested in me in a sexual way that it had clouded my thinking. Duh.

Lars grabbed my hand and said, "Honey, I'm in the same boat. I haven't been back for years only because I know the answer to *who am I*. And I don't like the answer. I go through life, trying to change my fate, but to date, nothing has worked."

"But, Lars, you're perfect. What's there not to like?"

"Nigella, I think you know me well enough by now to know that I can't seem to find my soul mate in life. As in wife, and as in marriage, and as in having children. Thank God that I found you. You're my best friend, and you're not looking for a husband in me anymore than I'm looking for a wife in you. My problem is that I'm married to my job, and I don't like it one bit when my little voice in the back recess of my mind reminds me of it. So, I stopped asking myself *who am I?* a while ago, and I just accepted my fate of being a 40-year-old bachelor that's happiest in a lab. That's why I wanted to take you back to Stockholm with me. I love you. I want you to be happy. And I'll be right beside you to pick up the pieces as they are bound to fall along your journey."

"Well, you summed that up perfectly," I said in a soft voice.

Anna, his mother, slammed both her hands down in exasperation, and the two men in her life started to laugh as I looked back and forth from one to the other. She exclaimed, "Damn it! Damn it all to hell! I was hoping against hope that Nigella was the girl for you! I'll never be a *mormor* at this rate!"

The morning passed, and as I helped Anna put a little lunch on the table for the boys, I realized that I was falling in love with this lovely, lovely couple that were definitely as much in love with each other as my own parents. The afternoon passed, and we all traded stories back and forth like we had known each other our whole lives.

As we left their apartment to be on time for the 14:00 hour tea in the dining room downstairs, I turned to have one last look around their cozy home. I could feel the love all around me; it felt just like my parents' home at 7 Russell Hill Road. I was so grateful to Lars for insisting that I come here. You just never know when and where the next little life's lesson is going to pop up.

As we dawdled through tea, I could see that Lars was getting antsy, and his elderly parents knew very well that their precious time with their son was coming to a close. I knew they hated to ask him, as they were afraid of the answer, but Anna came out with a timid, "Well, darling, I suppose we'll see you for Christmas, right? You will be coming down to see us, won't you?"

Lars looked at me, knowing fully well that he had already committed to spending Christmas with me and my family in Canada.

He met his mother's eyes and he took a deep breath to try to soften the blow.

I jumped in to bail him out. That's what friends are for. I said, "Well, that's what we wanted to talk to you about. Now, please know that what I'm going to say is our treat entirely, and it's Lars and my Christmas gift to you. You see, we want you to come to Canada and stay at my house over the holidays this year. We're treating. And we want you to come so that we can spoil you. And you'll just love my parents. They're in love with each other just as much as you two. And you'll be more than comfortable; I have a big suite for you on the main floor, so there's no stairs to worry about. We have been planning this forever, and you simply must come."

I could feel Lars's arm go around my shoulder, and Eliot followed suit with Anna who was trying to get up out her chair to give me a hug. I jumped up to put my arms around her as I plopped her back down in her chair.

What I had forgotten to consider in the heat of the moment was that I had already asked Maureen if I could treat her parents to come over from Ireland for the holidays. We were going to have a very full house at 49 Parkwood Avenue.

"So that's a yes, right?" It was all settled, with a resounding yes from the old folks as well as from a very surprised and beaming Lars. Eliot had many questions for Lars about taking their walkers, canes, and hearing aids with them, and Anna asked me excitedly if she could help prepare the big meal on Christmas Eve.

As I explained to them that we would be having a Swedish Christmas on Christmas Eve, a Canadian Christmas on the day of, but they may miss Hanukkah as it was going to fall from December 01-10 that year. I told them that although I wasn't really that involved with my religion, I was a Jew. They looked at each other, and Eliot said, "Well, this is going to be the most interesting and varied holiday we have had in our lives!"

I jumped into the conversation to add, "Oh, I should mention too that our nanny's parents will be joining us as well. They live in Ireland, and they're staunch Catholics, but I'm saving the best room in the house for you."

Lars started laughing, and he kissed me on the cheek as he said, "Folks, you have no idea. This one here is full of surprises. Just sit back and buckle up. We're all in good hands with Nigella Kaufman Hansson!"

***

As the Volvo headed northwest up to Oxford, he thanked me over and over again for the Christmas plans, and I felt myself giving in to the jetlag that was hitting me like a ton of bricks. The next thing I knew is that he was helping me out of the car. "We're home, honey. I'll get you into bed right away."

I woke up to darkness. He had left a light on in the hall, and I stumbled out to the living room where he was stretched out on the sofa, reading a book. We sat in his little kitchen in our pajamas as I wolfed down a sandwich and he explained the science behind jetlag flying east being a real bitch compared to jetlag flying west. He was a nerd through and through. He tucked me into his bed once again, and I told him that I was going to make him the best Swedish breakfast he had ever had in his life the next morning.

***

"Oh, please, Lars," I protested, "I don't want to see the quaint little shops. Take me to your labs and your lecture halls. I want to see where you work. I want to see what makes you happy. And I know that retail therapy is not you. Besides, just remember, I'm just as much an academic as you are. Give me a break. I want to walk the hallowed halls of Oxford arm in arm with their most handsome prof."

I watched his face and pretended to be listening intently as he droned on and on about this and that. You might say he was in his element. He was practically glowing. I've never seen him look so handsome. Or so unattainable. He was right. Me, or any other woman, wouldn't stand a chance to snare his attention long enough to build a solid relationship as long as his work was at his fingertips.

And the worst of it all was that his beautiful body and good looks were wasted on the fact that he was too full of ethics and morals to bend a little to give into being any woman's knight in shining armor in the bedroom, even if it was just a night here or there. Fuck. Fuck ethics. Fuck morals. What a waste.

I must admit, I felt no loss really that I was not the woman that could challenge his first love – his world of the life sciences. One day, God willing, he would meet the nerd of his dreams, and the two of them would be in science heaven for the rest of their days.

I put my arm through his and gave him a little smooch on the face. "Come on, handsome, I'm going to buy you a coffee."

***

The London-Stockholm flight was an easy-peasy two-plus hours, and we were both excited to see our old stomping grounds once again. We both wanted to visit our old university and to experience what was happening in *Old Town* which had been revitalized with charming cafes and shops thriving right on the waterfront. It had been a while for both of us. I had made a date to have lunch with my old boss the following day; I wanted to visit my Mor's grave to see the new headstone I had arranged for, and I had a little business to attend to at three of the old restaurants where my Mor had worked in the kitchens, from the time I was a baby to the time that she became a grandmother, at which time we could afford to have her stay home with the baby while I worked as a lawyer.

Our plans were in sync, and it looked like we could wrap everything up in the two-and-a-half days. Although it was going to be tight, we shaved a little time off here and there, agreeing to meet at certain spots in or near our old campus rather than going back to reconnect at the hotel. It would leave us one day to do a bit of sightseeing in London before I would go back to Toronto and he would go back to Oxford.

***

Lars nodded to let me know he had caught sight of my wave, and he strode down to the back of the coffee shop. He gave me a little kiss and said, "Well, how did it go at your old office? Did you see any of the old crowd? Where did your boss take you for lunch?"

I admit that I was acting a little like a drama queen, but even thinking about it now makes my blood boil. I put on the most disdainful face that I could muster, and I proceeded to tell him that my old boss was nothing short of a common pig. A boar. A despicable thug. A person that was slated to burn in hell.

I could see that my 'grand dame' speech hadn't had the effect that I was looking for, as Lars tried to keep a little smile from curling his lips up at the corners. He grabbed my hand and said calmly, "Okay, honey, okay. Start from the beginning. The very beginning. What's got you so upset?"

I could hear my voice getting louder and louder as I told the story, and out of the corner of my eye I could see that the other patrons were fully engrossed in my story as well as the two female baristas standing behind the counter.

Lars, by this time, trying to keep a somber façade as to not rile me up any further, said, "Okay, now I'm going to paraphrase just to make sure I've got your story straight. God forbid that I misunderstand what has gotten you into such a state, honey."

I had an uneasy feeling that he was teasing me, just a little, behind his phony compassionate face, but I was still seething with the events that had unfolded, so I just nodded curtly and he began the replay.

"So, after a few pleasantries and after saying a brief hello to a few familiar faces, your boss – no, excuse me – your married boss took you to the big, fancy hotel near the office and you were both laughing and having the time of your life, sitting in the middle of the big dining room, enjoying your second or third martini before the lunch. That was before the bottle of wine. Am I correct so far?"

I looked into his face, but he was clever enough to still have that phony face on. I knew where this was going, but by then I wasn't in the mood to back down. I dug my heels in with a stony face as he continued, "And then it was just after the cheese tray, somewhere between the second bottle of wine and the dessert, when he suggested that the two of you take the party upstairs to his suite."

I didn't even bother to nod, as I watched him pursing his lips tightly together in an attempt to hold his laughter back. My eyes narrowed and I thought to myself he wasn't being much of a friend when I needed one.

"And then – oh wait, honey – please correct me if I'm wrong, okay? Now this is when you stood up and loudly called him a lying, cheating bastard and his wife was going to hear about this. Now that's the moment that the whole restaurant became quiet, right? And then you continued with a few other names that you say that you honestly have never uttered before in your whole life. And then you opened up your handbag and threw two handfuls of kronars, one handful after the other, into his face and told him that you would die before you would allow him to buy you lunch. You followed that by saying, 'Who the fuck do you think I am? Cecilia Yang?' And then, as he stood up to calm you down, you used your outside voice and ordered him to sit. Then you straightened your shoulders, held your head up high, and stormed out of the restaurant before the cad could make any more excuses. Did I cover just about everything, honey?"

By then, my arms were crossed. I had evolved from the laughing woman in the middle of the fancy restaurant, evidently feeling the effects of her first-ever martinis and half a bottle of wine to a sullen pouter, on the way down from her first drunken bender.

The coffee barista came over and said to me, "This one's on the house, Sister. I hear you. There's just too many lying, cheating bastards out there, aren't there?"

I didn't realize at the time that as she stood there, slowly pouring me the free refill, that she was standing a little behind me, shaking her head back and forth and mouthing a firm 'no' to warn Lars not to laugh out loud.

Lars jumped up from the table and said, "Excuse me, honey. Be right back. I need a quick trip to the men's room."

He fled from the table and the coffeehouse was dead silent. I heard the men's room door slam shut. I'm sure that his howls of laughter could be heard two blocks away. Everyone immediately put their heads down, reading their menus very intently, and even the kind barista fled back to the front and disappeared somewhere beneath the counter.

I tried my best, through my still-drunken stupor, to get up to try to make it to the door with what was left of my dignity still intact. I remember speaking loudly to the middle of the empty counter where I suspected that the barista lay behind on the floor, peeing her pants with laughter, "Thank you very much for the coffee. Please tell my friend that I'm waiting outside."

***

He put his arm around my shoulders and said, "Come on, my Swedish princess. Let's get you back to the hotel and out of your fancy new suit and high heels. I think we have time to have a little nap before we venture out to savor all that our old stomping grounds have to offer us."

***

It was eight o'clock, and I was sitting across from Lars in the restaurant. We were both wearing jeans and hoodies, and I had my hair pulled back with a scrunchie, and I was wearing no makeup. I was suffering with my first hangover and I looked the part.

However, I was man enough to bring it up first. "Lars, about this afternoon. I'm so sorry for my bad behavior. That's the first time in my life I've ever been drunk, and I can guarantee you that it's my last. I made such a fool of myself. And you were so kind to me. What really hurts, though, is I know you're going to tease me about this until the day I die, aren't you?"

"You're probably right about that, Nigella. But let's make a deal. I'll go easy on the teasing if you tell me one thing."

"Anything, Lars. Shoot."

"Who the hell is Cecilia Yang?"

And so, I began. Right from the beginning. Right from my in-vitro fertilization pregnancy at age 23 but never having sex until I was age 30. My first time was with François whom I married three months after we had 'done the deed.' A year into the marriage, when our twin boys were nine months old, my husband was not coming home at night. When he did come home, he wasn't interested in making love to me or even having just plain, good, old sex either. My father caught him red-handed in his office one afternoon with his assistant, Cecilia Yang. I wrote up the divorce papers, but he died one week later in a fire.

By this time, Lars's face was full of empathy. "So your big Broadway debut today wasn't about the lying, cheating bastard boss at all. It was about your lying, cheating bastard husband. Am I right?"

"No, Lars. Not really. Not quite."

"Oh. Okay. So, if it wasn't the boss, and it wasn't the husband, your anger must have been all about the other woman, this Cecilia Yang person. Am I right?"

"No, Lars. No. Although I'm ashamed to admit it. It's not about the three of them at all. I'm just mad at myself. I'm finding out the hard way who I really am, and I'm not happy with the realization, that's all."

"I think we're past the teasing stage of this story, honey. Spit it out, and you'll feel better, and I promise I'll never tease you about it."

I told him of my shame of having my dad finding me perched on the edge of my desk, with my legs wrapped around a sleazy professor's waist as he stood there, jeans down around his ankles, fucking me like something you'd see in a porn film.

"No! Oh, honey! I'm so sorry! What did your dad say?"

"He took charge of things right away. He told me to pick my panties up off the floor and that he would be back in ten minutes to get the whole thing sorted out. And then he did just that. He gave me some wonderful advice, and he and Mom and I stuck together through thick and thin. And then, to top it all off, that was the same afternoon that Dad found François with his hand on Cecilia Yang's ass in their office. Go figure. Poor Dad. Life gets crazy. It always sounds like I'm making up these stories of my life. It's hard to believe. But back to my behavior; I can't forgive myself for that. And now I'm acting out in the middle of a big, fancy, expensive restaurant in Stockholm like a spoiled, bratty schoolgirl."

"So okay. Back to after your dad saw François with Cecilia. What happened next?"

"Mom and Dad and I immediately took the kids to Disney World for the week, and I prepared the divorce papers. François went to Vancouver on business. One week later, on the same night he came back to Toronto from Vancouver, he died in the fire at the farm, along with his parents."

By that time, Lars had pulled his chair around to my side of the table, and I had my face buried in his chest. He said quietly, "How did the fire start, honey?"

I wanted to speak, but I couldn't get the words out. I could hear my own cries get louder and louder. The restaurant manager came over quickly to ask Lars if he should call a doctor or an ambulance, and Lars asked him for help to get me outside to get some fresh air. They hustled me back out through the kitchen and Lars lifted me up over the doorsill. There was an old chair there that the smokers used, and Lars kneeled down in the dirty, old alley beside the dumpster, holding me and rocking me back and forth until I could stop crying long enough to spit out my nightmare of how my husband was smoking weed and how his live butt started the fire that killed not only himself but his innocent parents as well.

I ended my story with words that I hadn't said out loud to anyone; not even to myself. I said in a quiet voice, "I hate him. I hate him for killing his parents. I hate him for what he's done to my kids. I hate him for what he's done to my parents."

"I know. I know, honey. That's grief for you. It's a bitch and there's not a damn thing we can do about it."

With that, the restaurant's backdoor opened a little, and the manager came out with a huge takeout bag. He said to Lars, "You may get hungry later on. Please take this with you. I hope you're feeling better tomorrow, miss. I've called you a taxi, and he should be here shortly. Please come back once you're feeling better."

***

It was hours later, and we sat pulled up to the little desk in Lars's room. For the second time on our holiday, we ate dinner in our pajamas. I said, "I'll arm-wrestle you for the last kroppkaka. Come on. Let's go."

He eyed me warily and said, "No. You can have it. I'm a little afraid of you. After all, we've been in town less than 24 hours, and you've cleared two restaurants and one coffee shop. It's all yours."

I smiled a little as I popped the kroppkaka into my mouth. "Trust me, Lars, you have nothing to worry about. I'm officially on the wagon."

***

I quietly opened my hotel-room door, hands full of the juice and muffins that I had picked up from the café downstairs. I was intent on being a better travel companion to my wonderful boyfriend who, according to the loud snores coming from the open doorway to the adjoining room, was still dead to the world. I had also gone to the bank on the corner and took out the kronars I needed to slip into the envelopes for the kitchen help in the three restaurants where my mother used to work.

I jumped a little as he said behind me, "What on earth are you doing now?"

"Oh! Good morning! This is my little project regarding the three restaurants that I was telling you about earlier. I'm almost done. I just have to count out equal amounts of kronars for each envelope."

"It looks a little like you just robbed a bank, Nigella. Do you have something to tell me?"

"Silly. Listen, as we say in Canada, I'm paying it forward. Back when I was a baby right through until I was in my 20s, the dishwashers in those three restaurants made sure my mother took home enough food for us from the backdoor of those restaurants for years and years and years. Living on social assistance was a tough go, and those daily packets of leftovers and day-old treats kept our nourishment topped up over what our monthly social-assistance disability check could. And it ensured that I had a lunch to take to school every day. Remember, Mor was profoundly deaf. She was also mute in those days. She spent her whole childhood living in the orphanage, and from a very young age she worked as a dishwasher, going from restaurant to restaurant in her silent world to fill in extra shifts. Those kitchens were always very, very good to her, and she always had enough to eat as a young person, and then after she had me when she was 29, those kitchens nourished me as well. Sometimes I would go with her after school to speak up for her and to say thank you to the kitchen staff. That's how she taught me to mind my manners and develop humility which is the basis of dignity and two-way respect all around, isn't it?"

"I see. Okay. I'm taking notes down on your journey of finding out who you really are, and these three envelopes almost make up for the drunk and disorderly behavior from yesterday. However, what are these separate three envelopes over here for?"

"Good question, my dear Watson. I'm making three donations to Stockholm's food bank in the names of: one, the fancy hotel restaurant; two, the coffee shop, and three, the kind restaurant from last night. I'm using these three envelopes to deliver a note of apology and to let them know that a donation has been made in their name."

I turned around and looked at him. I really looked at him. He was standing there in his rumpled pajamas and his morning-shadow beard on his handsome face. He was looking into my face, all happy and relaxed. I was so grateful that, for some inexplicable reason, he had popped into my life. That's just the way the universe works, I supposed to myself.

I know I sounded exactly like Mom when I made my next move, but on second thought, it was exactly perfect for the occasion.

"Okay, handsome, I'm a way ahead of you this morning. There's juice and a muffin over there for a starter. Get your ass in gear. I'll meet you at the door in ten minutes. I'm treating my favorite guy to the best Swedish breakfast Stockholm has to offer. And then you're going to take me over to the university and impress the hell out of me with your brainiac ways."

***

I headed back to my room to pick up a scarf for him. He stood there, in the doorway, with a big grin on his face, and he said, "You know, of course, that you're becoming your mom, don't you?"

"And that's a good thing, buster. Who else is willing to put up with you and keep you from getting the sniffles?"

"Don't get me wrong, princess. If you are half the woman that she is, we're all in good hands."

***

Our last day in Stockholm was absolutely perfect. The weather was superb, and Lars and I really enjoyed checking off the last few points on our list.

We visited the old cemetery which was right in the heart of the city, with tall apartment buildings towering over the old stones, where I had buried Mor seven years ago. The new headstone that I had ordered beforehand stood gleaming from one of the small, narrow shards of sunlight that the tall buildings permitted. I had ordered Mor's new monument in the dark-gray granite, the same as Mom and Dad had used for the family in Mount Pleasant Cemetery in Toronto. That's where the likeness ended, however. This little patch of city land was nothing at all like Mount Pleasant. No, not in the least. It was a humble resting place for Jews. The old, downtown, burial ground was named *Aronsberg*. It had seen better days and was not especially well-kept. I purposely didn't design the new stone to show any pomp and circumstance. It was a small, plain work of art simply adorned with the Star of David at the top of it, my great-grandmother's name, Martyna Kaufman, spelled with the Polish 'y'; underneath that, Grandma's name, Milka Kaufman; then Mor's name, Martina Kaufman Hansson, spelled with the Swedish 'i'; followed by my own name, Nigella Hansson, and last, my daughter's name, Martina Hansson. It was exactly what Mor would have chosen.

We placed two small stones on it, and I repeated the Kaddish, with Lars's arm around my shoulders. I knew I wasn't following strict Judaic protocol with this prayer, but I could tell by the peace in my heart that what I had done suited God above, my *mormors*, my *mor*, and me to a 'T.'

While we were in the little children's park where Mor used to take me as a child, and then 20 years later where she took her grandchild, Martina, for a swing and a slide, I was running over to the teeter-totter, trying to get Lars on the other end of it. I forgot about my still-tender foot for a mere second, and I fell to the ground as the sharp pain ran from my toes up through my metatarsal.

Lars was immediately on his knees, taking off my boot to see what the problem was.

"It's nothing, Lars, it's nothing. It happens when I'm not careful. I've only been out of the cast for a little while and I forget to be careful sometimes. Look, your jeans are getting all dirty. Get up. I'm fine. Get up."

"Cast? What do mean a cast? What have you done to yourself this time, Nigella?"

Shit. Shit. Shit. Another wheel-barrel of teasing was going to be dumped all over me, and I knew it the minute he showed his concern. I couldn't lie. Not to Lars. He would see right through me.

As I told him of my temper tantrum of kicking François's vintage Alpha Romeo's spokes out of the wheel that ended with me breaking my foot, and the pursuant ride in the back of the ambulance, he changed positions from kneeling on his knees in the dirt to his ass situated firmly on the ground. His arms were behind to prop himself up, and his long legs stretched out in front of him. His head went back and his howls of laughter were even greater than the ones from yesterday that had been brought on by my drunken tirade.

I made my way over to the swings and it was a good ten minutes of me just pumping a little air into my ride before he could manage to get his laughter under control enough to join me on an adjacent swing.

***

I was on the upward glide, looking up into my hometown's blue sky, when, from a deep, deep recess of my mind, I remembered back to my four-year-old voice calling out, "Mor! Morsa! Push me higher, Morsa!"

***

We were an hour into our flight back to London, and I smiled at my amazing friend sitting beside me. Over the last few days, he had picked up the pieces while I was busy 'finding myself' without the slightest whine. He was reading the newspaper, and I said, "Just when I think you can't get any more handsome, you put your readers on. You look more like my dad right now than you ever have."

He pulled his readers off and calmly folded his paper in two. "Okay, okay, I can see that I'm not going to have a moment to myself until you're on your next flight. What's up now, princess?"

"Seriously, Lars, thank you from the bottom of my heart for this holiday. I now know what I'm supposed to be doing with my life, and it's all because of you helping me answer the age-old question of *who am I*. I'm going to make it up to you every day of our lives, starting right now."

"Well, well, well. Let's start off by you telling me who you are, shall we?"

"Up until five years ago, I was a smart, hardworking lawyer and single parent living in my own small world in Stockholm. Then I met my dad and mom, and my whole world opened up in every way possible. All on their dime, I should add. The world was my oyster, and I simply took advantage of my new circumstances. I fell in love, got married, and had the twins right away. I got the house of my dreams and was showered with gifts from my parents, including a full-time nanny to help me with the children. I never went back to work as a lawyer. One day I had the idea that I should do something more, so I enrolled in the graduate program at University of Toronto as an easy out to going back to work. I just didn't want to practice law anymore, and once the sex went out of my marriage, I didn't want to be married anymore either. My biggest eye-opener was not my husband's death, as you may think. No, not at all. It was when we were all on holidays in Disney World and I met Jacquie. She is the most amazing woman I have ever met; a very close second to Mom. And you know how amazing Mom is. So, anyway, back to Jacquie. She came up from Florida to Canada when François died, and she has been taking care of me and my whole family ever since. She even took me to Auschwitz so that I could follow my grandmother's footsteps from her dairy farm in Poland to Auschwitz and then on to Bergen-Belsen and finally to Foehrenwald, the displaced person's camp in Northern Germany. And, now that we're home again, do you know what she does? She meets up with my dad every morning, rain or shine, at 7:00 a.m., and they have a morning run and a coffee at the local café. All this happens while I'm still in my big comfortable bed, deciding what to wear that day. She is studying to get her Canadian medical equivalency to allow her to work as a nurse practitioner in Canada. She's left her whole life behind just to help me and my family. She too calls me princess, just like you. And don't get me wrong, I know the two of you aren't talking about the kind of princess out of a fairytale. But I deserve it."

Lars's eyes opened wide and his black brows raised a little. "Darling, are you gay? Is that what you're telling me?"

"Oh my God, Lars. No! No, not at all. I do love her, but not in that way. But wait, let me finish my story." And so I continued, "Then, out of the blue, I meet you, and you take over from Dad, Mom, and Jacquie, by treating me to this amazing holiday and self-discovery trip, spoiling me and loving me despite all my shortcomings."

"Well, what are you going to do about all this, princess?"

"For starters, I'm not going to go back to work as a lawyer. No, I'm going to be way, way too busy for that. Besides, I don't have to worry about money or living off my dad's money either. Francois's and my in-laws' insurance payouts ensured that I have enough money to do me and the kids for as long as we live."

"So? Don't keep me in suspense. What are you going to do with your money, brains, and good looks?"

"I'm going to step up to the plate. I'm going to be head of the family from now on. After all, I've got three children to parent, plus Jacquie's little girl to co-parent. Dad and Mom are still grieving the loss of baby Nigel, and now their best friends and son-in-law are gone too. Mom's also grieving for the loss of the bush, go figure. It's just a bunch of old trees, but it was her childhood home, and she's really struggling with the loss of it all. And here Jacquie is filling in for me, acting as grief counsellor for us all, listening to my dad spill his guts morning after morning as I just sit on my ass, watching her fill in for me."

He was nodding quietly as I continued, "So, I'm going to take over by getting Jacquie thinking of going back to school to become a doctor, never mind working the tough shifts of a nurse practitioner. I can afford it, so why not? And she's so smart, Lars. She can run circles around me. And I'm going to take over the greenhouse business that supports the food bank that has fallen on Mom's shoulders now that Papa is gone. And as far as Maureen, the nanny, goes, I'm going to give her a big raise and make sure that she takes holidays a little more often. And you, I have big plans for you, Lars. I now know how I can pay you back for all your kindness and love that you have showered on me ever since the day we met."

"Now we're coming to the good part! What's in store for me in the grand scheme of things?"

"Well, it's the gift of time."

"Time? What do you mean? You're going to come over to the U.K. to see me more often?"

"No, not you, especially. I'm talking about your parents. As soon as I met your lovely parents, I fell madly in love with them. They made me realize I was falling short with my own parents. So, for the rest of your parents' days, I'm going to make sure that I call them at least once a week and get them over to Toronto to stay with me as often as they can make the trip. And I'll go to the U.K. too on a regular basis to see them there. My kids will be the grandchildren they don't have. I'll be the daughter-in-law they don't have. I know that your schedule doesn't permit all that much time with them, so I'm doing this for you. I've got you covered. What do you think about that?"

"I think that it's just about perfect, but only on one condition."

"And what would that one condition be, Lars?"

"Don't think for a moment that you're off the hook as far as being teased about all your bad behavior over the past few days. I can't wait to tell your folks all about your drunken luncheon, standing there in your fancy new suit, throwing two fistfuls of kronars into your boss's lecherous face."

"Do you have to tell them?"

"Don't worry, princess. Knowing you, you'll get embroiled in some other little escapade soon enough that will make this one pale in comparison."

I sighed and said, "I've changed my mind. You're not as handsome as I thought."

"You're sounding a lot like your mom, princess."

"And you're sounding a lot like a pain in the ass, Mr. Know-It-All."

We both leaned back and I looked out to watch as we dipped down into a bank of white, fluffy clouds. I felt him take my hand, and I turned to see him lifting my hand up to his lips.

"Thank you, Nigella Kaufman Hansson, for the best holiday I've ever had in my whole life."

"Oh, Lars. Oh, Lars. I feel exactly the same way. I'm so grateful that we've met. I can't wait until Christmas when we're all together for the holidays. You'll love the kids, and I can't wait for you to meet Jacquie. I'm going to cook you the best Swedish Christmas dinner you've ever had."

"And you're not going to get into the martinis, right, dear?"

"Trust me, Lars, you don't need to worry about that one."

***

Chapter Fourteen
Feeling the Pinch

It all started innocently enough. Jacquie was examining my foot that had been out of its cast for several months, and while she was massaging it, she said, "You know, I think that maybe you should pop into a gym and just see if you could set up some exercise sessions that will strengthen your foot, just to be on the safe side. You'll want to go back to skiing and skating I imagine, so let's get you in shape. I'll tell you what, I'll go with you and we'll both do a little weight training or something. I mean, after all, we're not kids any longer, and, sadly, we eat like we are. What do you think?"

"Brilliant. But the kind of weight-training I need isn't readily available."

"Oh, I'm sure that nice big gym up on Avenue Road will be perfect for you. Are you whining already, princess?"

"No. But I know me. The weight-training I need weighs in at about 180 lbs. and has two legs and two arms. I can either lay under it or ride it. Either way."

We both laughed a little, and I said, "Seriously, Sis, it's been a while. And although you know I don't miss my husband too much, I really, really miss just plain, old sex."

"Well, don't look at me! I'm not about to switch to the other side! And besides, you have a perfectly good boyfriend in Lars Hansson who I still haven't met by the way. For some reason, you're simply not willing to jump his bones. You just don't know what you want, that's all."

"I've explained to you a million times. Lars and I just don't have that spark. It's not just me; he's too ethical, too straight, and too moral to have a one-night stand. It's all or nothing for him, and he thinks of me as a sister. It's unfortunate, but I'll just have to find another Blueberry Hill, that's all."

She laughed. "Oh my God, Nigella, that was the best night, wasn't it? I've never done anything like that in my life, and it was so perfect! It was like having sex like a man, or something. You know, wham, bam, thank you, ma'am. All times five of course. At least I think it was five times. I lost count."

"Well, it's a hell of a commute to Poland to try to replicate that sexy night. I suppose I'll have to put up and shut up until Mr. Wonderful or his near facsimile comes along."

***

He was the most overtly sexual male I had ever encountered. Jacquie was sitting on the bench in the big, fancy gym right beside me as he knelt down in front of me on both knees, his shiny, straight, long, blond hair tied up in ponytail fashion. He examined my foot tenderly with Jacquie, playing the nurse, pointed out the location of the breaks in my foot and toes.

Jacquie said, "Dan, what am I saying here? You're a kinesiology graduate; you know what to do here. I'm going to leave you two and jump on the treadmill."

I panicked a little as his hand moved from my foot to my calf as his deep voice said, "Flex your foot, Nigella." I wondered if he knew what his touch was doing to me. I opened my eyes, embarrassed at my reaction, and I looked down into his face, shaking my head a little to hear what he was saying.

Shit. Shit. Shit. I knew by the look in his eyes that he was fully aware of the fire that he was stoking. Oh, he was good. He was very, very good.

By the end of our complimentary hour at the beautiful, well-equipped gym, Jack and I both agreed that we would sign up for a membership and that we would start off with a series of five, individual, one-hour training sessions, each of us with a personal trainer. I couldn't take my eyes off his big pecs and his pumped-up biceps. I tried to be casual as I said, "This all sounds fine, doesn't it, Jack? I'll take Dan and you'll take another fitness instructor. Okay with you?"

***

I received a text from Sexy Dan, as Jack and I privately referred to him. He was asking if I could possibly change our last, final, personal training session so that it would correspond to the end of his shift. The big, modern gym was a 24-hour facility and he usually worked nights. He said that he would like to take his best student out for a protein shake after our session, but he didn't get off work until 11 p.m.

"Absolutely," I wrote back. "See you at 10 p.m. sharp."

***

We had tucked the kids in and Jacquie came into my room as I was packing my gym bag. She was carrying a plastic *Shopper's Drug Mart* bag which she handed to me.

"What's this?" I opened it. I had to laugh. I rummaged around in my bag, and I pulled out a box of the exact same brand of condoms.

She said, "Great minds think alike." She hugged me and said, "You are such a handful. You're definitely a high-maintenance, Sis, but I love you. Take care of yourself. And remember. He's a 24-year-old gym rat who spends his days admiring his beautiful physique in the mirror as he peacocks around the gym. Don't be falling in love with him. Just love 'im and leave 'im. Like we've said before, it's wham, bam, thank you, ma'am. Understood?"

I nodded my head with her sage advice. "Understood. It's Blueberry Hill all over again, and I can do this. I'm a big girl now."

"Well, hopefully he's a big boy, if you know I mean. By the size of the bulge in his pants every time he looks at you, I think you're in luck."

"And, Jack, we're not going to ever mention this to the folks, right?"

"I'm not an asshole, Sis. Get real. Now you remember, you are to text me at midnight sharp or I'm coming out looking for you."

***

It turned out that Sexy Dan didn't buy me a protein shake after all. After the hour session in the gym, which frankly was an hour of the most blatant, hottest foreplay that one could get away with in a gym, I took a quick shower in the change room, noticing that my sports bra and cotton panties were soaked through. I changed into a matching set of La Perla, a clean tee-shirt, and loose track pants, and I walked out to see my big-pecs-and-hot-ass personal boy-toy trainer waiting for me at the door.

On the way out of the gym, he explained to me that he took the subway and that he lived at home with his folks, so I casually took out my car keys and said, "No problem, Dan. I've got us covered."

I realized that I had become the older woman that was buying herself a gigolo for the night. To tell you the truth, I didn't give a damn. I was going to get laid, come hell or high water. I sidled up to him and smiled wide into his face, trying to think of a hotel between the gym and my house, where I could discretely check into, dragging my prey by the scruff of his neck right along behind me.

As we walked through the empty garage, I found out that Dan had his own plans. He was a young man that didn't leave anything to chance.

Dan waved to the underground garage attendant, and he said, "Hey, Joe. We're going to be a few minutes getting out of here, but we're all good. Take your break if you like; no need to wait for us to exit."

I grabbed back control of the situation by the time we had gotten into my big Volvo. I said to him, laughing a little, "You know, Dan, I think that I'd better repeat one of my exercises from my workout. I don't want to leave now, just to wake up tomorrow morning feeling that I haven't worked out all my kinks."

"Oh. And what exercise would that be, Nigella?"

"It's the one where you spot me while I spread my legs to do my squats."

"Oh yeah. I know that exercise well. And you're right. You do seem to need a little practice."

With that, I flung my door open and ran around the car and opened his door. He had found the button to push the seat way, way back to make room for me, and before I could straddle him, he had pulled my track pants, along with my panties, down around my ankles so that I could step out of them to free up my wobbly knees.

All at the same time, he lifted his ass off the seat as he slid his track pants down to his knees. He had pulled a condom out of his pocket, and he held it in his hand.

I smiled a little at myself as I heard my voice say, "Here, boss, let me do that. Let me wrap your big, beautiful erection up before I ride it."

It wasn't as good as Blueberry Hill, but at that moment, it was running a close second. He was begging me to slow down and he pleaded, "Wait! Hold up! Hold up, baby! I want this to last, and you're killing me! My God, you feel so good! No, wait, I don't want to cum yet. Wait! Stop! No, no! Fuck, no!"

I pulled away a little and he moaned, "Oh, fuck, man, that's not going to work either. Forget it. Just ride me, baby. Now. Just ride me hard. I'll make sure I get another big hard-on that'll keep you happy for days. Fuck! I haven't even touched your breasts yet and I'm acting like a teenager!"

Hearing the tremble in his voice, I pulled the elastic out of his hair, and I felt his smooth, blond hair run between my fingers. It was the icing on the cake. That, coupled with his boyish, eager erection, was all I needed to scratch the itch I'd been suffering with for too long. I put my head back and I gave voice to my pleasure that was washing over me, wave after wave.

***

I probably don't have to tell you that both Jack and I never showed our faces at that gym again, and Jack, true to her word, never mentioned my blond, 24-year-old gigolo to the folks. Kind of like what goes on in Vegas stays in Vegas, if you know what I mean.

However, once in a while and out of the blue, and if we were alone in the kitchen, finishing up the dishes, she would say, "I wonder who Sexy Dan is coaching now. I hope she appreciates his good service."

We would both laugh and she would say, "You are something else."

And I would remind her, "In Canada, the accessory-to-the-fact is just as guilty as the perpetrator, you know."

***

Chapter Fifteen
Family Ties

It was November, and Jacquie had sailed through the first segment of her Canadian Internationally Trained Nurse Practitioner Program. I had convinced her to take some time to go back down to Miami to list her condo as a rental property. She wasn't ready to sell it, and the rental income would at least cover the expenses until she decided what to do with it. She had already decided to make Canada her new home permanently, but immigration paperwork takes time; it's not like a simple student visa or work permit. I promised to take care of Zalia and reassured her a thousand times that I wouldn't have another hissy fit and break my foot once again by kicking any inanimate objects while she wasn't around to pick up the pieces. It was too bad that she wasn't going to be able to meet Lars who was coming in just for the weekend on his way to New York, but all was not lost; he had already promised to spend Christmas with us, which was just around the corner.

I dropped her off at the airport and kissed her goodbye. "I love you, Sis. Now, you know the drill. Bring me home a nice, sexy boyfriend, and don't do anything that I wouldn't do. Now go! Just go!"

***

"Just me!" I called out as I opened the front door. I noticed that Patou took his time coming to greet me, and it hit me that he was now five years old. Where had the time gone? He was an excellent pet, with the kids especially, but he was definitely slowing down. Especially when the boys would try to ride him. He was over the whole baby-watching scene and preferred to stay close to Mom or out in the backyard in the summer when he would station himself in the middle of Papa's water feature and let the water run over him for hours at a time. I loved him with all my heart.

Actually, he was the first dog I ever had, and I knew that the others all claimed him as their own, but in my heart, he belonged to me. Mom had originally bought the dog for Dad right after his heart attack, but, one by one, every member of the family automatically claimed him for their own. The dog was cagey enough to play favorites with whoever was holding the bag of biscuits.

However, Patou, our big, Great White Pyrenees, if the truth be known, missed Papa, Mama, and François, as well as the farm, right along with all of us. He was at his natural best on the farm, chasing the squirrels and disappearing into the bush for hours at a time.

The rest of us couldn't face the burnt-out farm at all. I flat-out wouldn't ever think of taking the children up there. It was a massive, 20-acre, charred, blackened hell. Who knew? We may never be able to face it. The wreckage from the fire had been extensive; the whole insides of the bush had burned out completely but stopped more or less at the meadow where the big stumpery ran the width of a hundred feet. The stumpery had acted as a barrier of sorts, and the fire had seemed to die out there. The wind must have shifted within the flash fire, because the back of the farm near the old railway tracks had been spared as well.

The fire chief wrote in his report that the probable cause was a cigarette. When he asked if anyone on the farm that night smoked, I said in a small, sickened voice that my husband had the occasional cigarette. Mom and Dad, who were with me at the time, didn't say a word. We never spoke of it again. I had known from the get-go the cause of the fire and the chief's report was merely a confirmation to my worst nightmare. After reviewing the report with the fire chief, it was obvious to all of us that late that night, François had taken a walk down to the old railway tracks where he loved to go, had had a joint on the way down, and had flicked his roach down on the ground without thinking. That's why his body was found on the far side of the fire, down by the tracks. That's where François died. That's why his body wasn't burned. He had at least been spared that horror. He had died quickly from smoke asphyxiation. Unfortunately, my in-laws, who were inside the trailer, had run outside to pull the beehives out of the fire's path, when a flaming tree crashed down on Mama. Papa died trying to free her. Their remains were found together.

Papa and Mama's big trailer, where we had spent many, many afternoons putting the boys down for a nap in the afternoon and all of us playing cards into the evening, was not touched by the flames, but the smoke damaged everything. There was nothing left inside it or outside it that we could hold onto as a memento of the family that had established our honeybee farm. It was the same for the big Mercedes that Papa used to transport all the produce down to the food bank and to pick up everyone from the airport. It was gone, all gone. Mom's old friend, Tom Oliver, who was an arborist, had been working day in and day out since then, removing tons and tons of the scorched remaining ashes and wreckage of Mom's beloved childhood farm. He took care of getting rid of the trailer and the big Benz as well.

Of course, the loss of the apiary business, the bush, and the trailer were of no real consequence. It was the loss of three members of our family, Papa, Mama, and François that still had us reeling. There were the mornings that I would stop in to 7 Russell Hill Road for a quick coffee, to find my parents wiping their red eyes as they opened the door to greet me. How much could they take? They had buried their baby son the year before, and, now, they buried Dad's best friend, Papa, Papa's new wife, Diep, and their son-in-law, François. I didn't want them worrying about me and the kids, so I put my own grief aside and buckled down to act as head of the family until they were able to move forward. Thank God for Jacquie. I knew my parents felt the same way about her. We would never, ever be able to repay her for the role she played in our lives at this terrible time.

I know that I loved François when I married him, and I know that he had adopted my daughter, and I know that we shared two, beautiful, little twin boys, but I also knew that our marriage had died right after the twins were born, and long, long before the fire.

***

The farm, actually, was one of the reasons why Lars was coming into town. When I told him the story of how our family started an apiary a few years back in the middle of an old bush that Mom used to live on when she was a little girl, he was fascinated with Chi's research and ongoing study of the relationship of plant life and human beings. Being educated and involved in the life sciences, our old farm was right up his alley. He had kindly offered to go up there with me to meet with Tom onsite to organize our next step in clearing the land from a scientific point of view. That's the kind of man Lars was. He ran a close second to my father for being sensitive, kind, empathetic, and wise way beyond his 40 years.

Mom had made a list of all the species of trees that she remembered living there, and she had quite a list for Tom and Lars to look out for and to work into our reforestation plans once we got that far along.

I was completely overwhelmed by the immensity of the task, but Mom somehow chipped away at it day by day, and her vision for a new forest was slowly but surely beginning to emerge. Dad and I were grieving for the loss of our loved ones, but poor Mom had such an affinity with that old bush that her grief was compounded by the loss of the old oaks, maples, chestnut, and pine trees that had stood tall and proud over all the years. She simply put her head down, got to work, and soldiered on. As Papa had told me many, many times, Denise Royal was the toughest woman he had ever met. And every time he said it, he said it with awe, love, and respect in his voice.

Dad slowly had begun to work with the town planners, environmental groups, and the local forestry department, ensuring that Tom Oliver's work met and exceeded all the municipal standards, as we gratefully accepted the whole region's condolences for the loss of our loved ones, the loss of our honeybees, and the loss of our bush.

***

I gave Patou an extra scratch around his ears, and I heard Dad call out from Saul's office, "In here, honey."

I stood in the door of Saul's office and smiled at him. By the looks of things, he was unpacking a new laptop, and I reminded him that reading the instructions came easier if he would just take his reading glasses off his forehead and wear them on his nose.

After five years of both Mom and I teasing him unmercifully about being the bumbling, nerdy intellectual that walked around in a fog, sometimes I think that he just played the part for the attention.

He explained the new device sitting on his desk that was half unwrapped. "I was just thinking; last year I bought Martina a new laptop to use when she came over here, but I had forgotten about it, and it's been sitting here on the shelf ever since. So, I went out this morning to pick up this matching one for Zalia in hopes that I can convince the two of them to sleep over a little more often. It will give Lars and me something to tinker with while he stays for the weekend with us. The two of us will get these two little laptops all set up with age-appropriate programs and the likes."

I burst out laughing at his little-boy charm, so excited that his good friend, Lars, had agreed to stay over with him and Mom rather than stay with me, Jacquie, Maureen, and four noisy kids.

"Dad, he's coming into town to see me. I know, I know, you talked him into sleeping here, but he's not in the least interested in putzing around with you all weekend. It's me, all me, he wants to spend time with!"

"I happen to know better. When I explained to him that your house was in a constant uproar, with four out-of-control kids riding their bikes throughout the house, along with three know-it-all women, he caught on pretty fast. Don't worry. He'll be more than comfortable in our nice guestroom. Mom's got it all set up for him, and she intends to spoil him rotten, cooking him all his favorites. As for you, you can come and go as you please, but all I'm asking for is a little 'bro time' with our new friend. You know that Lars and I speak the same language somehow. What you don't know is that he phones me all the time, just to shoot the shit like boys do, without the high maintenance that our girls seem to require."

I took a step into the room to lean down to give him a kiss. "You know damn well he's coming into town to give us a hand up at the farm. He doesn't want to be fiddling around with kids' computers, but have it your way. I must admit, I'm quite happy to share Lars with you, but as soon as the kids are all in bed, he's all mine. I'm taking him out around town this weekend, just us two. We have a lot of catching up to do."

Dad called me back into the room, "Honey, seriously, this is the first time that Lars is going to meet all the kids, and your mom and I didn't want your nerdy, intellectual, bachelor boyfriend to be scared away from us all. We can all be a little overpowering at times."

"Oh. You're the best. But first things first. I've explained this to you and Mom over and over again. We're not romantically involved, and we never will be, so give that little dream up right now. Please don't worry about his reaction to the kids. It's not like I'm asking Lars to marry me or anything like that. And he feels the same way. We just love each other as platonic friends, and that's not going to change. I'm not sleeping with him, you know."

Dad's hands flew up in the air. "Neither am I!"

We both laughed, and Mom came into the room to see what was going on. Dad continued, "I know, I know, sweetheart, but your mother and I just want to see you happy. That being said, we're so happy that Jacquie and Zalia are with you and the kids, but we're always hoping that you'll fall in love again."

"I'll get working on that little project right away, Dad. I'll be sure to mention right upfront to any perspective suitors that I live with four kids and a crazy girlfriend, and that I have an interfering, very nosy father. Meanwhile, we'll have to learn to share Lars until my Mr. Wonderful comes into the picture. Deal?"

"Deal."

I'd caught onto Dad's sensitive and loving heart a long time ago. Every time he bought a new bike for Martina, it was really me that he had in mind, his little girl that he never had the opportunity to spoil all those years ago.

And now, with Zalia and Jacquie living with us, he was at his best, always buying two identical items for his two 35-year-old girls, his two ten-year-old girls, as well as his two three-year-old boys. Mom was the same, always baking and making everything in multiple sets of twos.

Between us, even after losing Papa, Mama, and Francois, we carried on, slowly but surely. How lucky could I get? I had no option other than to share the newest member of the family, my heartbreakingly handsome good friend, Dr. Lars Hansson, with my dad who was still reeling from losing his best friend of over 30 years in the fire at the farm. A bromance was exactly what my father needed right now, and it was my greatest pleasure to be able to facilitate that.

***

I got the kids organized and headed straight over to 7 Russell Hill Road. This was Lars's second day in town, and it all seemed to be working out very well. He had been so taken with the children the day before, and Martina and Zalia, acting very grown up for all their ten years, were really minding their manners. Lars seemed to automatically fall in love with all four of the children, and he was taking his lead from Dad. I had to smile when I saw him peel a banana and give half to Warren and half to Noah as if he had been doing this all his life.

He was especially taken with Martina; I supposed because she looked more like me, with her African blonde ringlets and skin tones so similar to his own. Several times during that first visit, I watched him staring intently at her. And, thinking about it now, she was also taken with him. I thought to myself that maybe she was missing her dad. All in all, and for whatever reason, it seemed to me that they had bonded in some special, quiet way.

***

Mom met me at the door and tilted her head toward the family room. "Our brainiacs are in the family room, setting up the girls' computers."

All three of them, Rabbi Kleiman, Dad, and Lars, were bent over the two new laptops as if they were performing neurosurgery. I barely got a kiss from any of them, so Mom and I took it upon ourselves to put some coffee on.

I looked over at the men as they all started to cheer, as they got the Wi-Fi signal on both laptops. A few minutes later, I heard Lars ask, "What's this? It seems like email has already been set up on this one. Did you set this up this earlier, Nigel?"

"Oh yeah. I bought this one for Martina a long time ago before we even knew little Zalia. At the time, I tinkered around with it, and as you can see, I set up a little email address for her."

"But who has sent her a message?"

"Not me."

"Not me."

"Not me."

Mom and I both looked at each other, and we walked over to the boys sitting on the sofa, all huddled over the laptop with the mystery email boldly showing its face on the screen. The date on the email showed that it had been sent months and months ago.

I leaned over to see the sender's name, a little concerned that some unknown person had sent my little ten-year-old an email.

Rabbi Kleiman read out the sender's name and there was dead silence in the room. He read: "*Ancestry.ca. Alert regarding a matching gene that lives in Oxford, U.K.*"

I stood there, frozen, as the rabbi's innocent words filtered through my mind, and then the meaning of the words went down deep, deep into my heart. I leaned over the back of the sofa, and I put my arms around Lars. He looked around at me in puzzlement, and everyone listened as I started to speak. I struggled to keep my voice from wavering.

"I know what this email is all about. I'm responsible for this. You see, way, way back last spring, when I registered my Kaufman name with Ancestry.ca, for some crazy reason, I also signed up Martina under her own registration. I think, at the time, I was rationalizing that I may get some Kaufman information on her site too, doubling my chances of tracing the Kaufman family."

"Oh, so that explains everything then," Rabbi Kleiman said.

Dad and Mom, by this time, were bending down, looking into my stricken face. "It's okay, honey, it's okay. What's wrong? So, she got an email. Don't worry. We can cancel the email address if that's what you want."

By this time, I had started to cry, and with tears running down my face, I cried out, "No! No! You don't understand! This is a match to my daughter's other genes! It has nothing to do with my genes at all!"

Lars got up slowly from the sofa and came around and put his arm around me, concerned that I was upset. I delivered the news.

"Dad, Mom, I know you know this, but, Rabbi Kleiman and Lars, what I'm going to tell you will explain everything about this email." I looked up at Lars who was beginning to realize that something more than a stray email was at stake here.

"A long time ago, in Stockholm, Sweden, exactly nine months before Martina was born in September, 2000, I was impregnated through the state-funded in-vitro fertilization program and I used an unknown donor's sperm. I chose that particular donor, because he matched the physical description of my mother's one-and-only love of her life that she had had an afternoon tryst with in 1974, which resulted in me being born nine months after. The love of her life was you, Dad, as we know."

"We know that, honey. What's that got to do with anything?" Mom said.

I looked into Lars's face that was starting to register a little concern, but I continued with my explanation, "This email is an alert to my daughter, Martina Hansson, showing that she has matching genes that are registered in Oxford, England. If they were from her maternal side, I would have received the same alert. Her alert is referencing her paternal side who happens to live in Oxford,

England, the same as you, Lars. You also received an alert that you had matching genes that live in Toronto, Canada, Lars."

Lars's face, by this time, was as white as a sheet, and my voice was breaking as I said, "I have to ask you, Lars. Did you ever donate sperm in 1998 or 1999 in Stockholm, Sweden?"

As Lars's face reached his final shade of pale, his eyes slowly rolled back into his head and he collapsed at my feet in a dead faint.

"I take that as a yes," I said softly to no one in particular.

***

By then, I was on my hands and knees, smoothing his hair back as the rabbi ran to get him some water. Dad was on one side of him, and Mom on the other, shouting in his face, "Lars! Lars! Look at me! Look at me! Are you okay, Lars?"

His eyes fluttered a little, and he offered us a small smile.

I kissed his forehead. "Welcome to parenthood, Dr. Lars Hansson. You have a healthy, biracial, Jewish, and precocious ten-year-old daughter."

***

The five of us sat around the big copper table in the family room, and we all sat there quietly to allow Lars to start first. I figured that he and I could work out the logistics of our new connection after he had had a chance to digest it.

Lars began by saying, "Nigella, please know that as soon as I get back to the U.K., I'll set up a monthly direct deposit into your account to take care of full support for Martina. Whatever you want; it's all fine with me. I'll make sure I'm here once a month to visit her. I'll get a little apartment here in town so I won't be in your way. I just want to be a good father. May I share my idea of how we can tell Martina that she has a biological father that wants to be a part of her life?"

We all nodded as he continued, "I think that you, Nigella, and I should have a sit-down with her and explain how in-vitro fertilization really works. I'll start the story by telling her that when I was a young scientist, still in school, out of curiosity more than anything else, I donated sperm to the state-run clinic. Then, Nigella, you add in that right after that, on a different day altogether, you visited the clinic to purchase some sperm so that you could have a baby since you didn't have a husband. We'll both tell her that the rules of the clinic were that both parties never knew the other party and that the law prohibited any further connection."

I spoke up, "Lars, this is perfect. She's very smart, you know, and she's had enough sex education at home and in school to fill in the blanks. Back when François adopted her, I told her about the in-vitro fertilization and that François was not her birthfather, but she was only five at the time. She'll catch on immediately, but our little girl isn't satisfied with fairytales. She wants the real deal. Be prepared."

Lars asked, "What do you think, folks?"

Rabbi Kleiman said, "As we all know, this is God's work. Right from the get-go, with how you two met, of all places, at a Kaufman reunion. The writing was on the wall, somehow. Don't start worrying about explaining this to Martina; we're all in good hands because we all have loving hearts. Lars, you'll find out soon enough, a good deal of this whole story has to do with this big old house. My good friend, Saul Himmel, Nigel's father, invited me in for a coffee one day, and I've never been the same since. In a good way, of course, Lars, but there's magic here. There's love all around us here at 7 Russell Hill Road. You see the two big pictures over there? That's Saul, Nigel's father, and that's George, Denni's great-grandfather. Those two, they watch over us all here, right along with God above us."

Dad added his two cents' worth, "I have a suggestion for a nice little outing, but it's just for the three of you. Lars, with your connections here, or I can make a few calls on your behalf, but I'm thinking maybe to give Martina an active part in all this, the three of you could go down to a lab in the next day or two and have some blood work done. All together, like a little nuclear family. You can put some science into the story, Lars, as the tech takes the blood from each of you. And then, once the results are in and you get the formal piece of paperwork, you can put it in your new family scrapbook. And then you'll have the documentation that you'll need to amend her birth certificate as well, if that's possible."

Mom said, "And, Lars, I have a suggestion for you as well. We have a perfectly good apartment right here where our best friends, Chi and Diep, lived. Please move in there. It has a separate entrance, you can come and go as you please, and you're going to need a space of your own. It has two bedrooms, a large office space, living room, and a fairly new kitchen as well. Oh, and it's connected to the greenhouse. You're more than welcome to stay here in the house with us if that's what you want, but as you know, we're a big, noisy bunch and you're used to living on your own. We want you here, right beside us. We're family now. Right, Nigel?"

Dad put his arm around Mom and smiled into her earnest face. "Of course, honey. You're right. You're always right." With that, he gave Lars a wink. "It looks like you have a new apartment, Lars. You can't argue with the boss."

***

I filed up the stairs to my in-laws' apartment with trepidation. I hadn't been up there since before the fire, and I didn't want to break down in front of everyone. It would just get my dad and mom all upset all over again.

I stepped into the foyer, and I immediately was drawn to the sun streaming in through the kitchen window. I breathed a sigh of relief. Everything was going to be okay. Dad put his arm around me and whispered, "You okay, honey?"

"I'm more than okay, Dad. This is all meant to be. This is where Lars is meant to be. I'll make sure that he's happy here. Don't worry, Dad. I've got this."

Dad, Mom, and Jacquie, shortly after the fire, had taken care of clearing out my in-laws' possessions. They had saved some things for the kids in memory of their grandparents, along with all the photographs, and had put them away in their attic. They donated the rest to Goodwill. They had left Papa's beautiful, old, mid-century, Danish dining-room set and his colorful Turkish rugs on the floor. Papa's big, long, leather sofa was still there, along with a couple of Scandinavian armchairs. The big office, behind the hidden, sliding wall, was sparkling clean and empty, as were the two bedrooms.

We were all in the spirit of things, and the rabbi was whining to Dad that if he knew that Chi's apartment was up for grabs, he would have put his name on it long ago. I watched Mom and she walked Lars, arm in arm, through each room. She was suggesting to him that she'd take care of buying the two new beds and linens that very week to ensure that he would be all set up for his return next month for Christmas.

Lars looked down at her and smiled. "Yes, Denni, whatever you say. But I'll bring my own duvets. You know us Swedes, we like our Swedish down duvets and our Volvos. Everything else is your choice, Denni. I'll straighten up with you as soon as you're ready. Thank you, thank you so much. I guess this means that you're my landlady."

"No, Dr. Lars Hansson. This means we're family."

***

As we were leaving, I pulled Rabbi Kleiman back a little, and the others filed down the stairs first.

"Rabbi Kleiman, would it be possible for just you and me to install a brand-new kosher mezuzah here on the doorway, for my Jewish daughter's non-believing father?"

"Of course, child."

***

Chapter Sixteen
Addendum: Jacqueline Dixon

Jacquie knew it had to happen sooner or later. It was her first time ever on ice skates. She had, just for a split second, relaxed a little while she was being supported by Lars on one side of her and Alessandro on the other. She knew it was going to be a big, embarrassing fall. The minute she felt her skate tip click into his, she knew right then that she was going down. In all ways. She gave in to the fall, and her arms, high over her head, dictated her short ski jacket to slide upward. She felt the ice against her back. Her eyes watched him almost in slow motion and she felt him crashing down beside her, with his mouth wide open with laughter. She too was laughing as she looked up past his big shoulders, and her eyes rested on the North Star in the black Canadian sky, shining like a beacon amongst the smaller stars. She made a wish. She felt his hands come up to cradle her face, and his mouth was very, very close to hers.

He whispered, "You okay?" She felt her arms come from up over her head to wrap around his neck.

"I've never felt better."

She pulled him down into her face and gave him a kiss that he would never forget.

An eternity later, he pulled away a little, and they both started to laugh as they looked up to see all the skaters circled around them. Denni, Maureen, and Nigella started the chant, "Jacquie's got a boyfriend, Jacquie's got a boyfriend," and all the other skaters at Toronto's City Hall skating rink joined in.

Phone cameras began to flash, and Denni said, "This will be on the 11 o'clock news tonight for sure. This is like the Kiss-Cam down at the games. City Hall public skating could only dream of publicity like this!"

Nigella grinned. "Oh yeah. You know, Mom, this is a perfect example of the immigrant experience in Toronto. It reminds me of when François and I first met. My God, that seems like 20 years ago! Oh, Mom, I'm so happy that Lars and Jack have found each other."

"Never mind the two new lovers. I'm so happy to hear what you just said about François. Do you know that's the first time in over two years that I've heard you say something nice about him! Could it be that you're leaving the angry stage and entering the forgiveness stage of grieving, honey?"

The 36-year-old widow smiled at her mother. "You might be right, Mom. I've noticed a change in my attitude ever since I came back from my trip to Europe in search of my roots. I guess you might say I've found the answer to the age-old question of *who am I*."

***

From the bench, Lars's parents, Anna and Eliot, were both grinning from ear to ear as they watched the novice skater kissing their son in a not-so-novice manner.

***

Hours later, Jacquie managed to wait until she was alone in her room. The tears were rolling down her cheeks as she quickly closed the door behind her. She said to herself, "What the fuck! What the fuck!"

She had never ever in her whole life felt like that with a single kiss! Surely, he had felt the same! That one kiss had been building up between them ever since they met a few days ago!

She went over what had happened on the way home. All of a sudden, out of the blue, on the way home from the skating rink, he shouted out from the backseat, "Whoa! Is that our drug store? Are we at our corner? Let me out, please! I'll walk home from here. Thanks, thanks ever so much. No, no, I don't need any company. I'll find my way home. And no, I won't stop in for the hot chocolate. See you all in the morning. Thanks again."

He didn't even say goodnight to her. How could she have misread him? How could she have misread that kiss?

Once they got home, she had sat quietly through the hot chocolate that Maureen and Denni dished out, and, thankfully, everyone was slated for an early night. The kids went down without a whimper, and Maureen's parents and Lars's parents had left just herself and Nigella shutting out the lights.

Nigella said, "I'll do the tuck-ins tonight, Jack. I love you, Sis. Sleep tight."

Jacquie took the stairs two at a time to avoid Nigella's questions about the kiss between her and Lars.

Finally, all the exercise from her first time on skates took hold, and she could feel herself giving into Mr. Sandman, when, all of a sudden, her phone rang. She bolted upright out of bed and grabbed the phone from her night table.

Damn, she thought to herself, *Nigella wants to talk about it. Shit!* She clicked the phone on and she said, with eyes closed, "No, girlfriend, I don't want to talk about it."

His Swedish-accented voice was low and very, very sexy. "Jacqueline?" he said tentatively, "Is that you?"

Her heart stopped, and she managed to say, "Oh. Oh. It's you. Sorry, I thought it was Nigella. What's up, Lars?"

"I'm sorry I didn't even say goodnight to you in the car. I really am the absentminded professor, you see. I had something on my mind that was distracting me, and when I saw the drug store outside the car window, it was the answer to my prayers, and I just jumped out on an impulse."

"Lars, Lars, Lars. You are a scientist. Now really. Acting on impulse? I don't think so. I'm not buying that. Try another line. Let's hear a different story."

"Um…um…when I fell on the ice, I scraped my knee and I needed a Band-Aid, so when I saw the drug store, it reminded me."

"Please. As Denni would say, do you think I just fell off the turnip truck?"

She could hear the smile in his voice.

"Okay, what about this; I've got a big, hard piece of chocolate for you, just for you, and I had to go the drug store to buy a wrapper for it."

Her heart sang, but she tried to dial down her excitement, "How do you know I want your big, hard piece of chocolate?"

"Oh, I know you want it, darling. It was in your kiss."

"Well, can't this wait until tomorrow? After all, your big, hard piece of chocolate is two blocks away from me. And I'm not even dressed. I'm naked. And I just got out of the shower. And my body is all warm and soft and wet."

"Trust me, Jacqueline Dixon. This can't wait until tomorrow. I know hard chocolate – it will be all soft and not much good for anything by tomorrow. But enough about me, let's talk about you. Exactly how warm and how soft and how wet are you?"

"On a scale of one to ten, I'm just about even with your big, hard piece of chocolate."

"Oh. I see. You mean to say we're both feeling the same way? Like, all hot with a high temperature? Hmmm. I imagine, you being a nurse and all, that you have a thermometer, am I right?"

"Right."

"Do you make house calls?"

"As a matter of fact, I haven't in the past, but I'm willing to try it out."

"I'll leave the door unlocked. Can't wait to see you."

"You better wait, Lars Hansson. I'm counting on you."

***

She rifled through her drawers, looking for the beautiful, cream-colored, silk short nightie and matching robe that Denni had bought her a few months ago. At that time, she thought to herself that she would never, ever get to wear it on a night of pure, unadulterated sex. That only seemed to happen to other women. Not her. And now, out of the blue, her prayers were being answered. A handsome, sexy, available man was waiting for her. He had even gone out and bought condoms. Sexy as hell, and thoughtful too. And he really seemed to be into her. It was her night to howl.

She packed a small overnight bag, hoping that he would want her to spend the whole night. Yes, toothbrush, hairbrush, body lotion, an extra pair of her best undies, and matching bra that were also a gift from Denni, and a bottle of her favorite shower gel. And her nightie and robe.

She tiptoed into the girl's room and gave them each a light kiss before softly closing their bedroom door behind her.

She opened Nigella's bedroom door and whispered into the dark, "Sis, are you still awake?"

"I am now."

"Lars called me and told me that he had a big, hard piece of chocolate that's all wrapped up and waiting for me over at his apartment, so don't wait up."

Peals of laughter rose from Nigella's bed and she said, "Oh my God, Mom was right! We've been waiting for this moment ever since you two met. Go! Just go! Don't come home. Please stay the night. I've got you covered for the kids' breakfast in the morning. Lunch is at noon at Mom and Dad's. Enjoy yourselves. I love you, Sis."

"I love you too."

"Go get 'im, tiger!"

***

The night air was crisp and cold. Surprisingly, she loved the Canadian late fall weather, especially the nights. She started into an easy jog, and as she looked up, she saw him, waiting for her at the corner.

It was like in the movies. Slow motion all the way. She was running toward him, and he was running toward her. His arms were around her, and she felt her bag drop to the ground, and she put her hands under his jacket and around to feel his back.

The kiss itself was broken and entirely ruined with her laughter as she felt his bare skin and realized he was standing there in his pajama bottoms, with no top, just a jacket thrown over his bare chest.

He explained, "There was no time for clothes. I couldn't wait another minute. I just had to have you in my arms. Don't laugh at me; God forbid my sensitive dick hears you laughing. That will ruin everything."

He grabbed her hand, picked up her bag, and the two of them made a run for it.

***

They were both way beyond the politeness and all the niceties of foreplay. He was on top of her, and she could feel his hands tighten in her hair as he gave in to his pent-up sex drive that had been dogging him ever since he laid eyes on her. She could feel his chest heaving as he kissed her face over and over again.

He whispered, "I'm sorry, baby, I just lost control. I couldn't seem to stop and wait for you."

She whispered back, "So who's keeping count? We've got all night. And I'm going to show you exactly what I want, so I'm going to be way ahead of you when it comes to tallying up orgasms in the morning's light, honey."

"Okay, okay, trust me, I won't let you down. I've been waiting for you ever since puberty hit all those years ago. I'm all yours. Kiss me just like you did at the skating rink. Tell me what you like and what you need. Show me. Touch me. Touch yourself. I want to please you."

"Right now, I need your mouth on my breasts. Yeah. Like that. On my nipples. Oh, Lars, can you feel them? My nipples need you. See, they're getting hard and they're peaking, just for you." She gave a little laugh and she whispered to him, "Your recovery time is admirable. Keep up the good work."

"Is it better for you on top?" He rolled over, holding onto her. "I'm all yours. Ride me. Ride me all night long. Tell me what you like. My God, you're so beautiful. Your breasts are so perfect, so beautiful. Tell me what you need me to do. And I'll deliver until you're begging me to stop."

"Wait a second here, Romeo. You're saying that you'll deliver until I'm begging you to stop? Not me; I never cry, Uncle. You better get ready. Again. It's going to be a long night, Lars Hansson."

"Thank God, Jacqueline Dixon, thank God."

It was the middle of the night as they sat in his kitchen, waiting for the kettle to boil so he could make her a tea. She was turned facing him, sitting on his lap, and she leaned in a little to brush her breasts into his chest.

"That's what I love. Right there. I love to feel your chest hair. It makes me all wet for you. Feel me. See? I'm so wet and slick for you. You're my man. And I'm your woman. I need you right now, again. Deep inside me. Right now."

He cupped her ass with one hand and held the small of her back with the other as her head went back, crying out in pleasure.

***

She woke to slip out of his spoon, and she tiptoed her way to the bathroom. On the way back, she took a moment to look out the window. The late autumn's dawn was just beginning to lighten the night ever so slightly. Her heart was full. It was the first day of the rest of her life. She looked back over her shoulder to watch him sleep, but, instead, she met his eyes, wide open, just watching her.

"You're the most beautiful woman I've ever seen in my whole life. Where have you been all these lonely, lonely years, darling?"

"I was looking for you."

As she snuggled back into their spoon, he said quietly, "We belong together, and I'm never, ever, going to leave you. I'm going to set your soul on fire like never before. We're going to grow old together, and we're going watch our two, beautiful, little girls grow up and thrive, right along with Nigella's two little boys. I love you, Jacqueline Dixon."

"And I love you, Lars Hansson."

***

She drew her breath in to accept what was to come, and she felt Lars's arm around her shoulder tighten a little. It was just noon, and they had torn themselves away from each other to shower and dress in order to join the family and the house guests for lunch.

They had snuck in through the side door, hoping to blend into the crowd without a scene as they knew they were in for the teasing of their lives.

Nigel and Denni, Alessandro, Maureen and her parents, Tomas and Annie, Lars's parents, Eliot and Anna, and Nigella were all at the big copper table, and the four kids were sitting up at the poker table. Lunch was already on the tables.

All of a sudden, Nigella caught sight of them, and she announced in a loud voice, "Well, well, well, they have finally come up for air. Here they are, walking the walk of shame, the two of them, arm in arm, cooing like the love birds they are!"

With that, everyone started laughing and clapping, to Jacquie's embarrassment. Lars didn't seem to mind too much; he just kept hugging her and kissing her as they made their way down through the room to take a seat amongst their family. Lars's mother, Anna, was waving for Jacquie to sit beside her, and Alessandro was pulling out a chair for Lars right beside him. Everyone laughed as Jacquie wolfed down seconds of everything, and Nigella said, "Really, Sis! Quite an appetite! It must be from all the skating down at City Hall last night."

***

As everyone settled into enjoying the lunch and conversation, Jacquie watched Lars as he quietly pushed his chair back and made his way over to the kids' table. He kissed each one of them on the top of the heads, and then he knelt down beside Martina and whispered in her ear, "Hi, honey, do you know why I have this big smile on my face right now?"

Martina looked up at him and said with her 11-year-old-going-on-30 voice, "Duh, yeah, it's because you're in love with Auntie Jacquie. I'm 11 now, and I know about the birds and the bees, as grandma calls it. Zalia does too."

"No, no, honey, I'm talking about this smile, right here, right now."

"What? What are you talking about?"

"My big smile is because when I walked into the room, I heard you say *Hi, Dad* instead of *Hi, Lars*. That's what's made me so happy. I love you, and no matter where I live, you'll always be my daughter."

Lars then looked directly at Zalia, and he put his arm around her shoulders. "And you, Zalia, I love you too. I'm hoping that you'll call me Dad too. After all, you and Martina call yourself sisters, and I'm in love with your mom, as Martina points out, so it would make me so happy to have two little girls instead of one. I want to be your second dad, the same as I'm Martina's second dad. Would that be okay with you, honey?"

Zalia put her hands over her face and started giggling away. "Yeah, Uncle Lars – I mean Dad, I think it's a great idea."

Martina said, "But, Dad, what about the boys?" nodding toward her twin brothers still intent on gobbling up their lunch.

Lars explained as best he could, "I don't think I can, honey. No, you see, I'm not your mom's husband. And one of these days, your mom will fall in love again with a new husband, and then that man will be the boys' dad. It wouldn't be right for me to be so greedy, and, besides, your mom needs to have the boys all to herself right now. I have a feeling that you two young ladies will be enough for me to handle."

Jacquie, mother bear, who had been watching the conversation from her seat, came over and crouched down beside Lars. "What's going on here, Lars Hansson?"

Zalia piped up, "Mom, Uncle Lars wants me to call him dad, the same as Martina does. Can I, Mom, can I?"

257

Jacquie looked into Lars's face, raised her eyebrows very slightly, and gave him a look that laid out the unwritten terms of their new relationship. Lars got the message loud and clear. He nodded his head in acceptance to the silent deal that the single mother had articulated without using a single word. He understood the deal fully: *This is for real, buster; don't go messing with my daughter's heart unless you are going to make this arrangement permanent.*

* * *

That night after dinner, Jackie and Lars, just the two of them, went for a walk through the neighborhood. It was a cold, crisp night, so they walked along at a good pace, when, all of a sudden, there were two men right in front of them, blocking the sidewalk.

"Identification please. Name? Address? Do you live in this neighborhood?"

Jacquie immediately felt herself going back, way back to the time as a small, black girl living in the inner city, witnessing her brother being dragged from their house like an animal just because of his black skin. He died later in his cell as a result of the beating that he had received while in police custody. That memory alone was enough to set her into a rage. She then recalled all the years and years of being pulled over after having worked the midnight shift at the hospital, with the police questioning why a black woman would be out in the middle of the night, driving a car which was always presumed stolen.

The two undercover police officers stepped back, albeit almost imperceptibly as she spit out her words and much to the surprise of the gentle, calm, Swedish intellectual beside her.

"Who the fuck do you think you are? You first! Get out your ID! Now!"

The two officers' eyes were wide by this time, but they promptly complied by showing their Toronto Police identification.

Jacquie was relentless, "Do you know who you're dealing with? This man is Dr. Lars Hansson, a world-renowned Swedish scientist who is currently staying at 7 Russell Hill Road just around the corner from where you're standing. And as for me, my name is Jacqueline Dixon. I live at 49 Parkwood Avenue, also just around the corner from where you're standing. I grew up in the projects in Miami, Florida, and I know racial profiling when I see it. Don't mess with me or this wonderful man beside me just because of the color of our skin. Do you understand me?"

Jacquie calmed down somewhat with the plain-clothed officer's response.

"Ms. Dixon! Ms. Dixon! Please calm down! You are exactly right. We should have had our identification out even before we spoke to you. We meant no offence. We're stationed in this neighborhood because we're on a quiet, long-standing surveillance to watch over a property in the neighborhood."

With this, the second officer spoke up, "Dr. Hansson, are you living at 7 Russell Hill Road? Your name doesn't match up with our records of who lives there. Can you explain?"

Lars, by this time, had put his arm around Jacquie's shoulders, asserted himself, and said firmly, "Yes, certainly. As Ms. Dixon indicated, I'm a Swede, but I live in Oxford, U.K. I'm here, along with my parents, as a guest of the Supreme Court Justice, Nigel Royal, and his family."

The two officers, looking a little relieved, nodded to each other. The talker of the two officers began again, explaining that as soon as the address 7 Russell Hill Road was mentioned, they knew that their evening was about to settle back down once again to their quiet, boring, periodic surveillance that they had been assigned.

They told the indignant, impassioned, black nurse and the tall, calm, black scientist the story of how the surveillance of 7 Russell Hill Road began. Chief Justice Nigel Royal had suffered with hiding out under the Canadian Witness Protection Program for years until they managed to wrap up a specific case of international money laundering. They also told them that the judge had been victim of a home invasion by two out-of-towners that had endangered his whole family a few years ago, and that the judge was always worried about kidnappers now that he had grandchildren to watch out for.

They ended their story by saying, "A little bit of boring, quiet surveillance is the least that we can do for the old judge, after him serving Canada in our judicial system over all the years."

Jacquie said, "I'm sorry for my tirade. I'm an African-American, and my back is always up as soon as I interact with the police."

The taller of the two men started laughing. "Ms. Dixon, please! You don't have to tell me! Look at me! Look at my olive skin and my straight, black hair. I'm as Italian as they come. First generation. I grew up here in Toronto, and all through school, I was called a wop every day, day in and day out. The cops were always giving me and my buddies the toe of their boot for things we never did."

His partner jumped in, "Yeah. My mother is Filipina. All my friends in high school thought she was the family's maid. And I grew up never being able to get a date because I was shorter than all the girls. Nobody wanted a short, little, half-Asian asshole like me!"

With his self-described proclamation, the four of them burst out laughing.

After they all shook hands, the Italian, by then known as Marco, said, "Wait just a minute here. I've got an idea…"

And that's when Jacqueline Dixon, the American with the brand-new Canadian PR card that was about to marry a Swede, followed by becoming a mother of two, was nodding in agreement to be nominated to sit on the Toronto Police Race Relations Committee as the Forest Hill Community Spokesperson.

That's how Jacquie spent the rest of her days as an advocate for not only the African-Canadian population but for the Asians, the LGBTQ, the First Nations, and all the other marginalized sectors in the big, diverse city of Toronto, just north of the 49th parallel.

***

Chapter Seventeen

House Guests

"Of course, Dad, of course. Yes, it's a great idea. I'll make sure that we set three extra plates on the table for Christmas Eve dinner."

I listened to Dad's plans over the phone, smiling a little at his enthusiasm. "Dad, it'll be nice. Yes, they'll go to early mass in the afternoon, so we don't have to change the time. Yes, so there'll be a crowd, but Anna and Eliot and Tomas and Annie will be happy to see a few more adults at the table. The kids can be a handful for them. They're not used to the noise. And yes, don't worry. We'll keep the basketball out of the house."

I listened as he further explained his reasoning for inviting Alessandro and his parents to dinner, and I reassured him, "Dad, I don't know why I didn't think of this. Alessandro is always with you anyway, and I'll make sure he and his parents feel very welcome."

***

She was a short, plain-looking, older woman, with her gray hair pulled back intentionally into a bun at the nape of her neck. But there was something about her face. Behind the defense that she put up as a shield, behind that toughness, I saw something very deep and very loving in her almost-black, round eyes. Her husband had been a handsome man in his day, but he too gave the impression that they were fish out of water when it came to leaving their comfortable Little Italy neighborhood to go to dinner with complete strangers. My heart went out to them both.

Alessandro stood behind them, as handsome as ever, arms full of wrapped gifts, and two bottles of wine pushed down deep in his jacket's pockets. I watched as Dad took their coats, and Mom, Anna, and Eliot grabbed their hands and led them to the living room. Tomas and Annie had them all laughing within the first few minutes, claiming that they were all European with a bunch of crazy Canadian kids having Christmas Eve with the Swedes.

Jacquie added, "Of course! That's how things are done in Canada! It's quintessentially Canadian!" Lars, of course, knowing that he was in love with the most brilliant, witty woman in the whole world, was nodding in agreement, but Maria, with her lack of the English language, didn't seem to be enjoying herself as much as everyone else.

I had a hunch that I knew how to rectify that. I dug around in the kitchen, slipped on one of my European aprons, and then grabbed another one and waved it over my head as I stepped back into the living room.

"Maria, I need some help! Can you help me in the kitchen? No, Mom, not you. Maria and I can do it."

And that's exactly how Maria Camarra managed to take over my kitchen and give us all the best Christmas Eve dinner we ever had. It wasn't long until Maria forgot her shyness about speaking English, and she and Anna began a friendship right there and then at 49 Parkwood Avenue, six-thousand miles away from their own home bases far away in Europe. This friendship would last for the rest of their lives. I looked over at Alessandro who was having to shout a little into his father's ear, as he was hard of hearing. He was a good son, no doubt about it. Dad had told me one day a few months back that Alessandro took good care of his parents, and he felt responsible for their wellbeing ever since his older sister had died in a motorcycle accident when she was only 17 years old. There had been just the three of them from that day forward. That's why Alessandro lived next door to them, over in Little Italy.

By the end of the dinner, Maria Camarra had the four children calling her and Francesco Nonna and Nonno. She had invited all of us, all 14 of us, over to her house for New Year's Day lunch.

Martina and Zalia were wearing the little, gold, hoop earrings that their 'Nonna' had given them as they cleared the table after the last dessert. Dad had them in the kitchen, loading the dishwasher, and Alessandro had the boys up beside him at the table, laying out the two big Lego kits, once again from Nonna and Nonno. Francesco was sketching out how to brick a house on a scratchpad for Tomas and Eliot, and Maria was dictating a recipe to Anna as she wrote everything down under her watchful eye. Anna and Eliot were telling them how Lars took them to see a residence in the neighborhood as they were thinking of moving to Toronto to be nearer to the family. Lars couldn't let go of Jacquie who was very busy nuzzling his neck. There was a lot of love around my big table that night, and I was so thankful that the kids didn't seem to be missing their dad and their grandpère and grandmère that first Christmas without them. We still had Christmas Day to get through, but I had a feeling that Lars had already stepped in somehow to fill some of the void for the kids. You just never know.

Just when I was feeling a little like the only single person in the midst of all these loving couples, I felt Maureen slip her arm around my waist. She said, "Is Your Majesty ready for a coffee? I mean a real coffee – an Irish coffee. And I won't be stingy with the whisky either."

"Deal."

***

I'd never been to a New Year's lunch or a dinner quite like this in my whole life. Everybody shouted and yelled a lot. Everybody hugged and kissed a lot. Everybody around me was having the time of their lives, and I told myself not to be such an uptight princess. After all, this was Maria and Francesco's part of the world, and I should try a little harder to fit in.

I heard Dad's big baritone over everyone else's, as his team scored on the hockey game that was blaring from the old television in the small living room. He was having a great time with all of Alessandro's boy cousins, half of them on the floor and half of them standing around, watching the game.

Mom, Annie, Anna, Jacquie, and the older Italian aunties were in the kitchen, and Martina and Zalia were outside on the street where Sandro and his cousins were introducing Lars and the kids to something that they called ball hockey or road hockey. I watched them all out the front window, and I smiled as I saw Lars scoop up one of the twins and put him back on his feet.

I decided I'd better make more of an effort, so I plastered on a big smile and joined Alessandro's girl cousins and the younger wives over on the narrow stairs that led up to the bathroom. They made room for me and continued their conversation about nails and hair as if I had been there for the whole conversation. Before I knew it, two of them were redesigning my ringlets with their fingers while another was putting my hand on her lap so she could apply some red nail polish on my plain-Jane nails. The manicurist, Connie, looked up from my nails and she said, "So how long have you been dating Sandro?"

"What!" I realized that I had raised my voice, but before I could soften my tone, one of the older cousins had nudged her and she hissed, "For fuck's sake, Connie, she's a widow!"

Connie's mouth dropped open, and she, right along with three of the other girls, took a moment to cross themselves in true Catholic fashion.

I recovered from my surprise quickly and explained to them, "So sorry, girls, for yelling like that. I was a little surprised by your question. I didn't mean to be rude. You see, Alessandro is my dad's friend. Yes, he does come over to my house, but that's because he's my supervisor at school and he checks my research and stuff. That's all. And you're right, I am a widow."

One of the older girls asked in a hushed voice, "Do you want to talk about? When did your husband die? Was he black too? How long were you married?"

By then, I had found my sense of humor, so I laughed a little and said, "In answer to your question of how long I was married, well, girls, I'll tell you. I was married to him for too damn long! He was a son-of-a-bitch and I deserved better!"

Everyone broke into laughter, and from then on, I was one of the girls.

***

They all stood out on the porch as my big family, all 14 of us, scrambled into our three cars to head out across the city. Lars put his arm around me and said, "Nigie, would it be okay if Tony and Sandro dropped off a couple of hockey nets tomorrow? I'll make sure they're put away every night. It'll be good for the boys."

"Sure, Lars. Of course. Whatever you want."

Maureen copiloted as I drove. Everyone in the back of the car was dead to the world. She said quietly, "Thank God the holidays are over. I can't wait until our company leaves, the kids are back in school, and now that Jacquie is with Lars, it'll be nice just back to you and me again. Like it used to be. We've come through one hell of a year, Your Majesty."

"Yes. And I might add, we've come through with flying colors. Thanks to you, Maureen, you and Jack and Mom. I've never laughed so much in my whole life as I have over the past six months. Thank you. I love you. And we're going to have one hell of a good year going forward."

***

That day in Little Italy was the start of my boys' passion for road hockey. After all, they were Canadians, and having two dinted and ragged hockey nets resting in my front garden 12 months a year until the day they grew up and left home was all part of the package. My magnificent Magnolia tree and the two cherry trees beside it weathered the storm quite nicely, but House and Garden never came calling to photograph the gardens again once the hockey nets moved in.

***

Even though we were in the middle of a cold snap, I felt toasty standing there in my pajamas, my old Uggs, and the old Canada Goose jacket with the big, fur, trimmed hood that Dad had bought me the first year I came to Canada. The night air was cold on my face as I lifted my hood a little to blow out a puff of air to watch it fade away, just like the kids do. The long icicles on the northern eaves glistened and I could see over the roof that the full moon was on the wane, but it still illuminated the clouds that were scudding by. A few twinkling stars emerged from behind them. The street was quiet. It was after nine o'clock when all of a sudden, I heard a psst. Psst. Tap, tap, tap.

I looked up and Maureen was cranking the window open. She hissed, "Have you lost your mind? What are you doing?"

I waved to her to come down. She closed the window. Two minutes later, we both stood there in our pajamas and parkas, looking up at the roof line beside the garage.

Maureen agreed with me, Lars and Jacquie, who were camping out over at Lars's apartment over Dad's garage, was hard on Jacquie, sneaking in in the middle of the night to be here with Zalia for the mornings. She didn't feel right about having Lars sleep over at my house; she said it would be too confusing for the kids.

Lars had joined University of Toronto's Molecular Science Division and had just accepted teaching part-time hours until that fall when he would begin teaching a full cohort. He and Jacquie were planning on getting married in the spring, and Dad's old apartment was too small for Zalia to join them over there, and none of us could consider breaking up Martina and Zalia anyway. I decided that for their wedding present, I would build them an apartment, separate from the rest of 49 Parkwood Avenue, with the entrance on the side, a kitchen and living room and office on the ground floor, and two bedrooms above the garage. Our big loft, where the boys slept, would have an extra door that would connect their apartment to the loft, and we would have Martina and Zalia take the loft. After all, they were teens now, and it was time they had a little space of their own. Lars was, after all, Martina's biological daughter, and he had already filled out the adoption papers to adopt Zalia as soon as they were married. The four of them were a brand-new family unit, and if I knew Jack, I knew that she'd be pregnant right away. Yes, they needed their own space and their own privacy.

Maureen said, "So we would bring the twins down to the second floor with me, and Martina and Zalia would take over the loft."

"Exactly."

"I'm happy to move, Nigella, if you need me to. I can take a smaller bedroom on the second floor."

"No. But now that you mention it, Martina's old room, which she never went back to since Zalia came along, is much larger and has a nicer bathroom than yours. Why don't you think about that? I'm happy to have it all decorated fresh for you, but I'll need your input. And there's lots of room in there for your desk, your little sofa, and television too."

All of a sudden, we could hear someone coming around the corner on the sidewalk, and all four of us laughed as Dad said, "What the hell is going on here? What are you two doing standing out here in your pajamas?"

***

Two nights later, I stood in my kitchen, looking out through the kitchen doorway at the noisy crowd sitting around my big, Swedish, dining-room table. Dad and Alessandro had come over earlier to set up Dad's old drafting table in a corner of my living room. Mom had arrived along with the architect and the contractor that had built their big family-room addition on their house six years ago and then my big renovation when I bought 49 Parkwood Avenue.

Lars, Jack, Maureen, and Mom were talking to the designer that had helped me decorate the house when we moved in a few years back. Martina and Zalia were eager to work with Mom and the designer to choose their own wallpaper and paint colors for the loft. They wanted to boot their little brothers' asses out of the loft that night, but Lars and Jack put a quick end to that nonsense. They asked the designer if she would make them a big sign for the door. The loft was to be renamed the 'Babe Cave.'

Lars left all the structural talk to the architect, contractor, Alessandro, and Dad. The only thing that he insisted on was that he was paying for it. I've never seen Dad look happier. He was in his element, running the show, and I knew without a doubt that the new apartment would be spectacular. He caught my eye and came over to give me a hug. He said, "Do you know what today is?"

"Um…This is our third building project. Another new beginning?"

He looked at me and said quietly, "It's our sixth anniversary, honey. This is the day that we met out at the airport. I met my daughter and you met your father for the first time in our lives."

"Thank God for that, Dad. I love you."

"And I love you, honey. Happy Anniversary."

***

It was soon after we started building that I went over to Dad's house to speak to him alone. The words were no sooner out of my mouth when I knew I had done the right thing.

"Really, honey? You want me to go with you to open the new children's playground in Poland? Just you and me?"

"Yeah, Dad. Just you and me. Think about it. Over all the years, we've never had a little holiday, just the two of us. I want you all to myself. And this is my treat. You're not allowed to pay for anything. It's only for a few days. Do you think Mom can live without you?"

I shook my head and laughed as he started to bellow, "Denni, Denni, where are you? I've got big news for you! My daughter has invited me to go on a holiday – just her and me!"

***

It was 8:30 a.m. in Munich, and we dropped our luggage off at the hotel before hopping into a taxi to meet my grandma's old midwife, Renata Wójcik, for brunch, along with the historian that had arranged my first visit with her last year. That way, we could have our one quick visit in Germany before our jetlag would set in. We would be back in the hotel in time to rest before our flight out to Stockholm the next morning.

Since we were in Europe anyway, I planned to take Dad back to my hometown just to show him where I went to school and where Mor and I had lived in our little apartment. He had only been in Stockholm when he was working on the Nobel Prize Committee way back in 1974 and hadn't been back since. Since the day I had met my dad, we had never really discussed what went down between him and my Mor, so I thought it was time that he had a little visit with her even if it was at her gravesite. We all need closure, even if it was 37 years in the making. And, besides, I had a little surprise for him in Stockholm.

After Stockholm, we would then fly to Warsaw, Poland, and rent a car to drive to the town of Wloclawek to cut the ribbon on the children's playground, then get a direct flight back home from Warsaw.

It was pretty tight scheduling, but both of us didn't want to be away any longer than necessary. It would have been different if the whole family was with us, but this was just a quick trip in and out to take care of the children's playground in Poland. It turned out to be much more than that.

***

Renata Wójcik hadn't changed a bit. She opened her apartment door and just stood there, looking me up and down.

I held out my arms a little, and finally she smiled and said, "You haven't changed a bit. You're just as tall as ever. Just like your grandma was." She looked up at Dad and said, "And who's this?"

Dad said politely, "Hello, Mrs. Wójcik. I'm Nigel. I'm Nigella's father, and these flowers are for you."

He offered his hand, but she slapped it aside and said, "We're almost family. Give me a hug. Oh! You're a big one, aren't you!? Come in, come in. We've got company here waiting to meet you. They're joining us for lunch."

Olga, the historian from last year jumped out of her seat to greet me and gave Dad a big hug too. Rabbi Becker, who was Renata's new rabbi, seemed to be an affable chap, and we kept our coats on as Renata told us we were going to the restaurant just down the street, and the lunch was her treat.

We ambled along down to the restaurant for brunch, all of us taking turns walking beside Renata and her walker. Her walker, the new one that Jack and I had bought her the year before, was decorated with the German flag on one side and the Canadian and American flags on the other.

She finished her story of what had transpired over the last year with, "So now I'm a Jew. Once again. Simple as that. Thanks to you, Nigella, and thanks to Rabbi Becker here. You made this possible."

I said, "I'm so glad that you were able to trace your parents, Renata. That's exactly how I found you and my grandma as well. And I'm grateful for that."

Dad added, "And it was you, Renata, that gave our beautiful Martina Kaufman Hansson her first eight months of life and love. Thank you. We're flying out tomorrow morning to visit her grave in Stockholm."

The historian brought out the paperwork with the photos of the signage at the new children's park that I had emailed her, to show Renata exactly how we were honoring Milka, my grandmother, who was Renata's hero at Foehrenwald, the displaced persons' camp, way back in 1946.

And it was then, after lunch, when we all settled back in our chairs, that Renata told her story, the whole story, of when she met Milka and how she delivered her baby girl, Martina Kaufman, who was a big, long, noisy baby with a mop of thick, golden hair and bright, blue eyes. And ears that would never hear a bird's song or her daughter's laugh.

**

Dad had been quiet during the flight to Stockholm, and I leaned into him a little and said, "Everything okay, Dad? You seem quiet this morning."

He looked at me and said, "I'm just overwhelmed with my admiration for you, my beautiful daughter. I had no idea that you had paid the old girl's rent for the last year. And you and Jacquie buying her the walker. And then yesterday, paying her rent for the year ahead. You're the best."

"Just paying it forward, Dad. I wonder who taught me that."

***

We arrived in Stockholm, and after checking into the hotel, I took Dad to my old park.

We were sitting on the old leather straps of the rusty swing set, scuffing our feet through the last of the snow in the little park where Mor used to bring me as a child and then Martina years later.

Dad said, "I can't believe you brought me here. I feel somehow like I'm meeting a new part of you for the very first time."

I smiled and nodded before I said in a serious tone, "Dad, I have something for you, and I want to explain why I've never given it to you before now. You see, when I first met you, you had a separate, happy life and a beautiful wife far, far away from your week in Stockholm back in 1974. Out of respect for your wife and for your marriage, I tucked this away. It simply wasn't relevant to you, and so it's just now that it seems appropriate to give it to you." I handed him the old photograph, circa 1975.

He was silent for a long time, just staring at the photograph. Finally, he whispered as his tears ran down his cheeks, "I had forgotten how beautiful she was. And look at you. How old were you here? About eight or nine months old? Oh my God. Oh my God. Look at her! For years and years and years in my mind, she was my golden princess, but over time, I had forgotten exactly how beautiful she really was."

He slowly clasped the picture to his chest, and he raised his face up to the heavens. I had never seen or heard him like this before, not even when the Tran family had died. He was beside himself, and his big baritone sounded out across the playground with pain and loss.

I had no idea how to calm him down, or, even if I should. Maybe he needed just to wail it out. I stood behind him and put my arms around him and smoothed his hair back. I looked up into the sky and sent the message that I had wanted to send ever since the day that I had met my dad, *Mor, we're here. We're all together. The three of us. Can you hear us, Mor? Morsa? Can you see us, Morsa?*

All of a sudden, I felt a lightness about us, and I bent down and kissed Dad's face, and I said, "Dad, enough already. I've just spoken with Mor, and she said to dry your eyes, that's she's with us. The three of us are together."

He looked at me as if he didn't understand what I was talking about, and when he saw my smile, he blew his nose and he said, "All of a sudden, I'm the kid and you're the parent. But you're right. Let's both have a swing, and we'll pretend she's right beside us, just the three of us."

"Nothing has changed, Dad. She's always been right beside us. She loves us just as much as we love her."

We pumped higher and higher, and Dad was laughing when he said, "I haven't been on a swing for 50 years. And it feels damn good. Tell your mother that."

***

We entered Stockholm's world-renowned Nobel Prize office, and the administrator had my order set aside for pick-up. Dad was grinning from ear to ear. He had to open the yearbook right then and there.

"No! That can't be me! Look how skinny I was! Look how serious I look! Look how much my scar stood out! Oh my God, I look so much like Lars here!"

"Dad, that's you. The Nobel Prize Year Book for 1974 does not lie. There you are, right in the middle of the Canadians, looking as handsome as ever."

"Oh my God! Wait until Denni sees this. She'll die laughing. I'm so glad you ordered one of these for me. Did you have all this planned out before we came?"

"Yeah, Dad. It's called online shopping. You know. Your wife is an expert at it. I just arranged to pick it up in person rather than having it shipped to Canada."

We left the Nobel Prize office and went over to my old university. We couldn't decide if the coffee in the old cafeteria was any worse than University of Toronto's. Dad just couldn't keep the big grin off his face, and I was so glad that he came with me.

From there, we went to pay our respects to Mor at her gravesite, and as we placed the stones on her monument like Jews do, he said, "Let's take another look at her photograph now so I can let her go properly. I have been carrying her around in my heart for 39 years, and now I can finally say goodbye with love and respect, without all the pain I've been harboring."

"Yeah, Dad. I hear you. But think about it. Yesterday, we heard her story from the midwife who helped birth her and who loved her for the first eight months of her life. Today, we had a swing with her in our old park, and, now, we're paying our respects for her life lived. It's a full circle, and we've done a damn fine job wrapping it up."

***

I was snuggled under my covers, and Dad was sitting in a chair, tipped back, with his long legs up on top of my blankets, and I said, "Yes, trust me, these are the very same two adjoining rooms that Lars and I had when we were here a year ago. I booked them specifically for our trip, as I had such a good time here with Lars."

"This is too much. You mean to say when you and Lars shared your trip to London and Stockholm that you didn't sleep together – you had separate rooms?"

"You knew that, Dad. I always told you that there was nothing between Lars and me. We've always been just friends, and we've both been very happy having it that way."

"Oh my God. I owe Denni five bucks. Again. She was right. I was so sure that you and Lars would get together once you were away from the kids and us and everything."

"But aren't you glad now that I didn't sleep with him? Now he's so happy with Jacquie; it's all meant to be, you see. It wouldn't have worked out if I would have had to tell Jacquie that I slept with the love of her life. No, not at all."

Dad looked at me. "You're right, honey. And that's exactly why I'm going to ask you to keep the picture of your beautiful mother with you. I don't need to be showing Denni a picture of a 29-year-old breathtakingly beautiful woman who I fell in love with one afternoon in Stockholm, Sweden. Not now. Not ever. But, Nigella, please know that that picture is the best gift I've ever received in my whole life. It freed me from my painful past and allowed me to forgive myself for not knowing enough to run after her that fateful afternoon. Thank you, honey."

"You're welcome, Dad. And it's exactly what I needed too as your daughter. I'm so happy that the three of us were together in the park. Now I can let her go too, the same as you." I added, "Now, kiss me goodnight and get out of here. We have a big day tomorrow, once we arrive in Poland. I have a special place in Wloclawek to take you to."

"You mean the Children's Park, right?"

"No. Some place better."

"Oh oh. Should I be worried? What's the name of this place?"

"Blueberry Hill."

"Are you kidding me? We're going berry picking in Poland?"

"No, Dad. Relax. You're gonna love it. Trust me. I love you."

"I love you too, honey."

***

We picked up the rental car at the Warsaw Airport, and we found ourselves pulling up to the very same hotel in Wloclawek that Jack and I had stayed in last year. Filip and Jakub were standing there in the lobby of our hotel, waiting for us. I held out my arms, and Jakub grabbed me and danced me all over the lobby as Dad and Filip shook their heads at my squealing with delight.

As Filip gave me a kiss on the cheek, he explained to Dad that Jakub's greeting was not the norm and not to expect the same treatment. They waited for us to get checked in and then insisted on taking us out for a late breakfast before taking us over to the children's park so that we enjoy all the signage and get the lay of the land before the ribbon-cutting ceremony in the afternoon. Dad was so pleased to see that they were wearing their maple-leaf pins that Jack had pinned on them the year before. He said to me, all enthused, "Good thing I brought another bag of 100, honey. I can give them out at the park."

I sat there in the same beautiful little café that they had taken Jack and I to last year, listening to the three of them talk away as if they had known each other all their lives. I had forgotten how charming, smart, and mannerly these two young men were, and I wished that Jack could have been with us. She would have loved it. Dad was really enjoying himself, and I smiled a little at myself handling this lunch situation so well in spite of the fact that I had enjoyed a fair amount of nakedness and passion with this very man sitting across from me in his immaculate jacket and tie.

Jakub reached over and grabbed my hand, and he said, "I was, of course, so disappointed to get your email saying Jacqueline couldn't come this time, but I'm so happy to hear that she's getting married. Please give her my love."

Dad said, "Now, boys, let me clarify this. Jakub, the park is your dream, and you put the deal together, and, Filip, you're running the financing, so why is it that the mayor is heading up the ribbon-cutting and the photo ops? Why aren't you two front and center? I'm sure Nigella wants you to get the credit here, not some mayor that she's never even spoken to."

The boys tried to explain that it was a political situation, and the old mayor was counting on this to get reelected in the fall.

I said, "But this is your park, Jakub. You've nursed this idea for years. Why are you giving it away to a mayor that hasn't given you any support for the project?"

Dad said, "Listen to my daughter, boys. She's a lawyer through and through, and there's no arguing with her. Now, let's see. Why don't you run for the mayor position, Jakub? A man with your intelligence and charm should be in that position. I've just met you, and yet I know without a doubt that you can make even the mundane look exciting. And you could probably keep your town-planner position as well. And, Filip, you could be deputy mayor. Lots to think about."

Filip looked at Jakub and said, "See, it's not only me that thinks like this. That old, burned-out mayor needs to be put out to pasture. Our town deserves better."

I said, "Hm…we've got a couple of hours, and I can certainly adjust my little speech to include something to the effect that you're going to be running in the fall election now that your project is finally up and running. And I'm certainly not willing to take photos without the two of you on each side of me. We're the team, right? Would that help?"

Dad said, "We had lunch the other day with a wonderful historian in Munich, Germany. She assured us that she had arranged for Jewish press coverage that are coming in from both Germany and Warsaw to cover Milka Kaufman's story, so it's a perfect opportunity for you right now, Jakub. And your mayor doesn't know about this press that's coming. He thinks it's just a local ribbon-cutting photo op. This doesn't happen every day."

Between the four of us, we had Jakub's complete campaign for the fall election mapped out on the paper table-napkins in 20 minutes.

We pulled up in front of the children's playground. We looked at the signage, and after seeing Grandma's name up on the big, wrought-iron gates, Dad had a tight grip on my shoulders as I sobbed like a teenager. The big gates were open, and the carved name was arched high above them. It read:

Park dla dzieci Milka Kaufman

The splash pad's water fountain was up and running, the swing seats were ready, the teeter-totter was stationed, and the basketball hoops, one at each end of the park, had nets ready to go. There were bike stands and water fountains. The new trees had been staked, and they had green nutrient bags attached to their bases. Bocce balls and hopscotch courts were all laid out, and there were big, shiny, dark-green waste receptacles in each corner.

Grandma's story was mounted on the water-fountain platform. It was a large, bronze plaque, with the engraved letters blackened so the story stood out for everyone to learn about the young dairy farmer from Kaufman's Dairy in Wloclawek, who had survived the Jewish Holocaust and had a granddaughter and great-grandchildren living in Toronto, Canada.

***

By the time of the grand opening of the children's park later that afternoon, we were ready to go, and we were as cool as cucumbers.

During the ribbon-cutting, I stood for all the photo-ops with Filip and Jakub beside me, and a few with the mayor as well. I circulated around, handing out our little flyer, with Milka Kaufman's story on one side and Jakub Kowalski, town planner's, *A New Vision for Wloclawek* on the other side. The crowd started to build.

Filip was directing everyone to the food truck and the ice-cream truck for free burgers, drinks, and ice cream that he had arranged for on Dad's offer to pay the running tab behind the scenes. The food-truck operators only knew that Jakub Kowalski, the town planner who was running for 'mayor,' was picking up the tab for everyone.

Little did the four of us know at the time that it would be Dad, the tall, handsome, smiling, black man with the large scar hooked under his cheekbone and the graying hair, who was handing out the Canadian maple-leaf pins, would be the biggest hit of the packed children's park that afternoon. After all, he was the first black man that had ever set foot in the town, and he was an instant celebrity.

In the middle of all this, Dad leaned over and said to me, "I wish Brad could see me now. I think I've got him beat in the celebrity department. Right, honey?"

"Right, Dad."

***

He held the two blankets that I had snuck out of the hotel, along with the two bottles of beer that he had stuck in his jacket pockets, one on each side, and I held the flashlight.

"Are you sure, honey?"

"I'm sure, Dad. That's why I brought the two blankets since this is more like a winter picnic tonight. Just think of it as Swedish style. One to sit on, and one to put around our shoulders. At least it's not as cold as Stockholm was yesterday. Just follow me. You're in good hands."

***

He whispered, "I'm in complete awe. I've never been in a more spectacular setting in my life. This is a very, very close second to the night sky at the château."

I whispered back, "Yeah, Dad. I know. Maybe we'll see a shooting star."

He turned to me and we tapped our beers. "Cheers, honey. I love you."

"Love you too, Dad."

"But why the name Blueberry Hill?"

I started to sing the old Fats Domino song, and he joined in, and by the end of the song, he said, "Oh, now's the time when I miss Denni. I never realized that this was the town's lover's lane until you started singing that old song. Duh. I was thinking there was a blueberry patch up here somewhere. How did you find out about this place?"

I started to laugh, and he quickly interjected, "No, no, no. I don't want to know. Well, maybe it's not all that bad. If you were with Jacquie, and maybe those two nice young men that we spent the day with, just maybe, it would be okay. Yeah, I guess so. We all need to let off a little steam once in a while, don't we?"

"Oh, Dad. I know you don't want to hear about it, but please know; that night up here is one of my most favorite memories of all. It was magical. It is magical. It's these stars. Let me tell you what Jacquie decided when she was up here."

"What?"

"This is where she decided to immigrate to Canada. She told us the story of the North Star and how she followed it to Canada. And now she's with us. I tell you; this place is magical. What do you wish for, Dad? Anything at all. It's all possible. Look what we accomplished today! What do you want? The sky's the limit. Look up – look up and find the North Star. And make your wish. And get prepared for the abundance truck."

"I wish for your happiness, honey."

"Bingo! Immediate reaction! Look at that! I've never been happier!"

"What do you wish for, Nigella?"

I surprised myself as I heard my words tumble out. I wasn't prepared for it in the least. I said, "I wish for another baby."

Dad looked at me to see if I was serious, and then he said quietly, "And this is because three children plus Zalia are not enough?"

"I don't know why I even said that. It just came out. But I must admit, I have always wanted more children. You see, it is magical up here on Blueberry Hill. I'm blurting out things that I haven't thought of for a long time."

Dad raised his beer to tap once again, and he said, "What I'm going to say is worth tapping our beers over. I just read this in the stars, so it must be true. Are you ready for it?"

I nodded. "Go for it. I'm ready."

"I know of a plan for you to follow that will guarantee another baby for you. All you have to do is finish up your graduate program, and you will be pregnant three months after you graduate."

"Are you drunk? Are you hallucinating? How could you say such a thing?"

"Trust me. It's in the stars. Just like you say. The North Star is right there, honey. Just follow it. Finish your studies. Follow your heart. The baby will come."

"Thanks, Dad. As soon as I get home, I'm going to buckle down and wrap up my studies. One step at a time, right?"

"Are you ready to call it a day?"

"Absolutely. But, first, I just want to point out a last little tidbit concerning my grandma, Milka Kaufman. You see down there, to my right, where we parked the car. That's where the farmhouse was. And the dairy barn was behind it. The lower part of Blueberry Hill was pasture land. It wasn't until decades after the war that the town expropriated the farmland to build this big water tower up here. Last year, Filip and Jakub told me that lovers have been coming up here on top of this glorious hill for years and years and years. I'd like to think that my grandma had a few magical nights up here with some local boy that was in love with her at the time."

Dad leaned over and kissed me. "That's a wonderful way to remember her. Forget the horrors of the war. Remember her in the arms of some nice young man that loved her under this blanket of stars. It's perfect."

***

That spring was a happy one for me. The new apartment that we were building was almost finished. Every day, the architect and contractor would check in with me, and I followed Mom's suggestion of making lunch for the crew. It would keep everyone on track and I could stay well-informed on the timeline as well.

When the architect and contractor weren't dropping in, it was Alessandro. He was so helpful and knowledgeable. He was working alongside the contractor, and he had supplied the roofers, the plumbers, and the painters for those particular jobs. The Camarra cousins had a lot of businesses between them, and my architect and contractor were pleased to accept their bids on the project. Alessandro always had the twins and the girls involved. He had bought them all hard hats and would walk them through the construction site, explaining how everything was built as they went along. Dad and Mom were on site a lot too, and Mom was working closely with the designer, making sure that redecorating the loft and the boys' new rooms were done right away. Lars feigned interest over Jacquie's wavering choices on exactly what shade of blue was right for a specific room. Jacquie was so in love with him that she had forgotten that she was capable of doing something as simple as picking a color on her own. That being said, I was so happy for the two of them.

***

Jacquie and Lars were married in Mom and Dad's backyard at 7 Russell Hill Road on a sunny, late spring day in 2011. She was breathtakingly beautiful as she walked the red carpet on Dad's arm to Mendelsohn's *The Wedding March.* Lars was waiting for her under the white arbor of roses, along with Pastor Smith and his best man, Alessandro Camarra. I was the matron of honor, and our girls were her bridesmaids.

Lars had amended his Canadian citizenship application to include his new American wife and his newly adopted American daughter. Canada had already granted the three of them their PR (permanent resident) cards, and it was agreed that Lars would keep his dual citizenship between Sweden and Canada, and Jackie and Zalia would keep their dual citizenship between the U.S.A. and Canada. Just for a split second, as I stood there, I was a teensy bit grateful to François, as our marriage years ago had allowed my very own, as well as my five-year-old daughter's, Swedish/Canadian dual citizenship when we married, even though my father was a Canadian.

It was right after that that Jack and Lars discovered they were pregnant. Our girls, almost teenagers, would have a new sibling, and even our six-year-old twin boys were excited about having a baby in the house.

I noticed that there was more than the usual amount of testosterone in the house with Dad, Alessandro, and Lars peacocking around as if they were the first men on earth to have a pregnant woman in their midst, and so it came to be naturally that Mom, Jack, Maureen, and I spent even more time together. Maureen happily bitched daily that she was being thrown back into the diaper stage of things but wouldn't hear of it as Lars and Jack wanted to hire an assistant for her. The grandparents, Anna and Eliot, spent more and more time at either 7 Russell Hill Road or 49 Parkview Avenue, either in the main house or in the apartment, joining whoever was around at the time, trying to keep up with all the kids' schedules, school work, Shabbat at my house on Friday nights, and Sunday dinner at Dad and Mom's.

***

Summer arrived, and after all the excitement of building the new apartment for Jack and Lars, and opening the children's park in Poland, and organizing all the kid's summer activities and camp, I found myself not buckling down to wrap up my graduate program like I should have. I knew exactly what to do, how to do it, when to do it, but, somehow, I just couldn't settle into getting it done.

You might say I was in a bit of a slump. Dad, Mom, and Maureen all thought it was a delayed reaction to my husband dying, but I quickly assured them that François Tran had absolutely nothing to do with my current state of affairs. On the other hand, I didn't want to tell them that I was just plain lonely. But that was the honest truth. I was lonely. I knew that my whole big family adored me like no other, but I was a 36-year-old widow with three children plus Zalia. I needed a man to share my bed with. I wanted what all the loving couples around me had. Dad and Mom, Lars and Jack, Anna and Eliot. And then there was me and Maureen. Of course, there was Alessandro who always seemed to be around to pick up the slack when it came to the many, many games of cards we played over at Dad and Mom's house. He was a very genial and witty card partner, but he was Dad's friend and my Ph.D. advisor, or that's what I thought at the time.

Once again, it was September. Dad held the girls' birthday party as usual, and, gradually, I picked up the slack and got back to work on my thesis that was built around my research called, *Anthology, Stories Told by Canadian Incarcerated Women.*

***

I wasn't worried in the least about Hanukkah and Christmas that year. The kids and I had adapted to the Tran family's death, and, actually, Francois's name very rarely came up. When the boys started calling Lars 'Dad,' I was a little concerned, but the nurse of the family, Jack, put me straight. She suggested that we let nature take its course, and to leave it up to the boys, so that they could naturally gravitate to whatever choice they wanted, with no pressure from the adults to sway their feelings. Lars agreed wholeheartedly.

I made sure everyone had a wonderful Christmas holiday that year, and I insisted that Maureen go home to Ireland, as that was the only thing that her parents wanted from her. So, it was up to me, and I made sure that my big family had a great holiday. I took the time to shop carefully for all the gifts, and I knew Dad and Mom really appreciated all the thought that I put into everything. Alessandro brought Maria and Francesco over once again for Christmas Eve, and we all went to their little Victorian for New Years' lunch, just like we had the year before. Out of the whole holiday, our four kids were more excited to go to Nonna and Nonno's house in Little Italy than anything else. Go figure.

***

We were just nicely into the New Year, and my assumptions regarding Dr. Alessandro Camarra came crashing down around my head, with a huge fight of epic proportions between said handsome, charming, perfect-card partner and a certain temperamental Swedish princess.

***

Chapter Eighteen
The Old Victorian In Little Italy

He shouted as he came through the front door, "Yo! Wonder Woman! Are you ready for our meeting, or have you been just sitting around watching soap operas all week?"

I smiled at him, kicking his shoes off at the door, just like the boys would do. Yes, he was definitely all male. Not that I minded in the least. He was the exact opposite of my perfectly and immaculately dressed dear-departed husband who was always so concerned about not scuffing his shiny lawyer-shoes or wrinkling his $200 shirts. No, Alessandro's style consisted of a Maple Leaf's hockey sweatshirt, a pair of jeans, and slip-on loafers most days. Even when I used to meet him down in his office at the university, he stuck to a small-check shirt tucked into black jeans with a sports jacket and tie hanging on his coat rack in case he needed to attend a meeting upstairs at any given time. Of course, he had a nice athletic build, and with his black, wavy, long hair, he looked good in anything he wore. He never blinked about fixing the boys' bikes for Dad who never could really figure out anything mechanical. He would stop by and not even come in but would just wave as he shoveled the snow off the steps or bring in the garbage cans, regardless of what he was wearing. Both Dad and Lars were of a different ilk altogether; they simply didn't have that physicality and kinesiological drive that this particular sports nut had. Of course, due to his prosthesis, some tasks were a little more difficult for him, but I admired the way he skated with us all every weekend down at City Hall and he rolled around on the floor with Patou right along with the kids.

It just so happened that we were all in Mom and Dad's big family room the first time that Patou really addressed Sandro's prosthesis. Sandro was down on the floor, growling at the dog to provoke him into play when Patou seemed to have enough of Sandro's prosthesis that was always sticking out to the side, hindering Patou from jumping back and forth. The dog put his nose down on Sandro's ankle, picked the hem of the jeans up in his mouth. and began to growl while shaking the foot back and forth in mock anger. The boys jumped on Patou's back and were shouting at him to stop, trying to get the dog to release Alessandro's pant leg, and the rest of us were all laughing like lunatics, right along with Sandro.

***

"Good morning, Sandro. I just made us a fresh pot of coffee and the house is quiet. The kids, Maureen, and Jack are all at school, and Lars is down at the university at a meeting. We have the whole house to ourselves. And, yes, I've been working away, so there's no need to bitch or grouse at me this morning."

Indeed, I had kept up my studies, and Alessandro was my biggest fan, although he liked to play the tough guy with me at times. He was the perfect advisor but was constantly pushing me to wrap it up and set a date to defend with my final oral exam on my thesis based on my original research of Canadian women that had been incarcerated.

***

"Would you rather move into the office?"

"No, no, thanks. I always like working right here on your big kitchen table. I'm the same at home. I've got the whole house to myself, but I always find I work best right from my kitchen. I guess it reminds us of when we were kids, always doing our homework at the kitchen table, right?"

"You know, that's right! I never thought of it like that before. Mor and I always spread all my books out every night over the table. I think it's a generational thing though; my girls just take their laptops and seem to work from anywhere."

He put his coffee down and looked at me. I thought he looked a little serious. He said, "Okay, Nigella, it's time. It's time for us to stop dicking around and set a date for your defense. Some of your team have already asked for me to book them in, but I know that you are ahead of them as far as your work being done, so I want to book you in first. You're my most brilliant student, and I want you to succeed. I have no doubt that you will; it's just that it's time to double down and wrap it up."

"No need to be so serious. Okay. Let's make a date. Would early spring work for the committee, do you think? Wait a minute here, is there something else on your mind? You look like you have something to say to me. What is it? Are we okay? I'm pretty sure my work is up to date."

"Oh, it's not you. It's me. I'm not okay. I have two rather serious things to tell you about your defense, and they're not pretty. I've known about these two things for a long time, but I simply was a coward and didn't want to tell you before I had to."

I looked at his serious face and I said softly, "Well, spit it out, Dr. Camarra. I'm a big girl. I can handle the bad news. Doesn't the committee want to consider my dissertation?"

"Oh my God, no! No! For Chrissake, Nigella, you're the best of the lot! It's about me, actually. You see, usually I would sit on the committee, but in your case, there are two very good reasons why I cannot."

By this time, I had left the table and was leaning up against the sink, with my arms folded. I stared him down and I could feel myself getting very defensive, and a knot was beginning to form in my gut. I said quietly, "Well, spit it out. You think I've got all day?"

"Nigella, I don't want to hurt you or embarrass you, but—"

I interrupted him with an abrupt, "Just spit it out. What's wrong with you? Lay it on the line right now. Give me the first of the two reasons. Get on with it."

"Way, way back before I really knew you, before we had that nice talk in my office when we told each other who we really were, I submitted a request to the university to allocate that little office down the hall from mine to you; the very same office that you forfeited after only using it for a couple of months."

I felt my heart sinking, and I felt my arms go back to hold onto the sink to brace myself. Fuck fuck fuck. He knew about my tawdry sex act with the sleazy professor. I felt my face flush, but I couldn't take my eyes off his. I had to take my punishment head on. The only other person in the whole world I wouldn't want to know about this, other than my father, was Dr. Alessandro Camarra, my esteemed advisor.

Shit shit shit. How could I have been so stupid!?

My mind was racing, and I went back and forth, back and forth, trying to decide what side of the fence I would take. Part of me thought that it was like I was in court as a prosecutor advising my client on how to plead. The other part of me knew I was guilty, and that I should accept my punishment, but on the other hand, I knew the law pretty well. Maybe I could bluff my way out of this. May I should just grow a set of balls and play the defense to the limit. I didn't have anything to lose.

"Nigella, the first reason that I have to tell you why I can't be on the committee because I was the one that initiated the complaint against that dirt-bag professor that took advantage of you. The university doesn't put up with crap like that. And I had to speak up and put an end to it. If I sit on the committee, it may be construed that I am somehow involved with you in something other than our professional relationship, and I couldn't bear to put you in that situation. Do you understand?"

My nightmare was all coming true as I listened with horror on how he had known all along about my stupid, stupid, stupid, little, one-time-only-on-the-edge-of-my-desk affair when I was a married woman no less.

"Since the very day I met you, you showed so much promise with your research, and I just wanted the very best for you. I finagled that office for you so we could work closely together, and it broke my heart as I watched him, day after day, slink down the hall, two coffees in hand as he executed his next move to take advantage of you."

I saw my opening to squash and bury my shame and I took it, although I must admit, it came out all wrong. I didn't mean to be so harsh, but it was my lawyer-killer-instinct; to go right for the jugular in order to save my own hide. I wasn't going to allow him to start picking away at my behavior, no, no, no. I had to end this before he had me labelled as a common whore who didn't deserve my doctorate.

I heard my voice and it didn't sound like me. It sounded at best like a small child being caught with her hand in the cookie jar. I shouted, "So, you were spying on me! You deliberately put me in an office near yours so you could watch my every move! Fuck you! Just fuck you! Who do you think you are? You're nothing but a spy!"

By this time, he had jumped out of his seat and began pacing up and down in front of me. He said, "Nigella! Calm down! I wasn't spying on you! I—"

By then, I was fully into survival mode and felt I had an edge. However, as I heard myself blaming him for my own bad behavior, I was dying inside, knowing I was twisting the truth and I was too selfish to hear him out. I drowned him out mid-sentence and screamed, "Get out. Get out now. And don't come back. I'll get another advisor for my doctorate. I don't want to think that you're spying on me anymore. I've had enough, and I want you gone!"

He stood in front of me, and I could tell by the set of his jaw that he was now as mad as I was. He didn't say a word, and he stormed out of the door, down across the porch, fumbling in his pocket to get his car keys out.

I stumbled over something in the hallway as I followed him, shouting out to him like a spoiled 13-year-old would, "Good riddance to you!" When I looked down to see what I was stumbling over, I realized that he had stormed out of the house in his socks. He had left his shoes in the hallway. Normally, this would have been so funny, but it just fueled my anger over being caught red-handed, acting like an adulteress even more so.

I bent over, picked up the shoes, stepped out on the porch, and aimed. I threw his fucking shoes, one by one, as hard as I could in the vicinity of his car which, by then, was running. The shoes bounced off the hood of his fancy, black, souped-up Little-Italy-styled car, with the Catholic crucifix dangling from the mirror.

He turned the motor off and I watched as he slowly opened his door to address the assault on his baby. I asked myself, from my clenched teeth and hands on my hips, "What is it with all the fucking men in my life with their fucking love affairs with their fucking cars?"

I backed up a little on the porch as he got out of his car and gathered up his shoes with one hand and proceeded back toward me with murder in his eyes. To his credit, he didn't check the hood for dents at that point. He was obviously too enraged. I took a deep breath and my eyes widened considerably. I was sure I was a dead duck.

I continued to back up as he walked straight for me. I backed up through the doorway into the house, but I held my ground in my hallway. I stood there, just daring him, although I must admit I slowly removed my hands from my hips and changed my physical position from defiance to one of defense when I crossed my arms over my chest.

Although I didn't say a word, my stony face and my arms crossed in front of me warned him who he was messing with. His eyes didn't leave mine as he closed the door quietly behind him. He quietly moved toward me and I didn't budge. We stood nose to nose in the center of my big, square hallway, and the only thing you could hear was both of us breathing. I'm 5'10", and he isn't much taller than me, maybe 6' or 6'1", but at that time, he seemed to tower over me. His brows were thick and black above his brown, brown eyes.

Thinking back on it now, I know that it was not his physical height; it was his integrity and good moral judgment that dwarfed me.

He dropped his shoes in front of him, and I felt them hit my bare feet. We just stood there, staring each other down, both of us unwilling and unable to say a word. His eyes were very serious and mine were very defiant. I realized I was acting exactly like my pre-teen daughter, but I knew somehow, deep down, that this brilliant, caring, handsome man would take care of my worst nightmare that was going down between us.

He leaned into my face even further, and I knew his lips were almost on top of mine, but he was gentlemanly enough to give me a few seconds to back away if I wanted to. On the other hand, maybe he was afraid I would haul off and slap his handsome, strong, and smoothly-shaven face. I couldn't blame him. It was then that I had to close my lips a little to keep them from trembling as I felt my tears begin to well up.

All in the same second, when I didn't back up, he slowly put his arms around me and his lips rested on mine before I could ruin it. When I felt his lips trembling a little, just like mine, it was a struggle to keep from crying out loud. I put my arms around the back of his neck, and I gave in to him like I had never done before in my whole life. It wasn't a sexy kiss at all. No tongue. No torso. Just delicious, soft, soft lips. It was just pure love. And that one perfect kiss went on and on and on.

***

Deep down into my first realization of how much I loved this man, I was yanked out of my bliss, back into the real world. He dropped his hands from my back, and he stepped back away from me to bend over to slide into his shoes. I just stood there with my mouth still open with surprise. He stood up, and, once again, and I thought I was in for another one of his kisses. It was not to be. No, not at all.

He looked me straight in the eye and growled at me in a very low, quiet voice, "Enough. Enough now. You know where I live. I expect you to deliver your apology to me soon so that we can book your defense. And at that time, I'll tell you the second reason why I can't be on your defense committee."

He shut the door behind him, and I just stood there, unable to move out and away from under that one, long, perfect kiss. I was lost on a cloud.

***

It was three nights later that I found a street parking-spot a little up from his old Victorian in Little Italy. I had been to his house before, as his parents had us all over for a couple of New Year's Day lunches at their house, next door to him, when he had had us all in for coffee to show us his newly renovated bathrooms.

Since my visit was the exact opposite of a booty call, I made damn sure that my intensions were pure when I had sent him a quick email to ask him if I could drop in. I didn't wear any makeup, and I had put on a simple tee-shirt and a pair of sweats with my old Uggs. I was determined to make an honest, contrite impression. And I knew from the part of his story that I had allowed him to tell me that having sex was a definitely a non-issue altogether. I was dealing with an ethical professor who simply would not get involved with a student no matter what that kiss told us both.

I had spent the afternoon baking him some of his favorite Swedish cookies, and I had two bags of them, one for him and one for his parents, and I was determined to act like a lady, come hell or high water.

***

He opened the door and just stood there for a moment, looking at me with a little boyish smile. He ran his hands through his beautiful, wavy, black hair and I noticed he had a shadow beard. He was wearing a vee-neck tee-shirt and an old pair of sweats that had seen better days. He had on the First Nations moccasins that Dad had bought for him for Christmas; the same kind that I had fallen in love with when I first came to Canada when I always wore Dad's around the house.

He said softly, "Come on in, *Bella*. Let me take your coat."

I stepped quietly into my new life as if I had been born into that world. The Italian world. His world. The world of deep passions, loud voices, respect, and love of family above everything else.

I can honestly say that as I sat in his nice, homey kitchen, I loved it as much as my own big designer kitchen with all its fancy gadgets. Let's face it, it was because he was in it; that's the real truth of the matter.

As we sipped on the hot green tea and ate the Swedish cookies at his kitchen table, we were in no rush to talk it out. It wasn't because we were nervous, it was just that we didn't want to break the spell. We were both smiling as he would tell me the story behind this or that around the kitchen, and I teased him a little about his hockey idols, the *Maple Leafs*, who were dressed in full uniform on an old calendar that was hanging on the wall.

And so, finally, I began, "Alessandro, please forgive me for my terrible behavior the other day. I was so embarrassed to find out that you knew about what went down in my office that I acted like a kid trying to get out of being punished. I'm so sorry, and it'll never happen again. When I heard myself yelling at you to get out of the house, I couldn't believe my own ears. And then throwing your shoes at your car, your baby. That was the icing on the cake. I'm so sorry."

Alessandro started laughing and he said, "By the time I got around the block, I got over myself and laughed at your passion all the way home. Oh, my Nigella, my beautiful, full-of-life *bella*, you are quite a handful. But let's be clear about one thing. When you cut me off in your kitchen and I wasn't able to finish my story about what went on between you and that piece of dirt, who by the way is no longer at U of T, it wasn't about your participation, if any, that I wanted to address. I could care less about how many sex partners you've had in the past; it's simply not important in the long run. I just cared that he took advantage of your good, pure heart and your loneliness. And he'd done this before. And besides, back to you and me. We're mature adults. What the fuck. Ever since puberty, I've considered myself the Italian Stallion of Little Italy. The human basic sex drive is what makes us all tick. I'm not interested in either your sex history or my own. I'm interested in us sharing our hearts for the rest of our lives. I'm interested in sharing lovemaking with you, not just sex. I love your whole family's good, healthy attitude toward sex. Your mother and father can't keep their hands off each other. Your father is burdened by having to carry around a big boner every day of his life because he can't get enough of his wife. And she's the same. Do you know that when we play cards, she's always playing footsies with him underneath the table. That's why he's such a lousy card player. She has him in a dither and he can't think straight. And Lars and Jacquie. Look at them. It's all magic. And that's what I want to share with you. It's not really just about the sex, it's about the love. And that's what I have to offer you. Pure love. And a hell-of-a-good, constant hard-on that has just been going to waste ever since I laid eyes on you. I'm just sick and tired of masturbating day in day out to your perfectly round, beautiful ass and your long legs. I've had enough, Nigella. Enough."

He took my hand over the table and said softly, "I knew from your kiss that you were sorry. I could feel your remorse. I was a little afraid at the time that you would slap my face, so I had to get out of there quickly before you had a chance to rethink the kiss."

"So, does this mean that you'll forget what I said about not wanting you to be my advisor?"

"Done. So now let me tell you the second reason why I can't sit on your defense committee, okay?"

I nodded and he started with the story of how he fell in love with me the first day he interviewed me, way back in 2009, three years ago. He told me that I was the woman that he had been looking for ever since he started looking. I was the enigma, and he was always walking on eggshells when I was around, because he didn't want me to know how he felt. He said that his unrequited love was volatile, with many ups and downs. He said he almost died when he found out I was married, and then he was elated when he met my husband at my dinner party and realized that my husband was an asshole and it would only be a matter of time until I left him. He spoke of how much he loved me when I spoke at the Tran Family Celebration of Life Service and how he watched the squad take care of Cecilia Yang. That was what confirmed for him that my husband had been a player all along. That's when he fully understood the issue between me and the sleazy professor in my office. He understood that I was acting out over the hurt and pain of my failing marriage. He added that when my dad had told him that I was going to trace my grandma's life in Poland and Germany, he prayed to the Blessed Virgin Mary every day for my mental health when I was visiting Auschwitz-Birkenau and Bergen-Belsen, knowing that it would only compound my grieving process of dealing with the fire.

He finished his love proclamation by saying, "But I think what I really love the most about you are your beautiful kids. I think Lars is the luckiest man in the whole world, living in the same house as them."

"Yeah. I know. The kids. They are my greatest blessing. When I got married and got pregnant right away, I was so thrilled when I had the twins, because I wanted as many children as I could have. Unfortunately, their birth was what ended my marriage before it really even got started. My husband didn't really feel the same way about having children, and he planned his vasectomy without consulting me. I learned my lesson. The next time I get married, if I ever do, that will be my only request. More children. I can afford them, and I plan on indulging myself with my greatest pleasure."

"Are you sure you're not Italian?"

"I'm Canadian. That says it all. I'm white, I'm black, I'm a Jew, I have Christian children, I'm a Swede, I have a bisexual nanny, and I have an American sister. I'm happy to add being Italian to the mix."

He raised my hands to his lips, and we just sat there, grinning into each other's face in the silence of the old Victorian with the creaking, original, oak flooring and wide solid wood casings and millwork surrounding the doorways. The Italian-style oil-cloth that covered the solid kitchen table that we rested our entwined hands on assured me that I had found a new, solid foundation that I desperately wanted to carry me and my family forward into the future.

I sat there, at age 38 years old, and after all my searching for my roots and searching for my identity and searching for my true love, I had finally reached home base in the kitchen of an old Victorian, right in the middle of Little Italy on the west side of Toronto.

I nodded a little and continued, "Okay, in summary then, you are bowing out of my defense committee because you don't feel you're an impartial judge. Right?"

"Right. That's why I'm always urging you to wrap it up. I need to sign off on my advisor-student relationship so I can begin wooing you and so that I can ask you to marry me. I need you to fall in love with me so you'll marry me and give me as many children as you want. I need you in my bed so I can show you what making love to someone you're in love with is all about. I need to be your fire and not just another flame. I'm not a hit-it-and-quit-it kind of guy, and I've waited my whole life for you. I want to take care of you. We can live at your house. I know you love your house, and it's close to your folks too. I'll pay the bills. I have enough money to take care of us and all the kids. You can work or not. Whatever you want. I just need you in my life, *bella*. Not as my student. As my wife. I love you and I'll wait for you forever, but what I really want is for you to get your ass in gear and write your last couple of papers and be done with it."

"The kiss that we shared is a very good reminder of what's waiting for me, Dr. Alessandro Camarra. I think that I had better leave right now before I forget my newly established dignity. I can't ever let you down again. I'm going to make you proud. You'll see."

He looked at me a little shyly, and he raised his one hand up to the vee in his tee-shirt. He said quietly, "Another thing, *bella*. I've noticed that ever since you've sat down here at the table, your eyes keep going back to my chest hair." His face flushed and he pulled down the vee-neck and his dark, curly, chest hair came to light. "If you don't like chest hair, I'm very willing to have my chest waxed. I'll go tomorrow morning. Just say the word."

My mouth was open with surprise, and it took me a minute before I burst out in loud laughter.

He said nervously, "What's so funny?"

"Just me, Alessandro, just me. I wasn't even aware that I was looking at you like that. I was still digesting all that you were saying about making love with someone you love. But back to your chest hair. You see, I've never been with a man with chest hair before. But I know right now this very minute how I feel about yours. Please don't wax your very sexy, sexy chest. Don't ever do that. Please."

He smiled wide and said, "You sure?"

"I'm as sure as God made little green apples." I leaned over and smiled into his face, and, teasing him a little, I said, "When it comes to you and me, the only waxing that's going to get done is my regular bikini wax that will keep my vajayjay all nice and soft and silky and tidy just for you. Deal?"

He could barely control himself. He leaned into my face, and we just sat there for a minute, unable to wipe the grins off our faces.

He said softly, "Deal."

We sat there, and my man started goofing around a little, and with every few words spoken, he would pull down the neck of his tee-shirt a little, lean way back into his chair, and stick out his chest. His showing off just seemed to add to the fire somehow. I was giggling like a schoolgirl, and it took us a few minutes to settle down enough so that I could get out of there with my clothes still on.

***

I stood up to leave, and he said, "You see that old spoon jar up on top of the fridge?"

"Yeah."

"After I came home from the Tran Family Celebration of Life Service way back when once you had become a widow, and after listening to your wonderful speech about immigrants, and family, and about being Canadian, I went to see my mother, and she gave me something that I put in that old jar and it's been sitting there ever since, waiting patiently."

"Well. Don't keep me guessing all night. What's in there?"

"Take a look for yourself."

I reached up and tipped the jar forward enough so I could see what was in it. I took a deep breath and smiled as I carefully tilted it back into place.

"It was my grandmother's. I want to put it on your finger when I promise to love you and take care of you and the kids for better or for worse, the very minute you pass your defense. No dicking around, Nigella Hansen. I've waited long enough. Now it's up to you."

As he helped me on with my coat, I said, "Do you think you could find it in your ethical, pure, and infuriatingly moralistic heart to at least give me a kiss before I leave?"

He sighed. "I don't dare touch you. You are the flame to my mouth. If I kissed you right here, right now, I would never, ever let you go, and your children would grow up with having to commute to Little Italy to see their mother that would be lovingly chained to my bed. I'd better put on a coat, and I'll kiss you through the window of your car."

I got home and put my four-pronged plan into effect immediately. First, I threw out my birth-control pills in order to give my body the necessary few months to deregulate its current programming. Second, I set the dates for my upcoming mikvahs on my calendar to correspond with my defense so that I would be starting fresh spiritually when Alessandro and I would begin our life together. It didn't matter to me in the least that he was a Catholic; I knew what I wanted to do as a Jew to start my new life with my new love. Third, I worked through the whole night, finessing my current research paper. Fourth, I named my vibrator *Sandro, the Italian Stallion.*

My doctorate advisor, Dr. Alessandro Camarra, had certainly lit a fire under my ass. In more ways than one.

***

Jack and Lars's beautiful baby, Eliot Nigel Hansson, joined us, and all of us would line up for our turn to hold him. Even the rambunctious twins were thrilled. I was so happy for Jack and Lars and all of us, but, at the same time, their baby was a reminder to me of how much I wanted another baby. My biological clock was ticking and there wasn't a damn thing I could do about it.

The next three months passed with me acting like a woman on the mission of her whole lifetime. In a way, it was. Dad, Mom, Maureen, Jack, and Lars gave me their unspoken support. Dad arrived every morning like clockwork to take the twins to daycare, and Mom shopped for me on a daily basis, arriving with bags and boxes of the latest La Perla and multiple sets of new 1,000-count, silky, cotton sheets for my king-size bed. She had a painter come in and repaint my bedroom and en-suite, and bought all new, big, white, fluffy towels for my bath. Jack and Lars put the kids to bed every night and constantly asked if they could help with my research. Maureen told the kids every day how proud she was of me working so hard to complete my studies, and she warned them that she expected the same kind of dedication from them when it came time for their studies.

It was during this time that Maureen offered me a way out of a little dilemma that was bound to face me in my near future. She leaned over the kitchen table in my direction as she placed the hot tea in front of me and said, "Now, Nigella, listen to me. I'm thinking ahead here a bit, but you need to hear this. I know you're a Jew. But I'm a Catholic and I know Alessandro's family are diehard Catholics too. You want to start your new life out on the right foot with the in-laws. What I'm trying to say is when it comes right down to it, their priest may not marry you and Alessandro, because you're not a Catholic. That's the truth of the matter. And although I know Rabbi Kleiman will marry you, I've done a little research. I've asked my priest, Father Borsellino, if he would marry you and Alessandro in some sort of civil ceremony outside the church, and he said yes, even though I explained that you're a Jew. I just want you to know that you have options. This would make your in-laws very, very happy. Think about it. It's an option for you to consider. I love you, and I want the very best for you."

***

As for Alessandro, we also worked within an unspoken code. From that day on, he emailed me the upcoming dates of our meetings, and I attended each one at his office down at U of T under a friendly, cooperative but professional tone. We would still meet up at Dad's house for a game of cards, but we all kept it light and fun, with no teasing whatsoever about my current status as a single woman on the hunt for yet another 'friends-with-benefits' short-term relationship. It was almost like I was wearing a very visible stamp on my forehead that said 'TAKEN.'

It seemed to me that I was just beginning to recognize that I was being deluged with the loving respect that my family had always given me; it was me that had changed. I now knew that I deserved all the love that the world had to give me, and I was able to return it to each and every one of them. Yes, I had grown up and had clued into who I really was. Finally.

***

It had taken me three years to complete my doctorate. I couldn't have done it without the team, my advisor, and my whole family. It was 2012, but I was light-years past my old, unhappy life being married to François who never supported my academic life from the get-go. I reminded myself that my three beautiful kids were my biggest accomplishments regardless of this Ph.D. that was about to be conferred upon me. I couldn't believe that Martina and Zalia were going into high school in the fall, and the twins were seven years old.

As I sat there after the committee had wrapped up my oral examination, I was well-aware that my confidence and big smile had them all smiling too. They asked me to come back in an hour and they would give me their results right then and there. They said that they didn't have to reconvene at a different date to deliver their conclusions.

Mom and Dad were waiting at the university's local Starbucks for me, and they both started to tear up as I sailed into the coffee shop, smiling from ear to ear. I excitedly told them I had to report back in an hour. All of a sudden, Dad reached into his pocket and brought out the gift that he had tried to give me years ago in my office that I wouldn't accept. I unwrapped the beautiful gold pen, and it was then that I realized once again I had the best parents in the whole world. They had quietly gone out and bought another pen and had it inscribed with just my original initials, NKH. They had discretely left my old married 'Tran' name off the new pen and this suited me just fine.

As I left the coffeehouse, I said to them, "Dad, Mom, please don't be alarmed if you can't reach me for the next day or two. Today at four o'clock, my three beautiful Jewish aunties have arranged a mikvah for me, and then I'm going straight over to Alessandro's house. I'm starting my new life with the man that I love, and I know that we won't be able to tear ourselves out of his big bed for at last 48 hours."

The three of us stood there, arms around each other, and Mom said, "Honey, please know that we don't want you to wait to plan a big, fancy wedding. Just get married right away in Alessandro's living room or wherever you want. Let Maria, his mamma, buy you a dress. And the girls as well. I'll stick to buying my dress and Jack's if it turns out that we're invited. That being said, I was up at Holt's last week, and they have those new gold Channel slip-ons with the kitten heels in your size ten, so I'll pick those up for you, since you don't want to be taller than your groom. However, let your new mamma into your world. I don't need to be butting in here. Let's get you off on the right foot with your new in-laws. They're such good people. And your man is their only child. Let them give you this wedding. Your dad and I are happy to stay in the background. So, with us or without us in attendance there, please know that you and your man have our blessing."

Dad couldn't speak. He was boo-hooing like he always did and was dabbing his eyes with his hanky. He could only get out, "My little girl, I'm so proud of you. You are one hell of a woman, and I love you."

"I love you too. Now goodbye! I've got fish to fry!"

***

The committee all stood as I opened the door. They all said collectively, "Welcome, Dr. Hansson."

I was laughing; they were laughing, and I said, "Can we add hugs to the handshakes? I need to give each and every one of you a hug. I want to show you my appreciation for all your help you've given me. Thank you. Thank you from the bottom of my heart."

They explained to me that I would be officially notified that I had earned my doctorate, and it was then that I asked them for a little favor that meant a great deal to me. I asked them if one of them could send me a simple email stating that I had passed my oral exam so that I could forward it to a loved one. They all pulled out their phones, and, within 30 seconds, I had five congratulatory messages in my inbox that I quickly forwarded to Alessandro without any personal message attached. I sent it out once again to Jack, Lars, Maureen, Mom, and Dad just to brag a little to my family.

***

Aunties Renee, Phyllis, and Donna lovingly prepared me for my mikvah which is the Jewish expression of human sexuality which is a mantle in a Jewish marriage. I floated along with their love and their prayers, and they agreed wholeheartedly with me that it didn't matter that I wasn't technically getting married that very moment and that my man was a Catholic and not a Jew. It didn't matter in the least. What did matter is that I was willingly taking part of the spiritual exercise for married couples to prepare for procreation. I was definitely on cloud nine. I couldn't remember being this happy in my whole life.

***

He opened the door and smiled. "What took you so long? I've been waiting for you for three years."

As I pulled away from his mouth, I said, "Your hair is still wet. Did you just get out of the shower?"

"No, beautiful. I've been in the bathtub. I've been doing my research to prepare for your visit. Last year I put in the new en-suite so that we'd have a separate, free-standing tub for us to have our mikvahs."

I smiled wide and I whispered into his mouth, "Our mikvahs! Oh my! What do you know about mikvahs? You're a Catholic!"

"All I know is that I'm willing to do whatever it is that will make you happy. Research told me that married couples use a mikvah to prepare for babies, and for family purity, and that a mikvah is a celebration of life. I'm not a Jew, but it seems to me that today, of all days, is a very fitting time for me to have a mikvah."

He kissed me gently. "I love you, Dr. Nigella Kaufman Hansson."

"And I love you, Dr. Alessandro Camarra. And I am a little late because I too was having my mikvah downtown with my three Jewish aunties."

He took my hand and led me back to his kitchen where he had laid out a beautiful antipasto tray, with a bottle of champagne on ice resting beside it.

As we sat there, he fed me, as well as himself, and I couldn't help but tease him a little, and I said, "So, how do you know that you said the right prayer at the right time while you were having your mikvah?"

"I didn't. But in my case, it didn't really matter too much. My heart was in the right place, so I just asked the Blessed Virgin Mary to bless our union that's going to take place tonight. I asked her to bless us with the creation of a child."

"Oh. So that's how you want it."

"Yeah, that's exactly how I want it. We'll get married this weekend, and you're going to instruct me tomorrow morning on what to pack to move over to your house."

I laughed into his adoring, happy face. "Actually, you're getting a little ahead of yourself. I mean, after all, you haven't even officially asked me to marry you yet."

I had meant it as a little joke, but all of a sudden, hearing my own words, we both became serious. He stood up slowly and reached up to get the old spoon jar off the top of the fridge. He shook it a little, and the old, plain, gold band that spoke to his family history of strong united couples before us rolled into his hand.

He kneeled down on his good leg. His prosthesis stuck out across the kitchen floor at a peculiar angle, and he automatically adjusted his frame a little to pull it into line behind him. He looked up at me, and his voice was trembling as he said, "My beautiful Nigella, will you marry me? I love you. Will you be my wife?"

"Yes. Yes. Yes, my darling. I love you, and I'll marry you."

By then, we were both laughing a little as his hand was shaking so badly that he couldn't fit his grandmother's ring on my finger. I think it was because my own hand was shaking as well. All of a sudden, the old ring had a mind of its own and seemed to spring out his grasp, and we laughed out loud as it rolled around and around in circles on the floor, only to disappear entirely under the table.

Alessandro scrambled, with his prosthesis foot slipping and sliding on the shiny tile floor, unable to find traction. He finally got on his hands and knees to get under the table, and, by this time, I joined him down there to find the errant ring myself.

"Aha, here's the little sucker! Got it!" he said.

We were nose to nose, and both of us by this time had stretched out on our bellies so that we were leaning on our elbows, and he held the ring firmly in his hand.

He whispered into my lips, "Will you marry me?"

When I said yes, he grabbed my hand firmly and slipped the ring on my finger, and we both started to laugh and cry at the same time.

He got control of his voice, and he said softly, "We can go shopping for a proper ring whenever you're ready. This ring here just represents my love and devotion to you and the children, but I'll buy you whatever you want to wear for the rest of your life."

I responded, "I don't want anything else. I'm never taking this beautiful ring off my finger. We're going to use this as my wedding ring. And we can have one made that matches it for you to wear. Deal?"

"Deal."

I whispered to him, "I never really thought of the most romantic moment in my whole life as taking place underneath a kitchen table, but this works for me."

"Yeah. I was clumsy on purpose. I just want to keep you on your toes. I want you to know that you're marrying a very spontaneous, fun, albeit one-legged man, and not a dull boring professor who's getting married for the first time in his life at the astoundingly old age of 46 years old."

"So, what happens now? Do I have to help my old husband up, or can you wriggle out from underneath this table on your own?"

***

I was laying back on his bed, and he was taking his time, peeling off my clothes, kissing me over and over, and I whispered to him, "I want to help you take off your prosthesis. I want to learn everything about you. I want to learn what makes you happy. Show me what to do, Sandro."

"My beautiful *bella*, I can take care of my prosthesis. It's my big, hard, third leg that needs some attention."

He rolled over, stood up, and pulled his sweater up over his head, just like a Chippendale dancer would have done. He pulled his jeans down and I heard a clunk as his prosthesis hit the floor. He hopped over to the bed and said, "Really, *bella*, there's lots of time ahead for that. And I'm not shy. The only thing right now I should tell you is that when I get into bed, I need to know my crutches are close by in case I have to get up in a hurry. See? They're right here, as always. So, if you get up in the middle of the night, don't trip over them. Please don't worry, honey. Everything's going to be okay. You're my girl, and I'm your man. We've got our whole lives ahead of us. I love you."

"Okay, you're the boss. But what did you say about your third leg? Did you say it needs some attention?"

"Now you're catching on."

***

Now, I know as you read this, you might smile at what I'm going to say, but it's the truth. The whole truth without a lie.

He had the most perfect, the most beautiful, the best-working, the prettiest, and the very straightest pole-like penis that I have ever had laid eyes on in my whole life. I know that I'm writing this as a woman in love, but, trust me, he was, as Tina Turner belted out years ago, he was, *Simply the Best*.

"So," I said as we caught our breath between sessions of glorious sex, "you were telling me the truth. You really are a very spontaneous, fun, albeit one-legged man, even in bed. Who knew? And at your advanced age as well!"

Hours later, after crying out in unison, I crumpled against his chest as our latest round of pleasure hit the both of us like a ton of bricks. I protested a little when he wanted to get up and have a quick shower. "No, darling, no. I love the smell of your chest right now. It's all sweaty and full of pheromones and testosterone. I want to lick you and kiss you all over, and I love your natural scent. It's what makes me all wet and excited for you."

In true academic fashion, we conferred. He agreed to my solution. I came out of the bathroom, holding a hot, wet facecloth that I squished all over his penis and wiped around his testicles. We had agreed that I wouldn't touch his chest. He was immediately big and hard again, so, as he watched, I took the facecloth and slowly wiped under my breasts and then I wiped between my legs. I threw the facecloth on the floor, and as I went to straddle him, his big hands cupped my ass, and he said, "Wait, wait, *bella*. I need you to move up on my chest. Yeah, up further. I need to taste you. I love you. I love our sex. I want to pleasure you first. I want you to cum again in my mouth."

***

He was right. He wasn't shy. Not in the least. I watched him from his big bed as he strode around the room completely naked, with his natural foot and his plastic foot hitting the old wooden floor, sounding with a step-clunk, step-clunk, step-clunk between each stride. The moon, or maybe it was the streetlight, illuminated his big front bedroom with the bay window that faced the narrow city street below. His black, curly, chest hair, which narrowed down into a thin line at his naval, took my breath away. It was at its best, still damp with our lovemaking, and he was the sexiest man alive, hands down. Never mind what People's Magazine said about my uncle, Brad, who had been on the cover of said magazine several years in a row, claiming that title. They had it all wrong. They didn't know my sexy, sexy, Italian Stallion husband-to-be at all.

"Yo, Tony," he said into his cellphone, "hey, man, send me over one of your best pies. Yeah. Yeah. You got it. Thanks, Cuz. Yeah. Oh, Tony, good news here. Yeah. No, you idiot," he laughed a little, and then continued, "Tony, I'm getting married this weekend. Yeah. Finally. Yeah. You're right. It's been three years, but she's worth the wait. Yes, you're right. Dr. Nigella Kaufman Hansson. Who the fuck else would it be? Yeah, you met her at Ma's New Year's lunches and the hockey nets. What? Of course, she knows about my one-and-half legs. Fuck no. She's most interested in my third leg, you know, the big, bionic one that's chock full of baby-making juice. (More laughter ensued.) You got that right. I'm the luckiest bastard alive. Thanks, man. Yeah, I'll keep you posted. Oh, just a minute, she wants to say something."

He grinned over at me, and I said, "Please say hi to my new cousin, Tony. I'm looking forward to seeing him at the wedding. Tell him I love him."

"Yeah, Tony. She says hi. She says she loves you." More one-sided laughter ensued, and then with a quick, "Love you too, man," he threw his cell down on the night table and proceeded to kiss me all over my face again and again and again.

He got back into bed and put me back in his arms where he said I belonged. He explained that the famous Camarra's Pizza, up on Dufferin Street, was indeed a family business, owned by his cousin's family.

How lucky for us. We had built-in family-style pizza at our fingertips for the rest of our lives. The kids would be ecstatic to hear the news. I know I was. Pizza was my favorite food group, and Jack would be so impressed. She would say I was 'marrying up' with this new turn of events. I pulled him out of bed, and we put our robes on to go downstairs once again to his kitchen. I was starving.

At some point, I remember waking to his arms around me and him whispering to me over and over again of how much he loved me. I felt my eyes close, and I reached down to feel his big erection begging for my touch. Mind you, his big needs were no bigger than mine. I hadn't been the least bit shy in meeting all his moves and grooves throughout our first foray into the fine art of making love with someone that you love, as he had described it to me earlier.

I laughed out loud and he said sleepily, "What? What now, *bella*?"

"Nothing. I just realized that I've been so engrossed for the whole night with all our lovemaking that I haven't even thought of the kids once. You see what you do to me? I'm becoming an unfit mother just because of you and your sexy ways."

He nuzzled my neck. "Hold that thought about my sexy ways, my beautiful wife-to-be."

***

I woke to hearing him whistling in the shower. I rolled over to see if I could catch his scent in the sheets before I felt my eyes closing once again.

***

The morning sun was streaming in his bathroom window as I put on a little makeup after a quick shower. I smiled to myself as I listened to him as he shouted into his cell, "Pops, Pops, put your hearing aid in. No. No. I said, put your hearing aid in. Oh, fuck man, never mind, just put Ma on. Yeah. Ma? Ma. Nigella and I are coming over for breakfast. Yeah. Right now. No, this can't wait until lunch time. We've got a wedding to plan."

He pulled the cell away from his ear so I could hear the uproar from the other end. I laughed as I took the phone. "Good morning, Maria. I'm coming over right now and I'll help you make breakfast. Oh. Okay, Mamma. Yes. Got it. No more Maria. Just Mamma. Thank you. I love you too. Oh. Okay. *Ti amo*, Mamma. Did I say it okay?"

I looked up at Sandro, and he was smiling and shaking his head at me trying to speak Italian like the dutiful daughter-in-law. I continued my convo with my new Mamma, "Put the coffee on, will you? I've got a hungry man on my hands here."

As we left the bedroom to go downstairs, I looked back into the room. The bed looked like it had been through a war. His beautiful, Italian, soft, linen sheets were balled up, half on and half off the bed. The matelassé blankets were sandwiched between the footboard and the mattress. Two of the pillows were on the floor. I laughed and I pointed toward the bed. "Oh, oh, whoops! It looks like your headboard is broken. It's listing badly to one side."

He nuzzled into my neck and said, "Yeah. I can see the headlines of the local newspaper now:

Swedish Princess breaks Italian Stallion's headboard in monumental love fest. Baby to follow."

***

Mamma instructed Alessandro and her husband to nurse the bacon and the sausage in her kitchen, and then she took me by the hand and led me up the narrow, creaking stairs and into her little sewing room. I just stood there silently, unable to speak. I couldn't believe what I was seeing, and when I turned to look into her face, she took my hand and said shyly, "Do you like it, *bella*?"

She looked up at me for reassurance, and as I put my arms around her, we both started to cry at the same time. All I could say was, "Ma, it's the most beautiful dress I have ever seen in my whole life."

She had designed the exquisite, ivory-colored, Italian silk with a deep vee neckline and temporary basting to hold the side slit together. The long gown rested on the padded dressmaker's form, with chalk marks and pins marking the darts, all ready for me to stand for a fitting.

As I was carefully stepping into the gown for the fitting, I asked, "But, Ma, how did you know way back then when he asked you for his grandma's ring that I would marry him?"

By that time, she had regained her confidence and regular bluster, and she looked at me over the top of her glasses and said, "Of course I knew. I have been praying to the Blessed Virgin Mary every day since then."

She stood back, hands on hips, with her lips pursed, eyeing her pinned adjustments. I smiled a little, thinking of my three mothers. Mor, my first mother, the deaf mute, was probably the toughest of the three, although you'd never believe it to look at her, so loving, so quiet, so gentle, with her long, straight, golden hair. And then Mom, my second mother, who was an ass-kicker if there ever was one, so full of '*joie de vivre*' and who loved all of us with such passion. But, somehow, I had a suspicion that this older, smaller, hardworking Italian immigrant with the broken English and tough exterior standing in front of me was going to trump my two other mothers put together. I made a promise to myself to return all the love to her that she had doled out to her daughter who had died at the age of 17, and her 46-year-old bachelor son who had lived next door to her his whole adult life up until now.

I had one ace up my sleeve to win her over. And that would be the day when I would tell her I was pregnant. I couldn't wait.

She reached up and pulled her measuring tape away from around her neck and ordered me to stand still while she measured my hips, and I said quietly, "Mamma, we're going to try for a baby right away. We're not going to wait." The look on her face said it all. I smiled and whispered to her loudly, "Yeah. In fact, we started last night. But don't tell the priest!"

It was such a corny little joke, but she thought it was so funny. I grabbed her and started to dance around with her, and she was laughing and trying to push me away and yelling out loudly, "The dress! The dress! Be careful with the dress!"

I pointed to a shelf that housed all her bits and pieces of lace of projects long gone and I asked her, "May I take a look through this lace? Maybe I need a little to tuck down into the deep vee-neck. The dress is perfect the way it is, but you know, Mamma, out of respect for the priest. I have to start off on the right foot with you Catholics."

I could see that she was analyzing my ask, so I added quickly, "I could just wear the lace tucked in during the wedding with the priest, but I could take it out for the reception so I wouldn't spoil your design."

"*Si, bella, si.*"

***

Right after breakfast, the four of us headed up to College Street so that Alessandro and Papà could go into their butcher shop that also catered for family celebrations. Ma and I would go into the bridal shop to buy two dresses for the girls, then we would all meet in the bakery where we would order the wedding cake, but only if they could deliver within the week.

As it turned out, the beautiful bridal shop had quite a good selection of junior bridesmaid's and first communion dresses on hand in Martina and Zalia's size, so I dutifully allowed the very proud new Nonna to pay for the two matching white dresses that she quickly picked out. I loved her even more as it dawned on me that this wasn't the first time that she'd been in this bridal shop making plans for her two little step-granddaughters long before it was all official. Thinking back to the day before when Mom was urging me to let my new mother-in-law run the show, I was just realizing that the two of them had been working together to ensure that the dresses would be ready to go on a moment's notice. I smiled at the clerk as she nodded her approval of my gracious acceptance that this was my mother-in-law's world. I just had to step back and enjoy the older woman's authority in such matters. Mom had been right. This was a very, very small matter in the larger scheme of things.

When the clerk suggested that we take a look at some bridal veils, Ma gave her a look with raised eyebrows. She calmly took both her hands and reached up to fan out my blonde African ringlets up and away from my face. She said, "You're looking at my *bella* daughter here. Does it look like she needs a veil to cover her glorious hair? I don't think so. No. But thank you, *grazie, grazie.*"

As I stooped down to hug her, I said, "You're the best, Ma. I love you. Oh, I mean *ti amo*."

On the way back to her house, as I sat next to her in the backseat of their car, I said to her, "Mamma, since you don't think I should wear a veil, I know that my mom has some beautiful, vintage, hair barrettes that Dad bought for her in Europe years ago. Do you think they'd go with my dress?"

She patted my hand and nodded sagely. "*Si, bella, si.*"

***

My in-laws' old Victorian was packed. I looked across the room and caught Dad's eye. He was just standing there, with his arm around my father-in-law, Francesco, quietly watching me. He gave me a little wink that said volumes.

Jacquie, my Matron of Honor and Lars, Best Man were even more happy for us that Mom and Dad.

Jacquie came up to me and whispered in my ear, "Are you pregnant yet? You see, Sis, I'm always one step ahead of you. Our little Eliot Nigel is already three months old. What's taking yah? It's been a couple of days. Get your groove on, girlfriend. My son needs a playmate. And, by the way, this is the best damn wedding I've ever been to, other than mine and Lars. Congratulations, Mrs. Dr. Nigella Camarra. I'm proud of you. You've married into the family of the pizza kings of Toronto. Who the hell needs a Ph.D. when you've got that market cornered? I love you like no other. Look over at your husband. He won't let go of your six-year-old twin boys. I heard him telling one of his cousins that Nigel is handling the adoption papers, the same as he had done for Lars and Zalia. Alessandro is one hell of a man, Sis, and he just married the best."

Maureen joined us, and I noticed her face was all flushed as she said, "Whew! These Italian men are all so handsome and sexy in their white shirts and black, straight hair. And they're Catholics too. It makes me almost forget the side of me that prefers girls. What the hell! I never knew until today what I've been missing! I'm going to start hanging out in Little Italy from now on. But meanwhile, Your Majesty, are you pregnant yet?"

Mom joined the squad. "Well, girls, I'm having such a great time here with our new big family of loud and boisterous good-looking Italians. Maureen, honey, I hope to hell you wore your fancy underwear. There's a young man over there. He's a Camarra by the good looks of him. He's the one that you were talking to, and he was undressing you with his eyes as you were batting your eyelashes at him. These Italian men have got it going on big time. Sexy as hell. But Nigel filled me in on the family dynamics here. You see, all of Alessandro's boy cousins are old-school, and they all live here in Little Italy. But his girl cousins have all married, and they've flown the coop up to Woodbridge, just north of the city, which is all upscale Italian. There's a little bit of friendly competition here amongst the boys, old-school against the up-and-comers. I wonder what they think of Alessandro moving over to Forest Hill. That should shake up the status quo! But, never mind all of them. Nigella, honey, are you pregnant yet?"

I said, "Girls, girls, girls. Take a look over there at my very sexy husband, Little Italy's original Italian Stallion. I imagine it will be exactly nine months from now that we're having the priest over to christen the family's next baby. Ma just took me upstairs to show me Alessandro's old christening gown. She's had it packed away in tissue paper for 46 years. She's been praying to the Blessed Virgin Mary for a grandchild ever since Alessandro hit puberty. With a sense of purpose like that behind us, we should start looking through the baby-name books without delay."

***

I knew it was too good to be true. Here I was, standing in the middle of my brand-new family, looking like the nice girl – the girl that was wearing the white wedding dress – like a girl that never swore in her life – a girl that never lost her temper – a devoted new bride that was willing to be pregnant and barefoot in the kitchen of her Italian husband for the rest of their days. I was almost gloating in pulling off this pure, demure image. I could count on Mom and Dad and the rest of them not to tell any tales out of school. It was my day, and I was indeed the sweet little Swedish princess standing regally amongst her devoted subjects.

My handsome, charming prince, Dr. Alessandro Francesco Camarra, hushed the crowd with his big, joyous voice as he began his toast to his bride. That's where it all started to go wrong. I caught onto him within the first 30 seconds. Oh yeah, it was Alessandro's payback time. Ever since I threw his shoes at him and dented the hood of his baby, he had nursed this admittedly undeserved assault with the patience of Job. In fact, I had almost forgotten about it.

At first, my eyebrows went up in disbelief as the crowd began to roar with laughter as he told them of me temperamentally kicking his sorry ass out of my house. But the guests were literally on the floor, rolling around with laughter as he imitated me firing his shoes, one by one, 50 feet forward to hit the hood of his car.

One of his cousins called out, "And you, Sandro, without a leg to stand on!"

I tried to swat him away as he grabbed me, kissing me all over my face, and the crowd's laughter didn't subside as I rolled my eyes and tried to deny the whole story.

Another one of his cousins shouted out, "How'd you handle your little firecracker, Sandro?"

He broke out in a huge grin and shrugged his impossibly sexy shoulders. He raised both hands up with a nonchalant gesture "I just kissed her. I kissed her like she needed to be kissed. And then I left her to think it over. She came knocking on my door three days later."

The crowd went wild, and I could see over all the heads that even my best friend, Jacquie, had thrown me to the wolves. She had her arms around Mom and Maureen, and I knew that the squad would never let me live this one down.

However, I must admit that I deserved every bit of my husband's well-delivered tale of my passion. Our passion. As he put his arms around me to support my back, I leaned back into a submissive tango pose. I put my arms around his neck, and I felt his lips on mine. I accepted my fate as a woman in love with a man that knew exactly how to handle his spoiled, temperamental, shoe-throwing Swedish Princess like no other.

***

It was the first time that I had known life at 49 Parkwood Avenue to be so happy for each and every one of the four adults, five children, and the one child yet to be born. We were delighted to find out that we were pregnant right away, and although I was over the moon with the news, Alessandro simply talked of nothing else. Of course, the house was chaotic as ever, with the four kids always wanting their play dates to be held at our house and sneaking the basketball or bikes in to ride around indoors when they thought they could get away with it. Even Patou would get sick of the noise and wait at the door until someone would let him out so he could mosey back to 7 Russell Hill Road where he lived as a king with Dad and Mom.

Alessandro had built out the garage to hold all the sports equipment, but there were always bikes and hockey nets strewn all over the front lawn. We even had space made in our closet in our big bedroom to house his variety of prosthesis, from the Aqualimb, an extra Dry Pro model that he used in the shower, the used one, and an extra one, just in case.

Sandro would come home from work, and the boys would be waiting for him, asking if he would watch them shoot a few baskets, or, better yet, to get the hockey nets and sticks out for a game of road hockey before dinner. I wasn't one to stay in the kitchen. I would always go out to the porch and just watch my boys enjoying their time together. Even Lars would join in. Both Lars and my husband loved it when I would bundle baby Eliot up and take him out to watch all the action as well. Actually, I think all of them, including Sandro, spent most of the time just showing off for me and my growing belly, knowing fully well that that's what made me happy. I guess we're all pleasers in our own little way.

After the kids were in bed, that was my own magic time with my husband. Just him and me. I had always had a firm rule of no kids in my bed, and Sandro had to accept that. If one of the kids upstairs was having a scary dream, there were our two teenagers and our nanny to handle it. Once we said goodnight to all of them, it was just us. Our own little world. No more talk about summer camps for the kids or a new roof on the north side of the house. Just that precious intimacy that we shared during our time together.

It always amazed me, that with our busy lives, and at our age, that we were both so eager for the sex part of our life together. We turned off the whole world, including kids, including our baby that was beginning to kick and move around. We just savored each other's bodies, heart, and soul, night after night after night. The sex just got better with time, even as our baby grew. Sandro was a confident, skilled lover regardless, but he knew how to eke out deep emotions that were entirely new to my reserved Swedish personality. And the baby just made him all the more responsive. He was simply bursting with happiness. When it came to me pleasuring him, he was happy with whatever went down at the time; he was simply devoted to making sure that his wife had never been loved better in her whole life. And I just couldn't get enough of him, even with my big belly, full breasts, and all.

***

It was April, 2013, ten months after our wedding, when Ma's old priest christened Francesco Nigel Camarra who was dressed appropriately in his father's 47-year-old old christening gown. Our beautiful baby boy was exactly one month old. We named him after Alessandro's father and my father, both of whom cried on each other's shoulders like babies throughout the whole big-hoopla Catholic service.

Of course, the big, noisy party that followed the service was held in Ma and Pop's old Victorian in Little Italy. I remember at the time, slipping out of the party and standing alone out on the old porch and looking up the narrow, car-lined street, my eyes searching for a patch of blue sky between the rooftops and the big old trees. "Mor, Morsa, can you hear me? Can you see me? Can you see my beautiful kids? Can you feel the love? What do you think of me now, Morsa?"

***

It was to be the last family celebration that the old house would host for us. But of course, my loving husband, son to his rapidly ageing parents, had it all planned out that way.

***

Chapter Nineteen
49 Parkwood Avenue

It was right after the christening, in May, 2013, and Sandro and I had been married almost a year on the night, that all sat around Dad and Mom's dining-room table that we all seemed to use when we were having a family meeting. The days of just the three of us, Dad, Mom and me, together with little five-year-old Martina tucked away upstairs in bed were way, way behind us. There was a hell of a lot of moving parts to our family these days. Jacquie and little Zalia had joined Maureen, Martina, the twins, and me in our big house permanently in the summer of 2010, and Lars followed as soon as he found out he was Martina's biological father. His parents, Anna and Eliot, had immigrated to Canada that first Christmas that Lars met Jacquie. They had moved into a beautiful suite at the Senior's Residence a couple of blocks away from us, and they were very happy to be so close to all of us. Rabbi Kleiman, long retired, was almost a constant fixture at 7 Russell Hill Road, and, of course, our little look-alike twin boys, Noah and Warren, were not so little now. They were seven years old, and their new father, Alessandro, had them enrolled in hockey and soccer to go along with their swimming and art classes that Dad still took them to. And then there were our two baby boys to think about too. Eliot Nigel was a toddler, and Francesco Nigel was a greedy little baby, always demanding to be fed, every hour on the hour it seemed, and he was gingerly taking his first steps. Six kids and 12 adults. And, oh my God! Lars and Alessandro were constantly talking of the next two babies that they were planning on a daily basis.

Dad's big baritone asked everyone to focus on Alessandro, and Sandro grabbed the floor when opportunity knocked. He laid out his agenda succinctly. He told us that he needed our help and that we all had a part to play in the future of his parents. Just the week before, his dad didn't remember who the baby was when he had taken him over for a little visit, and his mom had taken to sleeping downstairs on the sofa because the stairs had gotten too much for her arthritic knees. They had refused the help of a PSW (Personal Support Worker) over the last few years that Alessandro had tried to set up for them. They wouldn't even allow a weekly cleaning lady to come in.

Anna and Eliot immediately said they should move into their senior's residence in our neighborhood so that we could all visit them on a daily visit. Dad and Mom agreed wholeheartedly. Jack and I said at the same time, "But you know, Ma, it's got to be her idea, or she won't budge."

I smiled a little as Anna slapped her hand down on the table and said, "Well, that's that. Let's do this the smart way. Let's start by having a few family get-togethers at our residence. Hold off on the weekend dinners at 7 Russell Hill Road and 49 Parkwood Avenue for a month, to give Maria the idea that she could be hosting all the parties in our nice, big, community dining room with the catered dinners at her new home. To hell with the stairs over in Little Italy. It's time for her to sit back and just enjoy all her grandchildren."

Dad spoke up, "Alessandro, Son, you know of course Denni and I have you covered for your extra expense here. We'll pick up the tab for their apartment."

"Nigel, keep your money in your pocket. With the way that Denni shops for all of us, your expenses are way, way more than mine. For Chrissake, man, I have tenure at the university, and I still have my police pension coming in from my accident 35 years ago."

He laughed a little and he whispered in a loud voice, "And, besides, you know that I'm a kept man. I married up. This humble immigrant here married a wealthy woman."

I said, "Thanks, Dad, but Alessandro is right. He's got this. But what you could do is take Pops out to Best Buy and treat him to a nice, big, new television so he can enjoy his hockey games in style. Get the kind with the earphones so he doesn't have to remember to put in his hearing aid. Mom, you get Ma out to buy them a nice new bedroom suite and a new sofa. I'll get Martina and Zalia to ask their nonna if they can have her sewing machine and her stock of material. She'll part with all her treasures if it's going to the girls, I know."

Maureen said, "I'll pick her and Pops up every Sunday and take them to mass over here at my church. I'll make sure she meets new friends there. They still ask for Father Borsellino after the wedding. No sense in her traveling all the way over to Little Italy for mass, now is there?"

I looked over at Anna and said, "Okay, starting this Friday. Instead of having Shabbat at my house, I'm going to go over to pick Ma up, and I'll bring her over to your apartment on Friday morning so she can help me prepare latkes and brisket and the challah. I'll ask her to bring an antipasto tray along so she can show Martina and Zalia how to prepare the first course Italian style. She'll take ownership, I'm pretty sure. Okay with everybody? Deal?"

"Deal."

***

It was after just a couple of family dinners being held at Anna and Eliot's senior's residence when my husband dropped in to check up on his parents over in Little Italy.

Ma had been thinking things over and had it all planned out. She laid it out on the table to her son, "Alessandro, I've been thinking that your father and I should move over to Anna's residence. It will be so much closer to all the kids, and it's time I started helping out a little more with all Nigella's Friday night Shabbats and the Sunday night suppers over at Denni's. Do you know how much an apartment over there is going to run me? Can we afford it? I'd be willing to sell this damn old house with the stairs if I need to. Anna's apartment is so nice and new and clean-looking."

Her good son put a stern look on his face and said, "Ma! Ma! You drive me crazy! Now you want me to move your whole house over to the other side of the city? Are you sure you want to be closer to all the noisy kids?"

"*Si, si*, Alessandro. I know exactly what I want. Now tell me, should I put my house up for sale right away?"

He gave her a long look and sighed. "No, Ma. No. If that's what you really want, we'll get it done. But let's take it nice and slow and easy. I'll get you moved in. And you don't have to pack up anything. Pops needs a new TV anyway, and I'll treat you to a nice, new, living-room set. You don't want to be carting this old stuff over there to your fancy new apartment. And, besides, over at Anna's, all your meals are prepared for you down in the big dining room. That's how Anna and Eliot do it. You don't need to cook if you don't want to. Just leave your old house the way it is, just in case you change your mind and you want to come back and visit it once in a while. After all, my old house next door is still here as well, and I didn't take any of my old crap over to Nigella's. We don't have to get rid of either house. One thing at a time, Ma."

Alessandro was encouraged by watching his mother nod her head sagely, and he continued, smiling a little, "Ma, remember, I have a good job at the university and my police pension. I'll pay your expenses down at your new apartment. Just tuck your old-age pensions away for the grandkids. And over at the residence, there's no tax bill and no water bill to worry about. And we won't have to shovel out front in the winter anymore. That's how Anna and Eliot live. Their son, Lars, works at the university, the same as I do. He pays for everything, and that's what we should do too."

"Well then. Let's get the ball rolling. Can you phone the residence right now and ask if they've got an opening?"

"Ma! Ma! For Chrissake! Let me finish my coffee! All right, all ready! I promise you! I'll have you moved in within the month!"

Her face was flushed with excitement as her son offered her another little tidbit to relay back to him as her idea at a later date. Alessandro tapped on his dad's arm, and he mused to both of them, "You know, Pops, I've been thinking. Tony's two boys finished up school last year, and they were telling me that they've both saved up a little money to get into the real-estate market to buy their first houses. They've both got nice girls now and it's time they leave Tony's house on Simonetta there behind us and get out on their own. I'm just thinking now, but one of the boys could buy my house and the other one could buy yours. That would keep the family all together, and they'd be a block away from their parents. You know, those boys are both in their mid-20s now, but they still play road hockey on Simonetta just like I used to right here out in front of us. They don't want to move up to Woodbridge. They like it here in the old neighborhood. But not now, Ma. We're in no rush to sell. Hell no. Maybe down the road a little bit. Yeah. Those two boys will just have to wait until we're ready. After all, we don't need the money with my job at the university. We could even give them a bit of a break on the sale price to get them started out. If you wanted to, you could even carry the mortgage for them. That would give you a nice little income. And, of course, you'd already have the down payment in the bank. If you wanted to. I know Tony would really appreciate that. He works so damn hard day in and day out up at the restaurant.

And those boys have done so well for themselves. Both of them graduated with honors from the university. Two good boys, that's for damn sure."

Alessandro could see the wheels turning, and his Ma said, "Yeah. It's a thought. I was thinking earlier that we could keep the two houses for Martina and Zalia, but they're still pretty young yet to be thinking about things like that."

Alessandro cried out, "Ma! For Chrissake! My girls don't even speak Italian! And they sure as hell don't play street hockey! They don't belong over here in Little Italy. They're little Forest Hill girls. And, besides, now that I'm one of their fathers, they won't be leaving the family house until they're in their 30s. Right, Pops?"

The good son smiled a little at his ma, and he said softly, "Ma, listen to me. Maybe, for now, you could give them your sewing machine and all your fabric and material, and you could teach them how to sew. God only knows their two mothers can't even thread a needle. It's up to you to teach them how to sew and how to cook a decent lasagna, right, Ma?"

"You're right, Son. *Si. Si.* You're right."

***

And that's how the elderly, good Catholic Italian Nonna with the arthritic knees and the rapidly failing husband found herself hosting the next few Shabbat dinners in her fancy new apartment resplendent with all new furniture. Her new sofa had the arm caps firmly in place to guard against the wear and tear of her husband and grandchildren, and the clear, plastic wrap was left in place over the new lamp shades, as all Italian women of her age are prone to insist upon. Her choice of her new furniture, in fact, turned out to be very similar to Anna's, her good Swedish friend who also lived on the third floor of their fancy Forest Hill senior's residence.

***

Ma telephoned me one day a couple of months later and told me that she'd been thinking things over. She told me that I would have to have Shabbat on Friday nights back at my house, as she was too busy playing Bingo and going to exercise classes with Anna to be worrying about making the perfect latkes.

315

She summed it all up perfectly when she flat-out told me her cooking days were over and that she had better things to do with her time.

"You're right, Ma. I'll have Shabbat here this Friday night. We'll pick you and Pops and Anna and Eliot up. Don't worry, Ma. *Ti amo*, Mamma, *ti amo*."

***

The early morning was quiet out on the porch, and Jack and I heard our husbands' conversation as clear as a bell as their deep voices quietly discussed Lars's problem from the front seat of the Volvo that was still sitting in the driveway. They weren't aware that their voices were carrying.

It started with Alessandro's soft laugh as Lars scrambled into the passenger's seat, saying, "Sorry I'm late, man."

Alessandro didn't start the car. He just sat there, grinning into his best friend's beleaguered face, and he chastised him, "Look at you. The absentminded professor. Just stop for a minute and look at yourself. You've got a big, fucking boner and now you're going to have to nurse it all day long. You look like what they say down at the police stables, '*It looks like somebody rode you hard and put you away wet.*' Did you sleep in? Didn't you have time to take care of your big fucking package?"

"Fuck, man. It's my own fault. It all started last night. We went to bed early because I just couldn't wait for her any longer. I just can't keep my fucking dick down when it comes to her. She's as bad as I am. We never slept the whole night. Fuck! I'm a mess!"

Alessandro laughed at his best friend's dilemma. "Hey, man, don't be so hard on yourself. I know, I know. I'm the same with my *bella*. We're the two luckiest bastards in the whole world. Listen, man, don't worry about being late. We've got enough time. Once we get down to the university, just slip into the men's room and jerk off before your first class, and you'll be good to go. Try not to think about her, or you'll find yourself right back where you started."

Lars shook his head. "No, Bro. Nothing helps. I constantly slip into the men's room on the first floor. I go into my favorite stall at the far end, and I pleasure myself three times a day and I still can't control myself. I can't even say her name without getting a hard-on. I'm a fucking mess. Most of the time I don't even care who sees me like this. She's worth it. She's worth all of it."

At that moment, I sung out loudly, "We can hear you…"

My voice startled the two of them, and they looked up at us. The four of us started to laugh. Jack and I ran over to the car, and as Jack leaned in through his window to kiss him, he whimpered, "Honey, honey, please, no tongue, or I'm going to cum right here, right now."

It was impossible for Sandro and I not to hear his protesting, and Sandro punched his shoulder and chuckled. He explained, "Bro, when your beautiful wife is trying to lay a little lovin' on you, just shut up and put up. Take it like a man."

Of course, Jack jumped right into the teasing, and poor Lars had to endure another round of us laughing at him as she tousled his hair and reached down to give his crotch a little squeeze.

Sandro put the car in reverse, and Jack and I stood there, arms around each other, waving goodbye to the two most wonderful men in the whole world.

As Sandro was looking back over his shoulder while he was reversing out of the driveway, he gave his best friend a grin, and we heard him say with admiration and love in his voice, "Lars, Lars, Lars. My good friend and brilliant scientist, you're nothing but a hard-on with a hundred-dollar haircut."

***

It had become Jack's and my routine. Sandro and Lars left early in the morning, sharing one car, and the two of us got up with them to kiss them goodbye in the driveway, followed by coffee on the porch to get our day organized. She still met Dad early morning as well, and they enjoyed their own little routine of a run and coffee down at the Aroma Expresso Café, down on Spadina Avenue, before the rest of the house was up and at 'em.

We both pulled our individual baby monitors out of our pockets of our bathrobes, along with our cellphones, and placed them on the side table. We snuggled back down into our chairs on the porch and put our big fluffy slippers up on the footstool. We raised our coffee cups in unison and said "To our husbands." I laughed as I teased her, "So, what's your secret, Sis? How do you keep the absentminded professor in such a teenaged tizzy? Come on now, 'fess up. As Mom would say, *I want details.*"

Jacquie was grinning from ear to ear and she said softly, "Oh, Sis, look at us. Just look at us. Sitting here in our big fluffy slippers after waving our two, brilliant, hardworking men off to their jobs. The same men that insist that we

317

don't go out to work; that we just stay home and enjoy the kids, day in and day out. Really, Sis, look at us. The kids will be waking up soon, and our amazing nanny will be helping us with them. I can't believe our girls will be going into high school this fall. And look at my baby. My perfect little Eliot Nigel Hansson. And your baby, Francesco, who has got to be the happiest, best-natured little baby I've ever seen. He's such a dead-ringer for Sandro, right down to the wavy hair. No little black boy there; he's Little Italy all the way. And think about it, our sons will never know what it's like to be hungry or to be a black man in America. And our days, you and me, as little black girls living on food stamps seem so distant now. Look at our beautiful, beautiful children. Look at how happy all our old folks are, and Nigel and Denni too. You and I are so, so blessed."

I raised my coffee cup up to her and said, "I hear you. I thank God every day for our lives and our lifestyle."

She started to giggle like a schoolgirl, and she said, "Yeah. And our husbands. Oh my God! How did we ever get so lucky!? I couldn't have ever dreamed up a man like Lars in my whole life, and I know you feel the same way about Sandro. Here I am, and I have a husband who tells me every day that I have perfect breasts. He doesn't think that they're sagging in the least. I can ride his magnificent, big, beautiful dick every night of the week. It doesn't get any better than this, Sis."

I started to laugh. "Poor Lars. Really, Jack. You could have, at the very least, given him a quick little hand job on his way out the door this morning."

She looked at me, and she explained to me with wide eyes, "I did, Sis! That's why he was late!"

I leaned my head back and roared with laughter, "You are one little hottie, Mrs. Jacqueline Hansson! And now while I think about it, our boys have got it right. They are the two luckiest bastards in the whole world."

She added, "Not so fast, Sis. I think you've got them beat in that department. Look at your parents. I've never met finer people in my whole life."

"They're not my parents, Jack. They're our parents. You know how much they love you."

"I'm not an idiot. I know. And I love them back just as much."

She started to laugh, and she said, "You know, speaking of Denni, I was thinking of her late last night when Lars and I were in bed. One of her favorite songs that Nigel turned her onto is called *Footprints on the Ceiling.* It's an old Etta James or Barbara Carr song. There we were, the two of us, Googling the song on my phone, and we laughed and laughed. It just added fuel to the fire, and that's why we didn't get any sleep last night."

"Now you're blaming your sex maniac ways on an old song?"

With that, Jack's phone rang which set up a series of events that would change her life forever. And not in a good way.

***

As she snatched up the ringing phone, she noticed the Florida state-area code on her screen. All the soft beauty that had been on her face from her night of lovemaking disappeared behind a new, tough, Miami project's black-girl mask, and she answered with a terse, "Hello."

I watched as if it were a movie in slow-motion. The call simply caught her off-guard. Normally, she could have handled it with aplomb, and I gently took the phone out of her hand as her beautiful, happy face disintegrated into a pain-filled, open-mouthed, silent wail.

***

"Hello. My name is Nigella Hansson, and I'm Jacqueline's attorney. How may I help you?"

"Oh. Oh. Police Officer Adams here in Miami, Florida. Ms. Hansson you say? Oh yes. I see here in the file. You're her sister, and you live in Toronto. Is that where you both are right now?"

"Yes. Spit it out. What's the problem?"

"I'm sorry to notify you, ma'am, but your father, Mr. Reginald Dixon, has been found dead. It appears that he died last night. I'm sorry for your loss, ma'am."

My infamous temper came into play as my heart was breaking for Jack's pain. It just came out of my mouth, and I immediately knew I shouldn't have said it.

"What! Another member of Jacqueline's family dying in police custody!? Is her teenaged brother's death in your file as well? I want the Miami Police

Department to explain exactly what happened immediately. This time it won't be shuffled under the carpet. Not this time. No. Not on my watch."

"Ma'am? Ma'am? Please, ma'am. Let me explain, ma'am."

"Shoot."

"Ma'am, we found Mr. Dixon in an alley behind a motel way off the beach at 4 a.m. during our routine police beat. He was already dead. He died of a hot-shot of heroin, and by the load that was in his system, he didn't feel any pain. He left us in a blaze of glory, so to speak. You are aware, aren't you, that Mr. Dixon suffered with substance abuse for over 50 years, aren't you?"

"Oh. Oh. I apologize, Officer. I'm sorry for my outburst. We'll be right down to take care of everything. Meanwhile, may I ask you to email me permission papers so that either I or Jacqueline's husband can act on her behalf if she's not able to handle the paperwork? Yes, and the address of the morgue. And your precinct's address. Yes, yes, have you got a pen? Thank you. Yes, please write my email down."

I pulled Jacquie up and out of her chair, and I put her on my lap. I rocked her back and forth as she cried and cried and cried. She finally calmed down a little and threw her hands up in frustration. She blew her nose and said, "Why am I crying now? I haven't cried over him for years and years. I knew this was coming. I've been waiting for the shoe to drop for years."

"Okay, honey, okay. We'll call Lars right away and we'll get the two of you on an afternoon flight."

She jumped up in protest and paced back and forth. "No! Absolutely not! I won't have it! I don't want him to be a part of that sad life. I don't want him to see me in that environment. He's much too sensitive, and it will break his heart to see me hurting."

"Okay, okay. You're the boss. I just thought that I should stay home and take care of little Eliot for you, that's all."

She looked at me and started crying all over again. "Yes, please. Take care of Eliot. I just want Nigel. He'll help me. I'll ask him this morning if he'll come down with me."

I nodded and picked up my phone. "Dad? Change of plans. No run today. Just come over to the house right away. We need you here."

Jack took the phone from my hands and started to cry. "Nigel, my father died. I need you. Will you come to Miami with me to bury him? Thanks. What?

No, absolutely not, Nigel, no. Just us. I'll call Lars once I'm down there. I don't want to upset him. You know how sensitive he is."

***

As Jack showered, I felt a little guilty sneaking into Lars's closet. I grabbed a few things, and I thought to myself that somewhere down the road, Jack would see the humor in me rummaging around in her husband's underwear drawer. I stuffed it all into my own carry-on and snuck it downstairs to stash it in my trunk, out of sight. It was Mom's job to call Lars at work to let him know what was going on so he could go directly to the airport to meet Jacquie and Dad there.

***

I looked in the rearview mirror and I knew she was going to be okay. Dad was right beside her, taking down all the dates regarding her father, including his army stints in Vietnam back in the '60s.

"How're you doing, Sis?"

"I'm fine. I'm fine. Sorry for the big breakdown earlier. I was a little surprised at my reaction, but we all know grief. It's a bitch. You never know what to expect. I just have a headache, that's all. In fact, I've had it for a day or two now. I'm just tired out. Lars and I were up all last night. I'll take a *Tylenol* once I get to the airport."

Mom reached back to pat her knee. "Was it the baby, honey? Is he okay? Is he teething or something?"

I piped up, "Mom, get real. That baby sleeps right through the night. Jack has to take full ownership for being tired. Her and her husband spent the whole night through, on top of each other. You know. Sex, sex, sex. And then more sex."

We all laughed a little, and Mom continued, "Nigel's going to be right beside you. Let him handle everything. But, honey, there is one thing you can do for me."

"Anything, Denni."

"Once you get on the plane, keep those goddamn flight attendants, male and female, away from my husband. It's been my experience that the minute he boards the plane, they start hovering. Tell them for me that he's taken."

I looked into the rearview mirror to see Dad grinning from ear to ear, and he said, "Now, honey, calm down. Just calm down. You shouldn't be swearing like that in front of our girls like that."

I pulled up into the Departure Level drop-off lineup, and as Dad was pulling the carry-ons out of the trunk, I saw Lars up near the Air Canada doors, looking exactly like the absentminded professor that he was. I watched him as he spotted our Volvo, and he loped down to where his wife was standing. Jacqui had a very surprised and happy look on her face. She gave the love of her life a little wave to let him know that she saw him. What a pair.

I shook my head and I mused to Mom, "Look at him, Mom. He can't live one day without her."

Or so I thought at the time.

***

Early the next morning, in my half-awake state and over the background noise of Sandro's morning shower, I grabbed my phone from the bedside table, noting that it was six o'clock in the morning. I was all ready to hang up on some random robo-call selling gutter replacement when I heard Mom's voice say, "Honey, I'm at your front door. Let me in."

***

I swung my feet over the side of the bed as my gut told me to prepare for the worst. But nothing, not even my gut, could have prepared me for the blow that was to follow. It was to be the worst day of my life.

Mom kissed me hurriedly at the door and said quietly as to not wake the kids, "Where's Sandro?" all the while rushing through the kitchen to make her way down the hallway to our bedroom.

Patou stayed by my side. I just stood there, unable to move, until Mom and Sandro appeared at the far end of the hall, with Sandro soaking wet from his shower, naked as a jaybird, only wearing his Dry Pro over his prosthesis, step-clumping, step-clumping up the hall with Mom following him, running a little to catch up to his stride. She was trying her best not to look as she held a towel out to him in order to give him a little coverage.

I know now that it was just my brain trying to shield me from the ugly truth of the pending matter, and that sometimes humor pops up in the most ridiculous manner, but I just stood there. I was fixated on his nakedness, and I watched him ambulate toward me. My eyes rested on his beautiful, pole-straight, long, and flaccid penis as it swung in time, back and forth, back and forth, with each step from his right foot and each clomp from his prosthetic foot.

Alessandro, on the other hand, had only one thing on his mind, and that was to try to buffer me as best he could from the bad news that was going to lay damage to my heart like never before. He just wanted to make it all better for the woman that he loved; the same woman that was about to find out that her best friend, Jacqueline Dixon Hansson, had died instantly in her sleep from a massive brain aneurism that had ended her 39-year-old life in the blink of an eye.

I buried my face into Sandro's wet chest as he managed with one hand to secure the towel around his waist, holding me tightly with the other. Mom put the coffee on, and we clicked on 'speaker' as we waited for Dad and Lars to pick up down in Miami.

Dad's big baritone soothed us as he confirmed that our Jacquie was gone. Lars joined in, trying his best to reassure us that he was okay.

Dad started at the very beginning, using his best judge's voice. He filled in the details of their visit to the police station, followed by the visit to the morgue. By the time they had reached their hotel, Jacquie was feeling very satisfied that, upon Dad and Lars research and convincing, the Americans had acknowledged and agreed that Reginald Jack Dixon, the decorated 'Nam vet, would be laid to rest in Arlington Cemetery right along with his brothers and sisters who had fought with distinction and honor for their country back in the turbulent '60s.

During their time at the police station, Dad had seized the advantage of his title of being a Supreme Court justice from Canada. Dad spent his 15 minutes of fame educating all the police officers that the chief could assemble on such short notice as to who Reggie Dixon really was.

After introducing Jack as one of Miami's best pediatric-nurse practitioners, and her husband as a world-renowned Swedish scientist, the honorable Supreme Court justice, Nigel Royal, told the packed assembly hall all about

Reginald Jack Dixon's life that he had lived long, long before the PTSD and drugs took a hold of him.

He told them of how Reggie didn't stop fighting the good fight when he got home from 'Nam as a decorated U.S.A. soldier in February, 1968. His simply changed the enemy's name from communism to racism.

Dad told them all – in uniform and out-of-uniform – black, white, Asian – of how Reggie was one of the dedicated civil-rights movers and shakers that had marched right along with Martin Luther King on April 4, 1968, in the March on Washington when his hero's life was cut down right in front of him.

Dad had ended his informational session by telling the audience that Reggie's daughter, right here beside him, was continuing the good fight up north in Toronto, Canada, where she had a seat on the Toronto Police Force Race Relations Committee, and, in fact, she was fondly known as the ass-kicker that knew how to get things done.

As the ovation went into standing mode, Dad pulled Jacquie up beside him and then stepped aside so she could gracefully nod her head in acceptance of the respect that her fellow Miamians were finally showering upon her and her late father.

***

Alessandro, Mom, and I listened to Lars's voice as he told the rest of the story.

Lars's voice was calm and he began telling his part of the story. After the three of them had finished their room-service dinner, Jacquie told her two heroes that she still had the headache and it was her plan to have an early night. It was then that Dad asked her to clarify her nomenclature. He said that he had been under the impression that she had been named after Jacqueline Bouvier Kennedy Onassis and not her father whose middle name was Jack.

Jacquie stopped and nodded her head. "Yeah. You calling out his full name like that today; it brought it all back to me. I had pushed it way, way back in my mind, but, when I was a little, little girl, my mom tried to shield me from my dad not coming home and always getting into trouble and in and out of jail. Mommy had, at that time, made up a new story of why she named me Jacqueline in order to save me from future embarrassment as I grew up with the firsthand knowledge that my dad was a drug addict living from hand to mouth on the mean streets of Miami."

At the time, she had laughed and continued, "I can't wait to get home to tell Nigella that she's not the only one that was named after a great dad. My poor dad just had the back luck to lose the fight to America's biggest threat – drug addiction. Never mind the racism. Fuck that! He handled that war perfectly! Imagine, marching with Martin Luther King, Jr.! That's the story that I'm going to tell his grandchildren from now on."

Nigel nodded and said, "Exactly, honey. Dante's La Vita Nuova said, '*Nominasunt consequential rerum,*' which means *names are the consequences of things*. And you are certainly not like that white lady in the white house with the teensy-weensy voice back in the '60s. No, not at all."

She insisted that they both come in to tuck her into bed, and her last words to each one of them was, "I love you. You're the best." When Lars had tiptoed in to check on her 15 minutes later, she was sound asleep with a little smile on her face.

Lars finished his part of the phone call to us by adding that he had woken in the middle of the night. They were in their usual spooning position, and he only realized that something was wrong when she didn't respond to his kiss on the back of her neck.

***

Once Mom had told Dad and Lars that she and Zalia would be on the noon flight so that Zalia could say her last goodbye before the autopsy and cremation, we hung up and Mom said, "Okay, here's what going down. Sandro, honey, you'd better put some clothes on before I run upstairs to bring our girls down. Nigella, can you dig out her passport and travel letter out of the firebox so they'll allow her to cross the border with just me?"

I said, "Good plan, Mom. One little thing though, I'll get both girls' passports out. There's no way that Martina will let Zalia out of her sight during this crisis. You know her. You'll have to take the both of them, and I'll stay home with Sandro to take care of the four boys."

Sandro added: "Yeah. Nigel will take care of Lars, and I'll take care of my wife. I'll text my assistant right now that I won't be in today."

***

The five of us all stood out on the porch, waiting for the airport limo to pick them up. Martina was nudging Zalia, and Zalia was shaking her head no. Finally, Martina spoke up to get the teenager's question answered by the official know-it-all of the family.

She said, "Grandma, you don't have to answer this if you don't want to, but Zalia and I want to know if Auntie died because she was having sex. Did it cause a heart attack or something? Both of them are not so young anymore, you know. Dad's way over 40."

Mom didn't bat an eye. She put her arm around Zalia, and she said matter-of-factly: "Well, now, girls. That's a good question. And now that you're 13, I'm going to tell you about your mom and dad. You see, even people your mom and dad's age have sex, hell – even people my and granddad's age still have sex, but when it comes to those two in particular, it's never just sex. What they had, sometimes even two or three times a day, if you can believe it, at their age, was not just sex. They were also making love. So, knowing that, I can safely say that no, your mom didn't die from having sex. And, you know, your dad told me over the phone earlier this morning that he was holding her in his arms and she didn't respond when he was kissing her neck, so she had already died in her sleep. Peacefully. Nothing to do with sex or making love. It's just God's way of telling us that he needs her to be an angel somewhere else in the world and that her good work here with us in our family is finished up, just like her dad's was. It's kind of comforting to know that God needed both of them at the same time, and they both died within a day of each other, isn't it?"

***

It was eight o'clock in the morning that summer day, and, after Sandro and I had given Zalia another condolence kiss and hug, we waved goodbye to the departing limo.

I could hear Maureen's sing-along Irish brogue float down from the twins' open window, "Top of the mornin' to ya, my smart, handsome, precocious prodigies. Time to wake up now. Tell me what you want for breakfast, angels, and remember to put clean underwear on after your showers. None of your

326

nonsense now, boys. Dad's car is still in the drive, so you may be in luck to shoot a few hoops with him in the driveway before basketball camp if you hurry."

I leaned my head on Sandro's shoulder and repeated the mourner's Kaddish for my lost sister and my best friend. He held me close and whispered amen as he crossed himself, like the good Catholic he was.

***

Somehow, we all survived, including our little Zalia. Lars made a point of spending extra alone-time with her, encouraging her to tell him all the stories about her mom that he wouldn't have had any idea of. Every day I thanked God that Lars had adopted her the year before. And our two babies, Eliot and Francesco, not only survived; they thrived. Lars decided not to go back to teaching at University of Toronto that September, and he encouraged Maureen to take on a full load that semester by offering to cover for her morning shift of getting the four big kids off to school. He morphed into becoming a full-time dad and house-husband of sorts, and both Lars and I were up early in the mornings, waving Alessandro off before we sat down on the porch, coffee in hand, to discuss our plans for the day ahead, just like Jack and I used to do.

However, it wasn't all smooth sailing. It was just a week after Jack had died, and I was in the kitchen, chopping up fruit for the babies who were in their highchairs with their trays full of Cheerios in front of them. I heard a terrible crash followed by Lars's deep voice wailing uncontrollably. I ran into the office to see him lying prone on the floor, with his fists pounding his laptop which was bouncing up from the floor with each fist that hit its mark.

I got down on my knees beside him and patted his back as he just lay there, one cheek against the floor, sobbing.

I had one ear listening to the babies in their highchairs in the kitchen, all the time just waiting for his painful attack of grief to ease a little. He just lay there, and I just sat there on the floor beside him.

He finally quieted down, and I whispered, "I'm going to check on the boys, but just stay right here. I'll be back in a minute. Don't move, Lars."

I waited in the kitchen for a few minutes to give him time to collect himself. When I stuck my head back in the office, he was gone, and his laptop was, once again, on his desk, with most of the lid closed. The other third of the lid had been deposited into his trash basket.

***

I had spread a blanket out on the family-room floor, and the two boys were rolling around, babbling and playing with each other, as I leafed through a magazine, trying to pretend that nothing had happened earlier. I heard him walking down the hall toward us.

He stopped in the doorway, and he just stood there, looking at me with such pain and heartbreak on his face that I could feel my gut tighten up with trepidation of what was to come. I didn't move. I just waited for him to speak.

"I got the coroner's report. She was five weeks pregnant."

***

It wasn't long after that that we took the kids up to Mount Pleasant Cemetery to inter some of Jacquie's ashes. Earlier, when Mom had taken the girls back down to Miami, Lars, Dad, Mom, and the girls had taken some of Jacquie's ashes to her mother's gravesite and buried them in with Jack's mother and her little brother. They had saved some to be interred with her father's ashes at Arlington Cemetery at a later date. Up at Mount Pleasant, Pastor Smith and Rabbi Kleiman said a few prayers, and, once again, we had the two doves fly out of the cage to make a little ceremony for the kids. I don't know how we all got through that day. All I knew, for sure, that it was important for me that the kids remember to celebrate the deceased's life in this small way instead of just grieving for them. It set them all up for a safe place to come together as a family in the years to come and to remember our family members of our diverse and complicated family structure.

Martina and Zalia asked their grandparents if they could celebrate their September birthdays differently that year. After all, they explained they were going into high school and had simply grown out of the old public-school party that they'd had over the last four years. They wanted a family trip instead.

And, so, it came to be that Dad, Mom, me, Alessandro, Martina, Zalia, Lars, Maureen, and the four boys went down to Arlington Cemetery to attend the formal U.S.A. army burial of 'Granddad Reggie; first, and after we had scattered Jacquie's ashes over her father's grave, we headed straight to Disney

World where we all had the time of our lives, albeit carrying the painful memory of Jacquie through every minute of every day, out at the pool, in the park on the rides, or our big, noisy lunches out at one of the many kids-friendly restaurants in the theme park. Of course, we all enjoyed every moment of the holiday which we all needed, but Lars and Alessandro, who had never been to the Disney complex in their lives, were more excited than all the kids put together. Alessandro strapped on his Aqualimb and water polo reigned.

Mom and I were sitting poolside on a couple of lounge chairs, watching all the kids in the pool. Dad, Lars, and Alessandro were sitting on the side of the pool, their feet dangling over the edge, laughing and watching the kids showing off for them. They could have been an ad for some sort of men's products or something. Handsome and laughing, Lars with his leaner brown body between Dad who had kept his muscle tone up from his boxing days, and Sandro, my sexy man, with the dark curly hair all over his chest with the beautiful athletic body and big thigh muscles developed from all his years of wearing his prosthesis. I noticed a few men swim up to them to ask Sandro about it, and Sandro told me later that they all thought he was a vet from Afghanistan or the Middle East. The twins also fielded questions from the kids in the pool. The boys were very outgoing anyway and always played up their identical looks with lots of pranks, so their dad's prosthetic leg was just another angle for them to work. It wasn't long before every kid wanted to play with them.

The hot Florida sun was shining down on them, and the pool's water was glistening in Lars's and Dad's curly hair, while Alessandro's was slicked back straight, jet-black and sexy as ever. Every single person in and around the pool that day couldn't take their eyes off the three of them, and it wasn't just because of my husband's artificial leg. No, not at all. They were simply Canada's own immigrant eye candy, and there wasn't a person around that could dispute it.

We sat there, smiling, our eyes glued to our men and our kids. Every once in a while, one of the kids would look up and over for us to make sure they still had an adoring audience. We'd give a little wave to either Noah or Warren, and Mom would say quietly, with her voice full of pride and admiration, "Look at the little idiot. He's going to try another backward flip off the edge of the pool."

Maureen was still in the suite with the two babies when Mom tapped me on the arm and said quietly, "Can you believe our three handsome men? Our poster boys. Just look at them, honey. How'd we get so lucky?"

I replied, "Yeah, Mom. I know. But take a closer look, and you can see their lives written all over their faces as well. Maybe it's just because we know them, but their loves and losses show on their handsome faces somehow. And we're used to Dad's big scar on his face, but it pretty obvious to anyone outside the family that it must have been a traumatic experience. And Lars, poor Lars. Ever since the day I met him, he had that handsome, vulnerable, sensitive face. That all disappeared the day that he learned that Jack was pregnant when she died. After that day, his face hardened, and I haven't seen that vulnerable side of it since. He's handsome in a different way now. Just by looking at the three of them, you know that these men have lived and loved and lost. They're not kids, that's for sure. Lars is looking a little thin though, isn't he? I know he's pretty lanky, but his face especially shows he's missing Jack."

"Yes, honey. He was so in love with her. I pray every day that he'll be able to pull through his grieving without too much trauma. But, you know, those three are quite a trio. Nigel and Sandro are right there for him. They have quite a bond, just like you and Jack had."

"Yeah. And I'm glad that the two of us are sticking together this holiday, with the three men hanging out together. It would be hard on Lars if we were coupled up, leaving him as a third wheel."

With those words, I looked at her and watched the tears roll down her face, thinking of how much Jacquie would have loved being there at the pool with our three men, our nanny, and our six kids.

I changed the subject with a more positive tone, "You know, Mom, thinking about our Jacquie, the family's very own nurse extraordinaire, she would be so pleased that you had your breasts done. I know that you must have got lots of push-back from Dad about your decision, but Jack would be pleased that you went forward with it. And look at the results – you're still the same, only better! I'm happy that you chose just the lift, with no implants. Who the hell needs more to carry around, right? Your originals are just the perfect size for your slim shape."

"Well, we don't want to look like we're trying too hard, do we?" She laughed.

"No, really, Mom. Both you and Dad take such good care of yourselves. And it's nice for any woman to have a little work done once in a while. It makes us feel more relevant somehow. And especially for you having had the grandmother role thrown on you at such an early age. You have always been so graceful about that. There you were, barely married one year, and then there was a precocious little five-year-old calling you *grandma* every five minutes. It couldn't have been easy on you back then."

She smiled and laughed. "Yes, I remember back then and going through a few stages of cringing whenever we were all out and I would hear the *grandma* word being directed my way. Thank God my husband caught on right away; he never ever even teased me about it. Actually, there was no one I could really even talk to about it; it was so ridiculous of me to be so vain about something so silly as a sweet little girl calling me grandma. My girlfriends, your aunties, Phylis, Renee, and Donna, would have slapped me silly if they ever heard me whining about it. However, here I sit today, so proud to be called Grandma, right along with Mom as well."

"But, Mom, really, that was only five short years ago. We've all come a long way with our new lives. I'm so grateful that Dad and you took us into your home and your hearts back then. As my father-in-law used to say, you're one hell of a woman, Denise Royal. But, back to your perky breasts for a moment, has Dad calmed down about your little nip and tuck?"

"Yes. I know how to handle him. As soon as my little stitches had healed, I stopped wearing a bra under my tee-shirt when we would spend our afternoons together at home. That's all it took. It gets him every time. Basically, though, he's such a wimp when it comes to me and my health ever since our pregnancy. If I even tell him that I'm tired, he's hovering over me like I'm a baby. If you or the kids ever got sick, it would kill him, I'm sure."

She stood up, threw her shoulders back, and said, "I agree with you. My breasts are fabulous. I think I'll sashay over there just to remind him what a lucky man he is."

***

I sat there, poolside, on the lounge chair, remembering when we had met Jacquie back in 2010 at Disney World. I remembered admiring my new friend strut around the pool. She did have a beautiful body, and she chose to wear skimpy, two-piece bathing suits, not the least bit shy, like me, who stuck to a one-piece tank suit at all times. I think it was because, at 5'10", I seemed to draw attention to myself, and I wasn't comfortable in the limelight like that. Thank God for Mom. Before we left for our holiday, Mom had taken our two girls out shopping and talked them into buying one-piece bathing suits as well. Our girls were also tall for their age, and they both were at the point where they were wearing bras. Thinking about it now, maybe that was what got Mom thinking about having her breasts lifted. Mom had kept her thumb on them over the past year, and they agreed that they would dress a little more modestly until they were into their teens and a little more used to their new curves. Mom was the perfect Grandma. The girls were little girls one minute, and precocious tweens the next, and she instinctively knew how to handle them. The girls adored her, and they went to her before they came to me or Jack for girl-talk. And Mom had no limits. She was happy to discuss every topic with them, from riding bikes, scrapbooking, to same-sex marriage. And, of course, they knew that their nanny, the esteemed Ms. Maureen O'Reilly, was bisexual.

So, it turned out that this holiday, Martina and Zalia were playing out the whole poolside scene a little more self-consciously as they realized their grandma was right when she had insisted on one-piece bathing suits for them. They too were getting a lot of attention that they weren't quite ready for. However, the water-polo games were another matter altogether. Both of them were competitive, just like Jack and me. But, most of the time, they stuck pretty close to Dad or Mom while out at the pool on this holiday. Our little girls were growing up.

***

It was the next afternoon, and Mom came out to the pool and I waved her over to a shady spot. Her white Irish skin didn't fare well for too long in the sun, so she usually parked herself in a shady spot after a few laps in the pool. She had a big grin on her face, and she was flashing a room keycard in front of me.

"What's up, Mom?"

"Well, I was thinking. Your dad gave me that look that he's missing me, so I went in to the front desk and got us a room. A room away from our suite. There's simply no privacy up in our big suite during the day, with all the kids running around, so I figure I'll go over and whisper the room number in his ear. We usually hook-up for an afternoon nap, and we're missing just the two of us. So, don't come looking for me. I'm off duty!"

Sure enough, she flip-flopped over to the edge of the pool and whispered in Dad's ear. She disappeared, and, a minute later, I walked over and sat down beside him, with my legs dangling in the pool.

"Go, Dad, just go. I've got you covered."

***

Other than two bloody noses caused by both twins falling off the beds during pillow fights, and a couple of scraped knees from Eliot, we all agreed that we'd have to make this an annual trip.

The first day back, we were all over at Mom and Dad's for supper, after picking up Anna, Eliot, Ma, and Pops, so they could fight over who got to have the two babies on their laps first. Even Patou was glad to see us all, although his days of letting the twins ride him had been over for quite some time. He wasn't quite as eager to allow the two new babies the same privileges it seemed.

***

Over the fall and winter, Lars and I were good for each other, spending our days quietly going about our business around the house, changing diapers, doing laundry, and putting the boys down for their naps. We found ourselves slipping into the habit of speaking Swedish to each other during the day, and we both found it comforting somehow. He rarely spent any part of the day up in his apartment. I invited him to use my office to complete his bits and pieces of research, and we fell into the natural rhythm of family life easily. It all suited me just fine, because I loved being a full-time mom to both Eliot and Francesco.

Most afternoons, Lars would take the babies over to see our four elders over at their senior's residence, and, other afternoons, Dad and Mom would drop over for a quick visit. We all still maintained the basic family structure of Shabbat every Friday night at my house and Sunday dinner at Dad and Mom's.

Of course, Lars and I both had our days when crying jags would be the norm, but as time went on, we figured out how to remember Jack in a more positive light. Zalia began to call me mommy, and all six of the kids called both Lars and Alessandro dad. It was a crazy setup, but it worked for us.

As for Alessandro, he couldn't have been happier. He brought home the bacon, took care of all the sports activities with the boys, and Lars was delegated to the homework table with the girls and the twins every night after supper while Sandro put his feet up to watch the hockey game playing out on the television.

Martina and Zalia were fully invested in their first year of high school, and I was happy to see that both of them were making new friends and always seemed to have plans for their Saturday afternoon or Sunday with them. The girls missed our nights where Jack and I would sit them down in the kitchen and we'd all do our African hair thing, patiently first applying the oil, then the curl gel, then wrapping each curl with our finger to stylize each curl between the four of us. Sometimes Mom would come over and try to help us out, but she didn't have the knack. Maureen would comment dryly, "Denni, face it, you're not a black girl. You're Irish. Through and through. Just stick to writing your books and your storytelling."

***

I remember the first time Lars mentioned it to me. It was well into spring weather, and I knew as soon as he said, "Nigella, I've been thinking about this for quite some time," that he was worried about something.

After hearing him out, I was quiet for a moment, giving myself time to formulate what I was going to say in response to Lars's worries. I replied, "Yes. You're right, Lars. He has lost weight, and I've noticed he's been missing that big gusto in his voice when Tony is over or when he's watching the kids out at the hockey nets. He seems to have lost his big appetite too. I make all his favorites, but he just moves the food around on his plate. And he's been curling up on the sofa, catching 40 winks in the middle of a game, which is something he's never done before. Maybe he's limping a little more than usual because his prosthesis is loose or something. He just seems to be tired and worn out."

Lars offered, "Leave it to me. I know what a peacock he is, always strutting around you like he's God's gift to women, so I think it's best if I mention his weight loss to him. I'll get him in to see his doctor for a checkup. Okay with you? Deal?"

"Deal."

It was a few days later when Lars filled me in on what went down when he broached the subject of the lost weight with his best friend. He warned me that the outcome of the conversation was worrisome.

"How so?" I asked.

"Nigella, he didn't even argue. He just said quietly that he'd book an appointment, and he asked if I would go with him and, meanwhile, not to mention to you what was going on."

"So now you and I have a secret."

"Exactly, my friend. I'm sorry, but as you know, Sandro drives a hard bargain. Of course, I will fill you in on every detail as soon as I can."

He reached over the table and patted my hand and said softly, "We've been through the worst together, and I don't want you stressing about this. I've got this. It's nothing. Do you hear me?"

I kept blinking my eyes and nodding my head to keep my tears at bay as Lars started to unload the dishwasher. I watched him with the kitchen chores. Not only was he known as our absentminded professor because he always had his nose in a book or was never looking where he was going, but he had become our very own Martha Stewart and always snapped on the rubber gloves to tidy up the kitchen. The girls especially teased him unmercifully about his highly organized and systematic approach to the chores. Personally, I had come to the conclusion that he was born to be a stay-at-home dad. He relished every single moment of every single day with all six kids. He was more and more like my dad every day. They went to the same barbers; they both shopped for their expensive Italian sportswear up at Harry's at Yorkdale; they both sat with their legs crossed at the knee when they were discussing the academic topic at hand. They were too much. And, without actually saying so, Lars was my dad's best friend. My husband, on the other hand, would have no part of their fancy clothes. He would graciously accept the shirts that Mom would buy him, but, then again, she knew his style, and she had the knack to throw in a few luxury items when he wasn't really paying attention. Once again, Lars was the glue between the three men in my life. Lars was my husband's best friend as well. We called the three of them *'The Three Amigos,'* and they were the perfect fathers and spouses. A blend of handsome, ethical, brainy, charming, and very sexy men.

As it turned out, I didn't have to wait for the results from Sandro's visit to the doctor. It was the next Saturday morning, and I had slipped out of bed earlier to make Sandro breakfast in bed as a little treat for him.

I pushed open the bedroom door, holding the breakfast tray, and I glanced up to see that he was sitting up, pillows behind him, with a big grin on his face, just like a king. He said, "Do you know what I really want for breakfast?"

"No. What?"

He laughed and he said with so much love in his voice, it took my breath away, "You on a bun."

I quickly put the tray down and jumped into his arms. "You really are just my Italian Stallion from Little Italy, aren't you, big boy? Now, tell me, what's this big hot sausage doing hiding under the covers? Is that all for me?"

He kicked the blankets off and held onto his big erection as he swung his leg over the edge of the bed. "Where are my crutches?"

"Wait, wait," I jumped up, "Let me. Please. What do you want?"

"The door, *bella*, the door. Lock it."

I turned around to face him, my one hand still sliding the lock closed. I stopped and just watched him watching me. I wriggled out of my pajama bottoms and threw them across the room. I slowly started to unbutton my top, one by one, just standing there, smiling a little.

"Mrs. Camarra, get your ass over here. Breakfast will have to wait."

He put his hands around my waist to coax me on top of him. He whispered in my ear, "Now, where were we?"

Afterward, we lay there, and he started to laugh. He said, "Remember that first night we were together and you were so crazy for me and my hairy chest that you broke my headboard?"

"Now you wait just a moment. Hold up now. That wasn't me! That was all you, my sexy husband."

He laughed and kissed me. "All right. Have it your way. But five minutes ago, all that noise that I heard; that was definitely coming from you. It's a good thing that I reinforced this bed when I moved in. Admit it, you're still crazy for me, aren't you?"

It was later that morning when the sun was pouring in through the kitchen window. I looked up from the sink, and he was standing in the kitchen doorway, quietly, just watching me. I have never in my whole life felt as loved and as cherished as I did at that very moment. We both held our ground, just savoring each other from the distance. It was only when he started to move into the kitchen's sunlight that I noticed that his face was a peculiar shade of yellow.

He put his arms around me and said, "What? What's wrong?"

"Honey, you're very jaundiced. Just to be on the safe side, I'm going to run you over to Sunnybrook Hospital so that we can get you checked out."

***

It was around 3:30 that afternoon when I called Lars from Sunnybrook, "Lars, can you come over to Sunnybrook right away? Don't bring any of the kids. Please ask Maureen to cover for me at the house. Pick up Dad and Mom on your way. We're in big trouble. Please come as soon as you can."

***

My magnificent, brilliant, sexy, kind, and loving hockey-nut husband was chock full of stage-four pancreatic cancer. It was inoperable and his prognosis of time left was between three and four months.

***

Strange as it may seem, I got lots of rest that first three weeks. We had a second bed moved into his big private hospital room, and I moved in that very day. It was lights out at 10:00 p.m., and Alessandro and I stuck to the schedule. On his good days between treatments, we would laugh and giggle as I would try to fit in his bed right beside him, and he was always so happy if the drugs allowed him a big boner that I could take care of for him. It was those times when I would smile, remembering Jack always giving Lars a hand-job before he left for work in the morning. I never shared that little story with my husband. After all, he was the original Italian Stallion from Little Italy, and he didn't want to hear about anybody else's big hard-on except his own.

337

They started the first of two massive trials of chemo immediately, with the hopes of buying the patient a little time. Lars and Dad and Mom shuffled the kids back and forth, and it almost seemed bizarrely routine as Lars helped with the kids' homework over in one corner, and Maureen would take the babies back home early in the evening.

Thankfully, Alessandro didn't suffer too much from the chemo, so he enjoyed all the company coming and going. His cousin, Tony, and his two boys that had bought the two old Victorians dropped in almost every day, and, of course, all the nursing stations on our floor had complimentary, hot, juicy pizza dropped off daily from Camarra's over on Dufferin Street.

It was in these first few weeks that Alessandro organized his funeral, and I wasn't surprised at all when he asked his cousin, Tony, to arrange for the mass to be held in their old church in Little Italy, followed with a big, noisy celebration of life service at their local funeral home where all the Camarras had gone before him. He didn't want a separate, non-religious Celebration of Life party afterward for his colleagues and our neighbors to pay their respects. They would all have to go over to Little Italy. Our own family would have a private, second interment at Mount Pleasant where the kids could run around and once again see all the names of our family members that had gone before us.

Thank God for Tony. I mean, after all, what did I really know about Catholic mass? I was a Jew. And Lars would be of no help either. He was a non-believer. As much as we both loved our Alessandro, we were in no position to run the show.

The interment of half the ashes was to take place in their old Catholic cemetery in with his sister; the same place that Ma and Pops would go when it was their time as well. Tony was to divvy up the ashes, half for the Catholics and half for me, to be interred up at Mount Pleasant Cemetery, along with our whole family, where half of us were Jews and the other half were Christians. There was always room for a good Catholic boy, right?

The hospital scene was just too much for our four old folks, and although Dad brought them up every other day, it was usually for just a short visit. They decided amongst themselves that they would visit more often once Alessandro got home where he had decided that he wanted hospice at home, with a round-the-clock shift of hospice nurses living in with us.

Mom had a brilliant idea that Alessandro and I agreed to right away. Since Alessandro wanted to be set up in the big family room for his hospice, where he could host all of the kids and all of his Little Italy family, we would set up another bed for me, right beside his, but, meanwhile, Mom would move my stuff upstairs to Jacquie's old room and she would move Ma and Pops into our big suite which was on the main floor. It would be their time with their son, and they would be right there at all times without shuffling back and forth from their apartment. Alessandro had started his life with them, and he would end it with them as well.

***

Hospice at home was a lot easier than the hospital room for all of us. Patou had come over the first day and decided that he wasn't leaving. He set up camp beside Alessandro's bed, and that's where he stayed for the next month. Uncle Brad came up for a weekend, and the next couple of days it was nothing but testosterone hanging around in our big family room. Sandro was in heaven. Tony and the boys came over, and between Dad, Lars, Brad, and a few other big noisy cousins, there was always a card game going on right beside Sandro's bed so he could be a part of it all.

Maureen, the only other good Catholic in the house, accepted the honor of arranging with her own Father Borsellino, to come in periodically and to take care of the last rites when it was time. She said to Sandro, "I'd be honored to take care of this, Sandro, but I have to ask you if I can add in my own special Irish blessing somewhere along the way. You know the one."

She also added in her matter-of-fact way that she had been reassuring the twins that we weren't all moving to a new home. She had told them that we were all staying put.

Alessandro smiled at the earnest Irish nanny. "How did Nigella ever get so lucky to find you? I love you. Thank you for all that you do for the kids. And, yes, I want to hear your Irish blessing loud and clear, whenever you think it's appropriate. And get the kids to join in as well. And whenever the kids ask you about moving, you tell them that I'm the only one moving and that I'm going to be living with God up in heaven, and although I'll miss them, and my spirit will always watch over them, my old body is ready to go now."

"Oh, of course, Sandro. About the kids joining in the prayers. They always do. We always join in with Nigella's Jewish prayers too, as you know. That's how we do things in our family, right?"

"Maureen, can you find my jewelry box for me – it's either still in our room or upstairs in Jack's old room; I want to give you something out of it."

I watched as Sandro put the thick gold chain with the big crucifix over her head and told her to wear it in good health. He told her that he always said a prayer for her that she'd find a good Catholic husband or a wife to marry and that he wished her at least a half dozen noisy kids. He ended it with, "I love you, Maureen O'Reilly. Thank you for being here over all the years."

The kids wandered in and out of the family room as if it was normal that their dad was propped up in a bed in the middle of the big playroom. Mom and Dad would drop in with Lars's parents in tow, and Ma and Pops felt right at home in their big suite right beside the family room. Dad had hired kitchen help that came in every morning, and Ma took charge of making sure that everything in the kitchen was exactly to her specifications. All the cousins from Little Italy came and went, and there was always lots of hugging and laughter and wrestling with the twins, all the while, of course, under Patou's watchful eye. We all had an unwritten rule that we would try to save the tears for later.

The twins, always eager for new targets for all their 'identical-twins' pranks, had a field day with their uncles that could never decide how to run a game of road hockey with them; would they be better off with both of them on the same team, or one playing to the opposite net. Lots of theories, but no concrete answers.

As Tony laughed to Alessandro, "Look at them, smart as a whip; they're way ahead of us, and they're only eight years old. I think your little pishers from Forest Hill have got us beat, Sandro!" He nodded to Sandro and added, "Don't worry, Cuz. I'll make damn sure there's a hockey net out front every season. Your kids will be the best road hockey players in your fancy neighborhood, trust me."

"Hey, maybe you could use them as ringers for your game over in Little Italy. Your opponents would never know what hit them if you played on their look-alike faces a little. You could pick up a few bucks with a side-bet going on. But, Tony, there is something you can do for me right away. Can you get the registration for my car out of my wallet, and I'll sign it over to you. I want you to give the car to that nice kid, Joey, that works in the restaurant. The one that's still in school. He could use a car and you or your boys sure as hell have no use for it, and Lars wouldn't be caught dead driving it. Shit. He barely knows how to put gas in a car. Snobby Europeans and their Volvos and Benzes. But before you give it to Joey, get it detailed, oiled, lubed, filtered, and the gas tank filled up."

"Got you covered, Cuz. And don't worry, I won't leave it up to Lars to get your girls their first cars when they turn 16. I love him just as much as you do, but you gotta admit, he's nothing but a scientist that believes in public transit. Don't worry. I'll take care of everything in the cars and sports departments."

Alessandro said, "But, you know, I've got to give Lars credit. He is one hell of an ice-hockey player. I think he's got me beat, although I'd never tell him that."

"That might be so, but you know as well as I do, he only gets out there on the ice for you. He'd rather have his nose in a book. He's just about as sports inclined on the whole as Ma."

"Actually, his strength is in being a father. He's one hell of a champ in that department."

Maureen, the girls, and I all instinctively babied our fragile and sensitive Lars, and Maureen had already cut back on her classes and was spending most of the day at home to give Lars a bit of breathing space. He started meeting Dad early every morning for a run and then coffee down at the Aroma Espresso Café, just like Jack used to do. It gave the two of them to a little private time to work through the upcoming loss of their best friend.

Dad and Mom's house was full most of the time too. All their out-of-town friends, like Auntie Catharine and Uncle Edouard, who flew in from France to have a couple of short visits with me and Alessandro, Ann-Marie and Walt came up from the farm in Marlbank for the same reason, and my three Jewish aunties, Renee, Phyllis, and Donna, of course were either at Mom's house or my house; just popping in for a minute or two.

To tell you the truth, at the end of the day, if I had had enough of the whole dying-husband routine, I would wait with one eye closed until Sandro was asleep, and I would turn on the extra baby monitor that I had set up beside Sandro, and I would sneak up into Jack's old bedroom to get a goodnight's sleep. The nurse was right there, and I knew that Patou would come and get me if needed. That was the only time and place in my big house where I could just let it out and cry until I couldn't cry anymore. For some reason, though, I was basically okay with everything. I just felt so loved by everyone, and I thanked God for my blessings and for my last minutes, hours, and days left with the love of my life.

***

Alessandro was propped up in his bed with all the pillows behind him, like the king he was, and he said to me and Lars, "I'm glad we don't have any company right now. It's so nice just with the three of us here."

"Well, what do you call that big lump of a baby that's sound asleep on your chest? And the other one, the toddler that's conked out on Nigella's bed right beside us?"

"Naw, you know what I mean, Bro. Ma and Pops are having their afternoon naps, and it's just us. No bullshit. I love you both more than life itself."

He continued, and he said in his most conciliatory, smooth-talking way, "Now what I'm going to say is going to make the two of you as mad as hell, but I want you to hear me out. Don't be waking up the babies with any objections. And after you listen to me, I don't want any response. I just want you to tuck this away in the back of your mind as it is of no great consequence at the present moment anyway."

I kissed him and smiled into his face. Lars nodded, and Alessandro grinned at the two of us. "Now, remember, don't shoot the messenger. Just sayin'…"

Lars was the first to explode. He jumped out of his seat and did a few circles, and, with hands postulating wildly, he exclaimed in an infuriated whisper, "What the fuck did you just say? Are you out of your fucking mind? Me? I'm supposed to marry her? And have more children? By this time, he was raking his hands through his hair, and he had started to cry in anguish and frustration at his best friend's request."

Alessandro laughed a little and he said, "Now, now, she's not all that bad. I know she's got one hell of a temper, but she kind of grows on you."

Lars snapped at him, "This is no joking matter, you son of a bitch! Of all things to ask of me! And me – who would do anything for you – anything at all – but oh, no, not you! Not good enough for you! You ask the impossible! Look at me! Just look at me! My wife died last year, I have a baby still in diapers, and one in the terrible twos. I can't keep up with the laundry, and now

342

my best friend is leaving me! I can't handle another thing on my plate, let alone marrying her!"

By this time, I saw the humor in Alessandro's delivery and Lars's impassioned response, and, although I didn't agree with the idea one little bit, I had to laugh at the sly insult initiated first by my husband and then Lars's resounding agreement that he'd rather do anything but marry me. I leaned my head back and tried to stifle my laughter so I wouldn't wake up the boys. I felt Alessandro pull me down into his arms, and the two of us laughed and laughed and laughed.

I gasped and said to my husband, "He lacks a sense of humor, I'd say."

And that was how Lars began his descent into his big, tearful, sobbing, heart-rending episode of grief for his best friend that hadn't even died yet.

He leaned forward in his chair and put his head down on Alessandro's bed and cried like he'd never cried before.

Both Alessandro and I smoothed his hair down and whispered, "There, there. It's going to be okay. Hush, hush. I love you. We love you. Don't wake the babies. It's okay. It's okay."

As Lars blew his nose for the umpteenth time, I smiled a little and said to my husband, "Now don't think for a moment that I agree with you just because I was being nice at the time and didn't want to argue the point. But listen up, and listen up right now, big boy. It's not going to happen. Not in a million years. So, as Mom would say, *put that in your pipe and smoke it.*"

Lars had to have the last say, and he added, "Yeah, Alessandro Francesco Camarra, the self-appointed Italian Stallion of Little Italy. Who the fuck do you think you are?"

Alessandro's roars of laughter woke up the two babies, and Lars scooped them up to take them away to change Frankie's diaper. As the two babies yattered away, each one from underneath Lars's two arms, he said to them matter-of-factly, "It's okay, boys. It's a good thing I'm on diaper duty today. Your other father is a fucking nutcase."

Alessandro wouldn't let up with the teasing, and he said, "Lars, don't you remember what you told me one day when I was swearing? You said in your posh accent in a high and mighty tone that *profanity is the sign of a lazy mind.* Remember that, Lars?"

"Fuck you, Camarra! Fuck you! Just fuck you!"

Alessandro said to me, "Where's something I can throw at him? That would really get him riled up. He's always so dignified. I remember the first time I took him over to Little Italy and we had a game of street hockey. He bumped into one of the guys on the other team and he said *excuse me*. Every single man was on the ground, laughing their heads off. He wouldn't say shit if it was in his mouth. Gotta love 'im."

"And you tease him too much. Poor Lars. You're such a bad boy, Sandro. And it's nice that he's a gentleman."

"*Bella*, you're talking to me. I know you like a bad boy. And I know you can out-swear anyone in this house. But back to Lars, honey, to tell you the truth, I know I've been riding him a little over the past week, but I've got to toughen him up a little. I can't have him falling apart at this late date. So, you'll have to be the tough guy with him once I'm gone. The two of you have six kids that need the two of you to get on with life. And I have no doubt that both of you will be just fine. I love you both, and I want the best for you both."

I looked down at my thoughtful, caring, brave husband. How did he ever pull that one off? He was laying there, at his most vulnerable point, and he loved the two of us enough to ask us to marry each other and to have more children. That takes a lot of guts at the very best of times, let alone in times like this. He held onto his composure, determined to play it cool right to the very end. I couldn't cry now. I couldn't crack his vulnerability in order to ease my own pain. His request to us was the most beautiful thing anyone had ever asked of me, and I had to respect his way of doing things. I smiled as he reached up to pull me in.

The kiss reminded me of that very first kiss in my hallway when I came to the realization that I loved him. That was the kiss where he set me straight as to who was the boss.

I took advantage of our privacy, and I slid my hand down under the blankets to reach for his beautiful, sexy, pole-straight penis to see if I could offer him a little pleasure down there in that department. I would save my tears for later.

We never spoke of his request that Lars and I marry and have more children again.

***

There were times when I must admit I felt a little left out. My husband, when you get right down to it, was a man's man. He loved nothing better than being with the boys. I would watch him light up when Tony and his boys came over to see him, and I would fade out of his sight as they would sit there, speaking Italian most of the time, as I would come and go, adding in my two cents' worth when it was appropriate. I spent my time bringing them snacks and drinks and making sure that the kids all traipsed in at some point of the visit to say hello to their big, noisy uncles. I knew that all of them over in Little Italy loved me, but when it came right down to it, I was Sandro's wife. I was a Jew; I lived in a fancy neighborhood, and I had a Ph.D., equal to my husband's. And, to top it all off, I was a few inches taller than some of them. That never goes over well. Of course, I knew exactly where I fit in the big scheme of things, and I ensured that I played my part as Sandro's wife perfectly. I was warm and friendly enough, but I maintained a little of my cool princess attitude to ensure that my husband had nothing whatsoever to be jealous about. Men. What can I say?

***

Alessandro had asked his lawyer to come in to discuss a few little changes on his will and his insurance policy with Lars and me present. Since I was to take over as executor of Ma and Pops' wills, Alessandro wanted it known that upon both of his parents' deaths, the mortgages on the two old Victorians that they held for both of Tony's boys were to be forgiven in full, if, in fact, the mortgages were still in play.

I firmly told him that I would not accept his life-insurance payout, regardless of who it was made out to. I argued my point quietly but firmly that I had my own money and that I wanted every single cent to go the children, in trust for their education and investments. Sandro agreed with one small change to the deal. His life insurance was to be divided equally between the existing six children in the family, plus all future children born to or adopted through a relationship between me and Lars. Upon hearing this, Lars just shook his head and smiled at his best friend.

"You're just like a dog and a bone, man. But when you're right, you're right. I'm going to change my will too, right now, if that's okay with you. Currently, it reads Martina, Zalia, and Eliot, but I'm going to add the twins and

Francesco. Jacquie would like that. And, Nigella, would you mind acting as my executor as well? That means that you would have to run my parents' estate the same as you'll run Ma and Pops if I should die before them."

I said, "Okay, okay, enough of this talk about dying. Boys, you're too much. Just count me in. Whatever you want. I'll do it. But enough already."

The lawyer said, "I wish all my clients were as organized as you are. And this isn't straightforward with six kids, three original parents, grandparents, adoption, and two full sets of elders! I'll drop off all the papers tomorrow for signatures."

Sandro added, "To tell the truth, after living in this big house with all these crazy kids, I don't know whose kids are whose anymore anyway. And all the kids call us both Dad. That's the way it should be. And, Lars, thank you in advance for all the years to come when you have to field all those dad situations. I love you, man, even though you're the worst basketball player I've ever met in my whole life. Thank God you can skate."

"You're so full of shit. You find it very easy to forget that I'm one hell of a scientist. I've got you beat in that department. And I may be a better ice-hockey player than you as well, but I'm too much of a gentleman to say so."

We all laughed a little, more in relief that we had managed to get through another sensitive topic without falling apart completely.

The lawyer got up to leave, and I stood up with him and said to the boys, "Enough of your pissing contest, boys, I'm going to bake us some nice Swedish cookies, the kind that I like. Never mind you two with your chocolate-chip requests. You're out of luck today."

Lars added, "Oh! Oh! Wait a minute! I know what we'll do! And this will keep everyone happy."

The lawyer and I took our seats once again. We sat there as Lars jumped up from his chair and spread out his arms. "First things first. I think we should do this as soon as possible. It will be good for the kids. Here's the plan. I think that Nigella and I should adopt any of the six kids that aren't our biological children so that all the kids will be legally on the same footing as each of their brothers and sisters, regardless of their biological parents. What do you think?"

Sandro smiled wide and nodded and I said, "Larsie, you're brilliant. Let's get Dad to arrange it for us. Now let's see, hmm…this means that I'll adopt Zalia and Eliot Nigel, and since you're the biological dad to Martina, and you've already adopted Zalia, you'll adopt Noah, Warren, and Frankie. Right?"

Sandro, with a satisfied smile on his face, said, "Honey, you'd better rethink baking those damn, plain, old, Swedish cookies. My good friend Lars deserves his favorite chocolate chips. He's the man!"

***

"So that's it, Doc? No more extensions?"

"I'm afraid not, Sandro. But I agree with you, you're doing the right thing here. You told me a month ago you wanted me to tell you straight up, and now we're at that point. So now you can go ahead and take full control of the day that you're going to leave us. I encourage you to go forward and put on a date on it so we can adjust your meds to make sure it all goes smoothly with as little pain as possible."

The doctor looked at both of us and said, "I'll see myself out, Nigella. You two have lots to talk about."

Sandro patted the side of his bed. "Come here, *bella*, let's just have the rest of the day to ourselves. And tomorrow too. I'll tell Lars tonight that we don't want company tomorrow. We'll get the kids off to school and then it's just you and me. Meanwhile, let's just get you up here with me so I can feel you beside me."

We lay there, and I had my arm resting across his chest as Sandro chose day seven to leave us. He didn't want to drag it out past that in case he suffered some sort of an incident where the nurse would have to call an ambulance and he would end his days in the hospital. The doctor had explained to us that the nurse would keep the drugs topped up and that Sandro would slip into a deep sleep for several days beforehand, but that it would be a peaceful transition. Sandro wanted to say goodbye to each of the kids individually before this last resting phase, and we decided to keep the children in school on the last few days to keep things as normal as possible.

I know it sounds strange, but that day with just the two of us was just so perfect. Sandro didn't even want the baby there. Lars and Maureen disappeared with the kids and told us that everyone was having dinner at Dad and Mom's later. They took Ma and Pops with them. The nurse floated in and out on her timed intervals. We snoozed, and whispered, and kissed, and laughed at little remembrances. It was just him and me. We only spoke of the kids in passing. Sandro had taken care of everything. This time was just for us. My husband and me. He would ask me small, insignificant details of my doctorate, and he told me of when we first met and how his heart would pound whenever I had emailed him research or a draft of something that I had been working on. He would print all my emails out so that he could take everything home and read it all once again from his bed that night.

I told him of the night when I got home from Little Italy and I named my vibrator, *Sandro, the Italian Stallion*, and he laughed and laughed. Over the next few hours, he would go back to my little story and break out into gales of laughter once again.

The next day, our planned 'date' when it was just him and me, was not to be so perfect. We shed many, many tears, and, finally, I asked the nurse to top up his meds to calm him down. I was so thankful that we'd had the quiet, intimate day before. I watched his face slacken as his sleeping aid kicked in, and that was the moment I went back into my stoic self, holding my memories of just the two of us close to my heart.

***

It was a beautiful summer day at the very end of the school year when the inevitable happened. Sandro left us. Before he went into his deep resting phase, he had spoken to each of the children individually. He was magnificent. The house quieted down, and Patou never left Sandro's side. He knew. Once Sandro went into his deep resting phase, just as the doctor had described to us, in unspoken fashion, Dad, Mom, Maureen, Lars, Tony, and I carried our cellphones in our hand, eating and sleeping without knowledge of either, just waiting for the call. However, just like when Jacquie died, we all survived it.

Lars didn't leave my side for a moment, and Dad and Mom and Maureen handled the kids. Tony and his boys took care of our four elders. Patou hung around for a few days after the big Catholic funeral, but one day he ambled over to the front door and whined a little for me to let him go. There's a time for all seasons, and Patou had had enough. He was going home around the corner to 7 Russell Hill Road where he could count on some peace and quiet and a little biscuit from the old judge when his much-younger wife, the real boss of the house, wasn't looking.

Lars watched me opening the door for the dog, and he said, "Sandro probably gave the damn dog instructions too. It seems everyone I've been talking to has a list of what to do next. Your husband is running us all, as usual, but from a distance. It's a damn good thing he was one a hell of a man, Nigee, that's all I can say."

We all pulled together to have a family-only afternoon up at Mount Pleasant Cemetery with the kids, along with Brad and our four old folks. Dad, Mom, and I had gone up earlier and interred his ashes, along with Father Borsellino and Rabbi Kleiman. The day with the kids there was to have the same ceremony as we had had for Jacquie, where we released the white doves from their cage. And, besides, Ma and Pops didn't need to know that their son's ashes had been split between Little Italy and Mount Pleasant Cemetery. Why rock the boat? Brad had made the trip up from L.A. and took good care of Lars and Dad for me, so it was Maureen, Mom, and I that stood together. Father Borsellino and Rabbi Kleiman said a few prayers and then Maureen said the Irish blessing. That was it. I think it was harder on Lars than all of us put together. The kids seemed preoccupied with the doves. Dad and Mom were crushed but were mainly worried about me. We just went back to 7 Russell Hill Road's beautiful backyard, and, once again, Brad fired up the barbeque, and all the kids got out of their good clothes, and Patou made the rounds to all the adults, giving each one of us a paw and a little whimper.

It was a few weeks later, and we were all over at Dad and Mom's. I looked around me as my nine-year-old twins pole-vaulted over the backs of the two sofas, and Martina and Zalia, now 15 years old, were chasing the two babies, Eliot, who was almost four, and Frankie, as we called him, going on three years old. I was thankful that all the kids were still young enough to bounce back from Alessandro's death in a healthy manner, like they did when Jacquie died the year before. Dad and Mom had aged considerably, as when they were just recovering from the Tran family dying in the fire, our Jacquie had died in Miami. Jacquie was just as much their daughter as I was, and they were still reeling from the loss, right along with Lars. And poor Lars. My beautiful, handsome, dear friend Lars had lost so much weight, and he still had a haunted look in his eyes that he just couldn't shake. Actually, by spending the last year at home with me day in and day out had really helped him. He had gained a little weight back, and his face didn't look so hollow somehow. At least he could function. But even Uncle Brad's good looks were slowly but surely ageing. It had been one hell of a year for all of us.

Our four elders, Anna and Eliot, and Ma and Pops, had been slowly declining over the past few years, and they relied on Lars and Dad for their daily visits. They had lost two children within the last year, and it hit me that they may suffer a quick decline with Alessandro's death. Lars had hired a PSW to visit them all on a daily basis when Jacquie died last year, but I knew our time with them was limited.

It was just before dinner and Dad asked all the kids to get in a circle, as he had a surprise for the whole family. I knew by the way Mom was rolling her eyes that she was in on it, but it was a surprise, and a very pleasant surprise, when Dad announced that he had ordered a brand-new eight-week-old Great White Pyrenees puppy from the château in France. The pup was a direct descendant of our own Patou's father, so we could expect a little white ball of fluff coming in on the plane in a few days.

Dad had his head laughing and enjoying all the commotion as all the kids immediately jumped up and wanted to name the new dog. Many, many names were tossed around, and then Dad said, "I've heard Denni and Nigella both say many times that Patou is the king of the house, so." He took a breath and prompted, "So, if he's the king, who is the male pup?"

The older kids all yelled out in unison, "He's the prince!"

And with that, the new pup's nomenclature was settled.

Everyone laughed when Maureen threw her hands up in the air and cried out, "Just what I need – I just got the last baby out of diapers, now I'm going to have a new pup pissing all over the kitchen floor!"

***

It was later that night when Lars got back from taking the elders home. The four boys were sound asleep, and the girls were up in the loft. Lars and I were sitting around in our pajamas in the kitchen, having a decaf, and Lars said, "Nigie, I've been thinking."

"What now?"

"No, this is good. Hear me out."

"Oh, well, spit it out. Don't keep me waiting in suspense."

"Okay, okay. Here's my idea. I think we should start shuffling bedrooms around again."

I smiled a little and shook my head. "Ever since I met you and Jacquie, all our bedrooms have had revolving doors. I just got my own bedroom back, after having Ma and Pops camped out over here. Count me in for anyone else in the house moving, but not me. I'm not budging from my own bed ever again."

He laughed a little and said, "Agreed. No, I'm thinking more in terms of Maureen. We simply can't do without her right now, and I feel like I owe her, right along with you, my whole life. She's so good to us all, but especially with little Eliot since Jacquie isn't here. She joined the family nine years ago and has always been so good about changing rooms when you've been shuffling kids around. She's 28 years old. She needs her own place so she can entertain her friends and her new boyfriend privately. I know that over the past little while, she packs an overnight bag on her days off and she stays over at his place. And he's one hell of a nice guy. I'd like her to take my apartment, and of course I'll pay that rent like I have been doing ever since I moved in there. I'll come with Eliot over to your second floor. I was thinking that I could take Jack's old room, and Eliot could take Zalia's old room, and we'll share that Jack 'n Jill bathroom between those two bedrooms. That way I can check on him in the night. You've got me all moved into your office here over the last year, so I think it would be nice for Eliot to be near the other boys in the mornings instead of being by himself up in the apartment. What do you think?"

"I think you're brilliant, Lars. It's the perfect idea! Oh! Speak of the devil! Look who's coming through the door!"

Maureen said warily, "Are you two talking about me? It had better be good. What's up?"

After listening to Lars's offer, she gave both of us a big hug and said, "First you buy me a car, now I'm going to have my own apartment. But I really don't need whole apartment with two bedrooms. It's too much for me."

Lars said, "Maureen, it's perfect. You can have your own office and your own lounge. I know, I know, in Canada they call it a living room. But you're from Ireland, you know what I mean. And you need one. You've still got a year left on your Ph.D., and then you're going to go through your one-year supervised practice, post-doctoral. By then, you'll retire from your job here or beforehand if you can't stand us any longer. And you've got a boyfriend in your life now. I'm so proud of you becoming a child psychologist, and all these years working day in and day out as well as studying. You need your own space that's more than what you have right now. And I need to be over here on this side of the house with Eliot. He needs to be with his brothers and sisters. And this way, we don't have to move the girls either. They'll continue up on the third-floor loft, and you'll just lock your loft entry door from your side so you'll have complete privacy. And our four boys will be all together on the second floor with me."

Maureen came up with the deal. When she said, "On one condition…" I knew that the real boss of the family had her own ideas about what was going to go down at 49 Parkwood Avenue.

"It's a deal, Lars, only if you'll go back to work. You've been staying at home now for a year, and I know you and Nigella love to be together, but it hasn't helped the two of you move past losing Jacqueline. And now we have to deal with losing Alessandro. Look at the two of you – you're both just too skinny – you've been moping around not taking care of yourselves. And we can't have that. The kids need two vibrant parents right now, so your moping days should end right now. Don't be griefy!"

I laughed and said to her, "Now, now, Maureen. You know damn well that *griefy* is not a word."

She retorted, "And you know damn well what I mean. Don't try to sidetrack me with semantics, Dr. Hansson. Now, Lars, I know the university wants you back, so I want you to call them and tell them that you're returning to work with the fall semester. That will give you a couple of months to prepare for classes. And, Nigella, as for you, you need to stay at home with the kids and put supper on the table every night for Lars and the kids. That's a full-time job. And we need you to start running every morning with your dad, just like Jacquie used to do. That would be good for you to build a little muscle. And your dad needs that too. He's the biggest baby of all of you, and it's been really tough on him. And I'll get the kids off to school in the fall. I've scheduled that I'm only in class and placements afternoons from now on."

Lars and I were so startled by her plan, we just sat there, stunned.

Lars said, "Absolutely. I feel like such a fool that you had to tell me this. I should have known this. Yes. Yes, to everything. It is time for me to go back to work. My days of diaper duty are over! I need to pick myself up to be a better father to the kids. My God! I've got six kids to raise! What was I thinking!?"

Maureen said, "Don't be so hard on yourself. We've all been through a hell of a year, and we've all done remarkably well. I'm thinking of the kids here, and we have to try to get back to something akin to normal, although in all my years here, I haven't got the slightest idea of what that looks like. And I know both Jacqueline and Alessandro would be so happy with these new arrangements. You know how much he loved having you down at U of T with him, Lars. And before he left us, he gave me strict instructions on how to handle the two of you. So, we've got a deal?"

I spoke up, with Lars nodding away in agreement, "Not quite so fast, super nanny. If Lars goes back to work, I'll take over his part with the kids. I want you to cut back on your nanny hours, and you're due for a raise too. I can handle this, and, in fact, I'm looking forward to it. You have no idea how I'm going to get off my ass and take care of the kids myself. So, from now on, run your schedule to suit yourself and I've got you covered at this end. We've got to be ready to do things for ourselves for when you graduate, or, for when you marry your handsome, sexy doctor boyfriend; whatever comes first."

Maureen smiled a little and said, "Thank you both for all your thoughtfulness and for loving me. We'll work it out. Just like we always do. And as for the apartment, you're right. I'm ready to host my own private sleepovers on my days off with my boyfriend in my own private apartment, as long as it's okay with you. But let's get one thing clear, he's not going to be here with all of you in the big house; he's all mine. Well, maybe if he has an individual invitation to attend a specific function, he might come, but you'll never see him other than that. You know that he's a new doctor in the first year of his practice in a busy clinic, and I want all his off-duty available time to be attending to my big needs in my private bedroom in my private apartment. Got it?"

"Got it! Deal!"

***

I sat there with Dad as Martina and Zalia started their pitch on how they wanted to handle their birthday this year. I had to laugh at Dad. When it came to his two granddaughters, he couldn't manage the slightest bit of a poker face. Of course, the girls knew how to work him and proceeded to lay out their argument in an organized manner.

Dad said, "So, let me paraphrase. You're turning 16. No party this year. None. No shopping with Grandma. You just want a car. A second-hand car that you two will share. And you'll use it to deliver to the food-bank produce from the greenhouse and you'll both shuttle your brothers around to basketball camp and hockey. Have I got this right?"

Martina was laser-focused on her granddad, just like I used to do when I was prosecuting in court long ago in Sweden. Zalia, on the other hand, looked over at me for a little support.

I smiled and threw my hands up in the air. "Don't look at me. You know that your birthdays have always been Granddad's deal. It's all up to the three of you."

The old judge sat back and he had to struggle to keep the grin down. He said judiciously, "Now, girls, I'll have to insist on an amendment or two to your plan here. About Grandma, you know she lives to shop for you girls. You don't want to take that away from her. When she wants to take you to the mall for back-to-school shopping, you just have to give her that. Trust me, I know your grandma. You don't want to disappoint her. And about the car. That's going to take a little research. Do you think that the three of us can have a few research sessions on your laptops in order to define the new car?"

It was these car-hunt sessions that made the girls realize they were stepping into new territory. For six years, they had shared everything, ate the same food, and were willing to let their grandmother dress them in matching sweaters. All of a sudden, those days were over. Martina wanted a white car, Zalia wanted black. Martina wanted a two-door sports car, and Zalia wanted a four-door hatchback. After every session, Dad would close his notebook and thoughtfully nod his head. Finally, he said, "Leave it with me, girls. I'll get Uncle Tony's input. He's the car guy of the family. We'll see what we can do."

***

The five of us, Dad, Tony, Lars, Mom, and me, sat out on the porch and we divvied up the workload. Dad was going to go down to city hall to get the permit to put in a small, paved, two-car driveway on the far side of the garage, to butt up against the hedge and the property line. Tony was going to get a paving crew together. Lars was to phone my Volvo dealer and order two, new, sporty, little hatchback models, one white and one black. Mom was to drive her little Mercedes over every evening to teach the girls how to parallel park, and Dad was to pay for everything. It worked like a charm.

Tony raised his glass and said, "Sandro's right here, right now. I can feel him all around us. This is exactly how he would have done it. Here's to Dr. Alessandro Francesco Camarra."

"To Sandro."

As I walked Tony out to his car, I said, "Tony, maybe you can help me out with something here."

"Anything, Nigie. What do you need?"

"It's this way, Tony. If Lars or Dad or Maureen finds out about this, they'll never let me forget it. This is between you and me."

"Oh, oh. What have you done now, Nigie?"

"I need you to get rid of the evidence for me."

He started to laugh, although a little nervously.

"I ran over the goddamn hockey net when I backed out the other day. My Volvo is just fine, but the hockey net is beyond repair. I dragged it up and put it behind the garage. Can you make it disappear for me?"

He was laughing so hard, he could barely speak. "Oh my God, Nigie! You're the best! Sandro would have loved this. This one is almost as good as when you kicked the spokes out of the Alpha Romeo and broke your foot."

"Yeah. Very funny, Tony. Can you help me out or not?"

"Don't worry, *bella*, I'll take care of everything for you. Your secret is safe with me. I'll be back tomorrow with a truck to take away the old one, and we'll replace it with a new one."

I could hear him still laughing as he drove up the street and turned the corner, out of sight.

***

Chapter Twenty
Guided by The North Star

We were out on our nightly walk, and I said to Lars, "I've got an idea for a Christmas present from both of us for the girls."

"Yeah, I'm at a loss. Whaddya' think?"

"Well, this might be a little sensitive for you, Lars, and if you don't want to do it, I understand completely."

"Just shoot, will you? I know your little tricks by now, Nigie. Don't try to sugarcoat this."

"Okay. Here goes. I thought maybe, just maybe, that you and I could take our four wedding rings into the jewelers, and we could make a pair of earrings for Martina from my and Alessandro's wedding bands, and have them inscribed in the inside with our initials and the date when we were married. And, the same for your and Jack's rings, to be made up the same way for Zalia. I know that every time I look at my set, I just cry. They just make me sad, and I don't want that kind of sad memory when I think of Alessandro. I know Martina would love them, and that way I have something to hand down to her. I have nothing for her from Mor, so I could fill in that gap."

Lars stopped and looked into my face. He said quietly, "I feel the same every time I look at Jacqueline's ring. And I still wear mine. And I shouldn't. The rings are just too sad for me as well. This is a perfect way to change a sad memory into a happy one. You're right, the girls would love them, and Jacquie didn't have anything from her mother to give Zalia either."

He reached out and gave me a big hug, and we both had a little cry, and then I said to him in a surprised voice, "Lars, I think we've just turned a corner. It's been weeks now since the last time you and I cried together! Yay!"

"I know. Being back at work is so good for me, Nigie. And I really appreciate that the two babies are always waiting for me to get in the door at night. I feel like a king. I know that that's you behind all of it, and I love you for it. Thank you for everything. Thank you for spoiling me." He smiled and he said, "But back to the rings for a minute. How'd you get so smart? Are you sure this wasn't Denni's idea? It sounds too nice and too sweet for you to dream up all on your own."

I pushed him to the side and I started to run. "Last one home unloads the dishwasher."

***

Hanukkah and Christmas didn't seem to have the big fanfare effect that I usually cooked into all the plans. Mind you, we all had a good time, and the kids were just as excited as ever, but it seemed to me that it was a bitter-sweet reflection for Dad, Mom, our four elders, and Lars and me. Although our elders never said much about themselves, Dad and Mom had been saying for the last six months that we needed to start thinking about different living arrangements for Pops. Dementia was coming into play, and Ma was beginning to lose confidence that she could handle it. And Eliot too was right behind him. A few times, the residence director had phoned Lars to advise him that his father had wandered off the grounds and now had to be placed on the 'watch' list.

But it was Ma that worried us the most. Her natural take-charge attitude had become unmanageable when it came to the PSW who stopped in every day to bath them and dress them. She complained all the time that the PSW was trying to steal from her and that she wasn't listening to her. Even mild-mannered Anna couldn't change Ma's mind.

So, we savored every moment of the holidays, knowing deep down it may be the last of all of us being together under one roof. Since Jacquie and Sandro's passing, the four of us took nothing for granted.

Lars was grinning from ear to ear, and he urged me to open my gift from him, at the same time as Dad and Mom opened theirs. Both gifts were wrapped in beautiful paper, euro style, and both felt like a big flat envelope. It was obvious that the three of us were receiving the same thing from him.

I tore mine open, urging Dad and Mom to keep up with me. We looked at each other in surprise, and Lars was jumping up and down like one of the kids.

As I hugged him, I could feel the kids all yelling in the background, "What is it, Mommy?"

He had it all planned out. It was to be a weekend in the Big Apple, just the four of us, no kids, no elders, no dogs – just us.

***

We had the time of our lives. We rented skates at Rockefeller Centre and went down to Mom's favorite restaurant, the Balthazar, down in Soho, for muscles and frites. I thought to myself that I had never seen Dad and Mom happier as when we were sitting there at the Motown Revue which was playing on Broadway, watching them sing along to all Mom's old favorites. It was late, late night when we made it into one of Dad's favorite jazz bars to catch a set. Mom gave me a look and shook her head as both Dad and Lars reached into their pockets to bring out their little notebooks to jot down their thoughts. Old habits die hard, as they say. As it turned out, the manager of the club had been watching us. He knew that we were out-of-towners, but he thought that maybe Dad and Lars were in the business. I mean, after all, they certainly looked the part. They were so handsome, so sexy in their expensive black leather jackets, with their euro-scarves wrapped around their necks and so into the music. The manager of the club thought they were music critics writing a review. He had the waiter drop a complimentary fresh pitcher of beer off at the table, and Dad, playing the part to the hilt, threw a big wad of bills on the tray as a tip. The band filtered over during their break, and Lars took offence when one of them asked me to join him out back for a cigarette.

The musician backed up and drawled, "Chill, man! I thought she was your sister! Fuck, man, relax! I meant no harm. We're all cool here."

The next bar we hit had a blues band on, with a little postage-sized dance floor. As Lars and I watched Dad and Mom get their groove on, we laughed a little at Dad kissing her. I knew that his tongue was in her mouth, and you couldn't have squeezed a toothpick between them. I grabbed Lars's hand and pulled him up.

"Come on, Larsie, let's get our groove on."

He smiled a little at me, and he warned me, "Okay, Nigie, but it's not gonna be like those two. You know the drill."

"No, Larsie, I don't know the drill."

He swung me around, and before I knew what was happening, he had pulled me up tight against him, and he told me the drill, point blank, "Friends don't get boners." With that he pushed me back away from his body and jumped back into the cool hipster image, dancing with me like I was his sister.

I looked into his eyes. I couldn't read him at all, and I knew that he meant it to be some sort of a joke, but there was something about it that didn't come across as funny. I smiled and said, "Okay, Larsie. Good to know. Now are we gonna dance or what?"

The most memorable moment of the weekend for me, though, was when we made the pilgrimage to Strawberry Fields, in Central Park, to pay tribute to John Lennon. It was Lars's choice to go there, and we all stood around the big mosaic circle that had been swept clean of the snow, and there were fresh rose petals strewn about. There were a couple dozen people standing around the circle, and a guitar player started playing *Let It Be*. Everyone joined in, and a few people in the crowd started passing around joints. Mom accepted the big, fat joint as if she did this every day of her life, took a big toke, and passed it along to Dad. He followed suit, and as I watched the Supreme Court justice hold his toke in for maximum results, I thought to myself, *Well, well, well. This is definitely a first.*

Lars quipped the old adage to him, "Don't bogart that joint," and by the time it came around to me, I was smiling so widely that I could barely suck the smoke down. It was my first time to toke on a joint, and to this day, it remains one of my favorite memories, right up there with Blueberry Hill.

***

I remember it was early May, because the magnolia trees were out in full bloom. The oriental cherry trees were right behind them, with their buds just begging to open. My father-in-law – no, not Francesco, I mean my first father-in-law, Chi Tran, had planted all my flowering shrubs that first fall so long ago when we had bought the house. I thought of him every time I walked around the yard, pruning carefully here and there, just the way he had taught me to do. Many of my neighbors would ask me who my gardener was or where did I get this shrub or how did I plan the color schemes of the different beds. It was all because of Chi. It's funny; I very rarely even gave my first husband, François, a moment's thought, but over the years, I cherished every little moment that I'd shared with Chi like no other.

It was just after I had driven Eliot and Frankie to daycare, and I was out there in the front yard, with my nose in a big magnolia bloom, when my phone rang. My heart sank as I recognized the phone number on the screen. It was the residence, and it was about Anna. Lars's father, Eliot, had died in his sleep the month before, and his beautiful, devoted wife, Anna, had simply lost the will to live. As much as the PSW, the doctor, the whole family tried to coax her to eat, she faded away right in front of us. We had just decided the night before to transfer her into a full-care facility that could put her on intravenous, but her will to be with her Eliot took control and the PSW had found her lying peacefully in her bed. She had stopped breathing some time before that.

At least they had both ended their days in their own comfortable apartment. Lars especially was so grateful for that.

Ma and Pops hadn't been so lucky. We had moved Pops into a long-care facility back in February, but he only lasted about a month. His time was up, no matter how good the care was. Ma had refused to move into the full-time care area of the residence, and it was so painful for all of us to watch her daily decline into dementia. For some reason, she would only allow Denni to visit her, while me, always her favorite, was banned from her presence, right along with everyone else. What could we do? We made sure she got the very best care, and Mom would pop in every day to listen to her scream and complain, (in Italian, of course) that this nurse or that nurse was stealing her money. By the time we had got her moved from the apartment into a full-care area, we could only pray that she wouldn't suffer any more from her newly diagnosed Alzheimer's disease. The drugs helped calm her down, and she died from the disease shortly after that. Ma and Pops joined their long-ago deceased daughter and son, my Alessandro, oer in the old Catholic cemetery in Little Italy.

Anna and Eliot's ashes were interred up under a new stone, right beside Alessandro's stone at Mount Pleasant with the rest of our family.

***

It was after we had interred Anna and Eliot's ashes that Dad, Mom, Maureen, Lars, and I had a heartbreaking, painful moment that day up at Mount Pleasant. As usual, we were keeping things very light but respectful as the kids excitedly looked for all the different names of our family on the different stones. We had always tried to instill a celebration of the person rather than one of grieving the loss. Besides, who really knows the right way or the wrong way to handle these things? All you can do is to try to do your best.

We listened as the girls were reminding all four boys of who was who, when little Frankie, still only three-and-a-half years old, ran over and stuck his little hand out and touched the name *Alessandro Francesco Camarra*. He was rubbing his fingers over the *Francesco* and was crying out in excitement, "Mommy, Mommy, this is me; this is my name! This is me! Look, Mommy!"

Our smart little boy was just beginning to read, and he had recognized the letters of his own name. However, what broke our hearts was what he didn't recognize. He didn't recognize that that the letters on the stone were for his father. At his age, he only knew Lars as his dad, and, sadly, there was no going back for any of us.

The tears ran down my face as I looked at my beautiful twins, Noah and Warren, when I realized that they probably didn't remember their biological father, François, either. They had been even younger than Frankie when their father was killed in the fire. And since then, they had buried their second father, Sandro, who had adopted them when we were married. I watched as Lars went over to the twins and put his arms around them. We were all on the same page.

Before Martina and Zalia could respond to Frankie's claim, Dad scooped him up and said in his big baritone, "You're right, little man! That is your name! How did you get so smart, learning how to read so well? You must take after your grandma. She knows everything. She's just as smart as you are."

It was later, as we were driving over to the Rainforest Café for an early dinner, that our bright little boy came up with a question that we laughed over for many days to come. He said, "Grandma, Grandma! Grandma, do you really know everything?"

His grandma gave her husband the look and then claimed her turf, "Yes, Francesco Nigel Camarra, I know everything. Now what about you? Do you know everything?"

He thought about it for a few minutes and then he said, "No. I don't think so, Grandma. I'm not like you. I must be like Granddad."

***

I stood there, holding the breakfast-in-bed tray, watching him as all six kids jumped into his bed with him, all of them singing 'Happy Birthday' loudly and off-key. Finally, one by one they made room for me to set the tray up, and the handsome, happy, grayer-by-the-day, stubble-faced, 46-year-old dad read each homemade card out loud as if he were reading out an acceptance speech for the Nobel Prize.

The kids finally wandered off, and I pulled up a chair, poured myself a coffee from the carafe, with my legs up and over his covers. By the time I really looked at him, I was a little taken back with what I saw on his face. His was smiling at me, but not with his usual wide grin when he was teasing me about something. This was all different. And his words sounded differently too. He was showing a tenderness about him as he thanked me for the best birthday breakfast he'd ever had.

I could feel my face flush, and all of a sudden, I was conscious of sitting there in my nightie and robe, with my bare legs up over his.

For some reason, I could feel myself panic a little, and I swung my legs back and put my two feet firmly on the floor, and I said in a matter-of-fact voice, "Okay, buster, are you going to lay around all day long, or are you going to get up and at 'em so I can get you out of this crazy house for your birthday surprise?"

"Where are you taking me?"

"It's a surprise. All you need to know is to be at the front door in 15 minutes. I'm driving. Just wear a pair of shorts and a tee-shirt, and bring a bathing suit in a bag. Dad, Mom, and Maureen are taking the kids on for the whole day, so you're all mine to spoil rotten."

He was grinning from ear to ear. "All right, already. I know when I'm beat. You're the boss, Nigie. Now get out of here so I can take a shower."

***

As I drove, he looked over at me with surprise on his face. "Wasaga Beach? Why Wasaga Beach? There's nothing there except for a few hotdog stands, a beer joint that sells chicken wings by the bucket, and a hell of a lot of sand and cold water."

"Exactly. Just like the lakes back home in Sweden. Cold as hell. Or so I've been told. I've never been there. Yet. So that makes us two Wasaga Beach virgins. Right?"

"You're putting me on, right? We're making a two-hour-plus drive to dip our toes in Georgian Bay and drink beer and eat a hotdog in the sand? No. Come on now. 'Fess up. What's really going on here?"

I laughed a little nervously, and I had to admit to myself that maybe I had made a mistake here. All I knew for sure is that I wanted Lars and I to have a day away from 49 Parkview Avenue, kind of like we had in New York last winter. We had both enjoyed that trip so much. I just wanted to see my wonderful friend and father of our six children to relax and have a fun day in the summer sun at a big beach with Swedish-like cold lake water. So, I said to him, "There's nothing going on here. Relax already."

"Bullshit, Nigie. There's something going on here. You're just not aware of it. Yet."

"Now listen up, Dr. Lars Hansson. Forget your deep analysis of a simple gift given from the heart, and just lay back and take like a man. D'ya hear me now?"

He leaned over and kissed me on the cheek. "You're right. You're always right, just like your mom. So, that does it. I'm all yours for the day. And, by the way, thank you just for being you. I love you, Nigie, mother of my six children."

I smiled at him and said, "Now that's what I like to hear. Now crank up some tunes, will you? We don't have any kids in the backseat, and we don't have to sing along to all those ridiculous kids' songs. You're the copilot and you're falling down on your job over there. It's all rock 'n roll today!"

As it turned out, we didn't walk out to Wasaga's big shoal, the sandbar, with the cool, silky water slipping over our thighs on the longest sand beach in Ontario until eight o'clock that night.

***

We were both laughing like kids when I swerved over to a parking spot to go into our first of three garage sales. We had spotted the signs for them, and both of us in our whole lives had never, ever been to a garage sale. We were so amazed at all the good stuff we could buy, priced anywhere from 50 cents to a 1.25, that the trunk was full by the time we had pulled away from the third sale on the street.

When we'd made it to the midway of the Wasaga Beach little carnival of sorts, Lars had slopped mustard down the front of his white tee-shirt, and he commented on the fact that he'd never seen my hair look quite that bad in all the years he had known me. All we could do was laugh. We bought a string of tickets for the rides and a string of tickets to win a hand-crocheted blanket. We rode the Ferris wheel and ate a back-bacon-on-a-bun along with a cob of corn. Poor Lars wasn't used to this kind of food, and I wiped his face off after he dragged me over to the edge of a tent where he threw up the dinner. I got us a couple of plastic cups of beer and a large pack of gum so that he could get that taste out of his mouth. I tucked him back into the car to get him to the beach in time for the sunset.

It was during the long walk out to the sandbar in the shallow water, holding hands and gasping a little as the cold water moved up our legs, when I said to him, "Larsie, look at the sunset. This is exactly why I brought you here. Just look. It's so beautiful."

He looked over at me and smiled a little, and he said, "You're lying like a rug. I know exactly why you brought me here, Nigie. And before we leave this God-forsaken place, you're going to admit it to me."

I looked at him, and all of a sudden, I didn't know what to say. I splashed him a little and said, "Well, I didn't mean to poison you with the carnival food or anything like that. Next time I take you out, I'll consider your delicate palate. You're such a wimp, Larsie."

He stopped walking out and pulled me to him, and he said softly, "Do I have to spell it out for you? Do I have to tell you why you wanted to get me way out here in the middle of a big, fucking, cold lake, with the sun going down on us? Do I have to do it all, Nigie? Do I have to tell you that you're finally ready to kiss me? How long do I have to wait for you? Do I have to beg you?"

My mouth was open, and I couldn't say a word.

He said gently, "Trust me on this. I love you. I would never ever rush you, but I know you, Nigella Hansson. I know you're ready now. If you can't speak, just nod your head."

I nodded my head up and down, and I felt his arms go around me. It took just that one, long, sweet, tender, and soulful kiss that told me that my life was going to take another turn, just when I thought it couldn't get any better.

I started to laugh that interrupted all the kissing, and I said, "You taste like spearmint gum. Thank God."

That started a splashing contest as we ran back to the blanket, and by the time the stars came out, we were snuggled up against one another, one blanket underneath us and one blanket over us. We talked and talked and talked. About all things, unimportant and important. I pointed up to the black sky with the thousands and thousands of twinkling stars above us. I said, "Do you know the story about the North Star?"

"I only know the science one. I want you to tell me the love one. The one that only you can tell."

I looked directly into his face to see if he was simply teasing me. Nope. His face was full of happiness and love, so I told him the story of how the African-Americans had called Canada the North Star, and I added my own little twist as well. I told him that I had been searching for a sign to give me the courage to move forward in my life, and that that same North Star that was shining so brightly down on us, that it was all that I needed to take the next step. I ended my story by saying, "I love you, Lars. I'm ready. I'm ready to share our love. I'm ready to have your children. I want to make love to you every morning and every night, and I want to make your breakfast and pack your lunch every day. I want to make you happy."

He kissed me gently. "I can add my own story about the North Star."

"What's that?"

"To me, right now and right here, the North Star is our catalyst. It's what's going to set things in motion. It's a deeply personal vibe that I'm getting from it. That star is all about Jacquie and Sandro giving us their blessing. They want us to get married. They want us to have more children. It's out of our hands. Our steps are ordered by something greater than ourselves."

"For a non-believer such as yourself, darling, that sounds pretty profound. But now is not the time to tease you about your heathen ways. I accept you just the way you are. But seriously, Lars, about Jack and Sandro. I feel it too. I feel their blessing. And I love you."

Lars lightened the conversation up a little, away from our deceased spouses, and told me of another of his personal signs that he had tried unsuccessfully to tell me about five months ago when we were in New York, but he couldn't quite pull it off, as he was too afraid that I might not be ready to hear it.

"So, tell me about it now. I'm all ears."

"When we were in that little blues bar in New York, and when you pulled me up to dance, I warned you that friends don't get boners. You see, all these years, I've loved you, knowing that we were friends and not lovers. I knew this because my big dick never lies to me. All of a sudden, last Christmas, about a year-and-half after Jacquie had died, and about six months after Sandro had died, I started having these huge erections every time you came into the room. My dick had spoken. And I've been dealing with all of these magnificent hard-ons ever since then. What can I do? My dick has been resurrected, and know I am to spend the rest of my life being deeply in love with the mother of my six children. The same one that didn't comb her hair this morning."

"Oh, I see."

"But, never fear! I have a plan now that I've seen our North Star. It happens to be shining at this very moment on a small, little motel on the main drag of this little beach town. I propose that we throw caution to the wind and stay over and explore all of our options. I'll even buy a toothbrush so I can kiss you the way that I need to kiss you and love you the way that I need to love you."

"I like the sounds of this. One question though, for the big scientist of the family."

"Shoot."

"How the hell did all this sand get into the ass of my bathing suit?"

"That calls for further inspection, darling. Right now, let's get out of here so we can get a room. And by the looks of the establishment, I think that we'd better splurge and get the deluxe room to ensure that we get a shower and a toilet that we don't have to share with anyone else. After all, it's my birthday, and you did say that today was your treat, right?"

It was a magical night full of loving and laughing and talking and times of pure sex and other times of pure lovemaking, the whole night through. It was like it was meant to be, all along. We laughed as we ordered pizza delivered to our door in the middle of the night, and we cried the next morning as we realized that we would have to get back into our day-old underwear and mustard-stained tee-shirts to drive back down to the city.

However, we both agreed that we wouldn't have changed any part of our day at Wasaga Beach. Well, that may be a small, white lie. We could have done without Lars puking all down the left side of his shorts.

By the time the morning light was peeking through the curtains of the dingy little room, we had agreed that it was better than the Four Seasons any day of the week and that we would make it an annual event to return to renew our love fest. As Lars said about our room, "It grows on you."

For some reason, I relished the time that morning in the tiny shower, just by myself. I suppose it was because I had just spent the most intense, emotional, loving last 12 hours with Lars, and I needed just a little time to myself to collect my thoughts. And to give God thanks for my new lease on life. I'm not going to lie; I took a moment or two, like anyone would do, to compare the lovers that had come into my life. Not that there were that many, but they all had had such an impact on me. Even Sexy Dan at the gym. Now I don't mean comparing them physically or even their varying degrees of mastering the skill set of having sex with a woman. All of them thought they were the best, and we all know that that's half the battle, isn't it? I wanted to take a moment to compare what each one of them had given me other than the orgasms.

I thought of Filip on Blueberry Hill and was grateful for the sense of freedom that I felt up there under the stars. And Sexy Dan in the front seat of my Volvo, giving me that sense of bad girl excitement that's always good. I even thought of François, my first, in New York, showing me, a virgin, what he needed me to do for him. And finally, I allowed myself to go there. My heart ached a little as I remembered Alessandro, my very own Italian stallion, who's deeply loving ways showed me how to make love with someone rather than just having sex. I remembered the way he would strut around stripped down naked, proud of his beautiful body. And oh my God, it was beautiful.

However, when I came to Lars, there was no comparison somehow. Maybe it was just a case of, like the old song says, "Love the One You're With," but I don't think so. Lars was just so – just so – just so himself. He was sensitive, caring, fun, genial, and very loving. He was very eager and very ready, time and time again, wanting nothing for himself. He just wanted to please me. And please me he did. Over and over again. Perhaps it was easy for us to get to that intimacy so quickly, because we knew each other so well, or maybe it was just that the universe had decided that our time had come. Who knows?

As I got out of the shower, I summed it all up perfectly. Lars was number one in all categories. And it was all because the others lacked that *je n'c'est se quoi*. That descriptor that we all use when discussing the great love stories of all time. When it's written in the stars. The Romeo and Juliets, the Liz and Dicks, the Napoleon and Josephines. They all had it. And Lars and I had too. In spades. We were, simply, soul mates.

***

We both got a bit of a surprise that morning, however, when we opened the trunk to throw the beach blankets in. We looked with amazement at all the garage-sale treasures we had bought, and we both said at the same time, "What were we thinking!?"

Lars spotted the Goodwill box on the side of the road, and I pulled over, popped the trunk, and we deposited our garage-sale treasures into the donation box before getting out of Dodge in a cloud of dust.

***

We were an hour into our drive, both of us quiet and reflective, with Lars silently passing my takeout coffee to me every few minutes. Just like couples do.

He said quietly, "Vivianna Grace Hansson."

I responded, "What if it's a boy?"

"No. It's going to be a girl."

"Okay, honey. Okay."

***

We were married under the big, old maple tree in Dad and Mom's backyard. Rabbi Kleiman officiated. It was a family affair, with everyone circled around us, holding hands as we said our vows. We exchanged plain gold bands. Mom had bought me a beautiful, ivory, silk dress, and I wore her old vintage hairclips in my hair. Dad had bought Lars and himself matching pale tan suits at Harry's. Mom, along with our two girls and Maureen, were wearing pale turquoise dresses, and our four boys all had new suits and clip-on ties. It was the same old crowd from all of our family celebrations, my three Jewish aunties, Auntie Catharine and Uncle Edouard were over from France, Ann-Marie and Walt were up from the farm at Marlbank. I noticed that Uncle

Brad with his oldest son, Madison, had taken Maureen's nice young doctor under their wing. Tony, his wife, his two sons, and their new wives attended, along with my team that I had graduated with, a few of our neighbors, and some of Lars's friends from the university were there. Both Patou and Prince had big bow-tied ribbons around their neck, and once they had figured out that there was a big bowl of doggie treats out for them, they stationed themselves on each side of that table so as not to miss out on a single crumb.

Dad and Mom had booked rooms for everyone down at the Four Seasons, and we all had a wonderful night with dinner, dancing, and the kids all joining in and running around, having the time of their lives. Martina and Zalia put on quite a show with their hip-hop moves, and everybody was in agreement that Dad had it down pat. By then, our babysitter had enlisted the help of Dad and Brad to carry our four-year-old Eliot Nigel and Frankie, our three-year-old, upstairs. They were all partied out.

I went over and put my arm around Maureen. "It's your turn next, Maureen O'Reilly. Every night I say my Jewish prayers that I'll be dancing at your wedding next. Don't wait, honey. Just jump in the deep end. You've got a wonderful man, and I want you to be as happy as I am."

The best part of it all was that everyone, and I mean everyone, right from Rabbi Kleiman to Patou and Prince, thought that this wedding was just the most normal turn of events in the whole universe.

"Of course," they all said, "I knew from the get-go that they'd end up getting married. After all, they had six kids, and they even have had the same last names since they were born, far, far away in Stockholm, Sweden."

Our getting married was as sure as the North Star that we had all followed throughout the years on our journeys of finding our way home.

***

"You're as bad as old Patou. How many times do you have to go through the whole house checking on all the kids? Please come back to bed. The boys will be up in a few hours, and you still haven't got any sleep."

He slipped back into bed and put his arms around me. "How do you expect me to sleep tonight after finding out that we're having baby number seven?"

"Lars, darling, we're just barely pregnant. The baby isn't due until next May. Now remember, we agreed not to say anything until we're checked out at the doctors, right? Can you keep that big grin down to a dull roar until our appointment next week, Mr. Wonderful?"

"I'll try. But we're all over at Nigel and Denni's tomorrow. And Nigel has always read me like a book. I can't promise anything."

I smiled at him and whispered, "You know I feel the same. Dad and Mom are going to be so happy for us. I love you."

"I love you too."

***

I sat there, with Lars right beside me. All I could hear was everyone saying, "Open it! Just open it! Tear the paper! Open it! I looked over to the long brick wall, and even the two, big, enlarged photos of Granddad Saul and great-great-granddad, George, seemed to be urging me to open my surprise gift."

Noah and Warren, my ten-year-old look-alike twins, were sprawled on the floor, and Eliot, now almost five, was crouched down with little Frankie trying to coax him into a wrestling match. Maureen, now age 29 years old and wrapping up her postgraduate studies of childhood psychology, was sitting next to Dad who was 65 that year. The nice young doctor that she had started dating over a year ago was still hanging around, and I noticed his car was always parked on the street overnight on her days off. Dad and Mom had made a point over the last year of inviting him over for Sunday night dinners, all done in such a casual manner of course as to not rile Maureen up, and he fit right in with the rest of us. He was just 32 years old, and a Catholic as well. Could he have been any more perfect? Both Lars and I felt ancient when he would tell us all a funny little story of what happened at the clinic that day. And although none of us came out and said so, we were all pleased that Maureen had settled on falling in love with a man rather than a woman. She had calmly told us all a couple of years ago that she had gotten over the whole bisexual thing and chalked up her experiences with women as being nothing more than a long, drawn-out case of being bi-curious.

The pup, our Prince, or 'Pincie,' as little Frankie called him, was up on Dad's lap, and I knew that he must have had a few biscuits in his pocket to have made that happen. Our almost-17-year-olds, Martina and Zalia, were coming over from the kitchen, each carrying a tray of drinks. Mom was sitting on a separate chair next to Rabbi Kleiman who was in, sitting on his walker.

Old Patou had decided that I was his favorite that day, and he had his paw up on my lap, scratching at the big wrapped present that Dad had put on my lap. At the age of ten years old, we had all agreed to stop trying to teach the old dog new tricks. Our old dog had led the life of a king. He was the real boss of the family and knew exactly how to mooch all his favorite treats from each and every one of us. And after all the years and years of true dedicated service to our whole family, trotting from 7 Russell Hill Road to 49 Parkwood Avenue on his own accord, he deserved every tidbit that we offered him.

As I peeled off the paper, strip by strip, the big heavy package began to present itself. I was laughing as I looked at Lars and asked him, "Were you in on this?"

He kissed me tenderly and said, "Of course I was. You know that I'm always one step ahead of you, darling."

As he went in for another kiss, all the kids were yelling, "Stop the smooching, Dad! Just let her open the present!"

I laughed and put my hand up on his chest to block him a little, and he continued on in his quiet, calm voice with the sexy Swedish accent, "We'll hang it on the front porch, right beside the mezuzah."

He lifted the big bronze plaque off of my lap so everyone could read out loud and all together, even little Frankie. I could hear all the separate and unique timbers of my family as they heaped their love all over me, line after line.

The plaque read:

49 Parkwood Avenue

This is Nigella's house.
We dedicate this property in her honor.

Martina, Zalia, Noah, Warren, Eliot,
Francesco, Maureen, Nigel and Denise,
Brad, Lars,
Patou, and Prince

September, 2016

I glanced at Lars and smiled a little, noticing that he had left space for our next baby's name to be added. He watched as my finger traced out *Vivianna Grace* right under *Patou and Prince*, and, as we shared a little kiss, I glanced up to realize that Mom had watched me trace our next love child's name out. She raised one eyebrow, smiled, and quietly tapped her heart to let me know that she knew our secret.

***

The End

Epilogue

The only opposition that Lars received regarding Zalia's 17th birthday request was from me. I just thought the girls were too young to be looking back into their humble beginnings.

Dad said, "Honey, we have two remarkable young ladies that are almost 17 years old, and since I've been doing their birthdays since day one, I'm asking you to reconsider. Our girls live very privileged lives, all because of the people that went before them. I want them to have a healthy respect of how they got here. Look at me, I'm 65 years old, and I've never even tried to find out who my birthfather was. I've never went back home to see the old homestead. I should have."

Mom said, "And look at me. I was 43 years old before I knew enough to forgive and forget my family and to get on with my life. And, Nigella, remember when Lars had the common sense to take you back home on your little self-discovery trip when you were 35? Trust me, it's time our girls got a little perspective."

Lars added, "Honey, you know this would be especially good for Zalia. When we sold her mom's Miami condo, we put that money aside just for her. She asked if she could take Martina on these two trips, to go back home for herself and her sister, and she wants to`pay, instead of her granddad who always pays for everything. It's good for her to want to contribute and to share with her sister."

And so that's how it came about that Lars took the two girls for a trip back to Miami, Florida, so Zalia could show her sister where she used to go school and where she used to live.

And that's how I ended up taking Martina and Zalia to Stockholm, Sweden, so Martina could show Zalia the apartment where she lived with her grandma and me, and the park where Grandma used to take her as a toddler to push her on the swings.

The girls decided that I would have the one hotel room in Stockholm, and they would share the adjoining other. After all, I was just pregnant, and they told me at my age I needed my rest. I had booked those very same adjoining rooms that Lars and I had shared, and when I told this to the girls, they looked at each other and back at me in disbelief.

Martina said, "Mom, are you telling us that when you and Dad came to Stockholm that you didn't sleep together? And you were both older and you were both single?"

"Yes. That's right. Your dad and I didn't have sex until his birthday, a few months ago."

"Really, Mom. Get real. We're not kids, you know. And, besides, there's nothing wrong with having sex once you get to a certain age. That's what Grandma says."

"Honestly, girls. Your dad and I met years ago, and we both liked each other, but it wasn't meant to be. He could have been gay for all I knew. And that didn't change at all, through our whole friendship, until he met Jacquie. And they immediately fell in love, as you know. It was love at first sight for them. You were both 11 at the time."

Zalia said, "Wow! So, my mom was dad's first love? He never loved you first? Wow!"

"Well, remember, your mom was a very beautiful woman. And your dad is a very principled and ethical man, the same as your mom. He had never been in love with a girl before in his whole life, and he was 40 years old. He's the old-fashioned type that has to be deeply in love with the lady before he gets serious with her. He's a very special guy."

Martina added, "Yeah. Him and Granddad. They're the best. That's the kind of man I want to marry to."

***

We were sitting on the swings, in the old park where Mor used to bring me as a baby and then Martina 25 years later. I brought out my old photo of Mor and myself, the same one that I had shared with Dad.

The girls huddled over the photo and both of them were in awe of Mor's beauty. I had to smile. They had no interest in the fat, little nine-month-old on her lap that was me, but they were totally absorbed with the beautiful golden angel with the straight blonde hair falling down past her shoulders.

"She was so beautiful. She could have been Miss Universe. Look at her!"

Zalia added, "I always think that Grandma is the most beautiful lady when it comes to white ladies, but Mor has definitely got her beat."

I said, "Well, girls, remember that Mor was only 29 years old in this picture. She is frozen in time and will never age, where Grandma is now in her 50s. Right?"

Zalia nodded and gave me a bone. She said, "Mom, you were very cute. I think that Martina looks a lot like you. When we get home, let's bring out her baby pictures and we'll compare."

I told them what their granddad had said about the picture, "Girls, Granddad says that Grandma doesn't really need to see a picture of his 29-year-old first love, since she'll never age and Grandma has aged. So, we're just going to keep this picture to ourselves, as we don't want to hurt anyone's feelings. Okay?"

"Yeah. That's right. Okay."

By the time we got to Mor's gravesite, we put the stones carefully on the monument, and I said a couple of Jewish prayers, and the girls and I repeated the Lord's prayer. We all took another look at Mor's photo to say a proper goodbye, just like Dad and I did on our trip down memory lane.

***

It was the end of a very successful few days in Stockholm, watching my girls navigate shopping for the latest fashions with the Swedish kronar, carefully calculating if it would be cheaper to buy it back home in Toronto. I sat there with them in the open-air café in the big square, enjoying the last few days of Stockholm's waning summer. I was just absorbing every moment, watching them watch the cute teenage boys strut their stuff down in Old Town. The three of us had had such a great time. I played the part of an old married woman and asked them to define some of the young boys that seemed to be strutting by our table with amazing frequency. As Martina and Zalia got into the game, we were all laughing as they tried to outdo each other with their descriptors. One boy was a hunk; the next was a stud muffin; the next nothing but a hoser. When I asked what a hoser was, Martina laughed and told me I wasn't a real Canadian if I didn't know what a hoser was.

I turned to Google, and my phone quickly translated the term, "Oh, in Swedish you mean an 'idiotisk'."

Zalia added, "Maybe hoser is being too hard on him. I'd up-classify him to a goofball."

It made me realize that I actually spent very little time alone with my two daughters. They were always busy with their friends, or Mom, and they were both very involved with the greenhouse picking and delivery of the produce for the food bank. They took their jobs at the greenhouse very seriously. I made a promise to myself to become a little more hands-on with these two young, witty, and impressionable girls.

**

I was already in bed, texting Lars, when I looked up to see Martina standing in my doorway, with a serious look on her face.

"What's wrong, honey?"

"Mommy, mommy, I want to get into bed with you. Something weird just happened to me in the bathroom."

"Did you just get your period?"

By that time, she was jumping under my covers, "No. I mean really weird. I was looking in the mirror, brushing my hair out, and I heard a lady's voice with an accent telling me to never, never cut my hair. She said it's my crowning glory and she said it's my blessing. It was really weird. It was like the ghost stories that Grandma tells me about Great-randad George."

I called out, "Zalia, honey. Can you come in here? I've got a story or two to tell you about Great-grandma Milka and Grandma Martina."

Martina's analytical mind was racing way ahead of the story. I had barely finished telling them that Mor used to say this to me when I was a girl, but then a few years ago, Grandma Milka came to me one night as a spirit and said exactly the same words.

Martina said in a hushed voice, "So since Grandma Martina never knew her mother because she died when she gave birth, that means that Grandma Martina must have heard this same story from her mother as a spirit, the very same one that came to me. Wow! I just heard from my Polish great-grandmother! Or maybe it was my Swedish grandma. I can't wait to tell Grandma this!"

Zalia added, "Wait a minute. It was your grandma, Milka, that went to Auschwitz when she was 20 years old, right?"

"Right."

"Well, maybe, just maybe, it was her mother that told her not to cut her hair. Maybe we're missing a generation of ghosts in this story. This could have been your great-great-grandma talking to you."

I added, "Yes, Zalia. That could be true. Great-grandma Milka, who was in Auschwitz, lived on a dairy farm in Poland. Her mother's name was Martyna, spelled with a 'y.' This first Martyna also went to Auschwitz with her daughter, Milka, and two little nine-year-old twin girls. But only Great-grandma Milka survived. Milka's mother is the lady that your grandma Martina was named after. So, Martina, that makes you the third Martina in our family."

"Mommy, I didn't know about the two little twin girls. That's horrible! Are you sure about this?"

"Yes, honey. The historian showed me their names on the Nazi paperwork. The paperwork listed them all as Martyna Kaufman, age 43, first twin girl Kaufman, age 9, second twin girl Kaufman, age 9, and then Milka Kaufman, age 20."

We talked and talked and talked. And that's how my girls found out the stories behind our family's long line of survivors. The Holocaust Survivor, the orphanage-raised profoundly deaf survivor, the Vietnamese boat survivors, the Irish famine survivors, the Underground Railroad slavery survivors, right down to Zalia's granddad, Reggie Jack Dixon, the Vietnam War and March on Washington survivor.

***

As I tucked them into their own beds, Zalia said, "Martina, remember that night when we were at the château in France? We know what to do when we're ready to make new plans or if we have a difficult decision to make, don't we?"

Martina replied, "Yeah. I remember. Auntie was amazing. She always told such good old-timey stories. Tell Mommy what she told us."

Zalia told the story, "One night on our holiday, after you and Mom had come home from Germany and Poland, Mom snuck into our room late one night, and she took us outside to the great lawn and we laid down on a blanket, just the three of us, all in our pajamas. We looked at all the stars, and she pointed out the North Star. She told us that African-Americans called Canada the North Star. She said that we could do anything in the world if we put our mind to it. And she said if we ever needed an answer to anything in the whole wide world, to just follow the North Star. She told us that when she was in Poland, she found the North Star, and that's how she decided to immigrate to Canada."

"Well, girls, I have a nice little North Star story for you as well. One time I was on a hilltop with Granddad, and I wished for another baby. Sure enough, I fell in love with Alessandro and I had our baby, Frankie."

Zalia added, "Oh yeah, I remember another time, way after our holiday to France. Mom had met Dad, and we were all skating down at City Hall. She said that night she looked up at the North Star once again and she told us that's how she knew that Dad was the one. She said the North Star is always the guiding light."

Martina said, "I wonder if Dad looks for the North Star. I mean really, look at him. He has led his whole life not even knowing who his birthparents were. He was a confirmed bachelor until he met our big, crazy family. But he's a scientist and also a non-believer, so maybe he doesn't believe in messages from the North Star."

I smiled a little and said to the two romantic teenage girls, "I'm happy to tell you two that your dad believes in the North Star big time! That's how we got married! We were up at a beach, late one night, and we were laying on a blanket under the stars. Your dad said that the North Star was telling him that both Alessandro and Jackie wanted us to get married and to have more children."

"No way! Dad said that?"

"Yes way! Dad did say that. He also said that the North Star is a catalyst, and that it sets things in motion."

"Wow! Who knew!?"

I smiled at my two 17-year-old daughters, and I bent down to kiss them goodnight. As I switched off the lamp, Martina sat up quickly and jumped out of bed.

"Wait! Wait a minute! I've got a great idea! Come on, girls!"

Zalia turned the lamp back on, and I started to smile.

***

The night concierge didn't say a word as he watched us sneak by him, with the hotel blanket rolled up and under Martina's arm.

Of course, the old park was completely dark and empty, and we stretched out dead center, in order to get a clear view of the stars above us. We lay there on the blanket, with me in the middle. I rested my hands, holding theirs, on my tummy to include my newest baby.

I whispered, "Girls, maybe it's just because we're here in our old park, but I feel like my Mor is smiling down on us from the North Star."

Zalia whispered back, "Exactly. I feel like Mommy is too."

Martina responded with, "Mommy, your mor is not only smiling down on us; she's telling me to do something, and it's not the message about not cutting my hair either. This is new."

"What's she saying?"

"My grandma is saying that I should go to university here in Stockholm."

"Oh my!"

Zalia said, "Let's make a wish."

And so, we did.

***